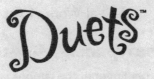

**Two brand-new stories in every volume...
twice a month!**

Duets Vol. #103

Popular Candy Halliday returns with a quirky
Double Duets volume featuring the identical Morgan
twin sisters—one who's zany and one who's serious.
Enjoy the fun as Madeline and Mary Beth encounter
double trouble with a pair of irresistible in-your-face
heroes who turn their lives upside down! Candy's
most recent Duets novel, *Winging It*, "has a number
of very funny scenes [and] a delicious hero,"
says *Romantic Times*.

Duets Vol. #104

Irish author Samantha Connolly serves up
A Real Work of Art, a wonderful story about a
heroine who impersonates her sister and goes from
uptight to fun and flirty—overnight! Samantha made
an impressive debut with her first Duets novel, say
reviewers. Joining her in the volume is talented
Jennifer McKinlay, whose writing "is fresh and funny,
with memorable characters and snappy byplay,"
notes *Romantic Times*. Jennifer's story
Thick as Thieves, a teasing road tale, was inspired
by her own cross-country trek several years ago!

Be sure to pick up both Duets volumes today!

A Real Work of Art

"Hello, sexypants," Megan joked.

She shook her finger at the famous statue of a Greek soldier. "You really got me in trouble yesterday, distracting me from my job like that."

The sculpture remained impassive, unlike Sam, who let out a snort of laughter.

Megan wheeled around. "I, uh, I thought…"

"Sexypants?" asked Sam with evident delight. "He's not even wearing pants," he said conversationally, "or is that what makes him so sexy?"

Megan was laughing, too. She turned to the statue and pointed her finger at Sam. "Get him, sexypants!"

Sam came to stand close beside her. "How do you think the display is looking? Are you happy with it?"

She wanted to reply, "I'm happy with you." Instead, she tore her eyes away from Sam's firm biceps and joined him in admiring the works of art. "I think it's great," she replied honestly.

He leaned over and elbowed her conspiratorially. "So, have you changed your mind about which one you're going to steal?"

Huh?

For more, turn to page 9

Thick as Thieves

"Jared, wake up!"

Cat was furious. He'd hardly spoken to her all day, he'd ignored her negligee and, to top it off, he snored! If she wasn't getting any sleep tonight, neither was he. When only snores met her demand, she reached for the extra pillow and smacked him with it.

"Ouch!" Jared grabbed her waist with one hand. His fingers tightened and then stilled as if registering the feel of her through the flimsy fabric she wore. His eyes popped open and he bolted upright, bringing his face within inches of hers.

"What are you doing on my side of the curtain, Cat?"

"I can't sleep," she said, pouting. "I want to talk."

"Well, get back on your side and talk from there." He pulled the sheet up to his neck, shifting away from her on the mattress.

Cat stifled a laugh at his prudence. "Don't be ridiculous. We can talk with me sitting here." As if to prove her point, she scooted closer to him.

Suddenly the hot look in Jared's eyes stopped all of Cat's movement. "Cat, I promise you if you come any closer, wearing that little thing you're wearing, talking is the *last* thing we'll be doing."

For more, turn to page 197

HARLEQUIN DUETS

ISBN 0-373-44170-3

Copyright in the collection:
Copyright © 2003 by Harlequin Books S.A.

The publisher acknowledges the copyright holders
of the individual works as follows:

A REAL WORK OF ART
Copyright © 2003 by Samantha Connolly

THICK AS THIEVES
Copyright © 2003 by Jennifer Orf

Visit us at www.eHarlequin.com

Printed in U.S.A.

A Real Work of Art

Samantha Connolly

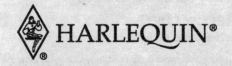

TORONTO • NEW YORK • LONDON
AMSTERDAM • PARIS • SYDNEY • HAMBURG
STOCKHOLM • ATHENS • TOKYO • MILAN • MADRID
PRAGUE • WARSAW • BUDAPEST • AUCKLAND

Dear Reader,

I have always been a sucker for stories of mistaken identity, so I just had to try writing one myself. A mix-up between sisters was the obvious choice for me because I'm lucky enough to have a sister who's also my best friend. I've never ended up in a predicament quite like Rachel's, but if I did, I know who I'd turn to!

Wandering through museums and art galleries is one of my favorite pastimes, so I really enjoyed creating a museum of my own, especially when the delectable Sam took up residence. As if Megan wasn't having enough difficulty without that kind of distraction! Those tricky situations and narrow escapes might have made life hard for her, but they sure were fun for me to write, so I hope you enjoy the story of how Megan met her match just by being herself (albeit in a roundabout way!).

All the best,

Samantha Connolly

Books by Samantha Connolly

HARLEQUIN DUETS
86—IF THE SHOE FITS

For Eloise

1

mostly to knuckle down to the actual work after driving in gorgeous, as she took, them to her drop to her room. She could no longer in that moment forget the vision...

She glanced as he moved with of motes on the desk in an electric to of the sun's warmth. She watched twenty-eight-eight lines, and a bit not really, even a bit...

"WHERE'S COPENHAGEN?" Megan looked around crossly. "It was right here. I had my hands on it and…oh great, now I've lost Copenhagen."

She flung her pen across the room and watched it bounce harmlessly against the door.

"How can two weeks worth of notes just vanish? Could somebody please explain that to me?"

She supposed if there was someone else in the room they might have, but there wasn't so Megan felt free to continue muttering.

"I hate this. It's too hard and I can't do it and anyway, I don't even want to."

She swiveled in her chair and looked up at the rows of books on the tall bookshelf behind her desk. It was crammed with guidebooks and pamphlets as well as an impressive collection of dictionaries in a multitude of languages, thesauri and books of grammar. And there on the top shelf, in pride of place, were the travel guidebooks she'd written. Out of the four hundred titles available in the Going Native series she was the proud author of five: India, Alaska, New Orleans, Austria and Tokyo. The book on Scandinavia would make six.

It wasn't everybody's idea of security, flitting off to spend eight months of the year in a strange country, but Megan loved it. She even loved writing about it afterward.

Just not right now. Much as she loved coming back to San Francisco, which was as much her home base as any place in the world could be, it was always a bit anticli-

mactic to knuckle down to the actual work after having an
adventure. In a few weeks she'd be back in her stride, but
the only way to get there was to do the work.

She glared at the messy stacks of notes on the desk in
front of her and on the floor around her. She'd already spent
a week sifting through them, trying to create some kind of
order, yet it seemed as if she'd made no progress whatso-
ever.

If only she was a little more organized when she was
traveling, but no, she scribbled disjointed paragraphs on
whatever came to hand, dotting the margins of her guidebooks with exclamation marks which now meant nothing
to her and jotting down helpful notes like *remember story
about kids in river*. She may as well have written *make up
story about kids in river*. All this and there was still a stack
of dictaphone tapes to be transcribed. The pages she had
already organized were festooned with yellow sticky notes
and cross-references and now she couldn't even find her
Copenhagen notes.

"I could be married," she said, sinking into a familiar
daydream. "I could be a suburban housewife. I could be
in my kitchen waiting for my husband to come home, and
my biggest dilemma would be what to give him for dinner.
Or no, wait, it's Sunday. We'd probably be in the park with
the kids. And I wouldn't care about Copenhagen or reindeer
or snow sculptures or Vikings or even Isak Dinesen because
I wouldn't have to write about them!"

She dragged herself wearily out of her chair and went
over to get her pen. She bent over to pick it up and smiled.

"Of course," she said. She picked up the bundle of notes
that the pen had landed on and offered up a little prayer of
thanks to the playful patron saint of travel writers.

She sat down again and rubbed her hands briskly together, still talking encouragingly to herself. "All right,
let's do this. Two more hours and we'll have the Copenhagen chapter in some kind of shape, and then, by tomorrow—"

She stopped speaking and looked up.

"I'm working," she said, and waited.

The doorbell rang again.

Megan squirmed. "I'm working," she said desperately. "I really am. I can't answer the door. I definitely have to do another couple of hours and then I've got all that transcribing and I haven't even begun to sort out the photographs and—wait, I'm here, come back!"

This last exclamation burst out of her as she flung open her front door and called to the person at the bottom of the stoop.

"Rachel?" she said, as her sister spun around and ran up the steps, sweeping past her and into the house. Megan frowned, rubbing her hip where she'd bumped it against a table in her mad dash to the door.

She followed Rachel into the kitchen and the two of them faced each other over the counter.

"Are you planning on robbing a bank?" asked Megan.

Rachel sighed. At least, Megan thought she did. It was hard to be sure since Rachel's face was swathed in a black scarf. She was also wearing a baseball cap and wraparound sunglasses.

Megan scratched her chin thoughtfully. "I know what it is. You've become invisible again, haven't you? How many times have I told you not to drink the—"

Megan abandoned the rest of the sentence because Rachel had unwrapped the scarf. Megan, open-mouthed, leaned forward to peer at Rachel's face, which was a distinctly unhealthy shade of blue.

"What is it?" she said.

"You tell me," snapped Rachel. She fished in her handbag and pulled out a small plastic packet which she thrust at Megan.

Megan looked at the packet which had a picture of a woman on the front. Her face was the same color as Rachel's.

"A face mask," Megan said. She looked up at Rachel. "You do know that you're supposed to wash these off?"

"Are you?" said Rachel in a threatening tone. "Are you really? Well, what happens when you wash it off and you find that your face has been dyed blue!"

"Where did you get this?" said Megan, flipping the packet over. The writing on the back appeared to be in Swedish.

"It was in that beauty pack that you sent me a few months ago. With the shampoo and body lotion? That was in the bottom."

"So you put it on and when you went to wash it off, your face…"

"Ta-daa," exclaimed Rachel. She sat down opposite Megan and pointed frantically at the packet. "Look, there's a twenty-four hour helpline number on the back, you have to call them, find out what to do."

Megan began to look as worried as Rachel. "I don't know if my Swedish is that good. I really only mastered the basics, how to order food, get a cab, find my hotel, that sort of thing."

"I don't care," snarled Rachel. "Get your dictionary and call them."

"Okay," said Megan. "Just run through what happened again. How did you follow the instructions?"

Rachel lifted her eyebrow sardonically. "Well, there was a picture of a woman with the stuff on her face so I kind of figured that that's what you do with it. And there on the back it says 30 which I guessed meant thirty minutes, so after half an hour I washed it off and ended up with this. I came straight over here and that's the whole story. I can probably sue them."

Megan was studying the packet. She nodded. "Yeah, see, that says thirty years of excellence, or excellent service to the public or something. You're actually only supposed to leave it on for, uh, two minutes."

Rachel's hands flew to her face as if to check it was still there. "Maybe I should go to the hospital?"

"Does it hurt?"

"No," said Rachel, still massaging her cheeks absently. The movement made them look so much like Play-Doh that Megan had to press her lips together to restrain a smile. "I guess you should get checked out although it probably isn't harmful. I got the beauty pack in a natural health store. They only used natural products. The body lotion was made from seaweed."

Rachel gave her a cold look. "That's terrific."

Megan looked down again at the picture on the front of the packet. "It seems to be made from some kind of berries. Unless they're suggesting that the woman is eating berries while she's relaxing." She looked up and met Rachel's eyes.

"I'll phone them," said Megan.

After ten tortuous minutes on the phone, Megan hung up. She hoped Rachel hadn't been able to hear the woman's peal of laughter.

No such luck.

"She thought it was funny," said Rachel.

Megan winced. "It was sympathetic laughter. Anyway, don't worry about it, because the good news is that it isn't harmful and it'll fade in a couple of days."

"Two days?" Rachel said with despair. She stood up and began to pace.

"Either that or two years," Megan added under her breath.

"I think I'll still go to the emergency room. They might be able to get rid of it."

"That's a good idea," said Megan. "What did David say about it?"

"He hasn't seen it yet. He's in San Diego, at a conference."

"A hotel full of banking executives," said Megan dryly. "There's a party."

"It's just as well really," said Rachel. "My behavior has been strange enough lately without this on top of it."

"What do you mean, strange?"

Rachel was still pacing, looking distracted. "It doesn't matter. Forget I said it. We're okay again."

"What? Were you and David having problems? I thought he was the ideal boyfriend."

Rachel looked abashed. "He is. It's just that...I thought he was cheating on me."

Megan rubbed her face. "I've been working too hard," she said. "And I've fallen asleep at my desk and now I'm having a very bizarre dream." She met her twin's eyes. "I can't wait to tell you about it tomorrow."

"Oh no," said Rachel. "Is this your dream? I was hoping it was mine. I was really looking forward to waking up."

Megan tried to get back on track. "But he isn't cheating on you?"

"No, he isn't, but who cares about that? I'm in real trouble now." Rachel pointed at her face.

Megan smiled reassuringly. "Oh, Rach, this will fade. In a few days it'll just be a bad memory and in a few, uh, years it'll be a funny story. Just take lots of showers. Come on, sit down. I'll make us some lunch."

Rachel stopped and put her hands to her head as if she had a migraine. Megan suddenly noticed that there was real tension in her eyes.

"You don't understand. I don't have a few days. This is one of the biggest collections of classical and renaissance art we've ever had in this city and we've already sold out the tickets for the first three weeks. We don't have any leeway, we've got to open on Saturday. But we still haven't got the catalogues back and the guest list for the sponsors' dinner is partially unconfirmed, so I haven't even been able to finalize arrangements with the caterers or the security staff."

She began to hyperventilate. "The music, the seating, the

floral arrangements—these are all in limbo because the art-work from Europe was delayed, so we haven't unpacked it all yet which means we can't sign off on the insurance nor can we start setting up for the dinner, not that we could anyway because we don't know for sure who's coming.''

Rachel sat down opposite Megan again and gave a shaky laugh. ''This morning was the first time in about a month that I took some time for myself. I was looking completely run-down. I thought, I'll have a facial, put some cucumbers on my eyes, lie down and listen to Faith Hill for half an hour and I'll be fresh for work again.''

Megan crinkled her nose sympathetically. She didn't know what to say.

''Okay,'' said Rachel. ''It's simple. I don't have any choice. I'll just have to go to Peterson and explain what happened.''

''How do you think he'll react?''

''Honestly?'' said Rachel with a catch in her voice. ''I think he'll react by firing me.''

Megan was surprised. ''What? That's ridiculous. He can't do that.''

''You're right,'' said Rachel miserably. ''He won't. But I'll be taken off the exhibition and Kenneth will take over. And I'm not sure where that will leave me afterwards. Peterson was the only member of the board who wanted me to have the job in the first place. The others think I'm too young and, of course, too female. I know I'm absolutely wonderful at this, it's the job I was born to do, but this is only my second exhibition. I'm still sort of on probation. If they see this…'' She sighed. ''Well, would you entrust even one Botticelli to this person?''

Megan thought quickly. She had traveled half the world and her boundless enthusiasm had gotten her into some tricky situations. She was adept at weighing up the pros and cons of a situation, pragmatically rather than emotionally.

''Okay, so you can't go in. But don't give up. This could

be gone by tomorrow and if not, you can surely call in sick just for one day."

Rachel laughed at her naïveté. "I've already called in sick. I'm supposed to be at work right now." Her fingers drummed an agitated tattoo on the desk as she thought out loud. "If only I'd brought my laptop home last night…or even the artwork files, I wouldn't get so far behind. It would almost be as good as being there. I could say I caught a twenty-four-hour bug and don't want to give it to anyone."

Megan brightened. "Can't you get someone to bring the stuff you need to your house?"

"I thought of that, but I'd still have to explain my appearance to anyone who showed up. I can't take that chance."

Rachel folded her arms across the counter and dropped her head onto them, groaning loudly.

Megan waited until the sounds of anguish had subsided slightly. She reached out and touched Rachel's arm lightly.

"I know we haven't done this for a very long time," she said gently. "But why don't I go in and get your stuff for you? You can tell me what to do and say."

"That's a great idea," said Rachel blithely.

"I'm serious," said Megan.

"Oh, come on, we're not twelve years old anymore."

Megan spoke calmly. "I'm just saying that no one there has seen us together yet."

"But they all know I've got a twin."

"Yes, but it's an abstract until they actually see us together, you know that. Even photographs don't do it justice."

Rachel looked at her. What Megan was saying was true. They'd seen the evidence of it time and time again. Regardless of forewarning or preparation, people were inevitably somewhat shocked when they met the two sisters side by side. Even with the evidence right there before them, it took a few minutes to accept that there were two living, breathing creatures that looked exactly the same.

Rachel ran her hands through her hair, pulling it back from her forehead. "It would never work."

"I don't see why not," said Megan. "I know a lot about the staff from your e-mails, I bet I'd recognize most of them. I know Jocelyn's red hair is the bane of her life. I know Helena always comes in hung-over and the head of the permanent exhibition is that English guy with the long name, uh, Bateman-Parker."

"Edward Parker-Bakeworth III," said Rachel.

"Right. I know the ticket staff and the shop staff don't mingle with the restaurant staff—what's that about anyway?"

"Beats me," shrugged Rachel.

"And the board members certainly don't mingle with anyone. Peterson has a strawberry birthmark on his neck and that guy Kenneth is always trying to cop a feel even though, a few months ago, Sidra 'accidentally' spilt hot coffee down his front."

Rachel's mouth twitched. "But what if someone asks you an art question?" she fretted.

"Rachel," Megan reminded her. "Who brought you to the Louvre? Besides, do they usually stop you and bombard you with specialist art questions?"

Rachel chewed her lip, a sure sign of her indecision, and Megan could see the hope surfacing in her eyes.

Megan tried not to look excited. "It's just an idea," she said, insouciance personified.

"Well, I suppose it is sort of your fault that I'm in this mess," said Rachel.

Megan narrowed her eyes, but she decided to let it pass.

"I guess we could go over to my place and get some clothes for you while I think about it."

Megan looked down at her leather trousers and snug black turtleneck. "What's wrong with what I'm wearing?"

Rachel sat down again. "Why am I even considering this?"

"I'm kidding. I'm sorry, it was just a joke. I'll do what I'm told. I'll be good and I'll wear your nice clothes and I'll behave. I promise."

Rachel looked at her. "I'm still only thinking about it."

"I know," said Megan.

"SO I GO DOWN the hall and it's the third door on the left."

"The right! Third on the right." Rachel peered at her. "Are you even paying attention?"

"Third on the right," Megan repeated dutifully, admiring herself in the mirror. She did a twirl. "How do I look?"

Rachel looked impressed. "I never realized how good I looked in that suit."

"So it doesn't make my butt look big?"

Rachel smiled. She put a few more hairpins in Megan's hair, tightening and adjusting the French knot. She plucked a thread from the shoulder of the jacket and handed Megan her briefcase.

"Now, don't forget to phone me as soon as you get in."

"I will," said Megan, with pronounced stoicism.

"And you'll wait in the office for about an hour so it looks like I'm working?"

"Yes, I've got it. And I'll cough and sniffle a bit when I meet people so they'll know I'm sick."

"And if anybody asks anything say you'll get to it—"

"Just give me ten minutes," finished Megan. "And then I phone you. I've got it, I'm fine." She was smiling confidently. "Don't worry, this will be fun."

Rachel grabbed her arm. "No. No, don't say that. It's not fun. Please don't have fun."

"Rachel, relax. What's happened to your sense of adventure?"

"I think it's gone down to the welfare office," said Rachel dryly. "To get a head start on the paperwork."

2

MEGAN TURNED the car into Rachel's parking space and switched off the engine. She pretended to be fiddling with her handbag while she scoped out the courtyard from behind her sunglasses.

There were a few men in suits crisscrossing the courtyard and a couple of tourists admiring the building's stonework. Two harried teachers were trying to organize a giggling mass of schoolkids and a security guard was explaining to some backpackers that they'd have to have their picnic somewhere else. No one seemed to be paying any attention to Megan.

She retrieved the high heels from the back seat and slipped them on, trying not to look furtive.

She got out of the car and wiggled her hips to smooth down the skirt which had ridden up during the drive. The pantyhose were also causing her discomfort but she restrained from adjusting them in the parking lot.

Look at me, she thought giddily, in my grown-up clothes, going to my grown-up job. She slung the handbag over her shoulder and picked up the briefcase and coat. Good grief, she'd carried less on her trek around Nepal. Squaring her shoulders she walked calmly toward the front door and then, remembering in time, she turned and pointed the keys at the car. It let out a chirrup which she presumed meant it was locked.

Walking up the wide stone steps, Megan couldn't help but be excited. She'd been so thrilled when Rachel had e-mailed her in Norway to announce that she was the new head of temporary exhibitions at the Hyder Gallery of Fine Arts and her weekly e-mails had been a continuing source of amusement and fascination. Megan had been looking forward to getting an insider's view of the gallery to which she'd been a frequent visitor, but she hadn't anticipated that her first foray would be undercover.

She tried to ignore the butterflies in her stomach as she walked through the ornate wooden doors and into the foyer. She nodded hello to the two security guards on the left of the door and when they didn't immediately jump up yelling "Impostor!" she kept on walking.

She kept a vague half smile on her face as she passed people, trying to look preoccupied. She didn't want to blank someone she was supposed to know, but neither did she want to grin inanely at a total stranger.

"Ms. Dean!"

Megan jumped as she was accosted from the right.

"Ms. Dean. Thank goodness you're here. Mr. Lewis said you were sick but the music people called this morning to check if you want the harpists as well as the string quartet. Oh, and Jocelyn said to tell you that they'll just play a standard classical score, unless you specifically want something unusual or modern, but she assumed you wouldn't."

Megan put her hand over her mouth and gave a little cough, which wasn't too difficult since her throat had gone very dry.

"I did call in sick," she said, raking her eyes over the woman in front of her. Black skirt, cream blouse, short brown hair. There was nothing distinctive about her except maybe her cute tip-tilted nose.

Megan quashed her rising panic. *Okay, I have no idea who this is but it's not a problem.*

"I do have a cold but I've just come in to pick up some things." She paused and put her finger to her lip, looking thoughtful. "I made a note about the music, I think it's in my office. Tell you what, come by in about ten minutes and I'll give you an answer on that."

Cute Nose nodded brightly. "Thank you, Ms. Dean."

Megan faked a sneeze and nodded as she buried her nose in a tissue.

Her heart was hammering, but she had no choice now but to continue following Rachel's instructions. She walked through the foyer, took the double doors into the hallway on the right and then, when she came to the third door on the right, braced herself and went in.

The room was empty and a quick glance at the photo of herself and Rachel on the desk reassured Megan that she'd come to the right place.

"Woo hoo!" she said triumphantly, closing the door. She flung down the bag and briefcase and took off the restrictive suit jacket, dumping it on the couch. She pulled up her skirt and fiddled with the pantyhose until they were no longer cutting off her blood supply. She pulled down the skirt, then let out a sigh of exasperation at the sausage of material bunched about her waist. How did Rachel wear these clothes every day? She pulled the skirt up, smoothed the blouse down over her hips and pulled down the skirt again.

She checked that none of the pearly buttons on the blouse had popped open and that the zipper on the skirt was closed and then she sat behind the desk and picked up the phone, humming the *Mission Impossible* theme tune.

Rachel answered halfway through the first ring, as if she'd been sitting at home gnawing her fingers to the bone, which, thought Megan, she probably had.

The music question was dealt with easily and ten minutes later, Cute Nose, or Rebecca as Megan could now call her, was given the requested confirmations.

Megan phoned Rachel again. "Just keep answering the phone that quickly and we'll be fine. I'll call you as soon as anything else comes up. Don't worry, I've done the hard part. I'll put in another hour here and then I'll see you at home."

IT ONLY TOOK half an hour for Megan to become restless. Buoyed by her initial success she was fully prepared to take on another challenge, and she braced herself hopefully every time she heard footsteps outside the door. But they always passed by, and Megan was left looking aimlessly about the office and tapping her foot against the leg of the desk.

She felt like an aggrieved child, sent to her room for something she didn't do. The whole gallery was just outside her door and other people were enjoying it. They were free to wander around, to look at whatever they wanted. In fact, thought Megan, the irony is that I have the most freedom of all since my face is a pass key to any room, any exhibit. I could see the new exhibit a week before it opens. If I could leave the room.

Her toes curled as she wrestled with her conscience. It wasn't such an outrageous idea. People expected to see Rachel and that's who they'd see. Everyone acted a little off-kilter occasionally and friends or co-workers assumed they were preoccupied or had a headache or were just having a bad day. There were hundreds of excuses for uncharacteristic behavior, and it was a paranoid person indeed who immediately jumped to the conclusion that they were dealing with a body-snatcher scenario.

But, on the other hand, Rachel would kill her.

She'd never know, said devil-Megan. Megan looked to her other shoulder. I dunno, said angel-Megan sheepishly, I kinda want to see the sculptures, too.

Because, thought Megan, formulating a final convincing argument, this is wrong. This is like visiting a new country and spending all your time in the hotel room. It's a crime, a crime against art.

"Good enough for me," said Megan, bouncing out of her chair. She put on the shoes but balked at the jacket. Then, with a deep breath, she stepped out into the hall.

SAM HARRISON looked disgruntled.

"That's no good either," he said. "It's still too cluttered."

The movers didn't say anything. They milled around, brushing their arms against their foreheads to wipe the sweat. Sam looked at the assembled statues, trying to visualize the arrangement that would show them off to their best advantage.

He looked over at one of the movers. "Did we use that low plinth, the one-footer? See if you can dig it out." He started directing them around again. "We'll put the centaur in the corner and try the bust in front of it, down low, and that way we can still have the Claudel by the window."

They set to work again and Sam himself cradled the sculpture in his arms as the marble base was pushed ten inches to the left.

"Careful with that," said a voice behind him. "Dropping a Rodin could really spoil your day."

Sam looked over his shoulder, still gripping the stone tightly. Aha, just the person he wanted to see. Maybe now she'd take him seriously when he said he needed more room.

"It's one of Camille Claudel's actually," he corrected her automatically.

She shrugged. "But who can tell the difference, right?"

Her flippancy confused him. "I was hoping you could."

She surprised him with a smirk. "I was just teasing you." She made a show of searching the floor around their feet. "You must have left it somewhere, oh, here it is." She picked up an invisible object and held it out to him.

He looked at her, frowning.

"Your sense of humor," she explained, patting him on the shoulder and giving him another smile.

The furrow between his brows deepened but Megan was already distracted.

"This is really impressive," she said, letting her gaze roam about the huge hall. She looked back at him and locked her eyes briefly onto his.

Sam was taken aback. All week she'd been almost icy in her professionalism and had slowly grown more so as they'd clashed over the allotment of space for the exhibit. But today her blue eyes were sparkling with pleasure and excitement.

"Thanks," he said gruffly. "But we could still use more room."

He watched her look reflectively at the statues and he felt his neck muscles tighten. He'd seen her do this before. This was where she pursed her lips and said she was sure he would work it out somehow with the space he had.

"No kidding," she said. "That corner is too squashed. The centaur should be on its own. You can't appreciate it with all the others drawing the eye downwards."

Sam couldn't have been more surprised if she'd opened her blouse and flashed him. He made sure the Claudel was secure before giving her his full attention.

"So you're giving me the extra room?"

A range of emotions seemed to flutter across her face. "Excuse me?"

Sam's eyes narrowed. "The extra room. You're going to let me have it?"

She nodded vaguely. "The extra room," she repeated slowly, setting Sam's nerves on edge.

"I'm glad you brought that up," she said at last. "That's mainly why I came up here actually. I just needed to check that you still wanted it before I made my final decision. Which I will be able to tell you tomorrow. Or," she said, brightening with enthusiasm, "maybe I could call you later."

Sam looked at her in confusion. "Call me?"

"Right. If I have to go home," she said, coughing delicately.

Sam breathed out through his nose. He was finding it increasingly difficult to be civil. "Look, Ms. Dean—"

"Oh please," she interrupted him. "Call me—"

She stopped abruptly and her eyes flickered. Sam had

never met someone who heard voices in their head, but he imagined they'd be acting a lot like this woman in front of him.

"You know what?" she went on. "Ms. Dean is fine. Yes, call me Ms. Dean. That is, continue to call me that."

Sam started to speak, but she cut him off again.

"And is it all right if I keep calling you…?"

She was holding his eyes now, her head tilted flirtatiously.

"Sam is fine," he said.

"Sam," she said, nodding happily. "Sam it is."

Sam couldn't believe it. She'd forgotten his name. He wasn't just puzzled anymore, he was becoming perturbed.

"Sam," she said with a sudden briskness. "I'm sorry. I know this must be frustrating for you. I promise I'll let you know about the room tomorrow, if not before." She looked at her watch. "But I really should go back downstairs now." She looked around the room again and her face twitched. "I'll just have a quick look around," she said with a mischievous smirk.

Sam watched her as she gazed reverently at the artwork. A horrible suspicion was dawning in his mind, and he continued to study her as she meandered among the statues, pausing here and there to put her hand to her chest with a sigh of satisfaction.

MEGAN EMPLOYED every ounce of her willpower to stop herself from blushing, but she could still feel the heat spreading across her face. She ran through the conversation in her head, trying to work out if she'd made a complete idiot of herself. Or, to be more specific, of Rachel.

She hadn't been able to help it. She'd taken him for one of the moving guys and had just been indulging in a little harmless banter, okay, flirting, before she realized she probably shouldn't have been talking to him.

But by then it was too late. By then she'd seen the sheen of perspiration on the tanned skin of his neck, she'd caught a glimpse of straight white teeth behind generous lips and she'd looked into his eyes. By then she'd heard his low voice and was completely flustered and had reacted by babbling even more.

She stopped in front of a statue of a Greek soldier and looked at the perfect nose and strong jawline. She wished she could study Sam with the same unabashed curiosity. She wondered if he'd felt it, too, that zing when their eyes had met. And what eyes. They were like caramel. No, like amber. She could gaze into them for hours trying to work out exactly what they were like.

Her gaze dropped to the exquisitely delineated muscles of the marble torso. Was there anything more inviting than a broad, strong male chest? Sam's muscles had been very well-defined through his T-shirt and he had long strong arms. Lifting statues was obviously excellent exercise.

Her blush deepened as her gaze dropped further. She sneaked a quick glance at Sam, then looked away quickly when she caught him watching her. She swallowed and folded her arms firmly as she felt heat spread to her neck. He was looking at her and she was looking at…honestly, these Greek soldiers found time to pick up a shield and a sword but they couldn't take two minutes to put on some clothes?

She took a few casual steps and found herself in front of a painting of Perseus and Andromeda.

In the full throes of passion.

What was this, an exhibition of erotica? She was about to turn away again but she forced herself to look at their entwined limbs, at Andromeda's expression of rapture, her head thrown back while Perseus pressed his mouth to her breast. One of his strong arms was tangled in her hair while the other was wrapped around her, his fingers digging into the flesh of her buttock as he pulled her tight against him, his hugely muscular leg thrust between hers.

Megan felt a pain in her arm. She looked down and realized she was digging her own nails into her bicep. She unfolded her arms and tried to calm down as she turned away from the painting.

She would have to leave. She really should go now. She squared her shoulders and tried not to stare at Sam as she walked toward him. She felt her heart racing, and he reached out to grab her arm as she stumbled on the unfamiliar high heels.

She giggled with embarrassment and put her hand flat against his chest to right herself. The warmth of his skin through his T-shirt made her insides contract.

She felt a sudden stab of desperation, as if she'd never see him again, and it made her blurt out the first thing that came to her mind. "Have you ever seen that old movie, *Heaven Can Wait?*"

He answered cautiously. "The one with Warren Beatty?"

"Right. You know, I love that bit at the end where he says something like, 'you might meet someone and even though he's not me there might be something in his eyes and if he's a nice guy you might give him a chance.'"

SAM DIDN'T SAY anything, instead he watched her walk toward the stairs. He shook his head in concern and amazement. Even though he didn't want to admit it, that last comment had confirmed his suspicions.

And he would have to do something about it.

3

"Honey, I'm home!"

Megan chuckled at her own wittiness as she dropped the briefcase and kicked off her shoes.

Rachel emerged from the kitchen just in time to see this last affront.

"Careful with those," she scolded. "They're Jimmy Choos."

"So what?" said Megan. "Does he want them back?"

She dropped Rachel's keys on the hall table and made her way into the living room, taking off her jacket and tossing it onto the sofa.

Rachel followed her like a fussy housewife, picking up the jacket and shaking it out before arranging it on the back of a chair.

She sat down opposite Megan and stared at her avidly. "So?"

Megan stretched out on the sofa and closed her eyes. "Doesn't the breadwinner deserve a little drink when she comes home?"

A heavy silence ensued so she opened her eyes again.

"You know," she said. "I think that this is the first time that the expression *purple with apoplexy* can be taken quite literally."

"I believe people also turn very interesting colors when they're being choked," commented Rachel.

Megan smiled broadly at her. "Rach, it was great. I had such a good time."

Rachel groaned and buried her face in her hands.

"No, don't be like that. It was fine. No one suspected a thing. No one questioned me or looked at me oddly and I got all your stuff. You can catch up, you'll keep your job."

Rachel stared, plaintive hopefulness all over her blue face. "Do you really think so?"

Megan spread her hands. "I'm here, right? If there'd been a problem they would probably, I dunno, have arrested me or something. So, please, relax."

Rachel let out an exhalation as if she'd been holding it all afternoon.

"And every time I met someone I made sure to sound very sniffly and cough a bit, but I didn't overdo it."

Rachel's face scrunched up with anxiety. "What do you mean? Who else did you meet?"

Megan paused. She didn't feel ready to mention Sam just yet. Rachel still looked a bit too tense.

"I just meant that secretary person, with the music question."

Rachel nodded. "Rebecca."

"Right. And I'm sure lots of people saw me coughing and sneezing so don't forget to have the tail-end of a cold when you go back."

She finished with an encouraging thumbs-up and was relieved when Rachel sat back and smiled.

Megan raised her eyebrows. "I'm waiting."

"Okay," said Rachel. "You're fantastic. You're the best sister in the world."

"Well, thank you, but actually I meant I'm waiting for my drink." She sighed in mock exasperation. "I hope David realizes what a hopeless wife you'll make."

Rachel laughed and jumped to her feet. She called out from the kitchen. "Beer or apple juice?"

"Surprise me," said Megan, rubbing her tired feet.

Rachel came out and handed her a beer. "To the incorrigible Dean twins," she toasted.

Megan clinked her bottle against Rachel's glass.

"The Dean twins," she echoed, wondering if it was now safe to broach the subject of the delectable Sam.

"The gallery is so amazing, Rach. The huge rooms, the high ceilings, the smell of old art. You must love working there."

Rachel grinned. She gestured for Megan to come and sit beside her. "Look at this," she said, switching on the laptop. She whizzed the mouse around expertly and conjured up a three-dimensional model of the gallery. She zoomed in and they were looking at an aerial view of the first floor.

"Gosh, it must be hard deciding where to put everything," Megan said subtly. "Do you have to do that?"

"We try to work out as much as we can before we start bringing in the works, but there's still a lot of rearranging once you see what it all actually looks like."

"So, that's part of your job, is it?" Megan persisted.

Rachel was still manipulating the gallery diagram on her computer and she answered absently. "Usually it's John Forsyth's job but this particular exhibition is so important they've got their own guy in charge of it. He does all the arranging himself."

Megan congratulated herself mentally. "Really? What's his name?"

"Sam Harrison," said Rachel, double-clicking the mouse.

"Oh," said Megan brightly. "He sounds nice."

Rachel stopped fiddling with the mouse and turned her head slowly. The look on her sister's face told Megan she'd blown it.

"I got your stuff for you, right?" she said in a placatory tone. "Everything's okay now."

"Is it?" Rachel asked icily.

"Of course it is." Megan moistened her lips. "The thing is, I just went and had a quick look at the exhibition."

"The permanent exhibition?" Rachel said hopefully.

"Well, no, the new one." Megan indicated the files she'd brought home. "Your exhibition."

"You went to the second floor?" said Rachel, making it sound like some distant planet. "And walked around?"

Megan nodded. "It's going to be a fantastic show," she said obsequiously. "That black marble centaur? Wow. And the painting of the seven muses. Incredible. And, of course, the Claudel."

"You did go up," breathed Rachel. "You are impossible. Have you ever considered just containing your curiosity?"

"I just had a quick look around and didn't talk to anyone. Well, anyone, except…"

"Except?"

"It might, possibly, have been that guy, Sam Harrison. Tall, black hair, the most amazing hazel eyes."

Rachel's own eyes had begun to bulge slightly.

"You talked to him? Please Megan, tell me it was just a conversation about the weather."

Megan thought quickly about what not to say. "It wasn't really a conversation. I just said everything was looking good and then he said something about needing an extra room and I said I'd get back to him about it tomorrow."

Rachel peered at her. "That's it?"

"Pretty much." Megan nodded convincingly.

Rachel made a face. "Well, he can't have the extra room. I told him that, it's already decided."

She clicked onto the aerial view again and showed Megan. "See, he wants to use this room on the left as well but that's where the dinner is going to be held."

Megan tilted her head. "Does it have to be there? Could you have it in the front of the main room?"

"But they've already set up most of the statues, as you saw," Rachel said pointedly.

"It's what? About fifteen statues? You could take out ten, open out a space. I bet he'd be glad to move them."

Rachel shook her head. "No, it's just too much trouble at this stage. I'll leave it."

"It might really be worth it," Megan persisted. "It might

be less trouble than you think. And I actually think it would look better.''

Rachel looked at her shrewdly. "You do, do you?"

Megan nodded.

"And that's the only reason you're being so persuasive, because you think it would look better?"

Megan shrugged. "What other reason could there be?"

"Oh, I don't know," said Rachel casually. "It's just that it would probably make Sam Harrison happy."

Megan widened her eyes. "Why would I care about that? I don't even know him."

"You just think it's the right thing to do for aesthetic reasons."

"Exactly."

"And not because, for example, me being nice to Sam Harrison now might smooth the path to you becoming his little love slave?"

Megan put her hand on her chest and swooned back on the sofa. "Rachel, he's a Greek god. A warrior. And I'm hopelessly impaled on his spear." She paused, grimacing. "No, wait, I didn't mean that the way it sounded. I mean, a figurative spear. A cupid's spear of love."

She looked at Rachel, who didn't seem to get it.

"Okay," said Rachel slowly, "I admit that Sam Harrison does give the impression of owning, under his clothes, a godlike body but you just met him. I mean, technically it's not a spear of love we're talking about here, it's a spear of lust."

"Not just a spear. A huge torpedo of lust. A blasting rocket of—"

Rachel put up her hands. "I'm begging you. Can we at least change to a different metaphor? I work with this guy. What on earth has gotten into you? He's not even your type."

"But he's lovely," said Megan dreamily. "Those strong arms, that wide mouth."

Rachel burst out laughing. "You know this morning

when I said that we're not twelve years old anymore? I think I might have been wrong about one of us. Anyway, forget it Megan, he's far too serious and reserved for you.''

''I didn't see a wedding ring,'' said Megan, undaunted. ''Is he involved with anyone?''

''Not that I know of,'' said Rachel. ''Although Helena has certainly been doing her best to snag him.''

''Helena?''

''I told you about her,'' said Rachel, referring to her e-mails. ''She wears those colored contact lenses.''

Rachel was enjoying the giggly conversation so much that she had almost forgotten the circumstances under which Sam and Megan had met. She suddenly remembered. Her face went a paler shade of blue.

''You didn't do anything or say anything that might have made him suspicious, did you? Please tell me you didn't act weird around him.''

''No, of course not.'' Megan's face was a mask of innocence.

''Good. That would really be a perfect end to a perfect day—to have Sam Harrison thinking I'm interested in him.''

Megan gave a hollow laugh. She decided it might be wise to get off the subject of Mr. Harrison for a while. Besides, there were the unanswered questions of Rachel's love life to be explored.

''Anyway,'' she said, ''what problems were you and David having?''

Rachel made a face. ''It was this stupid book that Helena brought into work, called *Is He Cheating on You?*''

''Oh Rach, you didn't.''

If Megan was known for her curiosity, Rachel's particular foible was her suggestibility. She could read an article about alpine explorers and days later she'd still be checking her toes for frostbite. Psychology or self-help books were a definite no-no.

"I only intended to skim it," said Rachel. "But it was all so familiar."

"So you decided David was cheating?"

"He bought me flowers for no reason."

"He likes you."

"He takes lots of showers and always smells good."

Megan laughed. "He's a clean guy."

Rachel joined in, laughing at herself. "Oh Megan, you should have seen me. I kept sniffing his collars for strange perfumes and examining them for lipstick smudges. I waved credit-card receipts in his face and got all suspicious when he gave me chocolates. The poor guy didn't know what to do."

"But you're okay now?"

Rachel waved her hand. "Oh yeah, we're fine. For goodness sakes, it's David. I'd trust him with my life."

Megan smiled, picking at the beer-bottle label. "I'm glad. I've always been so happy for you, having such a great guy. I think it's wonderful that—"

Rachel put up her hand as if to stop the flood of words. "What do you want?" she said, laughing.

"Just for you to introduce me to Sam, I mean, properly."

Rachel sighed patiently. "If I get through this week alive and I still have a job at the end of it, I'll personally fly you both to Paris. But right now I've got to do this. Don't you have any work to do?"

Megan slumped back on the sofa with thoughts of Scandinavian capitals pushed to the back of her mind. "I guess," she said, taking another swig of beer. A faraway look came into her eyes and a small smile played about her lips. Rachel shook her head and turned back to her own work.

When the phone rang it startled them both.

Rachel picked it up and Megan listened idly to her end of the conversation.

"Oh, hello Mr. Peterson...uh, yes I did...a cold, that's right...who?...Sam Harrison?"

Megan perked up.

"He said what?" continued Rachel. Her eyes shot to Megan's. "But that's…it's ridiculous…yes, I most certainly am denying it."

Rachel's brow was knitted and Megan could see that she was thinking hard. Megan was concentrating mostly on controlling the queasiness in her stomach.

Rachel spoke again. "I did take some cold medicine and felt a little light-headed, could that be…?"

She listened for a moment then started nodding. "Yes sir, giddy, I suppose I was." She shook her fist at Megan. "Kenneth? Oh no, that's not necessary. I'm sure this is just a twenty-four-hour bug, I think I'm over the worst… tomorrow morning…yes sir, thank you."

She hung up.

"That was Mr. Peterson," she said in a measured tone. "It seems your Greek god thought so highly of you today that he went straight to Mr. Peterson in order to express his grave concern because Rachel Dean came into the main gallery where he, Sam, was working, and she appeared to him to be completely blotto!"

Megan shrank back into the sofa. "What?"

Rachel nodded. "Yes," she said with fake amusement. "Apparently I was stumbling around, making jokes and talking rubbish."

Megan was stung. "I was not talking rubbish," she said defensively. "As for him running to Peterson, what a snitch!"

"Oh, don't try and lay the blame on him. I would have done the same thing."

Megan ducked her head. "Oh Rachel, I'm so sorry."

"You should be. Thanks to you I've now got an unavoidable morning meeting with Mr. Peterson. Since I've got a cold and am acting 'giddy' he's already inclined to pass my responsibilities onto Kenneth."

"I'm really sorry," Megan said again.

Rachel put her face in her hands. "I can't believe I'm

going to lose this because Sam Harrison thought I was drunk.''

Megan didn't say anything, just sat there, her stomach churning with guilt.

Rachel suddenly sat up as if she'd received a shot of adrenaline straight to the heart. She turned to Megan and an expression of pure joy bloomed in her face.

Megan drew back, unnerved.

"He thought I was drunk!" Rachel exclaimed triumphantly.

Megan looked like a deer caught in the headlights.

Rachel went on gleefully. "Don't you see? Okay, it's bad that he thought it was me, drunk, but, like you said, he never even considered the possibility that it wasn't me at all. He just said to himself, she's acting weird, she must be drunk. He thought you were me. You were a success."

Megan smiled warily.

Rachel reached out and yanked the beer away from Megan. "That's enough of that. You've got a big day tomorrow!"

4

MEGAN PULLED into the same parking space as she had the day before and looked up at the stone facade. Her nerves had been tightening the whole way over and now she was almost quivering with apprehension.

How could she possibly do a whole morning here?

That blue dye on Rachel's face must be soaking into her brain if she thought this was a good idea.

And it really didn't help that she'd have to see Sam again. Last night she'd almost been enjoying the thought of it. Imagining his face had given her little thrills of happy anticipation. It made a wonderful fantasy—but here, in real life, with all these other real people walking around, there was simply too much that could go wrong.

She got out of the car, trying to puff up her confidence. This can't possibly be as scary as yesterday, she kept telling herself, because today you'll be able to recognize people.

At least she was feeling a little more comfortable in Rachel's clothes. After her complaints about waistbands that got twisted around and blouses that bunched Rachel had put her into a simple sleeveless Donna Karan shift dress. She had also trimmed and conditioned Megan's hair—after Megan had, much to Rachel's annoyance, first made a great show of checking that the conditioner had instructions written in English—and it fell naturally to her shoulders with a little flick at the ends.

She smiled at the security guards as she made her way through the foyer and into Rachel's office. There she put down her bag and took off her coat and stood, peering intently at the map of the gallery that Rachel had printed out for her. Rachel's office was located on the east wing of the first floor and Peterson's was in the same area on the fourth floor.

There were three ways to get there. The first was a public elevator and staircase on the southwest corner, but using that would mean she would actually have to traverse the fourth floor. The gift shop was located there but it also held the lecture halls and restoration rooms so it was predominantly populated by gallery staff. Best avoided if possible.

There was a service elevator on the northeast corner, easy to get to and she'd be close to Peterson's office when she got off but it was a large slow-moving elevator, used to move paintings and other artwork between floors. For her to use it would be slightly unusual and a good way of drawing attention to herself.

So she had to go up the staircase on the east side of the building which meant first walking through the central office where the administration staff worked. Her scheme was to hone in on Rachel's assistant, Jocelyn, who would be the easiest to recognize because of her bright red hair. Megan would chat briefly with her and then make for the stairs without talking to anyone else.

She was almost out the door when she remembered the revised floor plan that Rachel had given her to show to Peterson. She grabbed the file from her briefcase and, squaring her shoulders, left the office.

She went into the administration room and quickly spotted both Jocelyn and the door to the stairs. Jocelyn came bustling over and gave Megan a commiserating grimace.

"I heard," Jocelyn said. "Anne told me."

Megan searched her memory. She was ninety percent sure that Anne was Peterson's secretary.

"Are you going up to see him now?" Jocelyn went on, whispering. "I couldn't believe it. Anne said it was something to do with Sam Harrison? That he called you a drunk? It's crazy and I'll tell Mr. Peterson so if you want me to."

Megan smiled. "No, it's not that bad. Sam said I was drunk, not *a* drunk." She rushed on. "Not that I was either. It's just a misunderstanding and I'm on my way up to see Mr. Peterson now and sort it out. I don't think it's too serious." As if saying it could make it so.

Jocelyn put her hand on Megan's arm.

"After you went home yesterday John Forsyth wanted to talk to me about..." She looked over Megan's shoulder then muttered, "Oops, speak of the devil."

Megan turned as a voice came behind her.

"Rachel, I'm glad I caught you. I wonder if I might have a word."

Megan turned to face a genial-looking man, only slightly taller than herself. He had thinning, sandy hair brushed back from his face and he was wearing a tweed suit.

"John," she hazarded, relying on what Jocelyn had said. "Could we leave it until later? I've got a meeting with Mr. Peterson and I'm cutting it fine." She glanced at her watch for emphasis.

Forsyth went on, regardless. "Just wanted to speak to you about my involvement in the exhibition. I understand this Sam guy is used to doing these things on his own, but I have explained to him that I'm available to help in any way. I just think he could make more use of me. I have been doing this for ten years, after all."

Megan nodded in understanding. "I'll speak to him about it, John," she said, edging toward the stairs. "Right after I see Peterson."

MEGAN STOPPED when she reached the fourth floor and took a few deep breaths. In the hallway she turned right and saw Sam immediately, standing next to a rotund man.

She understood now what Rachel had meant when she'd called Sam serious and reserved. He was dressed in a charcoal suit and, even though Megan wasn't usually a person to be impressed by a man's clothes, she could appreciate how good he looked.

Concentrate, she told herself. Even though the impulse was to hurry she deliberately kept her stride even.

She was Rachel, she was a professional and this was not a big deal although it was annoying and insulting to have been maligned like this. As if she didn't take her job seriously. Considering the fact that she hadn't actually *been* drunk the day before, Megan didn't really have to feign her indignation over the accusation. She lifted her chin a little and made them wait for her, putting on a pleasant smile as she approached.

"Rachel," said Mr. Peterson, "I'm glad to see you're feeling better. I was just telling Sam what you told me on the phone yesterday and I think it's cleared up the misunderstanding. I know you both have a lot to do so I really don't think it's necessary to spend any more time on it. Is that all right with both of you?"

Sam looked at her and she could see him taking in her polished demeanor and slightly steely gaze.

Yeah, what do ya think of me now? she thought smugly, resisting the urge to poke her tongue out at him.

"I think perhaps I should also offer an apology," said Sam graciously. "I certainly had no intention of impugning your reputation or of causing any trouble for you." He dipped his head, looking somewhat abashed. "I'm afraid that when it comes to the artwork I sometimes get a little overprotective."

His earnestness made Megan's heart flip over. She could feel a rush of affection rising in her chest, so she made a determined effort to quash it.

She settled for smiling warmly at him. "Oh please," she said, using Rachel's words, "I would have done the same thing. You were absolutely right. I'm sorry I put you in that position." She waved her hand airily. "I was really floating yesterday."

Then she caught Peterson's unimpressed gaze and realized she was being a bit too facetious.

Sam gave her a grateful smile. "Well, I'm glad to see that you're back to your old self again."

Megan nearly burst out laughing at his choice of words, but she held it in. Remember, she told herself, today's mission is to make a good impression.

She gave him a polite nod, almost as if bestowing benediction.

"That's great," said Peterson. "I'll leave you to it. Rachel, drop Friday's schedule up to me when you get the chance."

"Of course, Mr. Peterson," she said without hesitation, hoping that Rachel would understand the request. She held the new floor plan out to Peterson.

"I've decided to make a few changes to the layout of the works." She smothered a smile of satisfaction as Sam's head perked up. "It's a shame not to be able to utilize the end room, just because we want to keep it free for the dinner, especially when we really could use the space. I thought that instead, what we could do…"

She trailed off as Peterson held up his hand. "That's fine, give it to Sam. I'm leaving all that up to you two. You're the experts," he said jovially. He retreated into his office and Sam and Megan were left facing each other in the hall.

"We're going to use the end room?" said Sam, breaking the uncomfortable silence.

Megan smiled, feeling personally responsible for his hopeful expression.

"Yes. Despite the fact that you tried to have me removed from staff." She lifted her eyebrows to show it was a joke, "I've revised the plans. I hope it's not too late."

"Not at all," he said, taking the file and flipping through it. "This is great." He paused and looked up, meeting her eyes.

"I really am sorry about what I said. I hope it won't make things awkward between us. I want us to have a good relationship since we'll be working so closely together on the exhibit."

Megan put her hand on his arm, applying a little pressure. "Let's just forget about it."

And take your hand off him, she told herself.

He smiled, causing another frisson to run through her. "I think you've definitely made the right decision, Ms. Dean."

Megan crinkled her nose. "Oh look, you may as well call me Rachel," she said, hoping she didn't sound as begrudging as she felt. She would just have to wait for a while before she heard her own name in that delicious voice.

She indicated the file. "That shows the space I need for the dinner. We're moving it to the main hall. I've sketched in some of the artwork, but, naturally, that's in your hands. If you have any questions you can come to my office."

"I will," he said, examining the plan.

Megan tore her eyes away from him. "Uh, okay," she said. "I guess I better go do some work."

She turned away, but Sam pressed the button for the service elevator. "Are you going down?" he said.

Megan paused. It would probably look ungracious if she refused to go with him. He might think she was holding a grudge.

"Sure," she said as the elevator doors slid open.

On the way, Sam was still engrossed in the new floor plan and didn't seem to notice Megan's sideways glances at him. Apparently, that overwhelming attraction she'd felt *had* all been on her side. She sneaked another peek as he turned a page, nodding to himself. She shrugged mentally, trying to shake off her pique. He probably *was* too serious for her anyway.

The elevator stopped and Sam stepped out.

"See you later," he said absently.

Megan paused and watched him walk away. Okay, this was the second floor and he obviously wasn't expecting her to follow him. So I won't, thought Megan with a hint of bitterness. I'll just go back to Rachel's office. If you have any concerns, Sam, you can find me there. If, for example, you want to discuss the new floorplan which I worked so hard to get for you. It's okay, Sam, no thanks needed.

Just as she was about to hit the elevator button, the doors started closing of their own accord.

Uh-oh.

She realized, too late, that the metal buttons didn't have any numbers on them.

She felt the elevator descend and waited as the doors opened again.

This didn't look like the first floor. For one thing, the actual floor was bare cement.

A man in overalls came into the elevator. "Hi, Ms. Dean," he said cheerily, putting a key into the elevator controls and turning it. Megan heard a clank as the doors locked in the open position. She smiled weakly and suddenly realized she had no choice but to get out as other movers started loading in boxes. She swallowed and walked out, trying to convey that that had been her intention all along, as she desperately tried to get her bearings.

She was pretty sure she was in the vault, the huge underground storage area that also acted as a parking bay for the delivery vans.

Her complete knowledge of the vault was comprised of one sentence from Rachel. "That's the way down to the vault, but you won't need to go there so don't worry about it."

Well, she was here now and that elevator wasn't going anywhere soon. She noticed with relief that there were doors leading to a stairwell beside the elevator but reasoned that it would look odd to the movers if she just went straight up.

I'll just take a quick look around, she thought.

The vault was like a huge ancient library with paintings, instead of books stacked on towering shelves. Trying not to appear too fascinated, Megan went down the second aisle and, when she came to a gap, turned left into another aisle. Racks of paintings stretched out in all directions. Megan began by speculating that the numbers must be in the hundreds but, after turning onto yet another aisle, revised that to thousands. She ran her fingers through the dust that covered the tops of the frames, realizing that some of the paintings hadn't been moved in years. She loosened one and slid it out to have a look.

Well, that would explain it. She was no expert, but even she could see that the only thing the picture had going for it was that it was old. And, she supposed, if you had thousands to choose from, being old probably wasn't enough. She slid the painting gently back into place.

She decided she'd killed enough time, and she started back toward the stairwell, following her carefully remembered directions. Left here, then right, then right again.

Hmm, maybe not. Where she'd expected to see the elevator and nearby stairs were only more labyrinthine corridors. A mover came hurrying past and, after giving him a cursory smile, Megan pretended interest in one of the racks of paintings. The mover disappeared around a corner and Megan re-evaluated her position. Maybe it had been three rights. She'd just go around this corner and...no, this was no good either.

Megan felt a tickle of alarm but ignored it. She'd been in much worse positions than this. For goodness sakes, she could *hear* the movers and the mechanical clanks of the elevator. But the tall shelves distorted the sounds and they echoed from all directions.

She turned resolutely in the direction she'd just come and when she came to the intersection of shelves, turned right, her heels echoing as she strode along.

Another dead end. Megan let out a grunt of frustration and turned to retrace her steps.

Five long minutes passed and Megan began to wonder how far she'd walked. There were numbers and letters on the shelves but they were in no useful order that Megan could discern—probably had to do with the chronology of the works or something.

She turned another corner and faced another dead end. She stamped her foot. This was so stupid.

She walked back to an intersection again and stood, listening and searching the ceiling for inspiration. She heard footsteps and hurried down the corridor toward them. She would have to find some subtle way of asking for directions. She turned at the end of the aisle and found herself face-to-face with Sam.

She blanched, not knowing what to say.

SAM SMILED with relief. "I was just about to send out an SOS."

"I'm not lost," said Megan.

Sam faltered. "For me," he clarified.

She paused and then her mouth widened in a dazzling smile. "Right. For you. Of course."

Sam smiled awkwardly, embarrassed that his joke had fallen flat. He held up the piece of paper he was carrying. "I'm looking for CSEPK17679."

She took the paper from him and looked down at it, examining the number.

Sam watched her. She was wearing her hair loose today and a lock fell forward, curving across her cheekbone. Even in the muted light of the vault it shone with a golden gleam.

He blinked as she raised her head, and looked away hurriedly.

"That's no problem," she said, handing him the paper. "I'll show you where it is." She turned and walked to the corner, hesitating briefly before turning left.

Sam followed her, trying not to let his gaze linger too long on the soft sway of her hips. The dress she was wearing fit her perfectly, curving in to show off a slim waist.

She stopped and leaned forward slightly, peering at the numbers on the shelves. Sam stopped behind her and then took a step backward. He was suddenly acutely aware that they were alone and the silence and shadows of the vault somehow added to the intimacy.

"Here we go," she said, reading the shelf label. "PDEL86729."

Sam frowned and looked at his piece of paper again. "That's not exactly it," he said. "I need CSEPK17679."

Megan looked puzzled, then abashed. "Oh sorry," she laughed. "I was thinking of something else entirely." She put a finger to her head and made a face. "Short circuit in the brain."

"That's okay," laughed Sam.

"That's what happens when you're trying to think of a hundred things at once."

He nodded in wry agreement. "Don't I know it." He met her eyes and for a moment neither of them looked away. Her pupils were large and dark in the half light and all thoughts of work were pushed from Sam's head by the force of one big thought, which was to lean forward and kiss that soft, pink mouth.

Her lips parted.

Sam held her gaze, feeling his heart beginning to thump in his chest. He moved forward imperceptibly, searching her eyes for an invitation.

"CSEPK…?" she prompted.

Sam blinked, pulling back. He looked quickly down at the paper. "Er…17679," he croaked.

"Oh yes," she said. "It's this way." She brushed past him and Sam swallowed, trying to regain his composure before he followed her.

He was appalled. Another second and he would have kissed her. He put his hand through his hair, exhaling in relief at his narrow escape. He didn't know what had gotten into him. He'd acknowledged to himself when they'd first met that she was an attractive woman, but he'd also acknowledged that there hadn't been any chemistry.

But now, after that one little peek past her usual businesslike demeanor yesterday, there was chemistry fizzing and crackling all over the place.

"Here we go," she said, stopping again. Sam glanced at

her face, but she was focused on the shelf numbers. She didn't seem to have noticed anything untoward in his behavior.

"Wait a minute," she said with an annoyed edge to her voice. "It's not here." She put her hands on her hips and looked around crossly. "They must have moved it."

She looked up at him, shaking her head apologetically. "Sorry, I'm just talking to myself. They did some rearranging here a few weeks ago and I'm still not caught up with where everything is. I'll just call one of the guys." She tilted her head back. "Al? You there?"

Sam looked at her face, wondering if she really was confused or if she was just calling for a chaperone. In either case, there was no answer.

She shrugged. "Al must be off today." She tapped her finger thoughtfully against her chin. "Joe! Joe? Are you around?"

"Yeah?" came an answering shout. Megan smiled hugely.

"We need some help finding some works," she called out.

"Where are you?"

Megan lowered her voice. "Good question," she joked. She looked at the shelf, then called out, "Section D."

Sam felt relieved. She wouldn't have made a joke if she'd been nervous of him. It was bad enough that he'd been having libidinous thoughts about her, it would be intolerable if she'd realized it.

They heard footsteps and a mover in dusty overalls appeared around the corner. Sam handed him the paper.

"If I haven't seen you in a few hours," laughed Megan as she went in the opposite direction, "I'll send out the dogs."

INSIDE RACHEL'S office, Megan closed the door and collapsed against it, her heart fluttering like a trapped bird.

She was never going to leave this office again, not after that nightmare.

She jumped as the phone rang. Probably Rachel, looking for a progress report.

"Hello?" she said, sliding into the chair.

"Hey, sexypants," came a male voice in her ear. "Are you missing me?"

Megan froze. Why was Sam calling her from the vault? Then she realized that this really wasn't as important as the fact that he seemed to have skipped several steps ahead in the mating dance, *i.e.,* directly from nice guy to raving stalker.

"Rach? Honey, are you there?"

Megan closed her eyes, smiling broadly at her stupidity.

"David," she breathed. "It's you. Can I call you back in two minutes?"

There was a pause. Should she have called him sexypants? Or did he have his own name? Megan's nostrils flared with the effort of not laughing. Rachel and David had never used these pet names in front of her.

"I'm not still in the doghouse, am I?" David asked.

"No, of course not," said Megan, thinking that if he was, it wasn't her problem. "I've just got someone here. Let me call you back, okay?"

"Okay," he said. "I'm at the hotel. Don't be too long, peaches."

"Bye." Megan barely managed to put the phone down before her giggles erupted.

She dialed Rachel's number, her fingers shaking with mirth.

Rachel answered on the first ring.

"Hey, peaches," said Megan, still chuckling. "Or should I say, sexypants. How are you?"

There was a pause and then Rachel spoke in a voice overflowing with crossness. "Megan! What's gotten into you? You promised you were going to take it seriously today."

"David just called me," Megan said.

A much meeker Rachel answered. "Oh right. Er, David likes to make up pet names."

"Sure thing, banana-head," said Megan cheerily. "Anyway, listen up. You've got to call him back at the hotel, but first let me tell you about me. The meeting with Peterson went okay, he seems happy to say that it was a misunderstanding. And Sam was thrilled with the new floor plan, but then I went down in the elevator with him and I ended up in the vault by mistake. I'm okay but it was a little scary for a while. Oh, and John Forsyth wants to be more involved with the exhibition or something." She paused for breath. And Sam doesn't seem to like me after all, she wanted to say, but didn't. "Anyway, Rachel, my point is that you've really got to get me out of here as soon as you can."

"Okay, okay," said Rachel. "I'm working on it. I'm going to try this exfoliating cream that I've got and I'm going to mix it with a little cleanser. You just stay in the office, okay? Listen, I'll call David now and then I'll call you back later."

Megan put down the phone and drummed her fingers nervously on the desk. She rolled a pen back and forth between her hands and then looked down at the briefcase of her own work that she'd brought with her. Yeah, that's what she had to do.

Devil-Megan opened her mouth to speak but Megan quickly shrugged her off her perch. "I'm not going to mess up today," she said sternly. "So I don't want to hear a peep from either of you."

THERE WAS a sharp rat-a-tat-tat on the door before it swung open. Megan just had time to open a drawer, sweep her notes and photos into it and slam it shut before Peterson was standing in front of her.

"Rachel," he said. "Sorry to disturb you." He bent down and picked up a photo off the floor.

"Didn't know you were a skier," he said. "Where was this taken?"

Megan's eyes widened. "Oh, that's not me. That's my sister Megan, in Sweden. She sent me some photos."

"Ah," Peterson nodded. "The twin. Yes." He peered closer at the photo and Megan felt her mouth go dry. "Absolutely amazing really, isn't it? I bet people can't tell you apart."

Megan's polite laugh was tinged with hysteria.

"You know what?" he went on. "You should bring her to the opening, for a bit of fun."

"Uh, I'll see. She might be busy."

"Nonsense," blustered Peterson. "She wouldn't want to miss it. Of course she'll come."

"I'll definitely tell her," Megan said diplomatically. "Was there something you wanted?"

"Yes, Hank Rockwell just called me from a car phone. He and his daughter are nearby and he wants to have a quick look around. You don't mind taking him up, do you?"

It looked like he wasn't expecting a refusal so Megan didn't feel in any position to offer one. "Er, no, of course not," she said, glancing anxiously at the phone.

"Great," he said. "They'll be here in about ten minutes, meet them in the foyer, would you?" He turned back at the door. "And don't forget that I need Friday's schedule."

"HERE SHE IS," said the man in a cheerful, booming voice. "Our little expert."

"Hello, Mr. Rockwell," said Megan, trying to inflect her voice with confidence. "Good to see you again."

"Now we talked about this before," he admonished her. "Told you to call me Hank. Don't turn shy on me now." He rubbed his hands together briskly and then clapped Peterson on the shoulder. "I believe you've outdone yourself this time. I'm looking forward to seeing some marvelous pieces."

Megan waited nervously while the men exchanged pleasantries. She'd barely had time for a brief phone call to Rachel. Hank Rockwell fit his description perfectly, but could the girl with him possibly be his sixteen-year old daughter? She was tall and whippet-thin, with a sheet of shining blond hair. She glittered with expensive jewelry and her gorgeous face bore an expression of sullen boredom. Megan thought back to when she was sixteen. She was pretty sure that neither she nor Rachel had looked remotely like this until they were well into their twenties. And maybe not even then.

The girl's handbag, embossed with a discreet gold Fendi label, trilled and she answered her phone, vocalizing to the person on the other end, and to the assembled company, just how inconvenient it was to have this chunk taken out of her day.

"Well, Rachel," said Peterson. "I'll leave you and the Rockwells to it."

The emphasis on the Rockwell name was not lost on her. She nodded obediently and notched up her smile another few inches.

Mr. Rockwell turned to his daughter. "Tiffany, sweetheart, say hello to Rachel."

"Hi," said the glamour-puss. She wasn't looking at Megan as she spoke—her eyes were following the trail of workmen that was snaking up and down the main staircase.

"Shall we?" said Megan. She led them up the staircase, struggling to keep her breathing calm.

She knew she should be trying to remember what she could from her skimming of the catalogue (which at least she'd had the presence of mind to bring with her), but all she could think about was what she was going to do when Mr. Rockwell slowly turned to her and said, "Wait a minute, you're not Rachel, are you?"

They reached the top of the staircase and Megan saw that the movers were in a frenzy of activity as they coped with the rearrangements. The place looked more like a building site than an art gallery. She stood back as a man wheeled past a large metal bracket with a painting secured in the middle. Megan recognized it from the catalogue as a painting of Samson and Delilah, but compared to the catalogue illustration the painting took her breath away, the colors were so lush and vibrant.

It was a moment before she returned her attention to her guests, but they were fascinated by the sight of the exquisite works amidst the empty crates, straw and cardboard strewn about the place.

At least Mr. Rockwell was. The young Miss Rockwell was rather more focused on the flesh-and-blood treasures. She's like a kid in a candy store, thought Megan. Or should that be a testosterone store?

In order to delay the tour of the galleries and to grab another chance to talk to Sam (Megan wasn't sure which was the overriding motivation, but they were both pretty good) Megan led her guests over to him.

"Look," he said, showing her his clipboard. "I know you think it'll be easier to move smaller statues into the middle once the dinner is over but I've got a different idea. I think the *Laocoön* makes a far more impressive centerpiece. You'd be able to see it from the bottom of the stairs, even with lots of people around it. In the end it's the same amount of work. What do you think?"

Megan nodded. "Sure. That sounds fine. Whatever you think." She wasn't about to argue with him when she didn't even know what sculpture he was talking about. "Sam, this is Mr. Rockwell and his daughter Tiffany. I've come to give them a tour of the exhibition so far." She turned to her guests. "This is Sam Harrison, the exhibition organizer. This is the man who put the whole thing together." Megan could feel herself beaming, but she managed to stop short of exclaiming, Isn't he gorgeous!

Then she noticed that Tiffany didn't exactly need a heads-up in that department. She was looking at Sam the way a New Yorker looks at an empty cab.

Hmm, thought Megan, *maybe I won't ask Sam to accompany us around the galleries after all.*

"So," she held out a guiding hand to the guests. "Shall we go in?"

"You guys go ahead," said Tiffany imperiously. "I want to stay here and watch them move the statues."

Her father shifted toward Megan. "Okay, honey, don't get in anybody's way."

"I won't, daddy," said Tiffany, smiling up at Sam.

Ooh, you little vixen, thought Megan. However she had no choice but to follow Rockwell senior, so she hid her annoyance.

"Okay," she said. "I'm sure you won't mind babysitting for a little while, will you Sam?"

The pleading look he gave her made it almost worth it.

SHE FOLLOWED HANK into the first gallery and positioned herself in the middle of the room where she could keep an eye on Sam and Lolita.

"Don't be offended by Tiffany," Hank said to her. "I don't know if it's because her mother spoils her or if it's just a teenage thing, but she gets more willful every day. I'm just glad she agreed to come with me, I hardly ever get to spend time with her. Don't worry," he added. "You've got my full attention. I can't tell you how much I've been looking forward to this."

Megan smiled. When Rachel had told her that Mr. Rockwell was one of the biggest sponsors of the gallery, donating over a million dollars a year, she had focused, she suspected like most people, on the money.

Ridiculous as it was she hadn't been expecting someone who was actually enthusiastic and interested in art.

This was going to be fun, a nice saunter around the galleries with a fellow art-lover, rather than the ordeal she'd imagined.

Hank turned to her. "Where's the Titian?"

Okay, she'd relaxed too soon. She looked around the

room, trying to read the information labels that went with each painting.

This was made extremely difficult by the fact that they weren't there.

She turned back to Hank with a smile of pure panic.

"As you can see," she said, "many of the paintings haven't been labeled yet." Her eyes swept the room again. "And by 'many' I mean all of them."

Imagining that it was probably much too soon to resort to swooning she searched the room for inspiration before she remembered the catalogue in her hand. Of course. She wanted to slap her forehead.

Instead, she held up the heavy book.

"Lucky for us I brought a catalogue so we should have no problem finding the Titian." She laughed as if she'd just said the drollest thing.

"Oh, don't bother with that," said Hank, taking the catalogue from her. "If I wanted to read about the works I could have stayed at home, right? Let's just feast our eyes."

He tossed the catalogue carelessly onto a nearby crate and Megan looked at it the way a drowning person looks at a lifejacket bobbing away on the waves.

She turned back to Hank. "You know what, I agree with you." She snapped her fingers. "Who needs names and dates? Who cares who painted what? Let's just enjoy them as the works of beauty that they are." Megan would have happily stopped there, but her mouth seemed determined to run on without her. "In fact, I'm glad there are no labels. I don't want to be bogged down in details and useless information. Why, we can rely on our own judgment can't we? We can decide whether we like something or not just by looking at it. I'm with you Hank, let's forget about the names."

He looked at her for a long moment then started chuckling.

"Rachel Dean, you are priceless. I hope they appreciate you here. I've never known someone with such a boundless enthusiasm for their job and yet you always come at it from a different angle. Talking to you is such a treat.''

Megan gave a modest smile but inside she was punching the air. Wow, but she was good at this. Quick-thinkin' and fast-talkin', that was her. She was invincible.

"So, seriously," said Hank, turning away from her again. "Where is it?"

Megan looked at the back of Hank's head. A thought occurred to her. If he didn't know which one it was then it didn't matter which one she told him it was, did it? She looked around the room and picked out a nice pastoral scene.

She opened her mouth to start bluffing when Hank darted over to a corner. "Here it is," he said triumphantly. "Look at that. Incredible. His use of chiaroscuro always blows me away." He gave Megan a complicit smile. "I imagine that when Diderot differentiated between chiaroscuro and the representation of light and shadow he was thinking of Titian. The imagination of the painter!"

Megan clamped her mouth shut. He had a nerve. Pretending he was just interested in the "beauty" of art when all he wanted to talk about was chiaroscuro and Diderot and all those other things that, basically, Megan had never heard of.

What a phony!

So to speak.

Megan wished she was at home, in bed, with a book and a tub of vanilla fudge ice cream…oh, and a cup of cocoa. And maybe the television on quietly in the corner. And a hot-water bottle.

She sighed heavily.

Then she squared her shoulders and walked over to Hank.

"Marvelous, isn't it?" she agreed. "He's always been one of my favorites for just that reason."

He nudged her playfully. "You're just being diplomatic.

I know you prefer the darker shadows. I bet you've got a Caravaggio up your sleeve.''

Megan was amazed at her good fortune. Well, it was about time she caught a break. "Yes!" she exclaimed. "You're right. We have got a Caravaggio. Two actually.'' She paused before adding the cherry. "And I know where they are!''

Hank was chuckling again. "Lead the way," he declared.

Megan led him through the galleries until she came across the familiar paintings.

They were conveniently (for her) hung in gallery seven which led back into the main hall so, staying back in the shadows, she took a surreptitious peek out at Sam who seemed to be telling Tiffany about one of the sculptures. As she watched, Tiffany flicked her hair and gave a tinkly little laugh that set Megan's teeth on edge.

She's sixteen, she reminded herself, get a grip.

"I like the way you've themed the galleries. It makes for some interesting contrasts," said Hank, drifting back into gallery six.

"Yes indeed," said Megan vaguely. She took one last look at Sam before hurrying after Hank. She knew it was irrational of her to be exasperated with the sponsor, but was it too much to ask that he spend a little more time in gallery seven? Or with his daughter for that matter, since his little princess had deigned to come along?

She lifted her head as she heard a burst of laughter from the main hall. Curiosity won over decorum and she put her hand on Hank's arm and applied a little pressure. "You must come and see this," she purred, "before I forget."

He was too much of a gentleman to resist so she walked him back into gallery seven and positioned him in front of the painting which was directly opposite the door. She drew back from him and looked surreptitiously over her shoulder.

Hmm, Sam seemed to be drawing himself a bit of a crowd. A brunette had joined them, and, to Megan's eyes, she was wearing a blouse that was far too low-cut for the austere environs of the museum.

"I'm not really a huge fan of Van Dyck," said Hank. "His figures are too coarse and angular for me."

"Maybe you just need to spend more time with him," said Megan. "Let him grow on you." She glanced back again, her eyes narrowing. The brunette was smiling and tilting her head coquettishly.

"I think I'd rather spend time with the Rubens," said Hank, moving toward the central galleries again. He smiled at Megan. "Can't teach an old dog new tricks."

Megan forced herself to look amused. "I'll be with you in a minute," she said, moving over to the door and fiddling with the frame of the nearest painting. "I just have to…uh, fix this.…"

Hank disappeared into gallery six and Megan leaned sideways, trying to hear what Sam was saying.

A head appeared in the doorway and she jerked back in fright.

"Ms. Dean!" the mover called out jovially. "Sam needs you. He's thinking about moving the Tondo to the back of gallery four and he wants to talk to you about it."

Hmm, thought Megan, *who should I kiss first, this mover or Sam?*

"I'm on my way," she said, wondering what the heck a Tondo was.

Neither Tiffany nor the mystery woman looked too pleased when Megan stepped back into the central hall but Megan was delighted by the relief that was written all over Sam's face.

"Sorry to drag you out," he said. "I've just been thinking about crowd control. If we put it in the alcove in gallery four it'll be less disruptive than if we have it out here in the main hall. You don't want crowds blocking up the staircase."

Megan wanted to tell him that, for getting her away from Hank, he could put it over his mantelpiece, but she resisted.

"That's a good idea, Sam," said Megan. "We should do that."

"Look out," joked the brunette, touching Sam on the arm. "Genius at work."

Sam looked more embarrassed than flattered and Megan stared at the woman's bright blue eyes. That was definitely a color not found in nature.

"Helena," she guessed. "Did you need something?"

"Just taking a quick break," said the woman with another dazzling smile at Sam.

"Really?" said Megan archly. "Only one week to the opening and you've found yourself at a loose end?"

The woman tore her gaze away from Sam's face and focused on Megan. "Is there something in particular that you want me to do?"

Megan's heart stopped.

She'd walked right into this one.

The seconds ticked by as she tried to re-engage her brain. Say something, she thought desperately, anything.

"Friday's schedule," she blurted in a flash of inspiration. "Mr. Peterson wants Friday's schedule. Can you take it to him?"

"Which one?" said Helena.

Megan frowned. "Friday's," she repeated.

Helena's look of confusion deepened. "The conference schedule or the private viewings list?"

"Both," said Megan, trying to make it sound like the most obvious thing in the world.

"Okay," said Helena, still looking bemused. "See you later, Sam."

He nodded to her as she left, and Megan peered suspiciously at his expression. Did he look sad that Helena was going? Or lustful?

She dropped her eyes quickly as Sam turned to her. He opened his mouth to say something but was interrupted by Tiffany, who was determined to regain center stage.

"I'm certainly looking forward to the opening," she

said. "You should be able to pick me out of the crowd, Sam, I'll be wearing a gray Galliano. Sleeveless *and* backless."

Sam shot Megan another look of exasperation. Her smile flickered on before she could suppress it and Tiffany caught it in her laser stare.

"Is that Donna Karan?" she simpered, looking Megan up and down.

Boy, are you asking the wrong person, thought Megan. Still, Tiffany did seem to be an expert in this area.

"Uh, yes it is. I guess."

The girl nodded smugly. "I thought so. I just didn't recognize it initially because it's last season's."

She turned on her heel, flicking her mane of hair like the blade of a scythe and strutted toward gallery seven.

Sam looked at Megan.

She rolled her eyes. "I think I'm supposed to fall to the floor now, mortally wounded by the savagery of that barb."

Sam laughed. "I think it's a great dress," he said. "And you look great in it."

"Thank you." Megan sighed theatrically. "But it *is* last season's, so the only decent thing to do is throw it away."

"But won't you be cold for the rest of the day?" Sam out-quipped her.

Megan's eyes flashed at him. "I have to follow the Rockwells," she said. "Otherwise I could give you a proper scolding for that remark. Rest assured however that I will speak to you later."

He grinned. "I'll look forward to it."

Okay, thought Megan as she practically skipped after her guests, that was definitely flirting, wasn't it?

He *does* like me.

Doesn't he?

5

MEGAN HOPED she wouldn't look too conspicuous in the gallery restaurant. After her morning with the Rockwells and then another two hours hiding in Rachel's office, jumping every time someone passed the door, she felt as though she deserved a reward. There was a small cafeteria in the basement of the building for the staff, but Megan suspected there was too much chance of becoming embroiled in an awkward conversation there, so she'd come up to the bright rooftop restaurant instead.

It was only when she was in line with a tray of food that she realized she didn't know if she got a discount or not. Or even if she had to pay.

Luckily the cashier was being held in thrall by her co-worker's whispering—a tale full of "he said and then she said," so Megan was given little more than a cursory glance. Even the cashier's "Have a nice day" was followed quickly by a hushed "he didn't!"

Megan found a quiet corner table, slightly hidden behind an effusively leafed ficus plant and put down her soup and sandwich.

She had barely started when a shadow fell across the table.

"I see you're still dressed then?" said Sam, balancing a folder and a tray precariously.

Megan hid her nerves and strove for normality, hoping he didn't notice her blush. "I thought it only right that I should spill some food on it first."

"Of course," he said solemnly. "Mind if I join you?"

"Not at all."

"I thought I was the only one who snuck in here," he went on in a friendly voice. "This is good timing. I wanted to go over a couple of things with you."

Megan hid her dismay. "Oh look," she chided him. "It's lunchtime. Let's take ten minutes off, pretend we're just visitors here."

He looked surprised, then closed the file and pushed it to the edge of the table. "You're right," he said, looking pleased.

He leaned forward eagerly. "So, tell me, what does Rachel Dean do when she's not working?"

Megan smiled wanly. Maybe she should have stuck to talking about work. She didn't want to have to talk about Rachel's leisure time since it mostly involved being with her boyfriend.

"Oh, you know," she said evasively. "This and that, the usual."

He looked at her. "It must be hard," he said sympathetically.

She frowned. "What?"

"Being in the witness protection program."

Her burst of laughter drew curious glances from a nearby table.

"Okay," she said, meeting his eyes. "Maybe it did sound like that. I guess I just didn't want to admit that work takes up most of my life at the moment. That's kind of pathetic, huh?"

He shook his head as he swallowed a bite of his sandwich. "No, not at all. Well, maybe it is, but I understand. I'm the same. And I've always thought it's a better complaint than not enjoying your work at all."

She nodded her agreement as she added a sprinkle of pepper to her soup.

"So, what's your favorite part of the job?" he asked.

"The traveling, definitely," said Megan without thinking.

Sam paused in his chewing to look quizzically at her.

Megan tried desperately to think of a word that rhymed with "traveling" that she could pretend she'd used. The unraveling? The gravelling? Nope, curators didn't do much of those either.

"The traveling?" Sam asked.

"Back in time," Megan improvised. "Traveling through the ages, with the artists. I know that's a fanciful way of putting it—" understatement of the year "—but it's how I feel sometimes."

Sam raised his eyebrows thoughtfully. "I think I understand what you mean."

Really? thought Megan.

"You must get to do lots of actual traveling," she prompted him. "Taking exhibitions all over the world."

"Yes, I thought for a minute you'd read my mind. It's one of my favorite parts. I love seeing new places, meeting new people."

Me, too! thought Megan. She took a huge bite out of her sandwich so she wouldn't give herself away.

"Where have you been to?" she mumbled with her hand over her mouth.

He began to tick off on his fingers. "Egypt, Italy, Morocco, Australia, Japan."

Megan was wide-eyed with excitement. She was dying to ask him if he'd gone to the glass San'ai Building in Tokyo, but Rachel hadn't been to Japan and she was still Rachel.

She swallowed her food and had another spoonful of soup. "I'd love to go to Egypt or Italy," she said honestly. "Either of those would be next on my list."

"Where have you been already?" he asked.

Megan squinted, trying to remember Rachel's travel history.

"Uh, let's see, Paris and Toronto." She had a sudden dread that he would want to talk about Toronto, chitchat for which she was hopelessly ill-equipped so she hurried on. "And I visited my sister in New Orleans, Austria and India."

Sam scratched his lip with his thumb. "You have a sister who lives in three different places?"

Megan smiled. "Actually she's just come back from Scandinavia."

"Okay," laughed Sam. "I give up. What does she do?"

"She's a travel writer," said Megan proudly. "You know that series, Going Native? She works for them."

"What a great job," said Sam admiringly. "She must be very adventurous."

Megan blushed. "She is. And she's really funny and sweet, too," she added shamelessly. Well, it was possible that Rachel talked about her like this. "I think you'd like her. She'll probably come by later in the week, I'll introduce you."

Sam smiled. "Sure," he said casually. "So, did you walk down the longest street in the world?"

Megan looked at him blankly. What on earth was he talking about? A faint memory glimmered in the back of her mind. Of course, after her trip to Canada, Rachel had rambled on about some street in Toronto being in the Guinness Book of Records. Wasn't it hundreds of miles long though?

"Walked along some of it," said Megan disingenuously. "But first, why don't you tell me how you got into this line of work?"

It was an awkward segue, Megan knew, but she hoped he wouldn't notice. Men liked talking about their jobs, right?

"I got here through a series of wrong paths," Sam said, laughing. "I grew up thinking I was going to become an archaeologist, like my parents. I spent most of my childhood in Egypt and Greece, moving around with my parents to whatever dig they were working on and then we came back to Seattle to settle, and they both ended up working in the Museum of Natural History. So I spent a lot of time there and we used to go off on digs during my summer holidays."

Megan's eyes were fixed on him. She'd forgotten to eat. "It's so adventurous and romantic," she breathed.

"It was," he said, pleased. "I think I appreciate it even more now when I look back on it, how unusual a life it was. Anyway, I went to college to study archaeology, but even before my first year was out I knew it wasn't really what I wanted to do."

Megan tilted her head with interest as Sam went on.

"I'd just assumed that because I already knew so much about archaeology that that's what I should be doing. But after a lot of thought and a long talk with my dad I realized it was art I was interested in."

He paused dramatically. "So I enrolled in art college."

Megan giggled as he nodded self-deprecatingly. "Yes, I decided that if I loved art so much it must be because I was a great artist."

Sam interrupted himself to take a quick sip of coffee and Megan went back to her forgotten food. Before she resumed eating the sandwich, she asked, "So, were you a great artist?"

Sam offered her a statistic. "You know, that they say that the average art student paints about three hundred canvasses in his first year? I painted two."

Megan raised her eyebrows. "Two hundred?"

"No, just two."

Megan's eyes crinkled with amusement.

"But the year wasn't wasted," Sam went on. "All that time I hadn't spent painting I'd spent reading about those who could. At the end of the year I persuaded the dean to let me change my major to art history and that's where I spent the next four years. I worked at Seattle Art Museum for a while and then the wanderlust in my genes took over again and I followed a job to Sydney and after that I was headhunted by the Bonnington Trust who were sending an exhibit to Egypt. I had the qualifications and I spoke Arabic so I jumped at the chance and I've worked for them ever since."

"You speak Arabic?" she said in awe.

He nodded.

"That's a hard language to learn," she said.

He shrugged. "Not if you grew up there." He frowned. "Anyway, how do you know? Have you tried learning it?"

Megan cursed herself. She'd allowed herself to forget where, and who, she was again.

"My sister told me," she said. "I think she might have had a stab at it."

She leaned forward and he looked at her as she went on eagerly. "Megan has this game that she plays—"

"Megan?" he interrupted her. "That's her name?"

She looked at him in concern. He wasn't going to have an ex-wife called Megan, was he? "Yeah?" she said. "So?"

"Oh nothing, it's just…it's a pretty name."

Megan resisted the urge to reach across the table and give him a big kiss.

"The game?" he prompted, bringing her back to the present.

"Uh, right. Well, it's just this. You have to imagine that you're going to a foreign country to live and you can only learn ten words. What would they be?"

He leaned back, smiling thoughtfully. "That's a kind of personality test, isn't it, more than a game? I'd have to think about it. Is it long-term or just a holiday?"

"Long-term."

He nodded. "I see. Ten words to get me through life, basically?"

"Exactly."

"Well," he went on, "what if I said I didn't need any? I could be like that woman in *The Piano,* she didn't speak."

"Yeah, but she had her daughter to interpret."

"Oh, right."

"Wait a minute," said Megan in surprise. "You saw *The Piano*?"

"Yeah, so?"

"Did you like it?"

He shrugged. "Sure. I thought it was great." He laughed at the expression that crossed her face. "And no, I'm not gay."

She widened her eyes. "I wasn't thinking that."

"Sure you were," he laughed. "Everyone thinks it, if a man likes that movie he must be gay."

She looked him in the eyes. "Well, I assure you I don't think that."

He held her gaze. "Good."

Megan suddenly realized they were moving into dangerous territory, but before she could say anything he went on playfully.

"Besides, I don't think you can afford to be judgmental. What was that movie you quoted, *Heaven Can Wait?* I didn't think there was anyone under thirty who'd seen that."

Megan opened her mouth to answer then frowned in confusion. "Wait a minute, did you just accuse me of being over thirty?"

"No," he said, frowning in unison with her. "At least, I don't think so. I didn't mean to. Even though it's hard to believe you're not."

Megan's mouth fell open.

"I mean, because you're so experienced," Sam rushed on. "You're so good at your job." He stopped and put his hand to his forehead. "I think I've skated out to the middle of the lake here."

"Extremely thin ice," Megan agreed. "I tell you what, give me the first of your ten words and I'll let you back on dry land."

"My first word," he said meekly, "is *sorry*."

Megan laughed and gave him a little round of applause. He ducked his head and drank some more coffee.

"So," he said, "you like movies?"

She nodded. "Love them. Name a movie and I've seen it."

"That sounds like a challenge to me," he grinned. He straightened up as if he'd just thought of something. "By the way, what are your ten words?"

She put up her finger and waved it back and forth. "That would be cheating. You have to come up with your own ten first."

"If I can name a movie you haven't seen you have to tell me a word."

"Okay. But you have to have seen the movie you name."

"Of course." He thought for a moment. "*Jules et Jim.*"

She waved her hand dismissively. "Too easy. I went through that whole black-and-white-subtitle thing while I was a teenager."

"Okay," he said. "I'll try a different tack. *The Terminator?*"

She shook her head at him. "Schwarzenegger rules."

He chewed at his lip. *"Night of the Living Dead?"*

"Big horror fan," she said blithely.

He put his hand through his hair and shrugged. "Gosh, we could be here all day. Better start with the classics. *It's a Wonderful Life?*"

Megan didn't answer and Sam peered at her.

"You're toying with me, aren't you? You have seen it. Everyone's seen it."

Megan looked down and fiddled with her napkin. She looked back up again. Sam was looking at her hopefully.

She nodded. "Congratulations."

Sam spread his hands incredulously. "How can you not have seen it? It's on every Christmas."

"I know," she said. "But I always seem to be busy at Christmas."

"Busy?"

Yeah, busy being in another country, she thought.

"Sure. You know, you have to visit people, or there's guests to talk to, or cooking to do. I always end up missing it."

"You do know that it's out on video now, right?"

She laughed. "I know, but I can't do that. I can't mess with tradition. I have to watch it when it comes on television."

He smiled as he thought about it. "So you're going to wait until next Christmas and then attempt to see it again."

"Exactly."

He shook his head. "It's still pretty amazing to reach your age—" he caught her eye, "—whatever that may be, and not have seen it. I must have seen it ten times by now."

"Oh big deal," she retorted. "I've seen *Fargo* thirteen times."

He raised his eyebrow. "And you're boasting about that?"

"What?" she said defensively. "It's a great movie."

"Well yeah, but thirteen times? Anyway, stop trying to distract me. You owe me a word."

Megan thought for a minute. There was no harm in giving him her own list of words. It was so long ago since she and Rachel had played this game that she couldn't remember Rachel's anyway.

"*Sorry,*" she said.

He looked outraged. "Oh come on, a deal's a deal. You have to tell me one."

"That's the word," she said, grinning.

"Oh right. Really?"

She nodded, finishing off her sandwich.

"So, we agree on one word. One down, nine to go." He straightened up, looking excited. "I've thought of another one. *Help.*"

Megan crinkled her nose. "*Help?*"

He leaned back, stirring the sugar in the dregs of his coffee. "Yeah, definitely. If I'm trapped in a burning building or down the bottom of a mine I don't want to be yelling out Sorry! Sorry!''

Megan's eyes sparkled as she laughed. ''Good point.''

He looked smug. ''You didn't have *help*, did you?''

She caught her bottom lip between her teeth and shook her head.

''So what would you be yelling?'' he asked.

She ran through her list mentally and looked away from him. *''Antibiotic,''* she muttered.

''Shut up,'' she added as his laughter faded. ''Believe me, if you find yourself in dire straits *antibiotic* is a good word to have.''

''Sorry and *antibiotic,''* he mused. ''Already I'm building up a very different picture of you.''

''Well, Mr. Sorry-and-Help, it sounds like traveling with you would be one awkward situation after another.''

''I prefer to think of them as adventures.''

''Ooh,'' she said, thinking of something. ''I bet you like art heist movies.''

Sam blinked. ''Keeping up with you is a full-time job, isn't it? But, yeah, of course. You, too, I assume.''

Megan, on the verge of questioning his assumption, wanted to growl with frustration. It was so annoying having to keep reminding herself who she was supposed to be.

''Uh, of course,'' she said. ''What's your favorite?''

''The Thomas Crown Affair, I think.''

''Original or remake?''

''Original. What, you like the remake?''

She tilted her head indecisively.

''Oh, it's a Pierce Brosnan thing isn't it?'' he said knowingly.

''No, actually, it's a Rene Russo thing. What a woman.''

''Oh, and Faye Dunaway isn't?''

''Okay,'' she acceded. ''That one's a tie. Remake of *The Getaway?''*

He put out his hand, thumb downward. ''Why did they bother?''

"Although," she said, tilting her head, "there was James Woods."

"Always worth watching," agreed Sam.

They fell quiet. It was the first lull in the conversation since Sam had sat down and Megan was disappointed to see him glance at his watch. She realized with surprise that their food was all gone and she slid her chair back a few inches.

"I guess we should get back to work."

"Oh no," complained Sam, much to her satisfaction. "Do we have to? I was going to get another cup of coffee." He flashed her a complicit smile. "We could talk about books next."

She groaned. "Don't tempt me."

"Or," he said, reaching for his folder. "If you insist, we could talk about the insurance modifications, that way we can convince ourselves we're working."

She made her face regretful. "Sorry, can you bring it to me later?" She looked at her watch and rose out of her seat. "I really have to sort out…other stuff first, I won't bore you with it."

He went to get up and she put a restraining hand on his arm. "No, you stay here. Have your coffee. I'll see you later." She had to go and get another crash course from Rachel before he had a chance to ask any more questions.

"Okay," he said, sinking back onto the chair. "But this was fun. We should do it again tomorrow."

Megan faltered. It was ridiculous but she felt a real pang of jealousy at the thought of Rachel having lunch with him. Anyway, it was out of the question, he'd notice the difference immediately.

"We'll see," she said amiably. "If there's time."

She gave him another smile, successfully quashed the impulse to lean over and give him a peck on the cheek, and walked away.

Sam watched her leave. It would have been impossible for him not to. Her hair gleamed in the pale sunlight streaming through the glass walls and there was a spring in her walk that made her hair bob prettily on her shoulders. Sam shifted in his seat, annoyed with himself.

Then he was annoyed at feeling annoyed.

After all the talk about throwing away her dress and walking around naked it would have taken a superhero not to have had some kind of reaction. Especially when the dress fitted so neatly.

He leaned forward and rested his arms on the table. He had to change his train of thought right now, this was a family restaurant.

It wasn't even as if she'd been doing anything overt to cause such a reaction. Unlike, for instance, Helena. There was a woman who made no secret of her attraction to him, and yet it left him completely unmoved. But Rachel had merely to brush past him and every nerve ending was springing to attention. A quick smile from her and his ribcage suddenly felt too tight.

It was a heady combination to meet someone whom he both liked and admired so much. He had had dealings with inept curators during his career and Rachel Dean had impressed him right from the start, infusing him with confidence for the housing of the exhibition.

A thought nagged at his brain. He didn't want to be unfair, but she didn't seem quite as on top of things lately. It was as if she was distracted…or preoccupied with something.

He looked down at her cup with its smudge of lipstick, and an unconscious smile crept onto his face as snippets of conversation ran through his mind. *Antibiotic,* he thought, shaking his head in amusement. *It's a Wonderful Life.* How could she not have seen it?

He knew without a doubt that he'd be thinking of her next Christmas. Hoping she was watching it.

A waitress came and cleared the table, refilling his coffee cup and Sam stirred another half spoonful of sugar in. He leaned back, looking out the window. The view from the restaurant was magnificent. On his right the sharp point of the Transamerica Pyramid pierced the skyline while across the city to the left a few wispy remnants of fog trailed around the orange towers of the Golden Gate Bridge. But Sam wasn't seeing any of it. He was focused on a picture in his mind's eye of himself and Rachel, tucked up on the sofa beside a roaring fire. They had glasses of mulled wine in their hands, and she was shushing him as the movie started. He pulled her closer, and she snuggled against him as the black-and-white credits rolled.

Sam shook his head as the noise of the restaurant filtered through again. A carnal reaction was one thing, but domestic imaginings? That was really jumping the gun.

After all, he'd only known her a few weeks. And she hadn't even really started opening up to him until, well, until today.

And maybe she was just being friendly. Creating a more informal atmosphere to ease the tension of this busy week.

But Sam couldn't help thinking it was more than that. He would just have to watch her more closely in order to judge.

THERE WERE six people sitting around the oval oak table: Sam, Peterson, John Forsyth, Megan, Jocelyn and a man that Sam had introduced as Bradley Fielding, the authenticator from L.A.

Whatever that is, thought Megan. She didn't know what the collective word for butterflies was, but her stomach was definitely full of them. A queasiness of butterflies perhaps.

"First of all," Mr. Peterson said, starting the meeting without any aplomb, "Melissa Whitford's party, what can we do about that?"

"Melissa Whitford?" Megan blurted in surprise. She had read recently that the singer's album had just gone triple platinum. Then she realized that everyone was looking at her and that her surprise was a little misplaced. Jocelyn, who had opened a thin file, quirked her head and gently tapped the pages in front of her.

"Sorry," said Megan with a shake of her head. "I'd forgotten for a moment. Yes, of course, Jocelyn has it." She looked down at the table, desperately trying to affect nonchalance.

"Er, yes," said Jocelyn, looking down. "Whitford's P.R. said she wanted the 12th or not at all, since that's her birthday, so we spoke to Dogs Are People Too and, although they were pretty reluctant at first, they've agreed to take the 18th. Because of the short notice Whitford's party agreed to pay one and a half the usual which will cover the discount we had to agree to in order to keep Dogs Are People Too. Financially we're no worse or better off but Whitford's party will have national publicity so that's quite a coup."

Jocelyn sat back and smiled modestly. Megan glanced up from the table to catch Sam looking at her. Her eyes darted away and met Peterson's.

"Excellent work," he said. "Well-handled. Have you got the catering arrangements sorted out?"

Megan instinctively knew that the right answer to this question was yes, whether they had or not. She nodded with authority.

Then she frowned and turned to Jocelyn. "Dogs Are People Too?"

Jocelyn raised her eyebrows. "What about them?"

"That's the name...?"

"Of the charity," finished Jocelyn slowly, looking nonplussed.

Megan nodded, then looked down and straightened the files in front of her.

"Okay," said Peterson, looking down at his own files. "Have we come to an agreement on—"

"But they're not."

Five heads turned toward Megan.

"They're not people," she said falteringly, and yet unable to let it go. "They're dogs."

Four heads turned away from Megan to look alternately down at their files or at each other. Only Sam kept watching Megan, the corners of his eyes creasing in amusement.

She tried to justify her outburst. "I'm just saying—"

"What's the problem, Rachel?" said Peterson heavily.

She coughed. "There isn't one. I'm sorry." She picked up her pen and rested her hands on the table, trying to present a picture of attentiveness and total mental stability. "You were saying?"

Peterson gave her a look and then checked his file again.

"Okay," he said to Sam and Bradley. "How are the authentication checks coming along?"

"So far, so good," said Bradley. "Sam has comprehensive records from each home gallery, so rather than categorizing them based on our arrangements here, we're subdividing the…"

Megan tried to follow what they were saying, but the words quickly ran together. Her mouth was very dry. She had already finished the glass of water in front of her, but she didn't dare refill it in case her hand trembled.

She nodded intelligently as Bradley continued to speak.

He was a pleasant-looking man. About the same age as Sam and, although there was a peppering of gray in his dark hair, there was no denying that he was quite attractive.

And yet, she got nothing from him. He was well-dressed, well-spoken and had a nice smile, but none of it had any effect on Megan.

But when she looked at Sam it was like being pulled out of the path of an oncoming train. Her heart leapt into action and her skin flushed with the thrill of being alive. And, contrarily, it was also like sinking into bed at the end of a long day. It was hypnotic and calming and it made her want to sigh out loud with bliss.

Megan had never felt anything like it before.

She had felt rushes of attraction for men in the past, and

even become fond of some of them, but she had never been so completely overwhelmed by her feelings for one person before.

She rested one elbow on the table and tilted her head, rubbing at her temple, as John Forsyth joined in the discussion.

Of all the crummy times to meet the man of her dreams. She didn't want to be secretive and underhanded with him. For one thing, it went completely against her nature, and for another, she was dying to find out if she was having the same effect on Sam. She wanted to be able to talk to him properly, to ask him questions and be able to tell him honestly about herself.

"It's ridiculous," she muttered in exasperation.

A deathly silence fell over the table and Megan looked up.

"Ridiculous?" said Sam quizzically.

Megan tucked a strand of hair behind her ear and moistened her lips. "I didn't mean—"

"I knew you were opposed to the idea," Sam went on, "but I didn't realize you actually thought time-block tickets were ridiculous."

"I don't," she said strongly.

"You just said it," Peterson pointed out.

Megan bit her lip. "I know," she said. "But I was…I'm afraid I was thinking of something else. Sorry."

Her words seemed to intrigue Sam. He rolled his pen between his fingers and looked at her with a considering expression.

Megan felt as though he were seeing right into her brain. She surreptitiously wiped one of her sweaty palms on her skirt, looking everywhere but at him.

"So, the time-blocks," she said. "I think Jocelyn has the information on those." She looked over expectantly. "Don't you?"

Rachel's assistant looked worried. "No. I don't. You

said you wanted to…'' she trailed off and fumbled through her papers. ''Unless I mislaid it.''

Megan rushed to her defense. ''No. You're right. I did want to deal with it myself.''

She put one hand up, rubbing at her forehead. ''So, let me see. I don't think they're ridiculous but, as you said Sam, I am opposed to them.''

Sam locked his eyes onto hers. ''Why?''

There was an agonizing silence, broken eventually by the trill of a phone. Megan instinctively exhaled in relief before she realized that everyone was still looking at her.

She reached around warily and unclipped the phone from the back of her belt. She looked at the caller ID that was flashing and winced.

''Sorry,'' she mumbled, getting up from the table and moving to a corner of the room before taking the call. ''Hello?''

''Megan,'' came the voice of her editor, Marcus. ''How are things?''

''Fine,'' lied Megan. ''They're great.''

''How's the outline coming along?''

Megan thought carefully before giving a succinct answer. ''Not finished yet.''

''Is there anything you want to talk about?'' he asked. She could hear that her uncharacteristic reticence was making him curious. ''Anything you need to bounce off me?''

''No. Not at the moment.''

''Okay,'' he said after a pause. ''I just wanted to ask you if any of the maps you want to include need updating. Have you got your notes in front of you?''

''Not exactly,'' said Megan. She could feel her armpits starting to prickle with perspiration.

''Megan, is this a bad time? Where are you?''

''I'm at—'' Megan broke off. She'd been about to give Marcus a plausible excuse for her preoccupation, but she'd suddenly realized that she couldn't do that. As Rachel, she couldn't be seen to be lying.

"I'm in a meeting," she said reluctantly. She could imagine Marcus's brow furrowing as he processed this.

"A meeting?" he said. "What sort of meeting? Megan, are you thinking about leaving us?"

"No," she said. "It's not like that."

"I thought you were happy here. I thought we had a good relationship. Are you having a problem with the assignments?" he demanded. "Is that it?"

"No," repeated Megan. "Not at all. I just…I can't talk right now."

"Don't do anything hasty," Marcus said. "If there's a problem you can talk to me about it. We'll see if we can sort it out."

"I'll call you later," said Megan. "Don't worry."

She hung up and switched off the phone.

What an accomplishment. She was about to lose Rachel's job and her own; both at the same time.

She sat down again, her stomach doing flip-flops.

"So, what are we doing?" said Peterson testily. "Going ahead with the time-blocks or not?"

All eyes turned to Megan.

This is it, she thought in despair. This is where I get caught. I can't answer this. I don't even know what time-blocks are. A nervous tremor ran through her whole body and her stomach roiled. She pushed back her seat and stumbled to her feet. She didn't know if she was going to faint or be sick but she knew she had to get out of there.

"I'm sorry," she gasped. "I don't feel too good…"

"JUST BREATHE deeply," said Jocelyn.

Megan kept her head down and did as she was told. Jocelyn had followed her out of the meeting and ushered Megan straight over to her, Jocelyn's, desk.

Megan sat up, feeling her dizziness subside.

"Thanks," she said, as Jocelyn handed her a cup of coffee.

Jocelyn leaned toward Megan, lowering her voice.

"Would you prefer tea? Or water? You know, if you're in a…delicate condition." She indicated Megan's stomach.

Megan shook her head vehemently. "Oh no," she replied in an urgent tone. "It's nothing like that. Definitely not. I think I'm just tired." She lifted the cup of coffee. "This is perfect."

They were startled by a burst of laughter. Megan looked over and saw a group of women gathered around the water dispenser, Helena at the center of them. Helena caught sight of Megan.

"Ms. Dean thinks it's a good idea, don't you?"

Megan put on a pleasant expression.

"What's that?" she said.

"Asking Sam Harrison out."

Megan blushed, caught off guard.

She shook her head defensively. "Oh no," she said with a shaky laugh. "I already have a boyfriend. We're very happy."

Puzzlement crossed a few of the faces while Helena let out a laugh.

"Very funny. I mean me. Tell them." She looked around at the women. "She said last week that we'd be perfect together."

"There's no way, Helena," said one of the women. "I heard he's married to his job."

"What's the point anyway?" said another. "He'll be gone in a few months, as soon as the exhibition goes."

Helena shrugged mischievously. "That would be long enough for me."

Megan frowned as she stood up. "I don't know," she said in a concerned voice. "Now that I really think about it, I'm not sure it's a good idea."

They all looked at her. "Why not?" said Helena with amusement.

Megan made a face. "It's just the whole work thing. Work romances are never a good idea, are they? It could just result in a lot of friction being generated."

"That's what I'm hoping for," said Helena with a lascivious laugh.

One of the other women gave her a playful slap on the arm, and Megan had to put down her coffee in case it somehow found its way all over the front of Helena's smart blouse.

The door of the conference room opened and the women scattered as Peterson emerged.

Megan was anxious to escape to Rachel's office but Jocelyn restrained her with a solicitous arm on her elbow.

"Are you sure you're okay? You still look a bit peaked."

"I'm fine," said Megan as brightly as she could manage. "I just didn't have time for lunch."

"Skipping meals?" said Peterson behind her. "I don't like to hear that."

Megan turned slowly, biting her lip.

Sam was standing next to Peterson and he had just caught her in a bare-faced lie.

6

THE PHONE was ringing.

Loudly and insistently.

Megan's eyes fluttered open and she sat up sharply, blinking in disorientation.

What a terrible dream. She'd swapped places with Rachel and found herself in a series of situations that snowballed until she was...

She looked around Rachel's office and her shoulders sagged.

Oh.

She rubbed her face and grabbed impatiently at the phone.

"Hello?" she said, her voice croaky.

"What are you doing?" Rachel demanded. "It's eight o'clock."

Megan looked at her watch and then rolled her head, easing the kinks out of her neck.

"I must have fallen asleep," she said. "I just put my head down on the desk to rest my eyes for a minute. And that was at six."

"Oh no," said Rachel. "Did anyone come in?"

"Well, if they did, they didn't wake me." Megan bit her lip, regretting how cheeky she'd sounded. "Sorry."

"Tell me you made it through the day without being caught out," said Rachel, "and I'll forgive you."

Megan paused, remembering Sam's face. He hadn't said anything about the fact that she'd lied about lunch. He'd just held her eyes long enough to let her know that he knew.

"I think I did," she said cautiously, "but there were some really shaky moments. I'll tell you about them when I get home. I have to be honest with you Rachel, I am so glad that this day is over. I did manage to get some of my own work done but I'm really falling behind schedule."

Megan had returned her editor's phone call from the safety of Rachel's office and had eventually managed to convince him that she was perfectly happy with her job and no, she wasn't secretly applying to other publishers.

"How's your face?" she asked hopefully. "Almost clear?"

"Kind of. I was chatting to another woman on the internet and, wait until you hear this, her two-year-old son drew all over her face with markers while she was taking a nap. Isn't that terrible? He thought he was doing her makeup."

Megan smiled at the image.

"She gave me the address of a website that deals with removing all sorts of stains and I've been trying out some of their tips."

"Okay. I'm on my way home, I'll see you in a bit."

"Wait a second," Rachel said before she could hang up. "Since you're already there so late could you just run up and take a look at the galleries and check how many of the sculptures have been moved."

Megan made a plaintive sound.

"There won't be anyone around," Rachel coaxed. "They'll all be gone home. There'll be a few security guards in the foyer, but they won't take any notice of you. Please Megan, just to let me know the state of progress?"

MEGAN THREW an empty yogurt carton in the trash, put on her cardigan and picked up her briefcase and coat.

She looked around the office wistfully. Now that she was finally going back to being herself she could admit a certain enjoyment of her days of deception. Not enough to want to go through any more of course.

She closed the office door, locking it behind her and headed down the hall to the foyer.

There were two security guards sitting behind the information desk, chatting quietly. Megan nodded to them and then trotted up the main staircase.

In the evenings the art gallery was a very different place. There was an air of quiet and decorum and the impressive grandeur instilled a sense of awe in her.

She left her bag and coat by the door when she reached the center hall and turned left, going into the first gallery. The tapping of her shoes echoed loudly so she kicked them off and padded along in her stockinged feet, luxuriating in the quiet and stillness of the huge room. The temperature was evenly maintained for the protection of the paintings and the light was muted for the same reason.

Megan let her gaze drift over the walls. She smiled at the soft pink cheeks of giggling cherubs; over there a knowing Venus smiled down at her, and further on there was a woodland scene with dryads and nymphs.

In the next gallery were the more fearsome portrayals. A dark painting of Cerberus, three-headed guardian of the Underworld, Antaeus and Hercules locked in mortal combat and a few terrifying visions of Hades.

Megan, filled utterly with a sense of wonder at being alone with these priceless works of art, continued on to the next gallery where the sculptures were. This hall still smelt of dust and packing materials and there were empty packing crates left around, like the aftermath of a giant's Christmas morning.

Megan feasted her eyes on the statues she hadn't seen before. There was a roaring bronze dragon and she stroked her hand along his front flank, sighing in awe at the mastery of the work.

Then she came across the Greek soldier she'd admired on her first auspicious visit.

"Hello, sexypants," she joked, shaking her finger at him.

"You really got me in trouble yesterday, distracting me from my job like that."

The soldier remained impassive, unlike Sam who let out a snort of laughter.

Megan wheeled around.

She opened her mouth but couldn't think of anything to say that would make the situation better so she settled for stuttering idiotically. "I…uh…I thought…"

"Sexypants?" said Sam with evident delight.

Megan winced. "It's a sort of in-joke, it…oh, never mind."

"He's not even wearing pants," said Sam conversationally. "Or is that what makes them so sexy?"

By now Megan was laughing along. "What are the chances of you just letting this go?"

"Take a wild guess," he answered.

She turned back to the statue and pointed her finger at Sam. "Get him, sexypants!" she commanded.

"So, what are you doing up here?" he said when he'd finished laughing. "I thought you'd gone home."

She shrugged. "Just wanted to have another look around."

He came to stand beside her, folding his arms. "How do you think it's looking? Are you happy with it?"

She tore her eyes away from his firm bicep and joined him in perusing the statuary.

"I think it's great," she said honestly.

He leaned over and elbowed her gently. "So have you changed your mind about which one you're going to steal?"

Megan was caught off-balance. "What? I'm not going to steal any of them. Are you nuts?"

Sam laughed. "Relax. I promise I'm not wearing a wire."

"Uh, so what are you talking about?"

He looked a little shamefaced. "I overheard you talking to Jocelyn last week, about the fact that when you're walking around an art gallery you still like to pick out one piece that you'd steal.''

"Oh, right.'' Megan raised an eyebrow and, talking more to herself than to Sam, said, "Maybe I shouldn't say things like that any more. People could get the wrong idea.''

"It's okay,'' said Sam cheerfully. "I always thought I was the only person who did it.''

"What?'' Megan asked in consternation. "Thought about stealing paintings?''

"Thought about which one I'd like to take home, let's put it that way. Anyway, have you picked yours yet?''

"Looking at it with a fresh pair of eyes,'' she said with a grin. "I think it would have to be either the guys wrestling the snake or the painting of Samson and Delilah.''

He smiled, nodding. "You're right, we should get a painting and a statue. I'll have to get back to you though, I haven't even narrowed it down to five yet. By the way,'' he added with a smile, "you don't have to dumb it down for me. I'd know what you meant if you said the *Laocoön* and the Rubens.''

That makes one of us, thought Megan. Time to change the subject again.

"What are you doing up here all alone anyway?''

"I thought I'd let the guys go home at a reasonable hour tonight since they're going to be staying late for the rest of the week.''

"But you've stayed on?''

He looked around sheepishly, pointing at the packaging strewn haphazardly around the floor. "I figured I'd get some of this cleaned up—so we could get straight into the arranging tomorrow.''

"I could give you a hand if you like,'' she said, wondering too late if this was the kind of thing that Rachel did.

"That'd be great,'' he said.

She was about to start rolling up the voluminous sheets of heavy duty plastic but he stopped her.

"That plastic is filthy. You'll get covered in dust. Why don't you get the peanuts instead?"

She looked blankly at him. He was pointing at the small styrofoam bubbles that littered the floor.

Megan looked around. They were vaguely peanut-shaped but she would definitely ask Rachel what they were called before she went quoting Sam in public.

She picked up a sweeping brush and started to gather them into a pile. It was much harder than she'd thought because the slightest pressure made them skitter away. But she didn't want to go home, not when Sam and she had this easy repartee going between them.

She was so pleased with his sense of humor. All too often she found herself on the receiving end of puzzled looks when she got into a joking mood. But Sam seemed more than capable of getting her jokes and parrying with shots of his own.

That sense of humor would come in handy when she told him about the great switcheroo.

She paused in her sweeping to look at him. Maybe she should tell him now who she was. She was sure he'd enjoy it. They could have a laugh about it and get straight down to the business of becoming properly acquainted.

It was tempting.

Sam finished rolling the sheet of plastic and straightened up, putting one hand back to rub his spine.

"Are you okay?" she asked.

He waved his hand dismissively. "It's fine. Just tired, you know, it's been a long day."

She tilted her head. "I know something that could make you good as new. Especially if you're going to be working this hard tomorrow."

He looked wary. "You mean like a neck rub?"

Megan smiled. "Sort of."

"You comfortable?" she asked again, looking down at his prone form.

"You sure you know what you're doing?" he asked.

"Trust me. Now, don't tense up and try to hold my weight. Just relax and let me do all the work. The more you relax the better it will be."

"You're the boss," he said.

A few minutes later he was groaning softly with pleasure.

SAM LET OUT another sigh. He'd never had someone walk on his back before and the feeling was amazing. Her feet squidged and flexed his skin while her weight pushed out the stubborn knots of tension. She worked her feet along either side of his spine and he could practically feel it re-aligning. As he got used to the pressure he relaxed more and more and just when he thought it couldn't get any better she worked the balls of her feet into his shoulder blades. He let out another exhalation of pleasure as the aches melted away.

After fifteen minutes he was sorry to feel her step off his back. It felt as though he'd been there for an hour and it still wasn't enough. He heard her get down on one knee next to his face.

"You awake?" she whispered.

"Not really," he murmured. "Could you just leave me here until morning?"

She giggled. "Come on. Stand up. Wait until you feel the difference."

He grumbled amiably as he got up and straightened his back. He rolled his head from left to right. "It's amazing. Where on earth did you learn to do that?"

"I...my sister learned it in Japan and she taught me. It's fun, isn't it?"

"Can I have my T-shirt back?" he asked, smiling as she blushed.

"Oh, here. Sorry." She babbled on as he pulled the T-shirt over his head. "It's a good use of energy because it's no effort for me. I mean, using my weight to really

pummel those muscles. I couldn't give you half as much
of a massage with my skinny little arms.''

His T-shirt bunched and she reached out to pull it down
at the same time as he reached over to feel her bicep.

Her knuckles grazed his skin and he froze, his hand on
her arm. He held his breath, waiting for her to move but
she kept holding his T-shirt. They were both waiting for
the other to break the spell, to pull back and change the
mood, but with each second that passed it become more of
an impossibility.

He put a tiny amount of pressure on her arm, pulling her
toward him and, feeling it, she allowed herself to be pulled
forward. Her hand slid around to his side and he moved
his hand around to rest lightly on her back. The top of her
head was level with his cheekbone. There was still space
between their bodies but only a whisper of air between his
cheek and hers.

Her lips were parted and he could see that her breathing,
like his, had become more uneven. Her eyes were downcast, as if she was looking at his shoulder or neck. He
turned his head slowly, looking at the sweep of her neck
up from the dress. Strands of her hair moved as he breathed
and he could see her eyelashes flickering. She turned her
face a little more toward his until their mouths were only
centimeters apart.

Every inch of Sam's body was tuned to the feel of her,
the smell of her. He was afraid that he was going to start
trembling, his urge to hold her was so strong. She put her
other arm up to rest on his chest and he was struck by how
tiny and slender it was, even as the heat of it burned
through his T-shirt. He put his other arm around her, higher
up on her back, between her shoulder blades. He saw her
eyes close and he closed his as their lips touched.

It was little more than mouths meeting, but Megan felt
the effect of it all the way to her stomach. She moved in
and closed the gap between their bodies and the heat in-
tensified until it was almost unbearable. Then Sam's lips

began to move on hers. It was a gentle, tender kiss, as if
he was cherishing this first taste and didn't want to rush it.
Megan felt herself tremble and his arms tightened, pulling
her into the safe haven of his body. Her arms encircled him
and she gave herself up completely to the kiss, responding
with a matching warmth and ardor. His hand moved up
along her back and around to cup her face. His thumb
stroked the soft skin under her ear and she put one of her
own hands up to clasp at his hair.

He let out a small groan and Megan felt his tongue brush
against hers. It gave her a jolt like electricity and she
wanted to open her mouth to it, but she pulled back, her
breathing hard and ragged.

"No," she said. "I'm sorry. No, we can't."

He pulled his own head back and his eyes were glazed.
He looked at her in confusion but didn't restrain her as she
pulled out of his arms.

"I'm sorry," she said again and she meant it from the
bottom of her heart. She knew that the kiss had affected
him as much as it had her and her mind was a whirlwind
of desire and remorse.

Sam's look of confusion and embarrassment cut through
her. "I'm sorry," he said. "I shouldn't have...I thought..."

"No, that's okay," she said hurriedly, "I wanted you to.
It's just...it's a bit sudden, that's all."

Sam's breathing was slowing down. "I shouldn't have
grabbed you like that."

She looked at him, her eyes twinkling. "And I shouldn't
have put up such a fight."

He laughed, looking less embarrassed, and ran his hand
through his hair. "Phew, I guess it's been building up for
a while."

Megan felt her heart go cold.

"For how long?" she whispered. "I mean, since when?"

Sam looked uncomfortable. "Well, I guess it's only since
yesterday. I mean, before that, we were just working to-

gether, and then yesterday, you were so funny, and I know it was just the cold medicine, but it gave me a glimpse of what you'd be like, after hours, and I guess I just started thinking about, well, this.'' He grinned sheepishly. ''Typical male, huh?''

Megan smiled helplessly. ''Don't worry, I'm glad to hear it.''

He met her eyes again. ''I guess maybe I should ask you officially if you'd like to go out with me sometime.''

The full realization of what had happened was dawning on Megan and she drew back.

''Oh no,'' she said, putting her hand to her mouth. ''I really shouldn't have done this. I'm so sorry. It was a mistake. I...I have to go.''

SAM WATCHED in utter confusion as she turned and hurried out of the gallery. She had a small head start on him before he got his wits together and followed her. He was just in time to see her grab up her briefcase and coat and rush through the door. He stumbled on something on the floor and looked down. Her shoes were discarded in a lonely bundle. He picked them up and rushed to the doorway and spotted her at the top of the stairs.

I don't believe this, he thought.

I am running after a fleeing woman who has dropped her shoes.

''Rachel!'' he called out.

7

MEGAN STOPPED about halfway across the parking lot and looked down.

Well, that would explain why her feet were so cold.

She groaned, mortified. She considered just going but then remembered how ratty Rachel had been when she'd kicked her shoes off. Probably not a good idea to turn up without them altogether.

She turned back reluctantly and winced as she saw a silhouette appear in the doorway.

"Hey, Cinders? Did you forget something?"

Megan smiled despite herself. Sam came out to meet her and she leaned on his arm as she slipped the shoes on.

"I'm glad I caught you," he said. "I thought I'd be wandering around all day tomorrow asking strange women to try on these shoes."

Megan laughed and Sam went on. "You want to tell me what made you run out so fast? I didn't think I was that bad a kisser."

Her smile faded. "I'm sorry. It's not you. Well, it is you…and me." She bit her lip, trying to find the words. "I don't think it's a good idea for us to do this."

He looked down at her and she felt a tremor of excitement run through her. Gosh, he was gorgeous. She tried to ignore it.

"Can I ask why not?" he said.

"I just think it would make things really complicated," she answered honestly.

"A complication? Is that what this is? Because, from

where I'm standing it seems really simple. I like you, you like me, what's the problem?''

I'm a fake, she thought dismally, that's the problem.

"Unless…'' he said. "Is there someone else?''

She looked up at him, then away. "No,'' she said in a small voice.

"Then…?''

"Sam,'' she pleaded. "I'm tired and I want to go home. And I really am sorry but this was a mistake.''

A REALLY big mistake.

Megan repeated the words to herself again as she let herself into Rachel's house. Smells of cooking wafted from the kitchen, making Megan feel even more terrible.

How on earth was she going to explain it to Rachel?

"You made it!'' said Rachel, greeting her with a smile. "A full day. I'm so proud of you. Sit down.''

Megan looked around at the bowls of chopped ingredients and the pots simmering on the cooker. She was wracked with guilt. Rachel was going to so much trouble to look after her while she was out wreaking havoc on her sister's life.

Rachel wiped her hands on a tea towel and brushed a strand of hair off her face. "I can't wait to hear about today. Was it okay? What else happened? Tell me about the shaky moments.'' She laughed and took a seat on the other side of the scrubbed pine kitchen table. "I'm bombarding you, sorry. There's just so much I want to hear about. Anyway, go on, tell me about your day.''

Megan looked at Rachel's open, trusting, blue face.

"I…I—'' she stammered. "I have to tell you—''

She paused and frowned.

"What?'' said Rachel.

Megan tilted her head. "Your face, it's still blue.''

Rachel drew back defensively and put her hand to her cheek. "I think it's faded a bit. I think the light in here just makes it look...I mean, today, in daylight, it really wasn't so..." She trailed off and sighed. "I know."

"I thought you tried some new things on it."

Rachel made a face. "They haven't worked so far. This stuff has really soaked in good."

Megan leaned forward. "I don't know if I should tell you this, but there's also some patches of brown—"

"That's foundation," Rachel interrupted her. "I tried putting makeup on to cover it. Needed about three layers and I looked even weirder." She angled her face for Megan. "Are you sure it hasn't faded at all?"

"Hard to say," said Megan, peering closely. "Possibly a little bit."

Rachel slumped back. "But not enough." She jumped up and went over to the stove to stir one of the saucepans.

Megan dipped her finger into one of the bowls on the table.

"What is this?" she said, tasting it. "Teriyaki sauce?"

Rachel looked around. "That's apple chutney and corn flour with a spritz of window-cleaner."

Megan dashed over to the sink, spitting. She grabbed a carton from the fridge and gulped down some juice.

"Are you trying to kill me?" she spluttered.

"It's one of my mixtures," said Rachel. "Hey, get me the rosehip tea out of the cupboard, would you?"

Megan handed it over grumpily and then sat down again, looking around the kitchen in disappointment. "None of this is dinner, is it?"

"Dinner?" said Rachel absent-mindedly. "No, I didn't have time for that. Anyway," she went on, "I called Dr. Thomson today but the soonest she could see me was tomorrow morning." She split open one of the herbal tea bags and added the contents to her witches brew in the saucepan.

Megan looked at Rachel's back. "But you can work from home tomorrow, right?"

"Not really," Rachel said. "I've got a press tour."

"What's that?" Megan asked warily.

"It's just where journalists from different papers and magazines come in and I give them a quick preview of the exhibition and then they write very favorable articles about it." She looked over her shoulder. "It's pretty straightforward."

"Oh no," said Megan, leaning back. "No Rachel, I can't. I mean, I came so close to being caught so many times today. I really think I've used up my quota of luck on this thing. And I miss my own life and I'm getting really behind with work. And I can't get used to these shoes, my feet are killing me. The sooner you go back…" She trailed off as she suddenly realized she was being handed a chance to clear things up with Sam.

She wouldn't have to tell Rachel after all.

Like a deranged debater she rapidly switched sides. "Uh, but I see that it's impossible for you to go in, so maybe I have no choice. And I know more now than I did yesterday so tomorrow should be that much easier. So I guess I could do it, that is, if you really want me to."

Rachel shrugged. "I admit that I thought this was nuts to begin with but I have to give you credit, you're really carrying it off. And, hey, so far today I haven't had any phone calls about any strange behavior on your part."

Megan gave a choked laugh.

"If you're willing to do it," Rachel went on. "I can coach you for tomorrow. And if none of these work," she waved her hand around the kitchen, "I'm sure Dr. Thomson will be able to help. She might have some shot or something that will just make this dye disappear. Fingers crossed!"

"Fingers crossed," echoed Megan, uncomfortably aware that this was also the standard gesture for those perpetrating a lie.

THEY SPENT two hours trying to cram information into Megan's head before they finally realized their approach was wrong.

"I don't know why I didn't think of this before," said Megan in exasperation. "The whole point is that I'm in there playing you, and I don't even know what you're like at work."

She tapped her finger on the mock-up press pack that Rachel had made (since all the real ones were locked safely in the gallery). "I've been on this side of it, I know how these people will act."

This was true. Being a travel writer meant gathering information—from tourist centers, embassies or from anyone else who wanted to extol the virtues of their native country.

"Okay," said Rachel. "I'll act it out for you. You be the press and I'll be, well, I'll be me. Hang on, I'll throw some proper clothes on."

She was gone for ten minutes and Megan slipped into a dazed reverie about Sam, so she was caught by surprise when Rachel breezed back into the room.

"Hello people, how are we today? Have you all got packs? Hmm, Jocelyn, can we get some extra packs up here, please? Okay, I know you're all busy people so let's go straight in." Rachel made for the kitchen door then turned, her eyes sparkling with enthusiasm while Megan scrabbled to her feet, grabbing the press pack and a pen.

"I just want you to know that you're all in for a very big treat. I personally think that this is one of the finest collections of classical and renaissance works we've ever had in this city. This is the first time that some of these paintings have been out of their native galleries in over ten years." She tilted her head coquettishly while Megan tried to wipe the look of surprise off her face. "Quite a few of them will be familiar to you, but there are some delightful oddities among them, which I hope you won't skip over. Shall we go in?"

She swept into the kitchen and Megan was so entranced by the performance that she almost looked around for her fellow journalists.

Then she was given a tour which showed her Rachel's house in quite a different light. By the end of it she was prepared to believe that Bronzino's *Allegory with Venus and Cupid* hung over Rachel's bed and that a tall, virile Bacchus formed the centerpiece in her guest room. More importantly, she picked up a few useful tricks for dodging questions by referring to the press pack, providing distractions or, when all else failed, playfully inviting the questioner to guess the answer themselves.

They returned eventually to the living room and Rachel collapsed onto the sofa with a loud "Phew!"

Megan gave her a round of applause before sitting down herself. "Well, Ms. Dean," she drawled. "You take my breath away."

Rachel laughed and blushed with pleasure. "Did that help?"

"Definitely," said Megan. "You just swept me along and I was almost afraid to interrupt you with silly questions. That's exactly how I'll play it tomorrow." A slight frown creased her brow. "You'll still have to write that speech out for me though, there's no way I'll remember all those names."

Rachel considered it. "I guess I could do that, as long as you carry it as if you really don't need to, pretend that you're just checking it occasionally."

"And now," said Megan, going out to the hall to get her coat. "I'm going home for a few hours. If I'm going to be stuck here for a couple of days I'll need some stuff."

MEGAN WALKED into her apartment and looked around with delight at the familiar messiness. Rachel's house was lovely, but nothing beat the familiarity of having her own things around her. Her own books, her own plants, her own furniture and her own pictures and photographs on the walls. She shrugged off her coat and tossed it onto the sofa as she wandered into the kitchen to make herself a peanut butter sandwich, wondering what Sam would make of her apartment.

Because, she told herself optimistically, they would eventually sort out this mix-up and she'd be bringing him here.

She decided he'd like it. True, he sometimes gave the impression of being rather reserved, but Megan had seen the evidence of a playful sense of humor and his interest in other cultures would mean he would enjoy the fact that so much of her home was decorated with souvenirs from her travels.

She paused as she was spreading the peanut butter, staring into space. She could still taste him on her lips. The muscles in her stomach tightened as she remembered the feel of him pulling her against his body, the burn of his hands on her back. She let out a long breath, feeling again the sudden whoosh of desire course through her as if her body was a match that had just been lit.

Admittedly, kissing him while she was still Rachel had been a really bad move. Not least because now, Sam, if he was feeling anything like her, thought he was feeling it for Rachel. But it wouldn't really make that much difference in the end, would it? A rose by any other name and all that.

Unless he was falling for Rachel because of her job. No, that was ridiculous. It was Megan herself he was interested in, he'd practically told her as much.

She finished making her sandwich and put the jar back in the cupboard, unable to shake this new feeling of unease.

She'd been assuming all along that Sam would be amused when he found out about the switch, but she was slowly realizing that the kiss had changed things.

Wouldn't he be a little angry that she'd deceived him?

Even though it wasn't a very bad deceit? She wasn't, for instance, masterminding some great scam in order to rip him off or anything like that.

And she definitely wasn't deceiving him in order to make a fool of him.

It was an accidental deceit, that was it. He wouldn't blame her when he found out. He had a sense of humor, same as her. Hey, she wouldn't be mad if she found out he wasn't who he said he was.

She faltered. Would she?

Honestly?

She admitted it to herself. She'd still like him but she'd be pretty cross.

She poured herself a glass of milk, still fretting. It was killing her not to be able to tell Rachel. She remembered when Rachel had come to her to tell her all about meeting David and the reports that she'd received in the months that followed.

Much as she hated to admit it, she had been a tiny bit jealous. Of David, for replacing her as Rachel's closest confidante, and of Rachel, for having found someone to get that close to.

Megan had had boyfriends but she'd always known in her heart that none of them had half the importance for her as David had for Rachel.

But now, suddenly, she was feeling it for the first time. It was scary and exhilarating.

She wandered back into the living room and stood in front of a framed photo of herself that had been taken in a rickshaw on the streets of New Delhi. She swallowed a bite of sandwich and took a sip of milk, considering the photo. Whether Sam would be comfortable in her home was less to the point than would he be comfortable with her? The real Megan. She looked so different in the photograph to what he was used to. Her hair had been almost bleached completely white by the Indian sun and her face was weathered and freckled. But her grin was the same and her eyes were sparkling with happiness. She let her gaze wander over the other photographs. In some she was bundled up tightly against the cold, only her nose peeping out, and in others she was barely dressed at all in tank tops and cut-off shorts.

Would Sam, who was so used to the sleek, polished Rachel, even recognize this windswept traveler with her tangled ponytail and eyes brimming with curiosity? Did she look like someone he would be with?

"YOU SHOULD have brought her along."

"No offence," said Sam. "But this isn't really the kind of place you bring Rachel Dean to."

"Not into sports?"

The group of men in front of the big-screen television let out a roar of approval as another hockey player got his face mashed into the ice. Sam waited until the noise died down.

"Not into sports bars, let's put it like that."

Kevin, his friend and proud owner of the bar, leaned over the pool table and took his shot. He made a face as the ball rolled to the lip of the pocket and stayed there.

"Why do you always go out with these arty types?" he complained to Sam. "You should find a girl who knows how to let her hair down."

"I know it's hard for you to understand, but I happen to like a little sophistication in a woman." Sam walked around the table, eyeing the layout. "And, anyway, Rachel does know how to let her hair down, that's what I've been trying to tell you. She's got this whole other side to her that I'm only just finding out about."

He took the shot and then straightened up, exhaling in frustration. "I don't know what I did wrong."

"You should have hit it a bit harder," commented Kevin. "And you needed some back spin."

Sam gave him a look. "Not the shot," he said. "Rachel. I thought we were getting on so well and I was sure she liked me but then, when I kissed her..." He shook his head. "She couldn't get away from me fast enough."

"Maybe you misread the signals," said Kevin. He

dropped a ball into the sidepocket and then grunted in annoyance because he'd managed to snooker himself. He paced around the table, trying to find an angle.

"I really don't think I did," said Sam. He paused and shook his head. "I don't know. One minute she's beaming at me and there's all this eye contact going on, and then next minute she's putting up walls and warning me off."

Kevin took his shot without enthusiasm, turning away from the table before the balls had even finished moving.

"That's women for you," he said simply. "Besides, everyone's got their secrets, Sam. I bet you wouldn't want her to know what a terrible pool player you are."

He grinned wryly as Sam sank two balls in a row and lined up on the black. It dropped sweetly into the pocket.

"If I'm terrible," laughed Sam, "what does that make you?"

"A bigmouth," sighed Kevin. "Double or nothing?"

"It's your money."

Sam leaned up against the bar and sipped his beer as Kevin set up the table.

"There's just something about her," Sam went on, unable to stop puzzling it over.

"Something wonderful?" teased Kevin.

"Yeah, a bit," admitted Sam bashfully. "But also—"

"Something sexy?"

"Definitely." Sam took another sip of beer and stared into space, narrowing his eyes. "Something I can't put my finger on."

"Something funny?"

"She *is* funny," said Sam, deliberately misinterpreting. He paused in thought again and then met his friend's eyes.

"Yeah," he admitted. "There's something funny about her. I just haven't figured out what it is."

He chalked his cue and walked over to take the first shot.

"Yet," he added quietly.

8

THIS IS LIKE something out of *Groundhog Day,* thought Megan as she went up the stone steps to the gallery. I'm condemned to repeat this day until I get it right.

She looked around nervously as she went in, torn between wanting to see Sam and dreading it. At least Bill Murray got to make a fresh start every day—she had to work with all the mistakes she'd made the day before.

She still didn't know what she was going to say to Sam. When not cramming for the press tour, she'd outlined her options.

One: come clean. Tell him about the swap, tell him who she was and face the consequences. Which would be great if the consequences were laughs all round and then more of that delicious kissing, but not so much fun if Sam went to Peterson and exposed their fraud. She didn't think he would, and if it was only her career that was on the line she would risk it, but she didn't have the right to gamble with Rachel's.

So: second option. Continue the kissing. That was the most attractive option in the short term, but boy, would she be buying a mess of trouble for herself later. And it wouldn't be at all fair on Sam.

Face it, second option wasn't really an option.

Third option. Tell Sam it can't go on, that they should just ignore their feelings and concentrate on work. At least for this week. Nip it in the bud and there'd be no problem. It was the most sensible option and the least attractive.

Megan crinkled her nose in annoyance. Like an irresolute

dieter she knew what she had to do but she just didn't want to do it.

"Excuse me?"

Megan looked down at the elderly lady who had put her hand on Megan's arm.

Was she supposed to know this woman? With my luck, thought Megan wryly, she's probably Sam's mother, come to complicate life further.

"Could you tell me where the restroom is, please?"

Megan smiled with relief. At least this was a question she could answer. She was about to point the way when she caught a glimpse of Sam at the top of the stairway.

"Let me show you," she smiled at the woman, linking arms with her and walking her briskly around the side of the main staircase and down to the restrooms.

"Here we are," she said with a bright smile, holding the door open and watching out of the corner of her eye, ready to duck in if she spotted Sam.

"Thank you, dear," said the old lady, giving her a dubious look as she went in, as if she rather suspected Megan of marching her off to a broom closet. Megan decided that following her in would probably unnerve her even more so she let the door close. She walked carefully to the end of the little hallway and peered around the corner. Curious glances from people milling about in the foyer told her that she wasn't doing a great job of making herself inconspicuous so she straightened up and walked toward her office, speeding up into a trot as she reached the door.

"PRESS PACKS!" said Jocelyn brightly as Megan stood aside to let her in to Rachel's office. She *is* a good assistant, thought Megan. She helped Jocelyn put the packs on the desk and sat down behind it again as Jocelyn left.

She opened one of the press packs. Inside were a catalogue, various pamphlets about the Bonnington Trust and photocopies of gallery details, admission prices, joining the

Friends society and a brief history of the gallery. She pulled out one of the catalogues to refresh her memory.

"I've got to control this tour," she reminded herself firmly. "Show them what I want them to see." She banged her fist on the desk. "This is my exhibition and I'm a busy woman. Let's do this thing!"

She looked at her watch and exhaled in annoyance.

Not yet, however.

If anything was going to reveal her as a fake, this was it. But this was as ready as she was going to get. And, thank goodness, Rachel had typed out the speech for her. She fiddled with a pen in agitation. She hoped Sam wouldn't be around to see it. She frowned as she thought of him. It was a little strange that he hadn't come to see her by now. You'd think he'd want to talk about last night.

She tapped her pen absently. Was it possible that he was avoiding her? But why? Sure, she'd been avoiding him, but she had a good reason. The only reason he'd be avoiding her was if he regretted it.

She laughed shakily. How could he be regretting it?

She jumped as the cell phone in her briefcase rang. Rachel with some last-minute advice?

She answered it. "Hello?"

"Megan?"

Megan recognized the voice of her editor, but it took a second for her to get her bearings.

"Uh...Marcus, hi. Yeah, it's me."

He laughed. "You don't sound so sure."

She forced a laugh.

"Anyway, how's it going?" he said. "Tell me you're halfway through a first draft, brighten up my day."

Megan ignored the flush of guilt at not having done any real work since the weekend. "You're kidding, right? I'm still sorting out my notes."

"I see," said Marcus, sounding disappointed.

"Well, give me a break," she said. "I've still got three months, don't I? I'll get it done."

She could hear him moving paper around on his desk. "The thing is, something's come up. You're the first person I thought of because I know how much you've wanted to go, but it's not an option unless you've got a good start on the Scandinavia copy."

Megan frowned. "What are you talking about?"

"See, it's Roberta Weir. She was lined up for it, but she's been having some problems with her pregnancy. Nothing serious, but she's decided not to go. It's only a two-month trip, for the update, and we think you'd be perfect for it, however, you have to be ready to go soon."

"How soon? And where are you talking about?" Megan asked again insistently.

"Let me put it this way. We're looking at next week or the week after that at the latest because we've got to have you out there for the Carnevale festival."

Suddenly Megan knew where Marcus was talking about. And he was right, she'd been trying to angle a trip for years.

"Italy," she moaned.

"I knew you'd feel that way," said Marcus. "Now, it's a relatively short trip so I'll understand if you want to pass, but it could be a while before Italy comes up again. I'm going to need a yes or no from you by the end of the week. Have a think about it and see if you'll be able to do the Scandinavia work at the same time."

"Oh boy, that's tempting," said Megan. She looked around, suddenly remembering where she was. "But next week? I don't know if I'll be able to do that."

"Sure you will," said Marcus. "Just get your head down, put in a few long days. I'm sure you can get the outline to me. Only forty pages, that's all I'm looking for. It'll be tough but you've done it before."

"Okay," said Megan dubiously. "I'll get back to you in a couple of days and let you know, okay?"

"I'll be waiting. Call me with good news. Bye."

Megan put down the phone, dazed. Talk about bad timing. She'd been waiting for a trip to Italy for years.

So what's the problem, she thought. *Are you going to pass it up just because of some guy you only met a few days ago?*

But what if he's the one? Are you going to pass up true love for a trip to Italy?

But, then again, how could it be true love when he hadn't even come to see her yet?

And was Italy even physically possible?

She grabbed her briefcase and pulled out a sheaf of notes. Just the outline, Marcus had said. She spread out the notes across her desk. The opening chapters were simple enough, they just dealt with the practicalities: everything from visas to money to health and emergency services. Next came the chapters on the history, geography and culture of the country. And last, an area by area description of the best accommodations, restaurants and cafés, nightlife, sights, shops and activities, heavily interspersed with anecdotes and advice from the hundreds of locals that Megan had talked to.

She flipped rapidly through the pages, her eyes skimming the words while her brain raced. Holmenkollen Ski Festival, Briksdals glacier, Egeskov Slot, Gothenburg, hmm, nothing written about the midsummer festivals yet and only the barest sketch of Oslo.

She jumped as the door opened and Jocelyn came in. In a panic, Megan grabbed at the bundle of press packs and toppled it, spilling the packs all over her travel notes.

"Oops," she said, giggling nervously.

Jocelyn stopped and folded her arms, lifting a playful eyebrow.

"Something I shouldn't see?"

"What?" exclaimed Megan. "No, nothing like that. Just something I was working on. Not work work of course but just something personal…and unimportant."

Jocelyn nodded knowingly. She handed Megan a bundle

of pages. "Maps of the gallery, for the press packs," she said. Her eyes flicked to the desk then back to Megan's.

Megan could see that Jocelyn was curious, but she was determined to outwait her. Jocelyn hesitated for another moment, and then she smiled and went out. Megan put her head in her hands, giving vent to a little silent scream. Then she realized she hadn't heard the door close and she looked up to see Sam standing in the doorway, eyeing her curiously.

"Is this a bad time?" he said.

"Uh…" said Megan.

"Because I thought maybe we should talk about, you know, last night."

"Uh…okay," said Megan nervously, watching as Sam came in and closed the door behind him. Even though she'd had all morning to prepare, Megan still didn't know what she wanted to say to Sam. Well, she knew, she just didn't want to say it.

It seemed as though he shared her hesitancy because he wandered over to one of the bookshelves and picked up a framed photo. "Is this you? You didn't tell me your sister was a twin. Wow, which one are you?"

"Guess," she said with a shaky laugh, her mind still whirling with thoughts of Italy.

He looked thoughtful. "Well, let's see. I already know you so I think I have a bit of an advantage, but then again—" he raised an eyebrow "—we are talking identical twins here. Hmm, it's a tough one but I'd have to say that's you."

He pointed at the photo and Megan looked at it. She remembered when the photo had been taken. Rachel had been giving her a piggyback and Megan had unwrapped Rachel's scarf and put it around her own neck. As David took the photo Megan was laughing and Rachel was wearing an outraged grin.

Sam was pointing at Megan.

She paused, disconcerted. Well, so what, he'd had a fifty-fifty shot.

"I'm right, aren't I?" he said gleefully, noting her hesitation. "I knew it."

"Why do you think that's me?"

"I recognize the smile. Your smile is always so innocent but your eyes say 'catch me if you can.'"

Megan was very impressed, and quite flattered, so she hated to have to contradict him.

"Sorry," she said ruefully. "I'm the one on the bottom. The one on my back is Megan."

"Really?" Sam pulled the photo up closer to his face. "That's amazing. I would have sworn that was you."

Megan shrugged. "Well, you said it yourself. We're identical."

"You *look* identical," he corrected her.

Megan knew from experience that not many people made the distinction. Maybe Italy could wait after all.

"For instance, I bet she doesn't go around kissing men that she's only known for a couple of weeks."

Megan felt a blush rising. That was true. In her case it was more like a couple of days. Still, she couldn't let him get away with that.

"She might," she said defiantly, standing up. "It would depend on the man."

Sam nodded thoughtfully and put the photo back on the shelf. He turned toward her again and stopped right in front of her.

Megan should have moved back, she knew that, but she could smell his aftershave and she could see the shadow of dark hair curling under his pale blue shirt and, somehow, her legs wouldn't obey her.

"That's a nice shirt," she said inanely.

The corners of his lips tilted up. "Thank you."

She looked up and caught his eyes and that was her real undoing. His eyelashes were very long and dark and she was close enough to see the flecks of gold that gave his eyes such depth. They were sparkling with amusement, and if she hadn't noticed the way his breathing had deepened she might have thought he was only regarding her with mild curiosity.

Her mouth twitched and, before she'd even thought about it, she felt her own eyebrows lift invitingly.

He searched her eyes for a moment then lowered his mouth to hers, touching her lips softly. Megan felt a quiver run through her, resounding deep in her lower stomach. She put her hands on his chest and let them slide upward, past the jut of his collarbones and over the curve of his broad shoulders. Sam's hands slid around her back, holding her lightly as he kissed her again, catching her bottom lip between his. Megan kissed him back and it was like sinking into a tropical sea. Warmth suffused her and she leaned her whole weight against him, molding her body to his. His tongue pushed at her lips and she opened her mouth to his, searching and probing with her own tongue. She pushed her hands up through his hair and pulled his mouth harder onto hers. He brought his hands around to run them up along her arms and back down again, sending tingles shooting along her skin. His thumbs skimmed the edge of her breasts and the sensitive skin under her arms and she felt a burst of liquid heat low in her stomach. She moaned and his arms tightened around her again. She stretched up onto her toes, thrilling to the feel of his strong chest and shoulders. His hands ran down her back as she moved and slid over the curve of her buttocks. Her skirt stretched tautly over her thighs and she felt her heart thudding as he caressed her. She slid one of her own hands down and around his waist, running her fingers along the ridge of his spine. Tugging at his shirt she slipped her hand under it until she could feel his skin, splaying her fingers over the warmth of it. One of his hands snaked up to cradle the back of her head as he deepened the kiss while the other slid lower, holding her body tightly against his own.

The knock on the door startled them.

Their heads jerked apart and they searched each other's eyes as Jocelyn's voice rang out.

"Rachel, the press are here. They're downstairs waiting for you."

Megan and Sam continued to stare at each other as the sound of Jocelyn's footsteps could be heard moving away from the door. Then Sam's head dropped onto Megan's shoulder, and he exhaled hugely as she slowly slid her hand out from under his shirt.

"You okay?" he said, putting a hand on her shoulder.

She nodded, running her fingers through her hair, straightening it and fluffing it out. "I'll be fine. I'll just take a minute to fix my makeup and, you know, calm down."

He nodded, then surprised her by sliding his hand around to the back of her neck and dropping a gentle kiss on her forehead. "You'll be great. I'll see you later."

He stepped back and grinned sheepishly, straightening the waistband of his trousers. "I think I'd better go somewhere and, er, calm down, too," he said, making her smile again.

MEGAN'S LEGS were trembling as she walked up the main staircase carrying her speech and the bundle of press packs.

Right up until the moment it happened, if she'd been asked about the possibility of her ending up in a steamy clinch with Sam, she would have denied it vehemently and insisted that there was no way that she'd be that irresponsible (again!).

And yet, apparently, she was.

And did she even have the sense to regret it?

Logically, sure. It had been a very bad move.

But physically, her whole body was thrumming like a tuning fork, and she was afraid that if he walked too close to her in the gallery she wouldn't be able to resist flinging herself onto him as if they were magnetized.

She reached the top of the stairs to find herself faced

with a group of ten people, four women and six men, all chatting amongst themselves.

There was one thing to be said for almost ravishing Sam in Rachel's office—she'd forgotten to worry about this upcoming trial by fire.

She deliberately pulled back her shoulders and lifted her chin to get into character as she strode up to her audience.

"Hi everyone," she said self-assuredly. "Sorry to keep you waiting."

She dropped the press packs on a nearby desk and left the group to pick them up for themselves while she repeated Rachel's introduction from the night before word for word.

She went into the first gallery and stood in the middle, inviting them to gather around her. She hadn't counted on their natural curiosity and they spread out like an oil spill, filling the room.

"Is this a Rossetti?" asked a red-haired lady behind her. A few others interrupted their perusals to hear the answer.

"You know what?" said Megan, giving an impatient toss of her head. "We'll be here all day if I start taking separate questions. What I'm going to do is take you through, and I'll point out works of particular interest—" she imitated Rachel's flirty smile "—and, of course, my personal favorites, and you can be looking through your catalogues along the way and then, if there is anything you need cleared up at the end I'll be happy to answer questions." Unless, she thought, I conveniently get called away on an art emergency.

She could see a look of pique cross the red-haired journalist's face at having her question ignored, and she imagined the headline in the culture section the next day: Hyder Curator Is Rude and Unhelpful. Well, it couldn't be helped. Being unhelpful was preferable to saying I haven't a clue.

Megan made a beeline for the first painting on her list and glanced down at her speech, ready to deliver the first line. Which was, according to the pages she was holding,

"The magnificence of the fjords which cut into Norway's western coastline cannot be overestimated."

Megan flipped the page over in the futile hope that somehow she might have picked up Rachel's speech as well as her own notes, but no, of course she hadn't.

She looked up again at the ten expectant faces and smiled in terror. She looked back up at the painting and tried to clear her mind of jagged fjords and ferocious seascapes.

"Okay," she said, glancing surreptitiously at the label next to the painting. "This is a picture of, uh, Eros and a young girl. Eros is of course the god of love and the young girl…well, she's young so she hasn't experienced love yet." Megan was quickly realizing that it was one thing to read about a painting and another thing entirely to relay that information with any sort of erudition.

She struggled on. "So, see, Eros is trying to persuade her that love is a good thing and she should, uh, go for it, but she's pushing him away even though you can see that she's quite curious." Megan suddenly remembered another snippet from the catalogue. "Oh, and see the way the painter has made the path under their feet sort of rough and stony? That's because the path of love can be rocky. It's fun but rocky…so you have to watch out for it."

All the journalists were frowning slightly and Megan decided that the only thing to do was try and keep talking, in the vain hope of distracting them. She moved across the room and stopped in front of another painting.

"This is Mars and Venus," she said, hoping she had the right painting. It looked smaller than she had expected from the catalogue illustration. She ploughed on courageously. "Now, I don't know how many of you know this but Mars and Venus weren't even married. Venus was married to…uh, someone else so she and Mars were actually having an affair." She paused, looking at the doubtful faces. "Which is pretty funny really, isn't it? When you think of the whole Men-Are-from-Mars thing, eh?"

Nobody responded and Megan felt her throat tightening again.

"If you'd like to follow me," she said shakily, moving into the next gallery.

Okay, here was one of her favorites. Surely she could manage to say something intelligent about it.

"This is called *Hylas and the Nymphs*," she started confidently. "Now, at first glance what we see is a big, strong, tanned soldier and we're a bit worried for all these pale, half-naked nymphs in the water but the fact is that they are actually luring Hylas into the lake, where he'll drown. See the way they're smiling up at him and ever-so-gently grasping his robes and he's just on the verge of falling in." Megan sighed with emotion. "He's caught and he doesn't even know it."

She turned back to her audience but they didn't appear to be quite as enraptured as Megan, or for that matter, Hylas.

Megan swallowed dryly. This wasn't working. Time to try a different tack. "Okay, you see what I've been doing? I've been acting like someone who doesn't know anything about art. Someone who just came along and read the little bit of information on the wall and then looked at the painting. Just looked at it, which you don't need a degree in art history to do. Anyone can do it." Megan gave a small laugh. "I can see you're all a bit bemused but one of the things we're trying to do with this exhibition is encourage people to come, especially people who may not have visited an art gallery before, who may even be a little intimidated by it." She spread her hands expansively. "Sure I could stand here and reel off lots of technical information for you but it's all in the catalogue. I'm sure you'd prefer to use your time to actually look around for yourselves."

She smiled at them encouragingly, willing them to believe her. She had nothing left. If they didn't go for this she would definitely have to swoon. And the polished wood floor looked hard. The journalists glanced at each other and, after a moment's hesitation, they followed her suggestion, spreading out around the galleries, scribbling notes.

MEGAN AVOIDED becoming entangled in any conversations by flitting around and pretending to be checking the wall labels against the catalogue. Not giving them any chance to get restless she kept pushing them onward until they reached the final gallery where she was disconcerted to find Sam working.

Well, what did she expect? This was his job, wasn't it?

She nodded to him then looked away quickly because she could feel a betraying heat rising in her face.

But then a master stroke of distraction occurred to her that would take care of the press and Sam at the same time. "And now I'd like to introduce you to Sam Harrison, the overall curator of the exhibition. I'm sure he'd be happy to answer any quick questions you might have for him."

Her audience turned to Sam with murmurs of interest and Megan tapped nervously on her thigh.

Come on, come on, she thought.

Unfortunately, she soon found herself the object of interest again.

"Ms. Dean—" someone started.

Megan spoke over him. "Yes, Sam Harrison, that's H-a-r-r-i-s-o-n. Born into a family of archeologists and began his own illustrious career in the Seattle Art Museum. Since then he has curated exhibitions all over the world. Egypt, Japan, Australia, you name it. We're very honored that he's brought the exhibition here to the Hyder Gallery."

"You seem to know as much about him as the exhibition," one of the journalists joked.

Megan laughed along, thinking vengeful thoughts.

She shot a quick look down at the beeper on her waistband, then looked up quickly, not wanting to draw attention to the fact that she was waiting.

"Ms. Dean," the original questioner said again. "I notice there are no works by El Greco in the exhibition. Don't you think this is a rather glaring omission?''

Megan turned to him, relying on her common sense. ''There are over two hundred works in the exhibition. Obviously there are going to be omissions. It's certainly not because we think El Greco is less worthy or anything. Although, of course, it's Mr. Harrison's organization that collated the exhibition so if there are omissions, they made them.''

Realizing that this sounded rather accusatory she tried to lighten it with an attempt at humor. ''Maybe they don't think El Greco is any good, ahaha.''

When nobody else laughed she felt a finger of panic tickle her spine. Again she imagined tomorrow's headline, El Greco Is Garbage, Says Curator.

Followed a week later by the headline, Travel Writer Killed by Crazed, Blue-Faced Lunatic.

She tucked her hair behind her ear. ''Although, of course, I'm sure they don't think that at all.''

Beep me! she implored silently.

She jerked violently as her pager went off and scrabbled at her waistband.

''Oh darn,'' she said, looking at the journalists. ''I've got to get this. Please feel free to have another quick run through the galleries before you leave. If there's anything else, my assistant, Jocelyn, will be able to help.'' She gave them a shining smile. ''Oh, and there are a couple of complimentary passes in your packs, please come again and bring a friend. Thank you.''

She exited while they were still murmuring their thanks.

''How LONG?'' Megan asked despairingly. She'd been counting on good news from Rachel.

''She wasn't sure,'' Rachel replied. ''But she said it'll probably be at least a week.''

Megan put her hand to her head, rubbing her hairline.

"I don't understand, the help-line lady said it would be gone in a couple of days. It's been almost four now."

"Yeah," said Rachel. "Guess what. The recipes I got off the stains website? Bad idea. Dr. Thompson said they had some kind of reaction with the face-mask ingredients and sealed the color."

Megan let out a groan, filling Rachel's office.

"I know," said Rachel. "But I think I found something else, on this site about natural remedies. It's a really simple recipe of banana, peppercorns, carrot juice and finely ground grass."

"Ground glass?" Megan said in alarm.

"Grass, dummy. I said grass. Anyway, I'm going to give it a try."

"Are you sure that's a good idea?" said Megan. "What if it—"

"It'll be fine," said Rachel. "I'll try a test spot first. Anyway, tell me how the press tour went."

Megan gave her an account of the morning, and, even with all the bits about Sam cut out, she could tell that Rachel regained her sense of urgency about swapping back.

SAM WAS DISAPPOINTED not to find Rachel at lunch.

Seeing her in the gallery had been a delicious torture. He'd been glad he hadn't been in her place. He could see that she'd faltered in her speech a few times and he felt guilty because he was sure it had been because of him. Guilty, and quite flattered.

After he'd finished lunch he'd pay her a quick visit. Just to see if they could talk about what was going on with them.

And he'd behave himself—no amorous activity this time.

MEGAN LIFTED her head as he went into her office and her look of welcome warmed him. He watched as she moved a folder over what she'd been writing, and he frowned slightly. He thought he'd seen her do that before, as if she was working on some state secret.

"For the record," he said, sliding into the chair opposite her. "I happen to like El Greco very much."

She laughed and put her hands up to her face. "I know! I'm so sorry. Even as I said it I was imagining what they'd report."

Sam sat up straight and broadcasted, "Hyder Gallery says El Greco Sucks!"

Megan's eyes widened. "Well, I didn't imagine it being that bad, so thanks a lot. I can look forward to that."

"Why didn't you tell them we tried to get the El Greco from London?"

Sam had asked the question as an afterthought, so he almost missed her reaction. A fleeting look of alarm crossed her eyes, and she hesitated before answering with a casualness that seemed forced.

"It's the press, Sam, I didn't want to tell them anything I didn't have to. No point publicizing our failures, right?"

Sam sat forward, resting his elbows on his knees and looked at her searchingly.

"What's going on, Rachel?"

Her face stayed bright, but he could see unmistakable nervousness in her eyes.

"What do you mean?"

"I don't know," he said honestly. "You just seem so distracted or…confused lately." He let his concern come through in his voice. "I just need to know, is it to do with the exhibition? Or me? Is there something you're not telling me?"

She didn't answer straightaway, and he waited, giving her time to find the words and somewhat fearful of what she was going to say.

"You're right," she said at last. "I am distracted. But it's nothing to do with the exhibition. Or…or you. It's personal, Sam, it's just family stuff." She smiled ruefully at him. "It's not serious, just some things that have to be worked out."

Sam nodded, feeling oddly embarrassed that he'd imagined it had anything to do with him. "Is there anything I can do to help?"

She met his eyes, and her expression pierced him. It said that she wanted to lean on him, but she couldn't, or wouldn't, allow herself to.

"Thank you," she said with a warmth that he felt all the way to his bones, "but I'll be okay."

"Well, I'm here if you need me," he said.

She nodded again and then said awkwardly, "Uh…was that all you came in to ask me?"

He could sense she was trying to pull back again so he didn't badger her.

"I need the list of paintings you'll be displaying on the public access computers in the Reading Room. I just want to verify that we've cleared the reproduction rights."

Megan looked around her desk. She knew what he was looking for, if she could just put her hands on it. She shuffled through some files before remembering.

"Oh no," she said, putting her hand to her head. "It's at home."

"What?"

She looked apologetically at him. "I've had to bring stuff home occasionally to work on it, and I forgot it."

"That's okay," he said. "You can give it to me tomorrow. Unless you want to give it to me after I drop you home from our date tonight?" he suggested with a smile.

"Nice try," she said, smiling her appreciation at his joking tone. "But we're not going on a date."

He nodded. "You'd rather we just went on ravishing each other in secret?"

A smile tugged at her mouth, and he raised his eyebrows suggestively.

"Stop flirting with me," she said. "I'm trying to be practical here."

"So am I," he said indignantly. "If going out on a date isn't practical, I don't know what is."

Her smile widened. "I think most women would hope that a date would be romantic, Sam, not practical."

"Now who's flirting?" he chided gently.

She looked away and her smile dimmed. When she spoke it was to the desk.

"You're right Sam, and I'm sorry. I shouldn't have said that."

Sam paused, thinking. "Rachel, if you want me to leave you alone, I will."

She didn't look up and seemed to be undergoing some kind of mental struggle.

"That would probably be best," she said at last. "Let's just be work colleagues, okay?"

Sam was taken aback. He wouldn't have said it if he'd thought she'd actually take him up on it. He tried to make sense of her sudden distance. Maybe she was just worried that he was only after one thing and that rushing into something they weren't ready for would create an unbearable work atmosphere. He supposed it was a viable worry, considering the way his behavior had got away from him previously.

He nodded. "Okay," he said halfheartedly. "I understand."

She glanced up. "You do?"

Damn, had he misread again? Was he supposed to put up a fight for her? He shrugged, unable to convey his frustration. "Not really. But I'm assuming you have your reasons. Anyway, I like working with you, so that's enough for me. And if you decide you're ready for more, you know where to find me."

He went out and Megan slowly lowered her head to the desk, bumping her forehead gently against it a few times. She tried clicking her heels together three times, but when she looked up she was still in Rachel's office.

9

"Bo-ring!"

The girls in the front row tittered and Megan faltered in her speech. She had always been under the impression that you should talk to children as though they were adults, but she was beginning to see the inherent flaws in that theory.

She was pretty sure that if she were facing an audience of adults she wouldn't be heckled by one of them saying "Bo-ring" under his breath. An audience of adults wouldn't have giggled in response. In an audience of adults the man in the fourth row wouldn't have been yanking the ponytail of the woman in front of him and there wouldn't be two men in the back punching each other repeatedly in the upper arms. There wouldn't be note-passing and secretive giggling from the women in the ninth row and the man on the aisle seat wouldn't have been picking his nose.

Unfortunately Megan couldn't be too critical of them. It wasn't as if her motivations were so lofty. She just wanted them to stop making her look bad in front of the guy she liked.

She struggled on gamely. "The dynamism of Renaissance Art was partly due to the advent of increasingly enlightened patronage which encouraged the artists to develop their own personal styles."

She wondered for the hundredth time why she'd even allowed herself to be talked into this. Just one more day, Rachel had pleaded, promising that she could plan it out in detail.

Megan sighed mentally. She knew exactly why she'd

agreed to it. Because she'd been too much of a coward to tell Rachel about Sam.

She looked down at her whispering audience. And now she was paying for it.

The trouble was she agreed with her loudmouthed critic. The speech that Rachel had given her was kind of boring. All this reeling off of dates and countries of origin, it was all so dry and dusty and it would have had Megan chomping at the bit, too.

She glanced down at the rest of the page. It just went on in the same vein and since nobody was listening to her anyway she decided to cut it short.

"—which warranted his position as Venice's rival to Florence's Michelangelo. And so on and so forth. I'll give each of you a photocopy of this so anyone who's interested can read it. But now," she added recklessly, "does anyone have any questions?"

She gave them an encouraging look. Silence greeted her.

"Any questions about art? Or paintings…or anything?"

Some of them stared at her, others looked at each other or at the floor, but no one said anything.

"Oh, I know," said Megan, remembering a previous conversation with Sam. "I'll tell you something I like to do. When I visit an exhibition I always like to pick out which painting or statue I'd like to steal."

Dubious looks crossed the teachers' faces and a young girl piped up from the front row. "Stealing is wrong."

"Yeah," echoed a boy's voice and Megan located his concerned face in the crowd. "If someone steals something from you it makes you feel sad."

"And you have to go to jail," came another high-pitched voice.

Yikes, thought Megan, nothing like the guilt of little kids to make you feel truly awful.

"Stealing is wrong," she agreed, "and I'm glad to see that you're all so good."

She pointed to a boy who was holding his hand up, his fingers wiggling in the air.

"Yes?"

"How can you tell if a painting is wrong?" he asked eagerly.

"Wrong?" said Megan in confusion.

"A forgery," clarified one of the teachers.

"Er," said Megan. "Good question. Uh, there are many ways to tell if a painting is a fake and art experts spend years studying to learn these ways so they can examine the paintings and know if they are fake or real."

"Like what ways?"

"Uh…" Megan started to perspire, but an eager kid leapt to her rescue.

"Like," he said, "if someone's clothes are a different color in the fake, or they have different hair."

Others joined in eagerly. "Yeah, or if a dog has five legs or is facing the wrong way."

They were talking over each other, vying with each other to come up with more obscure differences, and Megan looked up to see Sam and another man watching her. It took her a second but she recognized him as Bradley, the authenticator from L.A.

Sam was smiling, and she realized that she was smiling, too, so she gave him a wink before returning her attention to the kids who were now all watching her hopefully. There were a few more raised hands now but Megan caught the gimlet eye of one of the teachers, a woman in a fuzzy sweater who had her hair in a long braid down her back. She had her hand raised but Megan got the impression that this was a mere courtesy.

"Er, yes?" she said.

"I think the children would like to know how you actually become a curator and get to work in a museum."

Most of the children looked quite disappointed with this prosaic question, as if they really just wanted to hear more about forgeries.

Tempting as it was, Megan refrained from telling them that forgery and imposture was exactly how she'd ended up doing this job.

"Well, first of all, there are lots of ways to work in a museum without being the curator. Why, we have more than…er, many people working here every day. Security guards, cooks in the restaurant, administration sort of people who work in offices…ahm…people who move the exhibitions around…uh, ticket staff and the ladies who give you the guided tour thing on cassette, you know, with the earphones…"

She trailed off. The teachers were looking at her as if to say it might have been in her interest to hire, along with all those other staff, a speechwriter. Even worse, the children were no longer giving her that shiny-eyed stare but had reverted to each other's company for amusement.

"But who cares about them," finished Megan recklessly. "Because being a curator is the best job of all. Because I get to talk to all of you. And I get to hear all your great questions."

A hand went up in the front row and Megan pointed at the girl.

"Yes?"

"My dad says modern art is all a pile of baloney."

The giggles rippled through them again and Megan smiled.

"I agree. Some of it is awful baloney. And it's okay not to like it. But just because you don't like it doesn't mean someone else mightn't like it. We all have different tastes and that's okay."

"Like cabbage!" a boy exclaimed from the fourth row. Megan looked at him, bewildered.

"Some people don't like cabbage," he elucidated.

"Oh right. Exactly," said Megan, grateful that she wasn't talking to the press today. There was another great headline for them. Art Is Like Cabbage, Says Curator.

"Anyway," she said, "the main thing about art is that

you look at it. So, your teachers will divide you into groups, and we'll all go into the galleries to look at the baloney, oh excuse me,'' she said over the laughter, ''I mean the art and you can try drawing some of the things you see.''

She directed one of the teachers to the first room and asked them to excuse her for a moment, going over to have a word with Sam.

''Were you laughing at my speech?'' she said sternly, her eyes twinkling at him.

He grinned at her. ''I've never enjoyed a lecture so much. Dogs with five legs? People looking the wrong way?''

''Ah yes,'' she said wisely. ''These are some of the lesser-known ways of spotting fakes. Just ask Bradley, I bet he knows them all.''

''It's true,'' Bradley said. ''Those are some of the first things we look for.''

Megan laughed along easily.

''We were just talking about the spate of robberies they had across Europe last year,'' said Sam.

Bradley nodded. ''Apparently Interpol still have no leads. Frankly, I don't think they'll catch them.''

''Really?'' said Megan. She didn't know the robberies they were referring to but that didn't stop her being interested.

Bradley looked at her. ''They were smart,'' he said. ''Going after lesser-known works like they did? Easier to take, easier to get rid of.''

Megan gave a noncommittal nod. ''I guess so.''

''Sam told me about the holdups in Madrid,'' Bradley went on with a smile. ''So I'm glad to see that they all arrived at last.''

Megan hesitated. Holdups? She hadn't heard anything about any holdup. Oh wait…she let out a breath. He meant delays, not robberies. Phew.

She nodded again, smiling inanely and looked over as the last of the giggling groups was led into the galleries.

"I'll leave you to it. I'd better follow them, they seem like an excitable bunch."

"Right," said Sam. "As opposed to your average seven-to-twelve-year-olds."

MEGAN WAS amazed at how bad most of the children's drawings were and how utterly unselfconscious they were about that.

They sat on the floor in little groups in the sculpture gallery, concentrating fiercely as they drew lopsided soldiers and took flamboyant liberties with mythical creatures. The teachers milled among them, as did Megan. Sam and Bradley did a walk-through, with Bradley checking the exhibits against a clipboard.

There was one other quiet occupant of the gallery, a studious-looking man who was circling the periphery, mumbling to himself and making notes. Megan had spoken to him earlier and now knew how the guided cassettes came into being. Someone actually had to narrate them, leading the viewer around the exhibition.

There were moments when Megan almost had to remind herself that this was not her job, not her life. She actually found herself enjoying it at times, being part of this team, feeling the privilege of working in such an atmosphere, surrounded by masterpieces.

She glanced up as Sam came back in through the far door of the gallery and she watched as he paused to look down at the drawings of a group of boys.

She smiled as he said something which provoked a little animated discussion among them. She continued to watch as he scratched his head and pointed at one of the coils of Medusa's deadly hair and then looked down again as the boys clamored for his attention. Megan put her hand over her grin. He was giving them his full focus, and Megan was sure that if she was among them she'd be tapping him on the shoe, too, grabbing his jeans, saying, "Look at me, look at my drawing."

She turned her attention back to the young girl who was drawing a picture of a man wrestling a snake (Megan now knew that when Sam mentioned the *Laocoön* this was what he was referring to). It looked as if the girl had only just realized that she'd transposed the man's head onto the snake's body and vice versa and she was undecided what to do about it.

"That looks great," said Megan.

"Really?" said the girl. "I think it's wrong."

"Don't worry about it. Things were supposed to get mixed up in mythology. Jupiter was always changing himself into different animals to sedu...uh, trick women."

"Jupiter?" said the girl. "Like the planet?"

"Exactly," said Megan magnanimously.

When she looked up again Sam had made his way through the gallery to join her.

"Hi," she said, smiling at him with her eyes. Then she tore her gaze away. No wonder he had such a hard time getting the message when she kept giving him such mixed signals.

"Having fun?" he said cheerfully.

She nodded.

"So, you want a few of these for yourself?" he asked, looking around at the carpet of children.

She looked at him. "I don't really think they're yours to give away, Sam," she joked.

He gave her a shrewd look. "Evading the question, eh?" he persisted. "Is that a no?"

Megan shrugged. "I don't know," she said vaguely. "I haven't really thought about it."

Another lie. Of course she'd thought about it, but she was always afraid that her peripatetic lifestyle precluded it. And she couldn't ever see herself giving that up. Not for children, not for a man.

Not for any man?

She peeked up again at Sam who was looking around in

amusement. He folded his hands and rocked slightly on his feet, thoughtful.

"I want kids," he said. "Two or three. Maybe four."

Megan felt oddly piqued, as if he was being deliberately obstreperous.

"Well, maybe you should get married then," she said contentiously. "I've heard that's the first step."

"I almost did once," he said.

Megan was shocked. He'd announced it so casually, and he looked completely calm, as if he hadn't just said something that had rocked her with jealousy.

"Really?" she said, fighting for nonchalance.

"Uh-huh," he said. "College sweetheart. Luckily we realized in time that marriage and kids was what everybody else wanted for us, not really what we wanted."

He glanced at Megan and smiled. "Few years later she met the right guy. They're living in Chicago now."

"And you don't mind?" she said, worried for him and wondering how that meshed with her response.

He shook his head. "No, I was happy for her. She wasn't the one for me." He didn't say anything else, just held Megan's eyes and she felt a sudden quiver, down low in her abdomen at the weight of meaning behind the words.

Her throat dry, she looked away.

What is going on with me? she thought.

He tapped her shoulder. "Hey, I thought of another word," he said.

She looked up at him in confusion. "What?"

"Another word? For my list of ten?" He lowered his head teasingly. "Do you want to hear it?"

I don't know what I want, she thought in despair.

"Of course," she said through a tight throat. "What is it?"

"*Yippee!*" he yelled, causing everyone to look around in interest.

Megan was startled—she didn't think she'd ever heard anyone shout out loud in an art gallery before. She looked up at the ceiling. Well, what did you know, the whole place didn't come crashing down.

She was about to respond but, before she could speak, there were a few echoing "yippees!" from some of the kids, apparently just for the sheer joy of it.

The teacher with the braid gave a warning "shush!" but the other teachers obviously felt, as Megan did, that they couldn't be shushing when, after all, Sam had started it.

Megan waited until the frivolity had died down and she looked at Sam.

"*Yippee?*" she said in a very grown-up voice.

"Sure," he said. "I'll need it for jubilant occasions, like when I win the lottery and break world records, that sort of thing. So, you know, yippee, woohoo, yay, yahoo, any of those would do."

Megan followed his train of thought in the opposite direction. "And what happens when you hit your thumb with a hammer?"

He looked abashed. "Yeah, I'll need one of those words, too, but I wasn't sure how to tell you."

"So." She counted off on her fingers. "*Sorry, help, yippee* and *expletive,* that's four. You're doing well."

"Thanks. You owe me two now."

Megan had to concentrate very hard to think of any of the words on her list.

"*Ice cream,*" she said.

He smiled and she explained. "I really, really like it."

"Couldn't live without it, eh?"

"Nope," she said, laughing. "And my fourth one would be *Megan.*"

"Megan?" he said.

Megan had a plummeting feeling. "I mean *Rachel.* My own name."

"So that's three?" he asked with innocent curiosity.

Megan's face felt hot. "Yes. The third is *ice cream,* my fourth one is *Rachel,* my own name and then the fifth is *Megan.*"

And the sixth is idiot.

However, Sam appeared to be distracted by his own considerations. "Of course. You'd have to have your name, that's an obvious one. Unless you want to spend all your time being called, hey you. Okay, that will be my fifth, my name."

Megan went on the offensive. "See, that's why I didn't want to tell you mine, because it influences you, which defeats the purpose. I'm not going to tell you any more."

I've got to call Rachel, she thought in desperation, she's got to get me out of here.

"MACKEREL OIL? Are you sure that's a good idea?"

"I know, it's pretty stinky, but the grass stuff didn't really have much effect."

Megan rested her elbow on the desk and put her chin in her hand, holding the phone to her ear with her other hand. Her nose was still crinkled at the thought of Rachel putting fish oil all over her face.

"I don't know," she said. "It won't be much good if it clears up your face but you end up too smelly to go out in public."

"Hey, thanks for the encouragement, okay? Don't worry, I'll stay out in the garden so I don't offend your delicate olfactory sense."

Megan was about to suggest that Rachel could take her acidic tone of voice and use that as an exfoliant but she thought better of it.

Rachel went on. "What's got into you anyway? I thought you'd be glad that I'm making an effort. Are you enjoying yourself so much that you don't want to leave?"

Megan groaned. "You couldn't be more wrong. I so want to go home. I want to be me again. And I have work to do, too, you know."

"I don't know what to say," said Rachel. "I mean, I can't make you stay. You could get up and walk out right now if you wanted to."

Megan sighed. "Please," she said. "Don't tempt me."

They were both silent for a moment.

"Did you have a bad morning?" Rachel asked hesitantly.

"No. It went very well, in fact. I was a hit."

"I knew you would be."

Megan smiled weakly, cradling the phone under her chin. "You don't have to butter me up. I'll stay. I said I'd do this day and I will. As for the rest of the week, I don't know, we'll have to talk about it later."

"Deal," said Rachel. "Thanks Megan, I really owe you big time for this. I promise, when I get back, that I'll definitely make sure Sam Harrison takes you out. Somewhere fancy."

Megan closed her eyes as Rachel rambled on, completely oblivious to her sister's discomfiture. "How are you coping with seeing him every day? Is it proving difficult to keep your libido under control?"

"It's going okay," she said guardedly. "I stay out of his way."

Rachel giggled naughtily while Megan dug her fingers into her thigh.

"Okay. Well, if he gives you any trouble you let me know."

"Will do," said Megan weakly. "Hang on, someone's here." She looked up as Rebecca followed her knock with a tentative peek around the door. Megan beckoned her in, holding the phone casually in her hand so Rachel could hear the conversation.

Rebecca handed her a slip of paper. "Mr. Forsyth told Mr. Peterson about the Venetian student works and Mr. Peterson said we should bring them up for Mr. Harrison to have a look at because he might want to use them."

She left and Megan turned the paper around, scanning the list of names and numbers.

"For crying out loud," she complained into the phone. "It's just one thing after another."

"Well, what did you think they paid me for?" said Rachel in her ear. "I heard what she said. The paintings are in the vault. Get a pen, I'll help you draw a map."

THANKS TO Rachel's directions Megan's second visit to the bowels of the gallery was slightly less traumatic. She was more careful about wending her way in and as soon as she found the requested paintings (which amazingly matched Rachel's descriptions right down to the frames) she wiped the dust off the top of the frames and enlisted the help of a couple of friendly movers who slotted them onto some wheeled moving-brackets. Megan let them go on ahead of her so she could surreptitiously re-check the numbers that Rebecca had given her against the shelf numbers. Satisfied that she'd got the right paintings, she made her way back to the elevator. All she had to do now was take them up to the second floor.

She got into the elevator and watched as the mover slid the last painting on, patting it like the flank of a horse. The paintings all had dust covers thrown over them and Megan frowned as she counted them. There was one more than she'd picked out.

"These are your four," indicated the mover, "And that one's the Corregio. Sam radioed down."

"Okay," said Megan dubiously as the mover rushed off and yelled at some guys who were unloading crates from the back of a truck.

One extra painting, she told herself, no big deal.

"Rachel!"

Her finger lingered on the elevator button for a moment, but then she took her hand down and looked out.

John Forsyth was hurrying toward her.

"Good timing," he puffed as he reached the door. He looked back, urging someone on. Megan could hear the rattle of a moving bracket being pushed over the cement.

"Can you take this up, too?" asked Forsyth. "The Corregio's going for cleaning so this is the temporary replacement.'' He stood aside and let the mover slide the painting in on the other side of Megan.

''The Corregio's going for cleaning?'' she verified.

Forsyth nodded. ''Yes, thanks. I'm trying to dig out those Bellano works that we got from the Ledwidge bequest. I think Sam might be interested.''

Megan couldn't help smiling at his animated expression. She was glad that he'd dropped the formality of 'Mr. Harrison.' He was obviously feeling useful at last.

However, she had to get going before anyone else waylaid her. She went to press the button for the second floor, then paused, moving her finger upward. She'd better go to the fourth floor and deliver the Corregio first, that was the important one.

In the few moments that passed while the elevator was ascending, Megan revised what she knew of the cleaning and restoration room.

Someone named Maggie is the head of the department, she thought, and…that's about it. That's all I got.

The elevator dinged and the doors slid open. Megan held her finger on the button and looked out hopefully. The elevator opened straight onto the restoration room. There were brackets and easels everywhere and the acidic tang of painting materials in the air. Megan gazed in fascination at the various people in white coats who were poring over paintings, focused intently on small areas of large masterpieces.

She caught the attention of a young woman with tied-back auburn hair.

''I have the Corregio for Maggie,'' said Megan. Then she offered her excuse. ''But I can't leave the elevator so…''

''I'll take it, Ms. Dean.'' The woman smiled, helping Megan wheel it off. ''Maggie!'' she called. ''The Corregio's arrived.''

Megan glanced over as a petite gray-haired woman

looked up from a painting. She took off her glasses and smiled at Megan.

"Rachel, dear, I won't be able to get to it until tomorrow. I hope that's all right."

"That's fine," said Megan. She pressed the button for the second floor.

"Mr. Harrison just wanted me to give some of his works a quick dusting. He's a lovely man," said Maggie.

Megan gave a smile and a wave as the doors whispered shut.

"Tell me about it," she sighed. She shook her head. Concentrate, she told herself sternly, don't mess up now.

The first thing she noticed when the doors opened on the second floor was the din. Movers were rushing around busily, wheeling brackets and shifting crates. Megan looked out uncertainly.

She lifted her hand as she spotted Sam. "Venetian works," she mouthed across the room. He nodded and stopped a passing mover, talking to him briefly before sending him over to Megan.

Megan smiled at Sam's calm in the midst of all the pandemonium and he gave her a thumbs-up before turning away again.

"These are from the vault, right?" said the mover, wheeling the paintings off efficiently.

"Those are the four Venetian works," said Megan, raising her voice to be heard, "and this is the replacement—"

"Corregio," finished the mover as he wheeled it off. "They radioed up. Thanks."

He waved over some others to help him and Megan stepped back into the safety of the elevator, letting out a huge exhalation of relief as the doors closed.

"YOU LOOK tired."

Megan made a face. "Thanks, Sam, thanks a lot."

"I'm just saying, that's another reason why you should take a break and have lunch with me."

Megan sighed, the thought of the huge folder of notes in her drawer weighing like a big anchor around her neck. She'd stayed up late again the night before, frantically typing up synopses on her laptop. The trouble was that she always got caught up with reliving her travels and lost track of time until the cramps in her neck and shoulders made her realize that hours had passed. And although she had to call her editor the next day, she still wasn't sure she'd be able to finish the outline in time to take the Italy job.

"I am tired," she admitted to Sam. "But I don't think avoiding work is the way to go."

"It's not avoidance," said Sam, breaking off his perusal of the books on the shelf to look at her. "It's replenishing the batteries. Come on, let's go outside for half an hour, have lunch in the park."

She hesitated. Replenishment was probably a good idea.

AFTER ONLY five minutes in the park Megan could feel her energy levels rising. She rolled her head from side to side to stretch out her neck muscles, then took another bite of her sandwich.

"This was a great idea," she said.

He smiled at her. "I know. I thought it might be good for you to get out. I don't want you to get overworked and have a nervous breakdown."

She laughed. "I'm nowhere near having a nervous breakdown." Not for the reasons you suppose anyway.

They ate in silence and watched people passing by for a while before Sam spoke up again.

"*Keraunophobia.*"

Megan looked around. "What?"

"*Keraunophobia,*" he repeated, eyes twinkling.

"Gesundheit," she said.

He laughed. "No silly, it's my sixth word."

She crinkled her nose. "But why? What does it even mean?"

"It's a fear of thunder and lightning."

Her brow creased. "And are you afraid of thunder and lightning?"

"Nope. Actually, I love it. But it was the longest word that I could come up with that contains all the vowels."

Megan peered at him. "And that's important...why?"

"I figure I can break it down and make other words out of it."

She laughed at his audacity. "That's cheating, you can't do that."

"I disagree," he said. "It's not cheating, it's imaginative thinking. And I'm keeping it." He gave her a rebellious look. "What are you going to do, disqualify me?"

"Okay," she said. "Fine. Have *keraunophobia*. I'm sure you'll fit right in with the natives when you go around using it. However, I think I'll stick with my own ordinary, reasonable words all the same."

He shook his head, feigning disenchantment. "Well, it would be best if you just stayed in San Francisco in that case."

Megan was still dying to tell him just how well she did fare in foreign countries, but she settled for giving him an enigmatic smile.

"Have you lived here long?" he asked conversationally.

She thought for a moment, to make sure she had her story straight. "All my life. We grew up in Russian Hill. The house was handed down from my grandparents and now I live in it."

"And your parents?"

"They moved out to Florida a couple of years ago."

"Does Megan live with you?"

"Uh, no, Megan has an apartment in North Beach." She smiled at him. "She likes to be closer to city life. When she's actually here. What about you?"

"You mean where do I live?"

She nodded.

"I'm almost embarrassed to admit this, but I think I've been living in hotels for almost two years now. I move around with work so much that it's never really seemed logical to get my own place. I thought I'd end up getting somewhere in Seattle but then I always find myself gravitating southwards. I love Monterey, Big Sur, all that area. I've been thinking about getting a little house down there, on the coast.''

Megan inhaled. "Oh, that's a great idea. You've got the beaches on one side, national parks on the other. It's so gorgeous.''

He grinned at her. "So, you'd come and visit me?''

"Try and stop me,'' she laughed.

Sam sipped at his coffee then went on, not looking at her as he spoke. "It's actually been the main cause of friction in my relationships with women, the fact that I move around so much. I mean, I would like to have a place that I could call home but I'd still like to travel with my job.''

He glanced at her. "I guess it doesn't make me a very appealing prospect, does it?''

"Oh Sam," said Megan. "I wish...''

"What?''

She shook her head, a big smile spreading across her face. "Don't worry," she said. "There are women out there who will find that very appealing.''

He looked down at the grass again, speaking lightly. "Maybe, but I was kind of hoping you would.'' He looked up at her again. "What are you laughing at?''

Megan was so happy she spoke without thinking. "I just can't believe it. Your lifestyle, your personality.'' She leaned toward him and looked into his eyes. "You. You're perfect for me. Well," she amended, "not for me exactly, I mean, for Megan.''

She leaned back and the disquiet on Sam's face made her revise what she'd just said.

"No, hang on, that sounds bad but it's okay, it's a good thing. Actually, you know what? Let's just forget I said that.'' She jabbered on nervously. "*Amnesia,* that's a good word, let's try that one.''

"I don't understand," Sam said slowly. "You're trying to fix me up with your sister?"

"No," said Megan. "That's not what I meant. Did I say that? No, I was just commenting on how similar you two are."

"But you said I was perfect for her," Sam argued.

"Did I? Well, in a way you are, you know. She travels a lot, too."

"Really?" said Sam with an edge to his voice. "And does she have the exact same personality as you?"

"No, of course not," said Megan hesitantly.

"Oh, that's too bad," said Sam. "But hey, she looks like you, doesn't she, so I'll never notice the difference."

"I didn't mean to offend you," she said in a small voice.

He looked at her with frustration in his eyes. "I'm not offended, Rachel, I just…every time I feel like we're getting close you say something to drive me away. If you don't want me, fine, I'll learn to live with it, but I really don't understand how you can think so little of me that you think I would even begin to consider a substitute."

He started to stand up and she put her hand on his arm. "No," she said. "Please wait. It was just a slip of the tongue, believe me, I didn't mean anything by it."

He searched her eyes for a moment and some of the hardness fell from his features but he didn't sit back down.

"You sure?" he said.

She nodded fervently and his mouth twitched.

"So you and Megan didn't do that as kids, pretend to be each other and swap boyfriends?"

She made a face. "Eeuw, no, that's a horrible idea." That, at least, was true.

"Come on," he said. "We'd better get back."

He glanced at her as they put their wrappings in the trash. "*Amnesia*'s not really one of your words, is it?"

"I wish," she said.

10

"SO, THAT'S THE MUSIC and caterers taken care of. Jocelyn said it works out cheaper with the catering if we let them take care of the drinks as well, instead of getting in separate bar staff. Will I give her the okay on that?"

"Great," said Rachel. "Did you give Peterson the insurance forms?"

"Done," said Megan, shifting the receiver to her other ear. She looked down at the list on her notepad. "What about the Coopers? Are they coming to the dinner?"

"I called them earlier," said Rachel. "At least there are some jobs I can do from home. Hang on, let me check."

Megan heard the sound of rustling paper and her eyes flicked to the desk calendar while she waited. Wednesday, only three more days to go to the opening. Rachel was still convinced she'd have recovered her natural face-color by then but Megan wasn't so optimistic. But what that meant for her didn't bear thinking about.

"Here it is," said Rachel. "Oh, that's right, they're in Maui. Put aside some extra complimentary tickets for them and they'll be over when they come back." She paused again. "I think that's all on my side for the moment. How are you doing?"

"Fine," said Megan, sitting back and swinging around in her chair. "I never thought I'd say it, but each day I find it a little less nerve-wracking."

"Well, don't get too complacent, that's a guaranteed way to slip up."

"Oh, I know. I'm just saying—"

Megan almost toppled off her seat as Peterson barreled through the door unloading a stack of newspapers on Rachel's desk.

"What do you have to say for yourself?" he said loudly.

"Gotta go," Megan said quietly into the phone. She hung up and blinked a couple of times to get rid of the image of Rachel going into cardiac arrest on the other end of the line.

Megan looked worriedly at the papers. "Uh, I haven't had a chance to look at them yet."

"Well, pick one," said Peterson, flinging himself into the chair opposite her desk. "They're all saying the same thing."

He was looking at her with a vague disbelief and Megan thought she was going to be sick.

She pulled a copy of *USA Today* toward her and opened up to the Arts section. Art Is for Everyone, announced the banner, and there were some photos in the middle of the article, one of which, Megan noted, was a rather nice photo of herself and Sam in front of the black centaur.

She skimmed the article frantically, aware of Peterson's eyes on her and when she got to the end she had to skim it again because she couldn't find the part where it exposed her for the forgery she was.

She lifted her eyes to Peterson's. He was nodding. "Isn't it great? And they're all like that. They loved you, loved the exhibition. I tell you, Rachel, we're going to have record numbers coming to this thing."

Megan opened another paper and skimmed through another glowing review.

"Wow, these are good. I don't know what to say."

"Credit where it's due," said Peterson, getting to his feet. "You deserve every word of praise in there, you've done a fantastic job on this, and I promise you, it hasn't gone unnoticed."

Unlike the fact that I'm not Rachel. The thought popped

unbidden into Megan's mind, and she clamped her lips down on a rebellious giggle.

Fortunately, to Peterson, it just looked as if she was becoming shy under all the praise.

He tapped the papers. "Don't spend too long basking, will you? Drop them over to the front desk when you're done. And keep up the good work."

MEGAN HAD GATHERED the papers in her arms and was about to rush up and show Sam when she remembered Rachel. She went back to the desk guiltily and phoned her sister.

Rachel's imagination had run riot in the five minutes since she'd heard Peterson's roar and Megan had hung up. It took Megan another ten minutes before she persuaded Rachel that everything really was okay, in fact, much more than okay.

Then she and Rachel spent another few minutes trying to work out how Rachel could go to a newsagents and get some papers herself. The mackerel oil hadn't been any more of a success than the grass and banana mush and the smell had indeed been repugnant.

"I still say you shouldn't try to cover it up," said Megan. "You look too suspicious with the whole scarf-and-glasses thing on. Just go in with a blue face and act like it's nothing."

"Great," sighed Rachel. "These are my options: I can have people thinking either that I'm a robber or that I'm mentally unbalanced."

"Wait," said Megan happily. "I've got it. You can pretend you're some kind of performer. Put on some clown makeup and just act as though it's normal, as if you're taking a break from a stint in the theatre around the corner or whatever."

"That's not bad," said Rachel. "Not bad at all. I think

I will do that. I've got to get out of here—I'm going stir crazy.''

"Just don't forget your cell phone," Megan reminded her.

AFTER A QUICK look through the papers, Megan gathered them together and went up to the galleries. Sam was deep in conference with Bradley, both of them poring over Sam's clipboard. Megan stopped, suddenly feeling a bit silly at her eager rush up the stairs, running to show off something which she really shouldn't be claiming credit for anyway.

Then Sam looked up, saw her and smiled.

Megan's heart did a little flip and she realized that feeling a little silly was the least of her concerns with this man. She was still wondering whether to go over, when Bradley gave her a friendly wave and said a few more words to Sam before going back into the galleries. Megan went up to Sam and put the papers down on a nearby work desk.

"I just wanted to show you these. The previews of the exhibition. Mr. Peterson is really pleased with them, and he said we can be expecting record crowds now." She showed him the paper she'd folded open. "Look, there's a picture of you."

He picked it up and she leaned in beside him to look with him. "Both of us," he said. "Don't we look somber and important? Two serious people engrossed in weighty matters of fine art."

This was so far from the truth that it made Megan grin at him.

He shrugged back. "Well, it's possible."

"Rachel!"

Megan was becoming more attuned to responding to this name and she was also, like a sufferer of amnesia, learning to look up with an expression of vague recognition while waiting for the other person to supply her with some more clues.

This time she didn't need any clues. She knew the person

calling her and her fake look of recognition fell off, to be replaced by a very real one of horror.

"Oh my God," she gasped. She looked back at Sam, completely flustered. "I…uh, would you excuse me…I have to, uh…"

"Okay. Can you leave these with me for a quick read?"

"Sure," she said hurriedly as she started to walk away.

"Will you be in your office later?" called Sam.

Megan saw David's eyebrows dip down in a frown and she looked quickly back at Sam.

She felt like a juicy bone between two dogs.

"Uh, I'm not sure, but you can leave them at the front desk," she said in a rush as she turned and hurried toward David.

"David, how nice to see you," she said. She searched his face for signs that he knew about the switch, but it was hard to read anything behind the glower.

"I wasn't expecting you here," she persisted. "Have you been home yet? Or over to my place?"

"No, I came straight here," he said. "I figured I'd done enough networking at the conference and I didn't want to sit through another day of self-congratulatory speeches so I caught an early flight home. I was going to call you later, but then I picked up a copy of the *Post* at the airport and I was so proud of you I decided to come by here and surprise you." He looked back at Sam who, Megan noticed, was still watching them covertly. She hoped he was out of earshot.

"Looks like I succeeded," said David.

"Indeed you did," said Megan, taking a step toward the stairway in the hopes that David would come with her. "But it's a great surprise. Are those for me? They're beautiful." She pointed to the bouquet of roses that he was holding awkwardly, but made no move to take them in case it gave Sam the wrong—or was that the right?—idea.

"Let's go to my office and put them in water," suggested Megan, putting a hand on his elbow and applying a little gentle pressure.

He resisted her efforts. "When were you planning to tell me, Rach?" he said. Even though his voice was low and controlled she could hear the hurt in it.

Megan was confused. "Tell you? Tell you what?"

David looked at Sam. "Don't even try to pretend anymore. I saw it, okay? I saw the way you two looked at each other. How long has it been going on?"

Megan shook her head. "David. No, you're wrong. There's nothing going on. Look, why don't we go down to my office and I'll explain—"

"Please. Stop lying to me," said David. "If you won't tell me the truth maybe I should just ask him—"

Megan's pulse shot into overdrive. She put her hand on David's arm.

"David, wait. I need you to look at me. I mean, really look at me."

With her back to Sam, Megan put her hand up to the side of her face and opened her mouth to allow David an unrestricted view of her molars.

David watched her and his eyes widened in amazement.

"Oh my God, you're Meg—"

She squeezed his arm and, abandoning all pretence of civility, pushed him toward the stairs.

"Mega-tired, that's right!" she exclaimed, drowning out David's voice. "But delighted to see you all the same. Let's go to my office."

MEGAN CLOSED the door behind her and fell against it, still feeling the adrenaline coursing through her veins.

She looked at David, who was peering suspiciously at her.

"Show me again," he said.

She sighed and opened her mouth, letting him examine the fillings that differentiated her from her twin.

When he was satisfied that it was her he rounded on her with alarm.

"What the heck is going on? Where's Rachel? Are you seriously pretending to be her? Why? Is she okay? Oh no, has something happened to her? What's going on?"

Megan put out a calming hand. "Rachel's fine, I promise. Please don't worry. But, well, it's kind of a long story. And yes, I am supposed to be her at the moment so thanks for nearly blowing my cover."

She let out a shaky laugh and flopped onto the sofa. "You wouldn't believe what I've gone through this week, the tests I've passed, and then what happens? Only you come along and just decided to shout it out to the whole gallery." She shook her head, laughing as her heart rate returned to normal. "You know what? I'm going to call Rachel, let her explain it to you. I think it'd be better coming from her."

She dialed Rachel, with David watching to make sure it was actually Rachel's cell phone number and put the phone on speaker.

"Hello?" said Rachel.

"Hi," said Megan. "It's me. I'm here in your office and there's someone here with me who wants to speak to you."

"Rachel?"

They both heard Rachel's sharp intake of breath.

"David? Is that you? But…what are you doing there?"

"I came to surprise you," he said wryly. "And it kind of backfired on me."

"You came to surprise me?" Rachel said happily. "That's so sweet."

"Yeah right," Megan cut in. "Except when he found out it was me he almost blurted it out to everyone."

"Megan had to do this gargantuan yawn to show me who she was," David interrupted, laughing, "and then she whisked me away before I could blow her cover." He smiled down at Megan who was swiveling idly in the chair.

"Just as well, really. I was about to start roaring at you. The minute I saw her and that guy togeth—"

Megan's finger came slamming down on the phone, cutting off the connection.

"—er I knew…" David trailed off as Megan looked up at him.

"Knew what?" she asked as David looked in confusion at the phone. Megan let the button up. The button for Call Waiting began to flash, but Megan ignored it.

"Knew what?" she asked again.

David tore his gaze from the phone. "Er, knew that something was going on."

Megan emitted a false laugh. "What? What makes you think that?"

David cocked his head. "Oh come on, it's so obvious."

Megan continued with the wide-eyed innocence. "What do you mean?"

David shrugged. "I don't know. It's a body-language thing. The way you stood together. The way you looked at each other. Anyone who watched you two for a minute would know at once that you're sleeping together."

"Ha!" Megan was triumphant. "Well, we're not, so there. Bang goes your theory."

The Call Waiting light went off, and, after a few seconds, started blinking again.

"Very well, I may be a little off on the timing but my theory is sound," insisted David. "There's definitely chemistry there. I bet you've already kissed." He stared her in the eyes.

Megan's gaze flickered away and it was David's turn for a triumphant "Ha!"

Megan jumped as David's cell phone rang.

"No, no, no," she said frantically as he went to answer it. "Don't tell her, okay, she doesn't know. I'll tell her. Please let me tell her."

She clasped her hands together in a supplicant prayer and gazed pleadingly up at him.

"Hello?" he said. "Hi sweetheart, yeah, sorry about that." He looked down at Megan. "No, it was just that someone came into the office so we had to hang up... No, it was nothing... Look, I just want to come over there and see you...we can swap stories then. You're at home, right?"

He paused and listened, then looked quizzically at Megan. "No, she didn't tell me anything about you, why?" He nodded. "Okay, great, more secrets. All right, I'll see you soon."

He hung up and looked at Megan. "I don't suppose you want to give me a warning about what it is that Rachel is hiding."

"Oh, I think it's best you see it for yourself," said Megan. She smiled gratefully at him. "Thanks David, for not telling her. I didn't tell her yet because, well, I wasn't sure what was going on myself."

"You'll have to tell her tonight," he warned. "I don't want to be responsible for letting it slip."

"I will," she said fervently. "I'll tell her as soon as I get home. To her place, I mean."

David picked up his briefcase and the roses. "I'll be taking these."

She laughed. "Probably should."

At the door he turned and looked at her again, puzzlement creasing his brow.

"Wait a minute. He knows who you are, right? I mean, he doesn't think you're Rachel, does he?" He laughed at the absurdity of his question.

Megan crinkled her nose and looked uncomfortable.

David blinked in disbelief. "Are you out of your mind?"

She scrunched her head protectively into her shoulders. "It's complicated."

"I'll tell you one thing," he said firmly as he went out. "This is absolutely the last time I ever try to surprise Rachel."

Megan folded her hands on the desk and put her head down on them.

"I'm an idiot," she muttered. "Rachel is going to kill me and Sam is going to kill me and…well, David will probably be too distracted by the fact that his girlfriend's a Smurf."

The thought brought a weak smile to her face and she lifted her head to rest her chin in the crook of her elbow.

"Come in," she said, in answer to the knock on the door.

"I was expecting you," she said as Sam opened the door.

"Were you?" he said, hovering in the doorway.

She nodded. "It's okay, you can come in. He's not here."

Sam came in, closing the door behind him. "I know. We passed each other in the hallway." He sat down opposite her and she straightened up to rest her chin in her cupped hands.

"Did you say hello?" she asked with a twinkle in her eye.

"We nodded to each other in a manly way."

Megan dipped her mouth behind her fingers to hide her smile. Even now, when it was all about to fall apart, she couldn't help flirting with him. What was the matter with her?

Sam rested his elbows on his knees and looked down at his hands. "I guess I'm supposed to ask who he is."

Megan looked at his downcast face. She loved the way his hair spiked over his forehead and the shadows that his cheekbones made over his jawline. He looked up again from under his brows and she felt her face heat as their eyes met.

She looked away quickly, awkwardly.

Sam gave a sad laugh. "It's okay," he said. "I think I've worked it out for myself."

Megan sat back and dug her fingers into the seat, agonizing over the words to use.

"Look," she said hesitantly. "It's not what you think. Well, actually it kind of is, but it's not as bad as you think."

He quirked an eyebrow. "Oh, I imagine it probably is."

She put her hands on the desk again. "Well, you're wrong. Although, you are also kind of right. It's just a bit messed up at the moment."

He didn't say anything until she'd looked up at him again. "Am I wrong about us?"

Megan felt a warmth spread through her whole body. She knew he was deadly serious. This gorgeous, kind, intelligent man was laying himself bare to her and asking her to do the same.

And much as she wanted to, she couldn't yet. She felt a surge of emotion well up in her chest and when she spoke her voice was husky but determined. "No," she said, holding his gaze. "You're not wrong about us."

He smiled slightly and nodded, then looked down at her desk while Megan fought to swallow the lump in her throat.

It seemed that neither of them wanted to break the silence that followed. There was no going back on what had just been said, but the way forward wasn't awfully clear, either.

Sam eventually spoke as he rose slowly to his feet. "I'd better get back to work."

He paused in the doorway and looked back at her. "Messed up, eh?"

She nodded apologetically.

"I know how that feels," he said sadly.

He gave her another one of those smiles that made her forget to breathe and he pulled the door softly shut.

WHEN MEGAN arrived home she found Rachel and David ensconced on the sofa. Rachel had her legs thrown across David's lap and they both looked up as Megan came in. Megan smiled warily, taking her time about removing her coat before sitting down opposite them.

David held up the remote and turned down the volume

on the television. He gave Megan a reproving look. "Rachel's face? I think you could have given me some kind of warning."

Megan looked at Rachel. Phew, she didn't know about Megan and Sam yet. Of course, that meant Megan still had to tell her.

Rachel spoke up. "Do you know what he did when he saw me?"

Megan shook her head.

"He laughed."

David ducked his head and Megan tried to join in with the banter. "You didn't!"

"Only for a second," he said. "Because of the initial shock. But then I was very sympathetic and understanding."

He bestowed an exemplary look of empathy on Rachel, but before long his lips started to twitch and a dimple appeared on his cheek and he had to look away again.

Rachel gave a pronounced sigh of forbearance.

"Anyway," she said. "How was your day? I can't wait to hear the full story of what happened when David came in. He refuses to tell me, said you could tell it better."

Megan looked at David and he raised his eyebrows impertinently. She gave him a tight smile. "It was a bit of a shock, but it worked out okay in the end. I managed to herd him off to the office before any damage was done, so everything's okay work-wise."

David cleared his throat noisily and Megan shifted in her seat.

"Although there is something I suppose I should tell you." She tucked a strand of hair behind her ear, running her fingers through it a few times nervously. "About work. Something that might be relevant to you, uh, that you should probably know about before you go back." She paused and swallowed, keeping her eyes on the coffee table. "It might just take me a minute to find the words."

She glanced up quickly at Rachel who was looking concerned. Unfortunately she was also looking a little steely, and Megan's hope that she might be speaking to a sympathetic ear vanished.

Megan smoothed her hand over her hair again. "Now, it will probably sound worse than it is—"

"Did you get me fired?" Rachel whispered in horror.

Megan brightened. "No, no I didn't. In fact—" she leaned forward "—and I think it's important that you keep this in mind, Peterson is very happy with you. He thinks you've done a great job with the exhibition." Megan spread her hands expansively. "As indeed you have. I mean, it's completely due to your organizational skills that I was able to play you this week. So, no, of course you're not fired. Gosh no, it's nothing as serious as that. That wouldn't be funny at all whereas I think you'll find what I have to tell you is, in a way, sort of funny, or at least you might find some way of seeing the humor in it—"

"Oh, for goodness sakes," exclaimed David. "She made out with Sam."

The only sound that followed was the creak of leather as Megan slowly drew back into her chair.

Rachel's face twitched through a variety of expressions before it finally settled into one of mild puzzlement.

"In front of you?" she asked David.

"Oh no," he said. "I just guessed it." Rachel's face started to clear, then fell again as David added, "But Megan confirmed it."

Megan forced herself to smile as Rachel turned a basilisk stare on her. "That's better than getting fired, isn't it?" she offered.

"You know what?" said Rachel. "I'm really not sure. How on earth did this happen? When did it happen?"

"I know it sounds kinda bad," said Megan. "But it really isn't. I mean, nobody else knows about it. It was in the galleries after work and we were alone and I'd given him this massage." She hurried on as Rachel's mouth fell open. "Let's not get into that right now, but there was a bit of kissing and then there was a bit of kissing the next day in your office—''

Rachel held up her hand. "Hang on a minute, I'm not following. When did you tell him who you were?"

Megan blanched and David tapped Rachel excitedly on the arm. "She didn't. He thinks it's you."

Rachel closed her eyes, and Megan glared at Sam. "Thanks a lot," she mouthed.

He nodded. "Oh yeah, this whole mess, it's my fault."

Rachel opened her eyes and Megan put on her contrite face again. Deeply, deeply contrite.

"Let me get this straight," said Rachel with a fresh and scary smile. "Sam thinks he's having a little fling with me. This is a perfectly reasonable assumption on his part because I've been giving him massages and kissing him whenever I get a chance. In the space of one week I have turned from a responsible, respectable, hard-working gallery curator into a shameless, sex-starved airhead."

"It's not like he was an unwilling victim," said Megan, offended.

Rachel held up her finger. "Don't even think about speaking to me right now."

They looked at each other, Megan switching between sullen and apologetic and Rachel maintaining a steady crossness.

"Okay," said Rachel at last, "I suppose you'd better speak."

Megan shrugged appealingly. "By the way, it's not a little fling. I wouldn't have jeopardized your job for that. We couldn't help it, it's the real thing. I think he's in love with me."

Rachel gaped and leaned forward. "He told you that?"

"Not in so many words but it's a definite possibility."

"And you're sure that it's *you* he loves?" David asked pointedly.

Megan gave him a look. "Yes."

"Because," said David implacably, "he doesn't exactly know who you are."

"Yes, but he knows me. This whole identity thing is just a minor obstacle. Will you stop laughing!"

"Sorry," said David. "So you think that when Rachel goes back next week he'll know immediately. 'Hang on,' he'll say, 'you're not the woman I love.'"

"Excuse me," said Megan archly. "But aren't you the man who was ready to punch Sam's lights out today because he was standing too close to the woman *you* love?"

David closed his mouth, suitably chastened.

"Besides," said Megan patiently. "He'll know the truth by then. I'll have explained the whole thing."

"Oh, you will, will you?" said Rachel enquiringly.

Megan met her eyes. "Are you saying you want to go back to work with things the way they are?"

Rachel winced. "It is your mess," she agreed. "You should be the one to sort it out."

"Don't worry," Megan reassured her. "It'll be okay. It's the real thing, Rach." She clasped her hands and let out a little giggle. "I've been dying to tell you about it. He's amazing. He's so smart and funny. You'll love him. And he's going to love this story. He'll understand, he really will, he'll think it's great."

Rachel looked doubtful. "This is terrible timing," she said.

"No kidding," said Megan.

Rachel narrowed her eyes. "I mean because of my job, not your love affair."

"Oh right, yeah, that's what I meant, too."

Rachel looked at her worriedly. "You promise me you won't tell him about the swap until next week at least?"

Megan's shoulders slumped. "But why not?"

"Because, for all intents and purposes, you don't really know him. This opening is the biggest event of my career. Are you willing to gamble it on the trust of a man you met a week ago?"

Megan twisted a strand of hair in her fingers, torn. She'd come across this dilemma before and the answer was the same. She'd gamble her own career but not Rachel's.

"You're right," she said, trying to hide her disappointment. "I'll wait of course."

"At least until after the opening," said Rachel, looking at her compassionately. "You can tell him next week."

Megan nodded, her eyes misting with frustration. "So, what's for dinner?" she said, changing the subject before she started blubbing.

"I was too lazy to cook," said Rachel, rearranging herself over David. "Let's order something."

As if on cue, the doorbell rang and Rachel looked at David with delight. "You did already?"

David shook his head and they continued to look quizzically at each other until Megan eventually stood up.

"I'll get it," she said. She muttered rebelliously as she made for the door. "I've only been working all day but don't worry about me."

She looked through the peephole and her hand froze on the lock. She took a couple of steps back, then spun and tiptoed hurriedly back into the living room.

"It's him, it's him," she mouthed frantically, pointing in panic toward the front door. "Sam's outside!"

They both looked at her uncomprehendingly as the doorbell pealed again. "You hear that sound?" Megan hissed, "That's Sam! Ringing the doorbell. Of this house!"

She turned toward the hallway and yelled, "Coming!"

Rachel scrambled to her feet, dragging David up with her. They started for the kitchen but Megan grabbed them.

"He'll see you there, go upstairs."

Megan made as much noise as she could while heading for the door to cover the sounds of two people sneaking up the stairs. "I'm coming! Sorry to keep you, I'll be there in a minute. Okay, here I am. Ooops, the lock is stuck. Hold on a second, ah, there it goes."

She opened the door and looked at her visitor with genuine surprise.

"Sam, what on earth are you doing here?"

"I'm really sorry to disturb you, but I still need the list of paintings that are going on the multimedia display. You didn't give it to me today so I assumed you'd forgotten it and I thought you might still have it at home." He looked sheepish. "Peterson gave me your address. And I've obviously disturbed you. I'm very sorry."

He looked so apologetic that Megan realized he was thinking that he'd caught her in flagrante delicto and she felt the need to reassure him.

"No, it's not really a disturbance. I was just...I had taken my clothes off, you see, so I had to put them back on before answering the door." Aware that this statement had just reinforced his misconception she went on. "I just mean, I'd taken them off because I was going to change into, you know, my jeans and sweater but, er, those are upstairs so that's why I had to put these clothes back on." She smiled brightly. "Would you like to come in and I'll get the list for you?"

"Sure," he said, after a slight hesitation.

She led him into the sitting room and headed straight for the coffee table to see if she could find the list and get him out of there.

Sam was looking around the room with interest and Megan followed his gaze anxiously. Relax, she told herself, there's nothing to be nervous about. It wasn't like they had a chart pinned to the wall with Master Plan for Operation Twin Swap written across the top.

She looked down at the coffee table again. Although it was strewn with documents and notes the list didn't appear to be there.

They both looked up as a thump sounded from the floor above him.

"I'm really sorry I had to disturb you," Sam said again.

"I know this is really bad timing, what with that guy coming to see you today and all."

Absurd as it was, Megan didn't even want him to think that David was here with her.

"Oh, that's not David," she said casually. "That's my sister. She's upstairs." And then, in case Sam wanted to meet her, she added, "In the shower."

She tried to think of a plausible explanation for such a situation. "She came over here because we're going to go out for dinner. Nothing fancy, just the two of us, sisters together." She thought for a moment. "So when I say that I was changing into jeans and a sweater I mean of course, very good jeans."

She smiled wanly.

"Sounds like you two are close," said Sam amiably.

"Oh, we are." She closed her mouth firmly before she could blurt out that she was about as close to Megan as you could get.

Sam wandered over to the bookshelf, giving Rachel's tropical fish tank a glance.

"Sweetlips?" he said.

Megan faltered. "Er…yes?"

"Aren't they? Oriental Sweetlips?" he said, pointing at the tank. "Or am I wrong?"

"Oh," said Megan, blushing while she looked at the myriad, multicolored fish flashing around. "Oh sure, you're right. Do you keep fish?"

"When I was a kid," he said, hunkering down. "What's that one called?"

"Which one?" she said, desperately buying time while she tried to remember some of the multisyllabic names that Rachel had regaled her with.

"The blue one, with the clear tail fin."

Megan dredged her memory. That one was something quite simple, wasn't it? Blue Dragon? Blue Fire?

"That's a Blue Flame," she hazarded.

He looked up at her. "That sounds familiar. Isn't there one called a Blue Devil as well?"

Aargh!

Megan nodded. "Yes, yes there is. These are sort of related, but much rarer. And actually, most people haven't even heard of these, even in pet shops, you know, or other places where you buy fish." She breathed in deeply. "I think I must have left the list upstairs," she said. "I'll just go and check. Pour yourself a drink if you'd like."

Darn, why had she said that? Now he'd have an excuse to hang around for a while. She felt a rush of guilt. Under normal circumstances she'd like nothing better than to have him hanging around. She'd be thanking her lucky stars.

She shook it off and hurried upstairs where, as expected, she found Rachel and David sitting on the bed, looking disconcertingly mischievous. Her sister looked up with wide eyes as Megan closed the door silently behind her.

Megan sat on the edge of the bed and they spoke in voices barely above a whisper.

"I told him you were in the shower."

"What on earth is he doing here?"

"It's a long story, he needs the multimedia access list. Where is it?"

"Why did you ask him here, to the house?"

Megan made a face. "Don't be ridiculous, this wasn't my idea. Where's the list?"

"It should be on the coffee table."

"I couldn't see it."

Rachel frowned in thought and Megan fidgeted with an incipient run in her pantyhose, making it worse.

"Oh, I know," said Rachel. "It's in the kitchen. I was looking it over at lunch."

"Great," said Megan, getting off the bed. "I can get rid of him."

She put her hand on the door handle, but a "psst" from David stopped her. Megan looked back to see his eyes shining with amusement.

"What?"

"Don't do anything we wouldn't."

She gave them a devilish smile before slipping out the door.

SAM HAD POURED himself a very watered-down Scotch and was thumbing through one of Megan's books. He smiled as he skimmed a paragraph about her experience of eating jambalaya in New Orleans. Her wry tone reminded him so much of Rachel.

He looked up as she came back in. Megan glanced at the book in his hands and gave him a wary smile before dodging into the kitchen.

"Here it is," she said, emerging a moment later and perching on the edge of the seat opposite him. She held the document out to him.

"Great," he said, taking it and putting it on the coffee table. He held up the travel book which had a little smiling photo of Megan on the back.

"You weren't kidding," he said. He indicated the shelf. "She really wrote all these?"

A proud smile popped onto her face. "Every one."

"How many are there?"

"Five and counting. Scandinavia is the sixth." She hesitated and then said, with a bashful expression, "You can borrow one if you like, to have a look at."

"I'd love to," he smiled. "I read a few bits. She's funny. She sounds like you."

He was amused to see her blush. "I guess she does."

Sam's smile widened. "I think I'll borrow the one she dedicated to you."

"What makes you think she dedicated one to me?"

He raised an eyebrow and she laughed and went over to the shelf. "Okay, here you go. *Going Native in Tokyo.*"

He opened the book to the dedication page and read. "'To Rachel. See you at the airport. Blue carnation and fake leopard-skin shoes.'"

He looked up questioningly, and she laughed. "It's an in-joke. She...I usually try to visit her wherever she goes, cheap holiday, you know, and when I was going to Vienna we were making arrangements to meet at the airport and...I said, but how will I recognize you? And we just cracked up. Now we take turns to come up with bizarre things that we have to wear or carry with us so we'll recognize each other." She shrugged. "It's silly, but—"

"Don't knock it," he said. "It's great to have someone to be silly with."

She grinned. "Yeah, it is. Do you miss that, being an only child?"

He shrugged. "I guess, sometimes. It's hard to judge, since I've never had it. But I've always imagined it must be great to have someone who's always on your side. And it must be even stronger with a twin." He smiled, feeling a bit foolish but asking anyway. "What about all those things you hear about twins being telepathic? Is there any truth in that?"

"There is a connection," Megan admitted. "But I wouldn't go as far as to say we're telepathic."

Her eyes drifted over his shoulder, then widened as her mouth dropped open.

Sam followed her surprised stare to the door.

"Hellooo, I'm not disturbing you am I?"

Sam rose to his feet as a woman came in. She was wearing black leather trousers and a tailored blue satin shirt. The whole ensemble was topped off with a turbanesque towel around her hair and a peach face mask which had, Sam noticed, an underlying hint of blue. He could only assume that this was the famous sister.

She stuck out her hand. "Hi, I'm Megan. Pardon my appearance but I thought it would be rude not to come down and say hello."

"Sam Harrison. It's nice to meet you. Rachel's told me a lot about you."

"All good, I bet."

Sam smiled. "Afraid so."

She nodded knowingly. "Rachel does like to talk me up."

Behind him, there came a brittle laugh.

Sam sat down again and held up *Going Native in Tokyo*. "Rachel's loaning me this. I've already had a quick look at it and I think I'm going to be a big fan."

She laughed pleasantly and joined him on the couch as she accepted a glass of wine from her sister. Sam didn't miss the meaningful glance that passed between the two women. He just wasn't sure what it meant.

He felt a hand on his knee. "Don't worry about letting anything slip," she said, leaning in confidentially. "Rachel's already told me all about your little tête-á-têtes."

There was a squeak from the seat opposite them, but Sam was amused and glad that he was getting on with Rachel's sister. "And she's told me that you made an attempt to learn Arabic." He offered her a simple greeting, and then wondered if he'd got the pronounciation right when she looked at him blankly.

"Oh no, you don't," Megan interrupted them. "I'm not going to sit here while you two talk about me right in front of me."

Her sister made a rueful face. "She's right. It would be a bit rude. But I'll definitely take a rain check. Sometime when I don't have goop all over my face." She smiled cheerily. "I'd better go wash this off."

The two women rose to their feet and Sam felt he had no choice but to follow suit. He drained his drink and picked up the schedule.

"Megan," he said, putting out his hand. "It was really nice to meet you. And Rachel," he added, holding up the schedule, "thanks for this. And for the book."

She walked him to the door. He was going to drop a kiss on her cheek, but she seemed distracted. Her eyes kept darting back toward the living room so he settled for a warm smile and a wave.

"What were you thinking?"

Rachel shrugged, unwrapping the towel from her head and using it to wipe the mask off her face. "I thought it might be good for you to get a real taste of what it's like when someone else is acting out your life for you. When you have no control over your own identity. And I really wanted to see this love thing that David was talking about." She nodded. "He was absolutely right."

Megan ignored this. "It was a pretty drastic way to teach me a lesson, wasn't it?" she croaked, still not sure if she was cross or amused.

"It's kind of liberating being someone else, isn't it?" mused Rachel. "I could do whatever I wanted, without regard for the consequences."

Megan was hurt. "I'm doing my best here! And I have to say, since nobody else is saying it, that I've been doing a great job." Her voice started to rise. "It's not easy, you know, acting out someone else's life. Always having to think before you speak, trying to keep your own personality from emerging, but being careful not to sound like a robot either." She threw her arms in the air. "Okay, so I slipped up, I admit it. But you don't know what it's like. My head is overflowing with fjords and European elks and sixteenth-century castles, and you want me to cram in all this art stuff as well as a whole bunch of new faces and new names and all you're doing is putting food on your face and fooling around with your boyfriend."

Megan collapsed onto the couch and put her hands over her face. "I can't do it any more, I want to go to Italy!"

"Whoa," said Rachel softly, sitting down beside her. "Oh Meg, it's okay. I'm sorry, I didn't mean to get cross with you. Come on, you know you deserve an award for the performance you're putting on. Look at me, I could barely play you for five minutes without being caught. You're a genius!"

Megan peeled her hands away and laughed weakly. Rachel went on. "I can't believe you haven't slipped up, and I really am sorry I gave you such a hard time over Sam."

Megan looked at her. "It's okay. I don't blame you at all. I would have completely lost it if you'd done it to me."

"You mean, started an affair with Marcus for you?"

Megan shivered theatrically. "Stop it."

"You'd have coped," Rachel teased her. "You would have just left the country as usual."

11
_____

MEGAN RUBBED her hand across her face. Only two more days, she reminded herself. She had stayed up late working on the final outline of the Swedish section and she would call Marcus tonight to tell him that she would be able to do Italy. For now, she had to concentrate on her alter ego as gallery person.

She looked down at her clipboard. "Okay, let's go over this stuff. The movers will bring tables and chairs up from the vault, starting at about midday tomorrow. The caterers also want a long row of tables for the bar, along the wall there. Is that okay?"

Sam nodded and Megan turned over a page. She didn't know as much as Rachel about her job, but she knew a hundred times more than she had the previous week. Still, she couldn't afford to let down her guard—one slip and she'd be caught.

She was about to go on when her phone rang.

"Sorry," she said, seeing Marcus's name flash up on the caller ID. "I'd better get this. Hello?"

"Where have you been?" Marcus squawked in her ear. "Didn't you get my messages?"

"Uh, yeah, sorry," she said, turning away from Sam. "I got kind of caught up in work. Is there something wrong?"

She winced at Marcus's sigh of frustration. "Gosh, no, nothing's wrong," he said. "Just wondering if you've thought about Italy at all? I need an answer Megan."

Megan put her head down, lowering her voice. "I've

almost decided. Look, this is kind of an awkward time, can I call you back? In about ten minutes?''

"I have a meeting now," he said.

"This afternoon?" she suggested meekly.

"And you'll have an answer for me?"

"Definitely," she insisted. He hung up, and Megan took the guilty look off her face and clipped the phone back onto her skirt before turning back to Sam.

"My sister," she said lightly. "Okay, the florists are coming in this evening so there'll be a lot of traffic through the main gallery. If you have anything else to do in there, you should probably do it this afternoon."

Sam nodded. "I'm finished there." He checked her face. "You're happy with it, right?"

She gave him a thumbs-up. "It's perfect."

"Aw shucks," he said, probably to cover up the fact that he really was grinning foolishly.

She nudged him playfully. "Concentrate," she said. "We're not there yet."

"How are you holding up?" he asked in a low voice.

"Okay. But I won't really relax until the dinner is over and we're all going home," she said, speaking the absolute truth.

"You've got to be looking forward to it a little bit," he said. "A chance to get all dressed up?" His eyes gleamed as he gave her an exaggerated once-over. "I know I'm looking forward to seeing that."

Heat unfurled in Megan's stomach. There was something about the way he looked at her, even when it was only jokingly, that made her want to pull him behind one of the smooth marble pillars and…wait a minute, what was that about dressing up?

Jeepers, she hadn't even thought about that. Of course it would be a black-tie affair. You didn't hire silver-service caterers and a team (a whole team!) of florists just so everyone could turn up in their workday clothes.

She was shot through with equal measures of anxiety and

anticipation. It would be wonderful to see Sam in a tux and she'd enjoy the chance to live up to his expectations and wow the socks off him, but how was she going to do that without a chance to go shopping for the perfect dress?

So little preparation time! And she'd hardly slept all week, she must look awful. She'd need to get her hair done and have a facial...no, maybe not a facial, but she'd have to find time to shave her legs and put on a fake tan.

But then again, Rachel would probably have her entire wardrobe planned out for her. Of course she would, and, let's face it, when it came to clothes Rachel knew what she was doing.

Still, it wouldn't harm anything to check, so she welcomed the arrival of Bradley, albeit looking a little less amenable than usual. It looked like the pressure of work was beginning to weigh on all of them.

"Okay, Sam," she said, moving off. "Don't forget what I said about the florists. See you later."

She left the gallery and was about to go down the stairs when she stopped dead. A peep of alarm escaped her. She vacillated between continuing on down the stairs or turning around and running back up and, like any body which is tugged in two opposing directions, hers stayed exactly where it was.

The object of her distress came to a stop in front of her.

"Rachel, hi," he said, taking her hand and shaking it warmly. "I don't know if you remember me. I'm Marcus Bennett, Megan's editor. We met at that launch last year?"

"Of course," said Megan remaining outwardly implacable, even though her mind was whirling. "How are you, Marcus? What are you doing here?"

He turned to introduce the woman at his side and Megan fought to keep her face neutral.

"We've come to have lunch at your fabulous rooftop restaurant. This is Claudia Liechtenstein, one of your sister's colleagues."

"Nice to meet you," said Megan shaking the woman's

hand and, with an extraordinary amount of restraint, not actually crushing her knuckles to dust.

There was a great camaraderie between the writers who worked for the Going Native series because they all loved their work and the world was a large place to be shared out, but Megan was immediately on full alert.

She knew that Claudia also had her eye on a trip to Italy. Megan's mind raced. Marcus wouldn't stab her in the back, but he did have to do his job and she hadn't exactly been cooperative over the last few days.

But the trip to Italy was hers! She wanted it and she couldn't wait around for another five years so, there, the decision was made. She would tell Marcus that she was the woman for the job.

And soon, before Claudia had a chance to persuade him that a bird in the hand was better than one who didn't return phone calls.

Stay calm, she told herself. Just get away and phone him.

"Well, I hope you both enjoy your lunch," she said. "And you must come back to see our new exhibition. It opens next week. I'll get you some tickets before you leave."

She made to walk away, but had to pause for a moment because Marcus and Claudia were performing a very familiar ritual. They were shaking their heads and looking at her as if she was a rather amusing zoo exhibit.

"I know," she said dryly. "It's amazing, isn't it?"

"I don't think I'll ever get used to it," laughed Marcus. "No matter how many times I see you. I'm sorry, I know it's rude to stare but I could be talking to Megan."

Megan shrugged and took another step away, but Marcus stopped her again. "Has Megan been around recently? Every time I call she seems too busy to talk to me. Or her phone's turned off."

Megan looked at him. "I know she's working very hard at the moment. Very, very hard. I've barely seen her at all. She just seems to be focused on work."

She tried to read his expression but he didn't look as excited by the news as she had hoped.

Megan had to talk to him now.

Well, obviously not now, but as soon as she could get away from him.

"Enjoy your lunch," she said again, turning and trotting down the stairs, thinking, *okay, first I'll call Marcus and then I'll worry about my clothes.*

"I DON'T UNDERSTAND," said Sam, frowning deeply.

"Unfortunately," said Bradley, "that makes two of us."

They were standing in the middle of gallery four of the new exhibition, looking up at a painting.

"This isn't the Corregio," said Sam again.

Bradley held out the clipboard. "But this is where it's supposed to be."

Sam waved the floor plan away. "I know it is." He looked around, skimming the other paintings in bemusement. Every other one was in its correct place.

"When did you hang this one?" asked Bradley.

Sam ran his hand through his hair, thinking back. "I didn't. Rachel brought it up from the vault yesterday with the Venetian student works, so I didn't even check it. I just told the movers to put it up." He looked at Bradley. "They must have put the Corregio somewhere else."

"I had a look through the other galleries. I couldn't find it anywhere."

Sam looked anxiously around the room, then back up at the painting, squinting as if he couldn't believe the evidence of his own eyes.

"So what we're supposed to have here," said Bradley, "is your Corregio, which has a value somewhere in the region of half a million dollars."

"Right," said Sam. A sheen of sweat had appeared on his brow. "But what we've got is a mediocre painting by a complete unknown, worth approximately—"

"A hundred bucks?" said Bradley. It was a facetious

suggestion but vocalized what they were both thinking. The sheer enormity of their potential loss.

"All right," said Sam, trying to rationalize. "It's just a mix-up. Our Corregio's probably gone to the permanent exhibition."

"A mix-up?" said Bradley incredulously. "Are you kidding me? We've got to call the police. This could be a theft."

"Wait, just think about it for a minute. If the Corregio's really been stolen," Sam indicated the painting on the wall with a scornful look, "is this supposed to be the cover? What kind of criminal mastermind would possibly think we'd not notice this? It makes no sense."

"Maybe that's the whole point," said Bradley. "That we would waste time puzzling about it and meanwhile the Corregio's being driven away as we speak."

"Give me five minutes," said Sam. "Let me just check the permanent exhibition. You know that even if it's all a mistake we'll still have to undergo the full investigation. Half the works will be recalled, especially the Michelangelo."

Bradley nodded, his face tight with anxiety. "Do it now."

Sam took one last uneasy look at the painting, then ran for the stairs.

MEGAN WAS in Rachel's office, dialing Marcus.

She waited for his phone to ring but the voice mail clicked on straight away.

"Nooo," she cried, hanging up. She glared at the ceiling, in the general direction of the restaurant. "Turn on your phone," she groaned.

She paced over to the window and looked out, arms folded.

Okay, his phone was off. She would just wait.

Yeah, wait while Claudia stole Italy right out from under her nose.

She groaned again and stamped her foot.

Then she laughed and turned to her desk, pulling some complimentary tickets out of a drawer and tucking them into a plain envelope.

"I must be getting old," she chuckled to herself. Her phone rang as she headed for the door and she grabbed it on her way out.

"Hello?... Oh hey, Rach, listen, can I call you back in about ten minutes? I just have to do something...no, it's nothing...well, Marcus, my editor, is here and I just have to talk to him for a minute."

She stopped at the door as Rachel babbled in alarm.

"Don't be ridiculous," Megan said. "Of course I'm not going to pretend to be myself." She paused. "Good grief, does that even make sense? Look, it's fine. I'll call you back from the office, okay? Bye."

She hung up. No reason to tell Rachel that it had indeed crossed her mind to switch back to her own identity just for a few minutes but, since she didn't have a change of clothes, she'd had to abandon the possibility and then had quickly realized that there was a much simpler option.

MEGAN PRESSED the button for the elevator again, aware even as she did how pointless it was. She fidgeted restlessly as the doors slowly slid open and she stepped into the elevator. As the doors started to shut she saw Sam come storming out of one of the galleries, an intense frown on his face.

He caught sight of her and she tilted her head and gave him a little wave. He didn't smile back. Instead, he started toward her, putting up his hand as if to stop the elevator. But the door whispered shut and, with a slight bump, the elevator began to rise.

Megan puzzled over the expression she'd seen on Sam's face. He'd looked somewhat upset, almost angry. And the way he'd focused when he caught sight of Megan, as if maybe she was the cause. She chewed at her lip, fretting. Had he guessed?

The elevator came to a halt and the door slid open. Deciding she could only worry about one thing at a time, Megan went out and crossed over to the wide doors that led into the restaurant and looked around.

She quickly spotted Marcus and Claudia. At her and Sam's table! The nerve.

She clicked her way across the floor and put her hand on Marcus's shoulder. "Here are some tickets for the new exhibition," she said. "It's going to be absolutely wonderful. One of our best yet. We've been getting some terrific reviews."

Marcus took the envelope. "Thank you so much, Rachel. You know we always like to give you a mention in our San Francisco guide."

She laughed and tapped his shoulder playfully. "Stop that, they're not a bribe. Anyway, listen, you won't believe it, but Megan just called me. I told her I'd seen you, of course, and she said she's been trying to call you, but your phone's turned off." Megan frowned convincingly. "She said something about wanting to give you an answer, that she was going to take the job?"

To her delight Marcus's face brightened. "Really?" He pulled his phone out of his pocket. "Oh, yes, I forgot I had it turned off." He started pressing buttons and the phone lit up.

Megan smiled. "Well, okay, I just wanted to pass the message on."

She couldn't help sneaking a glance at Claudia who was looking less than thrilled.

"That's great news," said Marcus, scrolling through his phone numbers. "I'll give her a call straight away."

Megan smiled again, then remembered the phone in her hand.

Her heart stopped.

"No!" she said, grabbing Marcus's phone out of his hand.

"I mean," she said, blushing under their surprised gazes, "that's probably a private call. I mean, I should leave you alone."

"It's really okay," said Marcus.

"Still," she said inanely, "best not to mix business and pleasure, isn't it? I'll leave you to it." She turned away.

"Rachel?"

She turned back slowly.

"My phone?"

She handed it over gingerly. "Ahaha. Sorry. My mind's all over the place today. Sure, give her a call. Gosh, I've got a lot to do, I'd better get a move on. See you later."

She turned away and could hear him apologizing to Claudia behind her.

"I'm so sorry, this will only take a minute."

She scurried through the tables, bumping into people and kicking bags over in her haste, with one hand clutched over the other holding her phone.

Her heart was beating triple time and she made a final dash for the door as the face of her phone lit up.

The ring followed a split second later as she ducked sideways out of sight. She took a deep breath and pressed her hand hard against her chest in a futile attempt to stop it hammering.

"Hello?" she said brightly.

"Megan! Hi, it's Marcus."

"Marcus, how are you? I've been trying to reach you." Jubilant now, at her mission accomplished, Megan didn't bother to disguise the smile in her voice.

"I know. I had the phone turned off. Sorry about that. I just spoke to your sister. She told me you'd called."

"Yes," she teased. "Having lunch at the gallery I hear. Did she give you some free tickets? I told her to." May as well get the credit for it.

"Yeah, she did. Thanks, they're great. You've got good news for me?"

Megan was about to answer when there was a jarring crash from inside the restaurant. She jumped and looked back into the restaurant, putting her hand over the phone.

"Sorry Megan, I didn't hear you," Marcus yelled. "Some waiter just dropped a tray. It's real noisy in here, hang on, let me just step outside."

Megan let out a strangled "eep" and turned to flee, running straight into a young couple. "Sorry," she mouthed, dashing down the hall as fast as she could manage in her heels. She was about to duck through the second set of double doors when Sam came through. She turned and saw Marcus come out of the restaurant and she tried to go through the doors but Sam was blocking her way.

"We need to talk," he mouthed. "Now."

She looked up at Sam's grim face and nodded, putting up a finger to forestall him and pressed the phone to her ear as Marcus's voice came again.

"Sorry about that," he said. "What were you saying?"

Megan hesitated. She and Marcus were at opposite ends of a twenty-yard hall and there were only a few other people around. It didn't look as if Sam was going to move out of her way either so she just kept her voice low.

"I wanted to tell you that I'd like to do that…uh, thing."

"The thing?" said Marcus. She could see him starting to pace and she began to sidle around Sam, putting him between her and Marcus.

"Yeah, you know, the Italy thing."

"Hey, that's great. But are you sure you'll have the time?"

Marcus was now less than ten feet away and Megan was afraid to answer. She inched another couple of steps around Sam. He was still glowering at her and, rather oddly, she thought, making no secret of the fact that he was listening intently to her phone call.

"Megan?" came Marcus's voice in her ear.

Megan gave a hum of deep contemplation and watched Marcus turn and walk away.

"Uh, yeah," she said, "I was just thinking about it. Yes, I'll have time."

"Because I don't want you to say yes now if you're going to come back to me later and say you can't do it after all."

Megan pushed her shoulders against the doors, in an effort to open them and they gave a loud creak of protest. Megan froze.

"I'll be able to do it," she said, desperate to get off the phone. She was almost certain now that Sam knew and he was about to say something. She leaned out slightly, peeping around Sam's shoulder. Marcus was on his way back, smoothing down his hair, not quite looking convinced. He looked up and their eyes met. Megan stiffened in terror and he grinned.

"Megan," he mouthed, pointing at the phone. She forced herself to grin back. He turned away and she continued quietly. "I promise, I'll be able to do it. Trust me, it'll be fine."

She glanced up and was surprised to see that her words had further inflamed Sam.

"Okay," said Marcus. "You've got it. I'll fax the details over to you."

"Okay, bye," said Megan tersely, hanging up. She looked up at Sam.

"What was that about?" he said, before she could speak. "That phone call?"

She frowned, resolved to play innocent for as long as she could. "I don't think that's any of your business."

"I think that's exactly what it was, Rachel," he went on. "Who were you calling?"

Megan was flummoxed. He'd called her Rachel which meant he didn't know about the swap. But what else could he be so upset about? Was it jealousy? Was it because he thought she'd been talking to David?

"It was my sister," she said.

Sam made a derisive face. "Oh yeah? Why were you talking about Italy?"

Megan's mind raced. What on earth was the matter with him? "That's where she's going next. I was just telling her that I should be able to get some time off." She shook her head in genuine bewilderment. "What's going on?"

Sam's eyes darted away from hers as if he was thinking about something then came back to peer suspiciously at her again.

"Why did you kiss me that first night?"

Twin spots of color rose in Megan's cheeks. "I don't know," she blurted defensively. "Why did you kiss me?"

Sam put his hands on her arms, leaning toward her and talking in a low voice. "Rachel, I need you to tell me what's going on."

Megan's breath became short. She was pinned by his stare. "I can't."

He let go of her and exhaled heavily, rubbing one hand across his brow. "Please don't do this. Just...just tell me where it is."

Megan frowned. "Where what is?"

Sam shook his head crossly. "The painting."

"What painting?"

Sam snorted. "What painting?" he said sarcastically.

Megan shook her head, her eyes wide with confusion. Then she looked over in alarm as Marcus and Claudia came out of the restaurant.

"Guess what," Marcus said in a friendly voice as they passed Megan and Sam. "Your sister's going to Italy."

Megan mustered a smile as they went down the stairs and looked back to find Sam's eyes boring into hers.

"You were telling me the truth?" he said.

Megan hesitated, then reminded herself that it was Rachel's job on the line. She nodded.

"So you don't know?"

Megan spread her hands helplessly. "Know what?"

He lowered his voice again, watching her carefully. "We've got a missing painting."

Megan felt all the blood leave her face and her legs turned to water. So this is what swooning felt like. She realized immediately that if Sam had merely accused her of being Megan she'd never have been able to fake such a convincing reaction. She rocked on her feet and put her hand over her mouth, staring at him in horror. The whole deception would come out and Rachel would be fired. And that would be the least of their worries. They might have to go to prison.

Sam, still watching her, obviously believed her reaction was genuine. He put his hand under her elbow and led her over toward the elevator.

"But how?" she mumbled in a daze. "Which one?"

"It's the Corregio," Sam said quietly. "The one I brought. Bradley and I discovered it missing a few minutes ago, and I went to the permanent exhibition in case there'd been a mix-up, but it isn't there. Your Corregio's being taken for cleaning but the mover didn't know anything about mine. And I radioed the vault but it isn't there, either."

Megan began to tremble with dread. "We have a Corregio?" she whispered.

Sam looked at her. "This is no time for games," he said threateningly.

Megan swallowed dryly. She was remembering John Forsyth's words. *The Corregio's going for cleaning so this is the temporary replacement.* Not Sam's Corregio, the Hyder Gallery one!

"I think your painting is in the cleaning room," she said in a small voice.

He stared at her. "What?"

"The cleaning and restoration room," Megan reiterated, unable to meet his eyes. "I think it's up there."

The elevator arrived and other people who'd been waiting crowded on while Sam just stared at Megan. The doors started to close, and she finally looked up as he jumped on, turning back to look at her with an unforgiving gaze.

"WELL, WOULD YOU LOOK at that," said Maggie, brushing a strand of hair away from her face. "How on earth did that get there?"

Sam was staring at the valuable painting, which had been slotted casually on a rack behind some unimportant works. He couldn't remember a painting ever looking so beautiful to him.

Maggie went on loquaciously. "I had no idea. I was expecting our Corregio so I just told one of my apprentices to put it away and I didn't even look at it. I wonder where my painting is?"

Sam smiled at her. "Don't worry. I was in the permanent exhibition just now and I saw them taking it down. I think it's coming."

After contacting Bradley by radio, Sam carefully lifted the Corregio onto a moving bracket and brought it over to the service elevator.

The whole way back to the second floor he was thinking hard. Rachel Dean's behavior was gnawing at his brain. He wasn't sure that he believed that this painting had been misplaced by accident. And once he'd allowed himself to consider the possibility that she'd been hoping to sneak it out of the gallery he found it was a very good explanation for the ditziness she'd been displaying lately. Because surely that was an act. He'd seen the evidence of her expertise and then, suddenly, she was playing it down and encouraging him with her wide-eyed admiration to talk about himself. The flattery, the flirting and practically the seduction. Was it all just to get him to let his guard down?

Sam knew why he was really mad. Not because she'd had the audacity to try but because, damn it all, it had been working.

MEGAN FELL onto her couch face first.

What a day. She felt utterly drained. Unable to face Rachel, she'd called her and told her she was going home for an hour or two before she came back to her sister's home.

She turned over, staring up at the ceiling as she pulled off her shoes. After the disastrous mix-up with the paintings she'd spent the day avoiding Sam like the plague. She'd explained the misunderstanding to John Forsyth and dispatched him to placate Sam and make sure that every painting involved in the whole fiasco was accounted for. Then she'd alternated between hiding in Rachel's office and hovering around Jocelyn in the central office.

After surviving today, Megan thought as she sat up, *tomorrow should be a walk in the park.* She padded toward the kitchen and opened the freezer, searching her stash. Mint chocolate or cherry ripple? She decided on mint chocolate and, grabbing a spoon from the drawer, dropped into a chair. She rolled her head from side to side, thinking about how different this moment would be if they hadn't found the painting. She ate another spoonful of ice cream, sighing with disbelief at her lucky escape and wondering whether Sam was still thinking about it.

SAM, SITTING in his car on the street outside, was actually wondering what exactly he'd hoped to achieve by following Rachel home. Although he'd convinced Bradley that it had all been a terrible mix-up, he hadn't quite managed to convince himself. He'd tried to accept that he was just being paranoid, but now his suspicions were aroused again by the fact that Rachel had driven to this house instead of her own.

He got out of the car and walked up to the door, still wondering what he was going to say. There were three doorbells and, shrugging to himself, Sam pressed the one for the first-floor apartment.

A moment passed and then Rachel, dressed in flared cotton hipsters and a loose T-shirt, opened the door. She looked at him in surprise as Sam realized his mistake. It wasn't Rachel.

"Oh sorry," he said. "I didn't realize this was your house. I'm Sam Harrison. We met at Rachel's house?"

He put out his hand, feeling more foolish by the second. "I thought I saw Rachel come in here."

She shook his hand, still gazing at him with wide eyes.

"Er, is she here?" Sam said sheepishly.

She let out an odd laugh. "Well, you saw her come in here, didn't you? I guess she must be."

Sam laughed along, puzzled by her nervous expression.

She seemed to hesitate, then stepped back from the doorway. "Would you like to come in and I'll tell her you're here?"

Sam followed her into the living room, dreading the conversation he was about to have with Rachel yet feeling more strongly than ever that his suspicions were going to be proved correct.

MEGAN CHECKED herself in the mirror once more. She'd put her Rachel clothes back on and brushed her hair. She really didn't want to go back out. There was a confrontation coming, she could feel it in the air like a storm.

"One more day," she told herself, striving to smooth out the worry lines from her brow.

She emerged as Rachel and found him standing in front of her framed print of a map of Anchorage, which portrayed the city as it had been fifty years before.

"Megan's been there," she said, coming to stand beside him.

Sam looked down at the legend on the map. "She's been to 1958?"

Megan smiled, but her relief was short-lived as Sam moved away and then turned to face her with his arms folded.

"I hate to ask this," said Megan, "but did you follow me here?"

Sam nodded, looking uncomfortable. "I'm sorry but I felt as though I had no choice. You'd been avoiding me all day."

Megan acknowledged the truth with an embarrassed grimace. "Do you want to sit down?"

They sat down opposite each other and Megan gripped her hands tightly in her lap, hating the troubled expression on his face and hating even more that she was the cause of it.

"I worked it out," he said at last. "It took me a while but I finally got it. I should have got it straightaway, of course, because it's the oldest trick in the book." He met her eyes. "Congratulations. You almost had me."

Megan frowned, confused. "The oldest trick in the book?"

"Distraction," said Sam. "Seduction. Enticement. Call it whatever you want. It was working, I was completely blind to what was really going on." He stood up and started to pace, shaking his head. "I just don't understand it, Rachel, why would you do it?"

Megan followed him with her gaze. "Do what?" she asked, utterly bemused.

He stopped and looked angrily at her. "You can drop the innocent act now," he said. "I know you're planning a robbery."

Megan couldn't help it. She pressed her lips together, fighting it, but the guffaw of laughter eventually exploded out of her.

Sam narrowed his eyes as she clamped her hand over her mouth.

"I'm sorry," she mumbled. "But that's just so ridiculous."

His expression didn't change and she leaned forward, appealing to him. "Are you serious? You really think I was planning an art heist?"

"Weren't you?"

"Of course not," she exclaimed. She spread her hands.

"That mix-up with the Corregio? You think that was my attempt? I mean, give me some credit, Sam. Don't you think I could come up with something a little more sophisticated than that?"

"I think you eschewed sophistication in favor of the simplistic approach."

Megan twitched her head in incomprehension.

"The whole seduction act," he said coldly. "Don't try to deny it, there's been something fishy about that right from the start. One day you're the epitome of professionalism and the next you're all over me, batting your eyelashes and giving me sultry looks. What happened, Rachel, why did I suddenly become so irresistible?"

Megan rose to her feet, holding his gaze. "You should know, you felt it, too."

His expression softened for a second. "Yeah, I did." A terrible hurt came into his eyes. "But in my case it was genuine."

Megan put out her hand. "Sam—"

"Don't," he said, moving back.

"No," she said, "you've got to listen to me. It's real, Sam, what I feel for you. Whatever else you think, you've got to believe that."

"Sure," he said. "I almost did. I admit it, Rachel, you caught me, hook, line and sinker. But I don't trust you at all, how could I?" He looked down, as if mustering resolve and then met her eyes again. "I just wanted to say that to your face, to make it clear. I guess I'll never know what you were really planning, but I know I'm out of it."

Megan felt breathless. Her eyes welled up and she struggled to find the right words. "Sam," she said, "I promise it's not an act. When I'm with you, I…" She faltered, remembering her promise to Rachel that she wouldn't tell Sam until after the opening. "I just can't—"

"You know what?" he interrupted. "It doesn't even matter now. Whatever it was, it's over."

He left swiftly and Megan remained where she was,

pushing her hands through her hair as she heard the front
door slam. She was stunned by disbelief at what had just
happened. She walked into the kitchen in a daze and sat
down at the table, staring sightlessly ahead of her as a sob
caught in her throat. Her eyes focused and she looked for
a moment at the tub of ice cream.

With a disconsolate cry she swept it from the table. She
dropped her head onto her folded arms as the tears over-
flowed from her eyes.

12

"GET OUT there!"

Despite Rachel's stern tone Megan continued to hover behind the door, speaking worriedly into the phone. "I really think I'm overdressed, Rach, are you sure about this?"

"Believe me, you couldn't be overdressed. Everyone will be dressed up for tonight, you're expected to look like that."

"I still can't believe you sent a hairdresser and a beautician here for me—it's so decadent."

"It was a necessity," said Rachel firmly. "Now will you please get out there before Peterson comes to find out why I'm hiding in my office."

"Okay, I'll call you later," said Megan, hanging up.

She took a deep breath and stepped out of the office, seriously hoping that Rachel hadn't misjudged the situation. She looked down again at the embroidered bustier of her Armani dress. It was truly beautiful and she'd been looking forward to having Sam see her in it. Not that there was any point now. On the few occasions when they'd had to talk to each other during the day he'd been polite but unreachably distant. She took a deep breath, willing herself not to cry again. There would be enough attention on her tonight without inviting more.

THE FOYER WAS resplendent with finery. The guests had begun to arrive and boy, was she grateful to Rachel. Women sparkled with expensive jewelry and the men looked dapper in tuxedos. There was a genial atmosphere as old friends greeted each other and strangers were introduced. There was a murmur of light conversation and an air of pleasant anticipation.

Security guards milled unobtrusively in the background and Megan felt as if she'd wandered onto the set of a Merchant-Ivory production until Peterson beckoned her over, reminding her that tonight she was part of the show.

She made her way over to the small circle of people. Her head was buzzing with Rachel's instructions. Make sure to mingle and have a few words with everyone, make a point of flitting around so you don't get caught up in any meaningful discussions. Thank people sincerely for coming and ask them if they're enjoying the exhibition, but please don't attempt to start conversations on any other subject.

She was just exchanging her first round of pleasantries when she felt a light touch on her shoulder.

She turned and got her first look at Sam in a tuxedo. Her heart skipped and she tried to keep her voice level. "Hi. You look…nice."

"Thanks," he said. "You look absolutely beautiful."

She looked up in surprise and their eyes locked. It took Megan a moment to remember that they weren't alone. She turned back to the small gathering of people who were watching them curiously. "May I introduce Sam Harrison, the curator from the Bonnington Trust."

He became involved in the handshaking and Megan took the time to get her composure back.

Sam's compliment had really knocked the wind out of her. It was hard enough being around him without him being nice to her. She reminded herself that all she had to do was get through the night. The blue on Rachel's face was almost gone—not enough that she could face everyone tonight—but, with makeup, she'd be back on Monday for the first day of opening to the public. Sunday would be spent clearing away things from tonight and setting up the ticket booths and guidestands so Rachel would get away with calling in sick for one day as long as she promised to be in early on Monday.

So this is it, thought Megan, my big farewell.

MOST OF THE guests had arrived, so Peterson made a little speech welcoming them all and they were led up the staircase to the second floor where flutes of champagne were handed out.

Sam lingered with Megan as they went up.

"Are you okay?" he asked quietly. "You look a bit bewildered."

She looked up at him, dismayed that her feelings were showing so clearly and still wondering why he was being so solicitous.

"Do I?" she said, trying a smile. "And here I thought I was a model of sophistication."

"Oh, that, too," he reassured her. There was an awkward pause before Megan went on.

"I have to give a speech later," she confided. "And I'm not sure I've learned it properly."

"I see," he said seriously. "Well, if you feel yourself forgetting your lines just give me a signal and I'll cause a distraction."

Despite herself, she smiled. "What kind of distraction?"

He shrugged. "Not sure. I could start singing maybe."

"Great," she said hopelessly. "In other words... I'd better not forget my speech."

SHE KNEW it was Rachel's glory, but she couldn't help basking in it a little. She had only spent one week in this unfamiliar world but her immersion had been so total that, without even noticing it, she had picked up so much and even felt a sort of pride for much of the exhibition.

As she moved among the guests and heard their appreciative murmurs and exclamations she felt as if the gallery

was her own personal mansion and she was the hostess of
the year's most glamorous party.

And she hadn't even had a glass of champagne yet.

And, if she was queen, then Sam was doing a good act
as king. They passed each other occasionally as they both
circulated, answering queries or giving short histories of
various works. It's just a fantasy, Megan kept reminding
herself, it's not your life.

AT DINNER Megan was childishly gratified to see that Tiffany Rockwell was sitting nowhere near Sam. Megan herself was flanked by two rather charming middle-aged men,
and, mindful of how easily Hank Rockwell's art expertise
had overwhelmed hers, she made sure to keep the conversation firmly on them, merely throwing in a few tidbits
about the gallery in order to maintain her facade.

Inevitably, her gaze did stray to Sam. Hmm, he was really getting on well with that woman on his left. Megan
took another bite of her roasted pepper and squinted at the
woman's hand. No wedding ring.

Megan nodded and smiled politely at something her
companion had said. No wedding ring. So what? That
didn't mean that she and Sam were about to run off and
get married.

But what's to stop him, said devil-Megan, making a
highly unwelcome appearance. Why shouldn't he talk to a
beautiful woman and laugh at her jokes? He's unattached,
isn't he? I mean, there's no one else making any commitment to him.

"Excuse me?" said Megan.

"I was just saying," said the man to her left, "that pri-
ority is given to national law over municipal in the accepted
hierarchy of interlocking legal systems."

"Really?" said Megan.

"Yes, and furthermore…" The man went on as Megan
returned to her anxious reflections.

She couldn't blame Sam for going off with someone

else—she was the one who was living a secretive double life. Sam was being totally aboveboard, merely conversing openly with a woman whom he found attractive.

How could he!

It doesn't matter anyway, she reminded herself, it'll all be cleared up soon.

By next week you'll be able to tell him the truth and then you'll be completely free to start dating each other with no obstacles and no complications. Oh, that's right, she added sarcastically, apart from the fact that he doesn't want you anymore.

She realized she was staring when Sam looked up and caught her eye, giving her a small smile before turning back to the woman.

And even if he did still want her, how could it possibly work? No complications? Ha! How about being on opposite sides of the globe, how's that for a complication? How long would it take for the thrill of e-mails and phone calls to wear off? How long before he found Ms. Dark-Hair's number in the pocket of his tux and decided, what the heck, no harm in giving her a call.

Megan stabbed at her wild mushroom cannelloni and chewed angrily.

What on earth was the matter with her? If it's that upsetting, she told herself, why don't you just stay here? Skip Italy altogether. She knew the answer to that. Italy was the safe bet, the sure thing.

And, of course, if she reneged on Italy, Marcus would never give her another assignment worth having. Ever. She had a thought that made her smile. If she wanted to skip Italy at this stage the only way she could do it was if she sent Rachel in her place. Talk about a tough assignment.

Her thoughts returned to Sam. Despite her confident protestations to Rachel all week, she really wasn't sure how Sam would react to the truth.

What if he felt tricked and deceived, and could she blame him if he did? What if he never wanted to see her again?

Maybe it would be better not to tell him at all.

HER PERUSALS took her all the way through dinner so it was only when Peterson rose to his feet that she started frantically running over her speech in her head.

"I would like to thank you all very much for being here tonight," said Peterson. "As you know, this is one of the most remarkable collections we've ever had in this city. The broad mythological theme encompasses many periods, from Classical Greek and Roman up to the Pre-Raphaelite works." He nodded at Sam. "I would like to thank the Bonnington Trust Foundation for allowing us to house the collection and extend a very special thanks to each and every one of you, without whom, it would not have been possible. I would also like to take this opportunity to formalize the appointment of one of our members of staff. She has put in a terrific six months' probation and I think her exemplary work on this project has more than earned her the position. May I introduce our head of temporary exhibits, Rachel Dean."

Megan rose to her feet amidst the congratulatory applause. Rachel hadn't warned her about this but then, how could she have? A bubble of joy burst in Megan's chest when she thought of how happy Rachel would be and it was followed by a sting of sadness that Rachel couldn't be here to enjoy this accolade for herself. At least it was no stretch for her to mimic the emotions Rachel would feel.

"Thank you," she said, with a proud smile. "This is a great surprise and I would like to say thank you very much to Mr. Peterson and the rest of the board for this position. It's a great honor and I hope I'll continue to live up to your expectations. I couldn't do it, of course, without a wonderful and dedicated staff and I hope they always realize just how much they are appreciated." Megan paused. Her throat was tightening and she took a deep breath, fighting the quaver in her voice. "I had an absolutely remarkable time working on this exhibition and even now, when I go into the galleries, it's as if I'm seeing some of them for the first time. I, too, would like to extend my thanks to you for your generosity in making this possible. And I hope you're all enjoying yourselves as much as I am tonight.'' Her eyes started to swim so she finished up quickly. ''Thank you again,'' she said, sitting down and blinking to clear the emotional tears. There was another ripple of applause and the man next to her patted her arm but all Megan could see was Sam watching her.

In that moment she decided to tell him.

THE PROBLEM was getting him alone. After dinner there was a short recital from the string quartet and then the guests were free to take a second, more leisurely ramble through the galleries.

Having come this far Megan was determined not to shirk her duties but her secret now burned in her chest like a hot coal and, having made the decision to confess to Sam, she wanted to do it immediately.

However, interruptions kept impeding her progress until she was beginning to wonder if it was really the right thing to do after all.

She found herself a quiet corner behind the tall sculpture of Daphne and Apollo and stood gazing at the cool white marble, trying to create a similar coolness and composure in her mind.

As had happened so many times in the past week the extraordinary beauty of the artwork became such a distraction that she was somewhat startled when Sam appeared at her side.

''There you are,'' he said. He twitched his eyebrow. ''Are you hiding?''

''No,'' she said, then added recklessly, ''Why? Were you looking for me?''

''I'm just making sure you don't go running off at the stroke of midnight,'' he said.

''Before my car turns into a pumpkin?'' she finished.

He made a somber face. "It would be a great loss to the gallery."

She looked up at him, nerves fluttering at the edge of her stomach.

"Sam, there's something I need to tell you." She looked into his eyes and was surprised to see warmth in them. It was just enough to give her the boost of courage that she needed.

She swallowed. "Phew, this is really hard. I'm going to have to take a big leap of faith here and trust you."

She paused and Sam seemed to take it as a reluctance to continue. "You can trust me," he said. "Absolutely. You can tell me anything. And there's something I want to tell you, too."

"Oh, I'm not sure you should yet," said Megan.

"I don't care," he said, taking a deep breath. "I'm going to. The truth is that I've fallen in love—"

Megan put her hand to her chest as a surge of emotion swelled in her. "Oh Sam, I have, too."

"—with your sister."

Megan blinked and then her voice echoed around the gallery like the crack of a pistol. "What!"

Sam gave a reassuring smile to the few other people interspersed among the statues and then looked back at Megan, his eyes dark.

"It's true," he said softly. "I've fallen in love with Megan. She's funny, generous, kind and enthusiastic. She's adventurous and sweet and she makes me laugh. I love her and I want to be with her."

Megan floundered as if she was in quicksand. "That makes absolutely no sense. I mean, you've barely spoken to her...I...when did this happen?... I mean, it couldn't have because...well, it's complicated, but I thought you...I thought that you and I..." Megan trailed off in dismay and then realized that Sam was watching her very calmly and very patiently.

And with a twinkle in his eye.

She frowned, searching his face and then her hand flew to her mouth. "You...you know?" she whispered, unconsciously leaning toward him.

He leaned forward, too, and nodded.

Megan pulled back, her eyes widening. "You know?" she gasped.

He nodded again, then straightened up as he looked over her shoulder.

"Mr. Peterson," he said jovially. "You should be proud of yourself, it's going very well."

Megan's heart kick-started again with a thud and then went into overdrive, banging against her rib cage.

She turned to Peterson, her smile frozen on her face.

"I think we can all be proud tonight," said Peterson, clapping Sam on the shoulder. "Rachel, just wanted to speak to you personally and say congratulations on the job."

Megan's mouth was bone dry. "Thank you," she croaked.

"Sorry your sister couldn't make it," Peterson went on. "And where's that nice young man of yours, why didn't you bring him?"

Megan swallowed. "He's out of town," she said. "On business."

"Never mind. Tell him I said hello." He turned to Sam. "Saw you talking to Jennifer Coolidge at dinner, lovely young lady."

"She was very charming," said Sam.

"Single, too," said Peterson, gazing around absently. "A man could do a lot worse."

"I'm sure," said Sam, taking the opportunity to wink at Megan.

She was too panic-stricken to respond and after a few more pleasantries, Peterson eventually wandered off, leaving Megan to repeat her earlier question in disbelief.

"You know?"

Sam checked to make sure that there was no one else in earshot before resuming their whispered conversation.

"Well, to be completely honest, I was only eighty percent sure until I saw your reaction."

Megan frowned. "What if I had been Rachel?"

He grinned. "Then that would have been extremely embarrassing for me."

Megan's head was swirling with questions. "How long have you known?"

"Since the first day, when you came up to the gallery and I thought you were drunk."

"No!"

"Well, no," he admitted. "I only really worked it out last night but that *was* the first day wasn't it? When I look back on it I'm amazed I didn't spot it. You were so different."

"I'm amazed that no one else spotted it. And I don't think anyone else has." She widened her eyes at him. "How did you guess? What finally gave it away?"

"It was the accumulation of little things rather than any one thing. Just lots that didn't sit right, from the stuff like fluffing questions in the administration meeting, the mysterious phone calls and the fact that you were so jittery with the press, right up to the whole mess with the Corregio." He laughed at Megan's grimace.

"That was such a nightmare," she muttered, shaking her head.

Sam let out a low rumble of a laugh. "You'll have to tell me the full story of what exactly happened some day. Anyway, I kept feeling that something was off but I couldn't put my finger on it, and then, of course, I thought I was just imagining things and getting distracted because of my attraction to you. And as I said, I just couldn't fathom why the Rachel I'd first met had suddenly become someone who gave me back-rubs and flirted outrageously with me." He smiled wryly. "You heard my explanation.

I'm afraid I really did think it was a ploy to distract me while you whisked the Corregio out from under my nose."

Megan couldn't resist giving him a teasing smile. "You have to admit that if it had been, it almost worked."

Sam shrugged guiltily, then went on, "I think it was visiting you at your house that finally did it. I was looking at that black-and-white photo of you and Rachel, the one hanging near the window, and I was thinking that if I hadn't met the two of you together I would have thought it was a trick photo. Then you came out of the bedroom that I'd just seen Megan walk into and something just clicked in my head. On my way home I suddenly realized that there was another explanation besides international art thief, even if it was equally bizarre. And another thing, which kind of disturbed me at the time, was that even when I met you in your Megan clothes, I felt it, as strongly as I do now, the connection that draws me to you."

"Oh Sam," she breathed. "I wanted so badly to tell you. I didn't mean to deceive you or anything like that. It's just the way it happened."

He was looking at her with intense fascination. "How did it happen? I mean, why did it happen? Was it a joke? A bet?"

"Are you crazy? I wouldn't do this for a bet. No... something happened to Rachel and she couldn't come to work so I offered to stand in. It was only supposed to be for a day originally."

"But it has been you all week?" he asked.

She looked into his eyes and read there the importance of the question.

She smiled, putting all her feelings into it. "It has been me—all week."

She could see him replaying bits of it in his mind. "And you are a travel writer?"

"Uh-huh."

"So all that stuff about the paintings?" he said, waving his hand around.

"Memorized frantically," she admitted. "Or, as a last resort, made up."

"And so, that morning in the vault, you had no idea where to find the painting I was looking for?"

Megan let out a guilty laugh. "Not a clue! And not only that, but I was also completely lost myself. I'd already spent fifteen minutes trying to find my way out."

He shook his head. "It's amazing," he said. "But what on earth happened to Rachel that she couldn't explain to Peterson?"

Megan told him and he didn't even attempt to look sympathetic, just burst out laughing.

"It's not funny," said Megan. Then, as he lifted an eyebrow. "Okay, it's a little funny but don't tell her I said that."

Sam was still laughing. "That's why she had the face mask on when I came, because she was blue."

"Right."

Sam looked at her. "So the fish aren't yours. When I said Sweetlips?"

She blushed. "I thought you were talking to me."

He ran his hand down her arm and laughed. "And that guy, David?"

Megan felt a huge relief at finally being able to explain. "David is Rachel's boyfriend, that's what I meant when I said it was complicated but that it was not what you thought."

"Complicated is right," said Sam. "So who else knows?"

"No one. Only Rachel, David and I. And I wasn't even supposed to tell you tonight but I...I just felt I had to."

Sam looked at her consideringly. "You were afraid I'd rat you out?"

Her eyes flew to his. "Rachel was. A bit. And I guess I wasn't sure."

"I guess you were right to wait," he said. "But I meant what I said. I'm in love with you, Megan. This has been the best week of my life, and the thought that I couldn't have you, that there was someone else, it was eating me alive.''

He looked stern. ''There isn't anyone else is there?''

''No,'' she said, smiling brilliantly. ''There's only you. I'm in love with you, too, Sam.''

''And you promise this isn't some elaborate art heist scheme?''

''I promise,'' she said, laughing.

''Well it should be a little easier now that you've got someone on your side. How much longer do you have to be a stand-in?''

''This is the last night,'' said Megan, even more upset by it now. ''Rachel is calling in sick tomorrow and she'll be back on Sunday.''

Sam grinned. ''I can't wait to see her here.''

''You be nice to her,'' said Megan with mock severity.

''I'll have to be,'' he said with a martyred expression. ''She's my girlfriend's sister.''

''Your girlfriend?'' laughed Megan delightedly.

''Of course,'' he said. ''I presume we'll be able to go out on dates now, as soon as you shed your secret identity.''

''You bet we will,'' said Megan. She laughed with pleasure and then her smile faded as she remembered where she was going.

''Oh but…oh no,'' she said.

He dipped his head. ''What is it?''

''It's work. Oh no, I'm going to Italy.''

''When?''

Megan's bottom lip trembled. ''Next week. On Wednesday.''

''For how long?''

''Two months,'' she said, heartbroken.

Sam looked concerned. ''Two months,'' he said. ''Hmm, in that case we'd better forget it.''

Then he laughed at her openmouthed expression.

"You're crazy. Two months is nothing. And I've been promising myself another trip to Italy soon anyway."

Megan breathed in deeply. "Really?"

Sam held her gaze, his eyes growing concerned. "You don't get it do you? This is the real thing, Megan, this is it."

He looked at the few people meandering around the statues.

"I think we could get away with a hug," he said conspiratorially.

Megan needed no encouragement. She flung her arms around his neck and arched her body into his as his arms encircled her. The tears that had been threatening all night dampened her cheeks as she felt his breath on her neck and heard him whispering, "I love you."

"I love you, too," she exhaled.

They pulled apart and Megan dabbed at her face.

She was about to ask him if he really was going to visit her in Italy, but he started talking before her.

"Guess what, I've got my last four words now."

She giggled, blinking away the last of her tears. "What are they?"

He reached down and took her hand, holding it between his as he looked into her eyes.

"Will you marry me?"

Megan's eyes widened and then she nodded in affirmation as she answered with a huge smile. "Antibiotic!"

Thick as Thieves

Jennifer McKinlay

TORONTO • NEW YORK • LONDON
AMSTERDAM • PARIS • SYDNEY • HAMBURG
STOCKHOLM • ATHENS • TOKYO • MILAN • MADRID
PRAGUE • WARSAW • BUDAPEST • AUCKLAND

Dear Reader,

I was inspired to write *Thick as Thieves* when I made my own trek across the United States, from Connecticut to Arizona, in search of new beginnings.

This undertaking is not for the faint of heart. I blame my parents for my wanderlust. When I was growing up, their idea of a vacation was to pack the car with kids and bags and drive across Canada or to Florida and back. I can't tell you how many hours I have whiled away staring at the car ceiling. As the youngest, I never got a window seat and always had to sit on the hump.

Like all moves, mine had the requisite events—a moving truck that broke down, a carsick cat (poor Chubby), cheap motels and bad food. Despite all that, driving across the country gave me an appreciation for this great nation and its beauty that I will never forget.

I hope you enjoy Cat and Jared's zany adventure as much as I enjoyed writing it. Keep on rolling.

Jennifer McKinlay

P.S. Online readers can reach me at jenymck@hotmail.com.

Books by Jennifer McKinlay

HARLEQUIN DUETS
74—TO CATCH A LATTE

For my son Wyatt
for showing me how joyous life can be.

In loving memory of Cay Culbertson, a dear friend
gone too soon. You were our butterfly. Flitter on.

1

_____

"WHY ARE YOU DOING THIS?" Cameron Levery asked, shaking his head in frustration. "I just don't get it."

"Cam, I've explained this to you a thousand times. I don't know what more I can say." Cat eyed her brother with the patience of the frequently nagged and resumed packing.

"Catherine, I didn't want to bring this up, but you're leaving me no choice." Cam cleared his throat as if stalling for time. "Are you leaving because of Matthew?"

Cat sat back on her heels and sighed. Her beloved, older brother only used her full name when he was feeling particularly paternal. Which seemed to be all of the time lately. She felt a bead of sweat trickle down her neck, and she reached for her glass of lemonade. Sipping the cool, tart liquid, she considered her brother's question.

Matthew Gerard—or the big dumb jerk, as she liked to think of him—had been her fiancé. Six months after their engagement, she'd caught him with his pants down, literally, in his accountant's office. She winced when she thought of it. His accountant, a buxom brunette, had control of more than just his taxable assets. When Cat had confronted him, the big dumb jerk said she was boring, that he felt strangled by their relationship.

It had been a sock in the ego to be rejected, but much to her surprise, relief had crept in. Matthew was right. She'd been a clinging vine, entwining herself so tightly about him and his needs that there had been no room left for herself. She'd become a bore.

By focusing so much energy on Matthew, she'd managed to alienate most everyone else. She'd lost touch with her friends and dropped most of her hobbies. The only constants in her life outside of the big dumb jerk were her job and her family.

"Hello?" Cam waved his hand in front of her face. "Are you in there?"

"Yes." Cat shook her head. "I am leaving because of Matthew, but I'm also leaving because of you."

"Me?" Cam gaped at her in confusion.

"Yes, you," Cat repeated. "And Julia, and Mom and Dad, and everyone else who's been taking care of me for as long as I can remember. I'm twenty-six years old. I need to be on my own."

"But to move to Arizona," Cam argued. "Isn't that a bit extreme? If you have to move, why can't you stay in Massachusetts or at least in this time zone?"

"Because Sally Jenkins, the teacher I'm swapping positions with, lives in Copper Creek, Arizona," Cat replied.

"I don't like it." Cam frowned. "I mean what kind of school system hires a teacher they've never even seen?"

"The kind of school that has all of my records and that has interviewed both me and my principal over the phone," Cat answered, putting down her lemonade and taping up the box.

"Why do you have to drive? Why can't you fly there and have your things shipped?" he asked.

"Because I have never been out of New England," Cat explained for the umpteenth time—no longer as patient as she'd just been. "This is my chance to see the country. How could I pass it up?"

"Well, can't you find someone to go with you?" Cam asked desperately. "Julia and I were talking, and we thought maybe you could take a friend."

"Cameron," Cat groaned in exasperation. Honestly, he could be such an old woman at times. "Don't you understand? I don't want to take anyone with me. This is my chance to prove I can take care of myself. Besides I won't be alone, I'll have Lucy with me."

"That puppy? Be serious. If a burglar broke in, she'd probably hold the flashlight for him." Cam picked up the box she'd finished taping and piled it with the others. "Catherine, you need someone to take care of you."

"No, I don't," she argued, resisting the urge to tape his mouth shut.

"Do you want me to list the reasons?"

"No, I..."

"You're a lousy judge of character, you're naive, gullible, entirely too trusting, and you have a horrible sense of direction."

"I am not, and I do not," Cat argued through clenched teeth.

"Was it or was it not you who befriended an ex-con and ended up driving the getaway car when he held up a convenience store?"

"I was sixteen, and he seemed like a nice old man. It could have happened to anyone," she protested.

"And when we went camping for the weekend, were you or were you not the one who got lost in the woods for six hours while looking for firewood?"

"I was eight, and I was not lost. I just took the scenic route," she huffed.

"Baloney. You could get lost in your own bathroom." Cam waved his arms impatiently. "And now you want to drive across the country. You're giving me an ulcer."

"Consider it a goodbye present."

"Not funny."

Cat took in her brother's distressed appearance and felt a chuckle bubble to the surface. His sandy brown hair stood on end, his hazel eyes were wide with worry, and his mouth wore the wobbly line of a man who knew he wasn't going to get his way and didn't know what to do about it.

Cat's chuckle burst forth, and she wrapped her brother in an enormous bear hug. Not an easy task as he was twice her size. He'd been her chief tormentor and protector since the day she was born. It broke her heart to leave him, but she knew this was something she had to do.

"Have I ever told you you're the best big brother a girl could ever have?"

"Yeah, right," he muttered, hugging her in return. "That's why you're leaving."

"I love you, you know," she said.

"I love you, too, Sis," he sighed in defeat.

CAT EXAMINED her small Cape-Cod-style house, satisfied that it would pass even the fussiest housekeeper's inspection. She wanted Sally to feel at home when she arrived, so she left most of her knickknacks out, packing away only the most fragile and sentimental of mementos.

Despite the nonchalance Cat adopted with her family, she was frightened by the prospect of leaving everything and everyone she'd ever known. Frightened being the understatement of the century. She was freaking out!

But she forced herself to breathe and discovered that with the anxiety, there was also a giddy sense of excitement. To strike out on her own, like a real pioneer, and travel west. Was there any greater adventure to be had? Of course, her covered wagon was a rented van with emergency road service.

Still, she was following the path of millions of settlers before her. If they could do it then, surely, she could handle it now.

Or so she tried to convince her worried family. She'd spent the weekend with her parents at their house on Cape Cod. They weren't happy. They'd even managed to make Cam's henpecking seem negligible by comparison.

Tonight she was going to Cam and Julia's for dinner. She knew it was going to be just as difficult. Flash flood warnings would probably be issued for the outlying area if she began to cry again.

"Come on, Lucy," she called to her black Standard Poodle puppy, who was gnawing on one of her old sneakers. "We have one more goodbye to make."

Cameron's house was across town from Cat's. A white ranch house, it sat back in the woods secluded from both the road and neighbors. Cat braked the car and hopped out with Lucy in tow. Not bothering to knock, she bounded through their front door.

"Hello. Anybody home?" she called, wandering through the foyer and into the living room.

Lucy leapt ahead of her, looking for a treat. As Cat rounded the corner into the kitchen, she saw Julia sneaking the puppy a fat slice of bologna.

"What's Lucy going to do without you to spoil her?" Cat asked as she hugged her sister-in-law.

"As if you don't." Julia hugged her in return and eyed her expectantly. "Tomorrow's the big day. Are you ready?"

"As I'll ever be." Cat laughed, dropping onto a stool beside the counter. "What can I do to help with dinner?"

"Nothing." Julia tossed her thick, black hair off her shoulder and waved for Cat to stay put. "Cam's out grilling the steaks and everything else is just about finished."

"Julia, do you think I'm doing the right thing?" Cat asked, knowing she could trust Julia, not just her sister-in-law but also her friend, to give her a truthful answer.

"Yes." Julia's tobacco-brown gaze met hers. "You're going to have the most incredible adventure. I envy you. If we weren't settled in this house, which I love dearly, I'd want to do what you're doing."

"Really?"

"Yes," Julia answered, mixing her pasta salad. "But

don't tell your brother I said that. He's going to miss you and so will I."

"I know," Cat answered, feeling a lump well in her throat. "I'll miss you both, too."

"Julia, is she here yet?" Cam's voice boomed from the other room.

"Yes, I'm here," Cat answered for her sister-in-law and left her seat to go hug her brother. "You didn't think I'd stand you up, did you?"

"No, but I was afraid you might get lost," he teased, wrapping an arm around her shoulders. "Catherine, there's someone I want you to meet."

He steered her toward the porch, and Cat caught a glimpse of the man silently stepping through the open door. He was tall and broad with the kind of frame no woman could ignore. Hours in the sun had left their mark upon him with darkened skin and a thick thatch of sun-bleached, blond hair that disreputably dusted his forehead.

When his brazen, blue gaze and cocksure smile focused on her, Cat felt a nervous flutter start in her belly and shimmer all the way to her fingertips. Jared McLean! She hadn't seen him since Cam and Julia's wedding five years ago. He was even more devastating than she remembered. Much like the first time she'd met him, her mind went blank and her tongue went numb.

When he clasped her hand in his larger one, she felt his callused palm rub against her own. His grip was firm but gentle. Cat quickly removed her hand, before it started to sweat.

"Cat, you remember my college roommate, Jared?" Cam asked. "Did you know he lives near Copper Creek?"

Jared's smile was pure devil, and Cat felt a tingle start at the base of her spine. He was the kind of man your mother warned you about and with good reason. Common sense and Jared McLean were not likely to appear in the same place at the same time.

"Nice to see you again." Jared's voice was as deep as a gravel pit and just as treacherous. "I hear we're about to become neighbors."

Cat licked her dry lips and tried not to sound as breathless as she felt. "Yes, I'm leaving for Arizona tomorrow."

"Really?" His disturbing voice drawled, making her insides spasm. "I'm heading back myself in a day or two."

"How are you getting back?" Cam asked him innocently. Too innocently.

"I haven't made any formal plans as yet," Jared answered.

"Maybe you could drive out with Cat," Cam suggested with a wide-eyed glance from Jared to Cat. "What do you think, Sis?"

Cat ripped her gaze away from Jared and eyed her brother through narrowed lids. "I think I want to talk to you, Cameron. On the porch. Right now!"

Cat disengaged her brother's arm and stalked to the porch. As soon as Cam shut the door behind him, she crossed her arms over her chest and began her interrogation.

"What are you up to?"

"What do you mean?" Cam blinked.

"I may be naive, Cameron, but do you really think I'm stupid?" she sputtered furiously. "Do you really expect me to believe this old chum of yours, who lives in Arizona, just happened to be here the night before I leave on my trip?"

"But it's true," Cameron protested. "Jared comes to New England every summer to escape the desert heat. He has a cabin up in Maine, and he always stops by for a visit."

"Then how come I've never seen him on one of his 'visits' before?"

"You were always with Matthew, you never had the time."

"Oh."

"I swear." Cam raised his right hand in a mock pledge. "This is a total coincidence."

"And I suppose it's coincidence that he lives near Copper Creek?" Cat glared at her sibling, unwilling to let him off too easily.

"His family has a place halfway between Copper Creek and Phoenix."

"It's mighty suspicious." Cat frowned.

"Would I lie to you?" Cam asked.

"Are you kidding? Aren't you the one who convinced me I could fly off the garage roof if I flapped hard enough?" Cat retorted.

"Hey! I signed your cast and said I was sorry. Jeez, that was twenty years ago, don't you forget anything?"

"No." She resumed her chastising. "If this is a coincidence, then why are you trying to pair us up for my trip out to Copper Creek?"

"It just seemed like a good idea." Cameron shrugged. "Hey, if you don't want to carpool, I'm sure Mother Nature will understand. And just because Jared seldom has enough money to buy a plane ticket, that's no reason for you to give him a ride. I'm sure he'll be fine if he hitchhikes as usual."

"Hitchhikes?" She frowned.

"Yeah, Jared likes to live on the edge," Cam explained. "Now, me, I wouldn't be able to handle that. Never knowing if the next car that picks you up is some psycho, just waiting to make you the highlight of the evening news. Nope, I couldn't do it. But that's just me."

Cat bit her lip and frowned.

CAMERON WATCHED THE CONCERN flit across her face. He hated lying to her, but it was for her own good. He knew his sister well enough to know she was incapable of abandoning a stray. So, if he had to lie to get her to adopt Jared, like she'd adopted that dog of hers, well, that was a small price to pay to insure her safety.

Jared was the most honorable man he'd ever known. Cameron knew he could trust him with his sister. In fact, there was no other man of his acquaintance who he would trust with his sister.

She didn't need to know that Jared was as poor as Queen Elizabeth and about as likely to hitchhike. If Cat fell for this line, there was no telling what a professional con artist could do to her. Nope, even if she was mad at him until she was sixty-five, he was going to con her into taking protection. Protection that answered to the name of Jared McLean.

"I'm sorry I doubted you." Cat said. "Of course I'll give your friend a lift to Arizona. I've waited this long to be on my own, I don't suppose another week will kill me."

Cameron felt a pang of guilt, but he shrugged it off as a necessity to achieve the greater good. A woman shouldn't drive three thousand miles across the country alone, especially one who believed the pile of bull he'd just shoveled her.

"Thanks, Cat. I'm sure Jared's going to appreciate it." Cam turned to the grill and loaded the steaks onto a platter. Leading the way into the house, he called, "Let's eat!"

CAT STOOD ON THE DECK, watching dusk envelop the trees surrounding the house. The crickets were tuned up and blaring their nightly symphony, while the moths waltzed around the yellow porch light.

"I wonder if Arizona is like this in the evening?" she mused.

"In some ways it is," Jared answered from where he sat in a lawn chair, studying her.

"Oh!" She started and a becoming blush flooded her cheeks. "I thought I was alone."

Jared glanced over her. He'd met her once before at

Cam's wedding, but his memory was obviously playing tricks on him. He remembered her as quiet and awkward. The one time he'd tried to speak with her, she'd squeaked like a mouse and run. She didn't look or sound like a mouse now.

Her disobedient hair shunned the clip she tried to tame it with and framed her face with winsome curls, a pale brown with streaks of gold and copper. Her eyes were just as mysterious. Not blue or green or gray, but a kaleidoscope of all three, and they were enormous. Her elfin face sported a pointy chin and a delicate nose, making her large eyes all the more startling.

She sighed, and Jared's gaze was drawn to her body. From the small but curvy proportions that filled her tank top to the slender legs that tapered from her shorts, she was much more well-rounded than he'd remembered.

She had the face of an innocent, but the body of a temptress. She was the kind of woman who could blend charm with sensuality, never knowing she had either.

And he was supposed to be stuck with her in a rented van for the next week? Heaven help him, he had a feeling this was going to be the longest trip of his life.

When he'd agreed to do this favor, he'd been under the misconception that he'd be baby-sitting a nerdy, absent-minded professor type. Cameron obviously suffered from the brotherly disorder of not seeing his sister as a strikingly attractive woman.

Jared understood. He had a sister of his own. But this was not his sister, and the response she kindled within him was anything but brotherly.

She sat beside him, sitting on the edge of the chair as if uncertain of her safety within such close proximity to him. Smart girl. The scent of her faintly floral perfume lingered in the air between them, teasing him.

"Cam told me that you intend to hitchhike home," she

began, her voice softly chastising. "That's not a wise thing to do."

"He told you..." Jared shook his head in disbelief. He had a feeling Cameron Levery was going to owe him one after this. "I...uh...of course, you're right."

"That's why I think it would be a good idea if you drove out west with me," she offered.

"Is that an invitation?" he asked, amused by her matronly disapproval.

"Yes, it is," she assured him.

"I'd be happy to make the trip with you," Jared lied. He would just think of her as a surrogate little sister, he told himself. That should cure any attraction he might feel for her. Absolutely.

A gnawing sound drew her gaze from his.

"Lucy?" she called to the puppy at the end of the deck. "What have you got? Lucy?"

The puppy turned her back to them and continued chewing, but not before Jared recognized the object.

"Hey, that's my sneaker!" he shouted and jumped from his chair.

"Lucy!" Cat scolded as she approached the dog. "Drop it."

The black fur ball just looked at them and wagged her tail. Cat snatched the sneaker and handed it to Jared.

"Bad dog," Cat scolded. "Bad."

Lucy cocked her head and licked Cat's hand. Jared didn't think she looked a bit remorseful.

"She didn't do any damage, did she?" she asked.

Jared slid the sneaker onto his bare foot. He looked down and saw his big toe staring back up at him.

"Oh, I am so sorry," Cat said. "I'll buy you a new pair."

"Don't worry about it." He shrugged and resumed his seat. "They were old."

"No, I insist," Cat said. "It's the least I can do." Her

little black puppy followed her, collapsed onto her Keds and began snoring.

Glancing down at the furry bundle draped across her feet, he asked, "Is she going with us, too?"

Her gaze followed his, and she smiled. "I hope you like dogs."

Jared was more of a horse man, but Cat looked so cute with her big eyes, he had to lie. "Sure."

He reached down to scratch the dog's ears and was distracted by the soft puppy fur that covered the little head. He was gentle, stroking the puppy's forehead with his thumb. A large, jaw-popping yawn was his only reward.

"Do you know what route you want to take?" he asked.

"I had a travel agency draw up a plan for me," she said. "I then created a whole system devised on color-coded index cards—places to stop to eat, where to get a hotel, alternate routes in case of construction, that sort of thing. I know exactly how many miles we have to go each day in order to make good time."

"Make good time?" he asked.

"Yes, school starts in two weeks and I have to be there. What? Is something wrong?"

"No, it's just that all of that planning sort of takes all of the sport out of it."

"Sport?" she asked. "I'm uprooting my entire life. That's more than enough sport for me."

She blew out an exasperated breath and Jared was intrigued by the way her lips pursed. She had a great mouth. Her upper lip curved toward the center in a pouty line. It was an invitation to tease. Her lower lip was full and defined, looking like it might melt under too much pressure. It was an invitation to taste. The desire to kiss her was as unwelcome as it was unexpected. Jared choked it down with a sip of iced tea.

Thoughts like that weren't going to make the next week any easier. He had to remember that he'd promised Cameron that he'd take care of Cat. It was a promise between friends, and Jared respected the unspoken guy code that stated friends' sisters are off-limits. He knew he'd kick any friend's butt who made a move on his sister. He suspected if Cameron had any idea that his thoughts were traveling this path, Cameron would call the whole thing off and ship Cat to the nearest convent.

"Have you lived in Arizona all of your life?" Cat asked him.

"No," he answered, watching as she twisted a thin gold bracelet around her wrist.

When he didn't elaborate, she cast him a look that screamed frustration. She'd been probing him about his life since before dinner. Jared didn't talk about his life. It wasn't that he had anything to hide, he just didn't talk about it. He knew his silence made her uncomfortable, and he felt bad about that, but he couldn't break the patterns of a lifetime just to put her at ease.

"What time would be good for you to leave tomorrow?" she asked. "That is if leaving tomorrow is okay with you? I'd like to leave tomorrow, because, you know, it's a long drive, and we'll have to stop frequently for the dog. Because she is a dog and well, they need to be walked, and I—"

"Cat!" Jared cut her off before she made him dizzy, but softened his tone, "I can be ready whenever you are."

"Oh, good," she sighed.

"Now, just hold up," Cam said as he and Julia walked out onto the porch, each carrying a tray of dessert and coffee. "We were counting on having breakfast with you."

"Cam, I really think I…we…should make an early start," Cat said.

"I want to check over the van and make sure you have all of your maps and such in order," Cam insisted.

"I checked through it and everything seems fine," she said.

Cam eyed her repressively. "We'll go over it tomorrow."

Cat shrugged helplessly at Jared and smiled at her brother. "If it'll make you feel better then all right."

Jared replaced his iced tea with a steaming cup of coffee and a fat slice of apple pie. The exchange between brother and sister was enlightening to say the least. It seemed Cat wasn't a scatterbrain but a pushover.

Jared knew Cameron Levery was a compulsive worrier when it came to those he cared about. After all, he had nagged Jared through four years of college. It was one of the reasons Jared trusted him, and Jared seldom trusted anyone.

He could appreciate his friend's concern for his sister. His own sister, Jessica, had caused him endless worry at times. But where Jessica would tell him to shove off when his concern became too stifling, he suspected Cat would rather cut off her left arm than risk hurting anyone she cared for by a show of independence.

He watched Cat as she closed her eyes and chewed a bite of pie. She moaned a guttural purr in her throat. Jared dropped his fork onto his plate. He'd never met a woman who moaned when she ate. He felt the tips of his ears grow hot, and he cursed the loyalty that brought him here.

The need to be on his ranch, surrounded by nothing but horses, was tempting enough to make him debate running away. Unfortunately, running away seemed like the coward's way out and Jared was no coward. With a silent curse, he retrieved his fork and dug into his pie.

CAT DRAGGED HERSELF OUT OF BED before the sun had a chance to lighten the horizon. Second thoughts had chased away any chance she'd had of a decent night's sleep. With the bags beneath her eyes weighing in at a pound each, she stumbled for the coffeepot.

As soon as the coffee started to drip, she began to revive.

With her eyes focused and brain beginning to function, she could feel a pair of soft baby browns boring into her with anticipation.

"Oh, all right," she agreed, walking over to the kitchen door where Lucy sat thumping her tail.

She opened the back door, and Lucy bounded out, her nose pressed close to the ground. Cat watched in amusement as Lucy tracked all of the various scents, never wandering far from Cat's side.

The morning air was already thick with humidity, leaving everything feeling weighted down and wet. Even the short, cotton nightshirt she wore felt oppressive and damp.

Lucy dashed across the yard to retrieve her favorite toy, a red rubber ball. Clamping it between her teeth, she trotted back, dropping it at Cat's feet. She barked and danced around, waiting for Cat to throw it.

"Okay," Cat sighed, forcing her sleep-deprived muscles to bend. Scooping up the ball, she tossed it overhand down the path toward the lake.

She'd miss the lake, she realized as she began to follow the path. She'd miss her walks along its banks and her evenings of contemplation, spent under the old maple tree on the shore, her feet dangling in the water's cool depths.

Cat laughed when Lucy, clutching the ball in her teeth, splashed into the lake. She couldn't blame her. The summer heat was already coating her skin with a sticky sheen of perspiration.

"Come on, Lucy." She clapped to draw her in. The puppy gazed at her with big brown eyes. "Come here, Lucy."

As if trying to bark around the ball in her mouth, Lucy jerked her head back. The ball hit the water with a plunk. Lucy barked at it bobbing gently.

"Get it, Lucy." She pointed and Lucy barked. "It's your favorite toy, if you want it, you'd better go get it."

The red ball began to drift farther out into the lake. Lucy

barked and leapt for the shore, shaking water all over Cat and gazing at her with pleading brown eyes.

"I don't believe this. You're a water dog, you're supposed to like to swim," she scolded the puppy. Lucy thumped her tail and whined. "Oh, all right, I'll go get your stupid ball."

JARED LEFT his borrowed car and followed the sound of the barking. Cat had been determined to get an early start, and he couldn't agree more. The sooner they left the sooner they landed in Arizona. And, frankly, after a restless night's sleep caused by big eyes and a pointy chin, he was more than ready to have this trip over and done with.

He reached the path, and a soggy puppy immediately pounced on him, looking for affection.

"Where's your owner, girl?" he asked, squatting to scratch the downy head. As if in understanding, Lucy barked at him and raced back to the water's edge.

Cat was waist-deep in the lake with her back to him, but the water carried the sound of her voice, and Jared heard her muttering about a "stupid red ball" and "no Milk-Bones for you."

"That's all right," he assured her. "I prefer eggs for breakfast."

Cat whirled about at the sound of his voice and let out a horrified wail. She flailed her arms as if trying to chase away a bee and, even as Jared was registering the problem, she hit the water with a splash and disappeared from sight.

"Cat!" he yelled and Lucy barked.

Before he could panic, Cat shot up from the water as if she'd been launched and howled, "Ah! That's cold!"

Jared couldn't help himself. He tightened his lips, looked away, trying to keep his laughter from escaping, but it just came out his nose in a chorus of snorts. He glanced back at Cat and saw her blow a soggy strand of hair out of her face. Her lips curled with annoyed disgust, and Jared turned his head away, trying desperately to suppress the hoots and howls that shook his shoulders.

"Ha ha, very funny!" Cat sniped, letting him know he hadn't fooled her. "What are you doing here anyway?"

Her cotton nightie clung to her curves, and she tried to cover herself by crossing her arms. An embarrassed flush stained her cheeks a lovely shade of pink, and her eyes darted to the bushes as if debating the feasibility of hiding amongst their leafy limbs.

Jared could have told her not to bother. Instead, he fastened his attention on the puppy at his feet and forced his chuckles to cease and desist. "I thought you might need a hand getting ready this morning, so I came over early."

"Well, you could do me one favor." Her voice was a tart blend of shy embarrassment and chagrin.

"What's that?" he asked, his gaze fixed on the dog.

"Could you go get my robe?" she asked. "It's hanging on the back of the bathroom door."

Jared glanced up. She stood hip deep in the water, unable to come any closer to shore. He could only imagine why. Swallowing to moisten his parched throat, he said, "Sure."

He got no more than four steps away when he was hit in the rear by what felt like a rock.

"Ow!" Spinning around, he glanced down and saw a red rubber ball rolling on the ground. Lucy pounced on it, and Jared glanced up to see Cat blinking at him. She looked as innocent as a kid standing next to a broken window, holding a slingshot.

"It's the first door on the left at the top of the stairs," she instructed.

Rubbing the sore spot on his rear end, Jared turned and marched toward the house with a grin parting his lips and Lucy racing around his feet.

IT TOOK THE BETTER PART of the morning for Cat and Jared to convince Cameron they were ready to go. Cat's house had been gone through and locked up, the van was examined and found to be in order, and the route was double- and triple-checked. Lastly, the "AZ or Bust" sign was hung on the back of the van. It was time to go.

Cat handed Cam the keys to her house and her car. "Please give these to Sally and be nice to her. She doesn't know anyone here, and she'll need some friends."

"I will," Cameron promised.

Cat felt the lump in her throat swell until she couldn't speak, and the tears behind her eyes burned with the need for release. Her brother, despite his henpecking ways, was her best friend. She relied upon his unconditional love to give her strength during the hard times and laughter during the good times.

"What am I going to do without you?" she whispered. Before she could stiffen her upper lip, she felt her face crumple. Hugging her brother close, she felt all of her uncertainty shudder through her. And much to her dismay, she bawled.

2

———————

"ARE YOU GOING to be all right?" Jared asked the sobbing woman seated beside him in the van. He could barely see her behind the wad of tissue she clutched to her face.

"F-f-fine." She sniffed.

"Is there anything I can do to help?" he asked.

"No." Cat waved a tissue at him. "I'm fine. I'm just not very good at goodbyes."

"No kidding?" he asked, relieved to see a watery smile brighten her blotchy face and red rimmed eyes. "I was beginning to think there wouldn't be enough left of you to soak up with a sponge."

"That bad?" She grimaced and stroked Lucy's soft head where it rested in her lap.

"Yeah." Jared nodded. "I'd say it's about the worst display of tears I've seen since Lassie left home."

"Sorry." She bit her lip and studied his profile warily. "I'm not usually such a sniveler."

"Don't be sorry. Maybe if more people were capable of sharing their feelings, the world wouldn't be such a mess."

"That or we'd all be walking around in hip waders," she joked.

Jared smiled, relieved to see she'd recovered her sense of humor. She was quite a woman. He knew it would be years before the vision of her saying goodbye to her brother would fade from his memory.

Wrapped in Cameron's arms, she'd wept into his shirt as though the anguish of being parted from her loved ones was just too much for her to bear. Julia had broken down and cried while Cam had remained stoic, although his lips had wavered a bit. Jared had been surprised to find his own eyes dampened at the sight.

Her sobs had ripped into him, and he was sure he'd never heard a more forlorn sound in his entire life. One thing was certain, no one could accuse the woman beside him of lacking feeling.

"Where are we anyway?" Cat asked, glancing out the window at the highway that stretched before them.

"We're nearing the New York border," he said.

"That's it? We're already behind schedule," Cat fretted. "I had this all planned out." She reached into the glove box and pulled out a set of colored index cards. "Oh, this is not good."

"What?" Jared asked, trying to read the card over her shoulder.

"Twelve o'clock," she read. "Twenty-minute stop for lunch. And if we're not even at the border, then we can't use the rest stop I'd planned. Well, that obviously needs to be revised."

"You're kidding, right?" he asked.

"Kidding about what?"

"Kidding about being behind schedule and designated rest stops."

"No, I'm not kidding," she said. "Organization is the key to any large undertaking."

"No, flexibility is the key," Jared disagreed.

"I'm flexible," she said.

"No, you're a control freak," he said.

"I am not," she said. "I just like order."

"Life isn't a lesson plan, Teach," he said. "You have to learn to relax."

"I am relaxed," she argued.

"We'll make it to Arizona in plenty of time," Jared promised.

"Well, goodness knows, stimulating conversation certainly won't get in the way of making good time," she chided him.

Jared raised an eyebrow and glanced at her, but said nothing.

An awkward silence settled between them, leaving Cat to wonder if he'd even grasped the insult she'd tossed him. She let her gaze drift to his hands where they gripped the steering wheel at two and ten. She could see the prominent blue veins on the backs of his hands that flowed in between his square knuckles. His fists were tanned and weathered from long hours of hard work. His fingers held the steering wheel loosely, but with total control.

She imagined that was how the mysterious Jared McLean lived his life. In total control, but always on the fringe. Never in the center of the turmoil. She'd noticed during the past twenty-four hours that Jared was not a talker. He was a watcher. He discussed neutral topics, but any questions directed at his personal life were sidestepped, deflected or ignored. Boy, did his aloofness bug her. Every conversation was a one-way street to nowhere.

A wet lick across her palm jarred her from her thoughts, and she glanced at the wriggling puppy in her lap. Lucy was full of energy from her long nap, and Cat dutifully rolled down her window to let Lucy stick her head out, while keeping a firm grip on her collar.

"I think somebody has to make a pit stop," she called to Jared over the noise of the open window.

Jared glanced at the tail gleefully pounding his shoulder and back at Cat. "There's a rest stop coming up in a few miles. We can probably run her around there."

Cat nodded and turned her attention back to Lucy. Her ears were flapping in the breeze, her mouth was open and her tongue was hanging out as if she were laughing. What a knucklehead, she thought, feeling a rush of tenderness for her baby.

The rest stop was crowded with campers and station wagons. Noisy children chased each other in the summer heat while their parents reclined in the shade.

Clipping Lucy's leash, Cat climbed down from the van. Jared grabbed the cooler Julia had packed for them and led the way to a large patch of shade beneath a nearby tree.

The late afternoon air was sticky with humidity, and the grass they sat upon clung to their skin. Lucy lapped greedily at the water Cat put in her bowl.

"Sit, Lucy," Cat ordered as she pulled a bag of dog treats out of the cooler. "Let's practice your new trick."

Cat knelt in front of Lucy and raised her right hand.

"High five, Lucy," she said. "High five."

Lucy patted her paw against Cat's hand.

"Good girl," Cat said and rubbed her ears. "Good girl."

Lucy scarfed her treat and flopped onto the cool grass with her chew toy. Cat glanced up and found Jared watching her.

"Isn't she smart?" she asked.

"Not bad for a sissy dog," he agreed.

"Sissy dog?" Cat protested.

"Well, she is a poodle," he said.

"A Standard Poodle," Cat corrected. "They're special."

"Hmm," Jared grunted and handed her an ice-cold pop and a fat turkey sandwich. Cat peeked into the contents of the cooler. Julia was a wonder. There was enough food in there to last them three days.

"My brother has excellent taste in wives, don't you think?" she asked.

"No doubt about it, he's a lucky man," Jared agreed, taking a healthy bite out of his sandwich.

"How come you aren't married?" she asked, curiosity beating out good sense.

"How do you know I'm not married?"

"No ring."

"So?" he challenged her.

"What kind of wife would let her husband hitchhike across the country?" Cat asked in exasperation. "Or, for that matter, let him drive three thousand miles with another woman?"

"Are you planning on eating sometime today?" Jared eyed the sandwich in her hand.

"I was just asking." She shrugged. "You're not very open about yourself, are you?"

"No," he answered between mouthfuls.

"Why?" she persisted.

"Eat," he ordered and nudged her sandwich up against her lips.

Cat frowned, bewildered by his reticence and more curious than ever. She couldn't help it. His silence intrigued her. He kept everyone at arm's length—even Cameron.

She bit into her sandwich and continued to ponder her traveling companion. During the past twenty-four hours, she hadn't learned one tangible fact about him. She didn't know anything about him, really, except that he was an old friend of Cameron's and he lived in Arizona.

Cat watched Jared take up Lucy's leash and walk her toward a copse of trees on the other side of the rest stop. She smiled at the unlikely pair as they were accosted by a group of children. Lucy was in her glory. Flopping onto the ground, with her belly in the air, she couldn't get enough of the small hands eager to pet her. To Cat's surprise, she saw Jared doing the high five-trick with Lucy. The kids were amazed and took turns trying it as well.

The quiet giant soon had a gaggle of children tugging on his arms and clinging to his legs. He looked like a big, blond tree that had sprouted children. She chuckled as he tried, to no avail, to disentangle himself from his fan club. It wasn't until their mothers called them that the children reluctantly left their new friends. Cat tried to hide her laughter by repacking the cooler as Jared and Lucy returned.

"What are you laughing at?" a deep voice growled in her ear.

"Me? Laughing?" Cat turned to find her face just inches from his. She felt her smile collapse as her pulse pounded in her ears. Those dimples of his were surely lethal.

"Yes, you." His voice dropped to a whisper as if he, too, was disturbed by their close proximity.

A cold nose and slurping tongue was thrust between them, and they both reared back when a wiggling Lucy tried to kiss them at the same time.

"Yuck! Dog germs," Jared teased, wiping his face with the back of his hand.

"My dog does not have germs," Cat retorted with mock pique. "Come along, Lucy. Let's wait for him in the van."

Jared watched as she strode back to the van with her nose turned up in the air. The curve of her lips gave her away, and he found it difficult not to laugh. Except this was no laughing matter, he'd come dangerously close to kissing her and this was just their first day out.

She was his best friend's sister. He wasn't supposed to want to kiss her. He tried to think of what he'd done recently to deserve this sort of torture, but nothing of this magnitude came to mind. He watched her settle the puppy into the van.

Her curly hair shone golden in the sun as it escaped the ponytail she'd tried to force it into. The formfitting white tank top and denim shorts she wore left enough of her skin visible to distract a monk. He sighed.

He wasn't surprised she'd asked him again about his personal life, only that it had taken her so long. She was, he noted, curious by nature. Like her brother, she was a meddler, a well-intentioned do-gooder who wanted happiness for those around her.

If he searched the whole world over, Jared knew he'd never find anyone more his polar opposite. He didn't share his feelings, secrets, fears or pain with anyone. He'd learned early on that to care was to be hurt. People could be ripped out of your life in a heartbeat. It just wasn't wise to care too much, because you never knew when someone would be taken away. Jared wasn't interested in that kind of pain.

Cat probably wouldn't be happy until a man bared his soul to her. Jared would never be able to do that. Sometimes it was best to know when to beat a hasty retreat. He'd deliver her to her job in Arizona, but that was it. He wasn't going to talk to her, touch her or care for her. And he was definitely going to stop picturing her as she'd looked this morning, with her sodden hair pushed back from her face, her soaked cotton nightgown clinging to curves she'd tried to hide with her arms, and stray droplets of water running down her skin like so many fingers. Yeah, he was definitely going to stop picturing her like that.

With the desperate resolve of a man trying to hold back the tide with his hands, Jared strode toward the waiting van. He replaced the cooler behind the passenger's seat and turned to find Cat studying him.

Her eyes were a pensive blue, but flecks of green were still visible. He didn't like the gleam in her gaze. It boded ill for his peace of mind and his privacy. She grinned at him, and he felt the hair on the back of his neck rise. She held out her hand, and he stiffened.

"What?" he asked.

She wiggled her fingers. "May I have the keys, please."

"What for?"

"It's my turn to drive," she answered, following him around to the driver's side.

"I don't think so." He chuckled.

"What do you mean 'you don't think so'?" she mimicked, her voice low and short with temper.

"I'm fine. I can drive the rest of the day," he explained, motioning her toward the other side of the van. Lucy watched them through the window with her head cocked to one side as if listening.

"You can't drive all day," she protested. "You'll be exhausted."

"I'm fine," he assured her.

"Well, I'm not. I want to drive," she argued.

"Too bad. I'm doing the driving on this trip," he answered, his own temper igniting at her stubbornness.

"It's my van." She glared at him. "If you weren't here, I'd be driving anyway."

"But I am here," he said and opened the driver's door. As he went to climb into the seat, she dashed behind him and wedged herself between him and the back rest.

"I'm driving!" she called out in victory.

"Catherine!" Jared unconsciously used her full name to reprimand her. "You're making a spectacle of us."

"Then let me drive," she retorted.

"If I lean back, I'm going to crush you," he threatened.

"Give it your best shot," she dared him, as if she knew he wouldn't.

"You're behaving like a two-year-old." Jared looked to his left and saw her fanny wriggling just beneath his elbow. The sight was so tempting he had to grit his teeth.

"And you're being a male chauvinist," she answered, laughing when Lucy licked her face.

"I am not. I'm just being practical."

"Practical?" She peeked at him from beneath his right arm.

"Your brother told me how you drive," he answered.

"Cam's just sore because I'm a better driver than he is," she informed him and puffed out her lower lip to blow a wayward curl out of her eyes.

"Uh-huh," he answered dubiously.

"Oh, come on, let me drive," she pleaded, looking squashed between him and the seat. With her big eyes and pointy chin, she appeared so eager and earnest, Jared felt himself begin to cave. Rats!

"On one condition," he answered, trying to sound stern. "You obey all of the traffic signs and drive the speed limit."

"Of course, I will," she snorted in disgust. "Sheesh, you make it sound like I've never driven before."

"Have you ever driven anything this big before?"

"Well, no, but I'm anxious to try it." She beamed at him.

Terrific. On top of being a meddler, she was a daredevil, too. Was any man ever so cursed? Jared slipped from the driver's seat and walked around the van. If she did one thing, just one thing, wrong he was going to take over.

Cat winked at him as he slid into the passenger's seat. "Now, was that so tough?"

He glared at her.

A bang from the back of the van sounded, and they both started.

"I haven't even started the engine yet." Cat raised her hands in innocence.

"I'll check it out," Jared offered. He disappeared and Cat adjusted her mirrors and tightened her seat belt.

"Something must have shifted," he said as he climbed back into the van. "I think it was that purple box back there."

"What purple box?" Cat asked. "I didn't pack a purple box. Are you sure it was purple?"

"Yes, I'm sure," he said. "It was purple."

"But I don't remember packing a purple box," Cat said. "What size was it?"

"I don't know," he said. "Smaller than a bread box, bigger than a shoe box."

"Are you sure it wasn't blue?" she asked.

"I think I can identify the color purple when I see it," he drawled. "Come on, we're burning daylight here. Let's go."

"But I'm sure I didn't pack a purple box," Cat said. "Maybe I should go look at it."

"Too late," Jared said. "I stuffed it in another box for safekeeping. Besides it's probably a present from Cam and Julia that you're not supposed to find until you get to Arizona."

"Oh, I wonder what it is," Cat mused. "I love presents."

"Well then how about you give me the present of getting this van in motion?" Jared asked.

"Fine, you big spoilsport."

"Hey, I'm just trying to maintain your schedule," he said. "We wouldn't want to fall behind, now would we?"

"Hmm." Cat switched on the ignition and pulled out of their parking spot. The van was bigger than anything she'd ever driven before, and contrary to her blithe appearance she was a teensy bit nervous. The large steering wheel wobbled in her hands, but determined not to lose face, she patted the puppy on the head and cruised down the on-ramp.

Once she'd merged with the westbound traffic, Cat cast a swift glance at Jared and sighed with feminine appreciation at the way his Levi's clung to his lean hips and his blue T-shirt stretched to accommodate the movements of his muscle-hardened shoulders. He was masculinity personified.

Too bad he had a white-knuckle grip on the edge of his

seat and his face was set in stiff lines as if he were bracing for a ride on a roller coaster. Humph! He was definitely one of those strong silent types. Well, strong was nice, but silent was boring. Cat was determined to have him gossiping like an old woman before the week was out.

They reached a motel in Pennsylvania just after nightfall. They'd caught up to the schedule Cat had mapped out. Cat's eyes were burning, her arms and legs were shaky with exhaustion, but she was pleased with the way she'd handled the van. Even Jared had relaxed his death grip on the dashboard.

The sign outside the motel blinked vacancy in red neon. Cat had never been happier to see anything in her life.

Parking just past the office, she switched off the engine and turned toward Jared and the puppy snoring loudly across his lap.

"I'll go get us a room if you'll stay with her," she offered.

"A room?" Jared repeated.

"Well, with your financial situation, I figured we'd share a room," she explained with as much tact as possible. Her budget didn't allow for two rooms and she couldn't just abandon him.

"I don't think that's such a good idea," he said. "I can sleep in the van."

"Don't be ridiculous." She waved a hand at him. "It won't cost any more for an extra person. I'll be right back."

JARED WATCHED HER GO, feeling the manacles of Cam's lie snap shut around his wrists. To tell her the truth was to expose Cameron's plot, and to perpetuate the lie was to subject himself to the torture of sleeping in close proximity to her. It was a lose-lose situation.

Thumping his head against the windowpane on his right, Jared grimaced. When and if he survived this little excursion, he was going to catch the next plane back to Massachusetts and strangle his old buddy.

The puppy in his lap began to whine as soon as Cat disappeared from sight. No amount of cajoling on Jared's part would distract the dog from her steadfast gaze on the office door. Jared reluctantly let his gaze mirror that of the dog's. Thankfully, the dog was the only one drooling.

CAT RANG THE OFFICE BELL and waited. There was no one behind the desk. She rang the bell again. No one appeared. Huffing out a frustrated sigh, she was about to pound on the bell again when a door behind the counter opened and an old man shuffled out. He was wiping his chin with a napkin. He was short and skinny and bald. He reminded Cat of a plucked chicken wearing overalls.

He squinted at her and Cat smiled. He frowned.

"Hey, mister," he said. "You only need to hit the bell once. I'm not deaf, you know."

Cat glanced behind her, There was no one else in the lobby.

"I'm sorry, sir," she said. "Do you have a room for two available?"

The old man narrowed his eyes and studied her. "Keep your shirt on, young fella. The sign said vacancy, didn't it? Of course I have a room for two."

Cat bit her cheek to keep from laughing.

"Yes, sir," she said. No one had confused her for a boy since she was four years old and insisted on dressing just like Cameron.

"We run a quiet place here," the old man said. "If you want to get drunk and bust up your room, do it some place else."

"We'll be no trouble," she promised.

"See that you aren't."

As the paperwork was processed, Cat browsed through

the motel's brochure. On the back in bold type she noticed the words NO PETS ALLOWED.

Not a rule breaker by nature, Cat almost told the man to cancel the room. But as the old codger handed her the key, Cat felt herself smile and leave. Lucy was a good dog. No one would ever know she was here.

CAT CLIMBED BACK INTO the van, and Jared noted the way she worried her lip between her teeth.

"What's wrong?" he asked.

"We have a situation," she confirmed.

"What?" Jared snapped, fearing the motel was booked solid, and they'd be forced to share one tiny single bed. He'd rather be tied to a rack.

"They don't allow pets." She frowned. "We're going to have to sneak Lucy in."

"That's all?" he asked.

"Yes, why? What did you think?"

"Nothing," he answered, feeling foolish and giddy with relief.

"How are we going to get her in there?" Cat wondered aloud as she steered the van around to the back of the motel.

"Don't worry about it," Jared reassured her as he pulled his sunglasses and baseball cap off the dashboard.

"I am worried," Cat said, switching off the engine and turning to face him. "I'm too tired to try and find another motel."

"Not to worry," he repeated as he fussed over Lucy. "Voilà."

With her poofy tail thumping against the back of the seat, Lucy tipped her head and gazed at Cat from beneath a hat brim and sunglasses as if pleased with her new attire. Cat glanced up at Jared and burst into laughter. Just the reaction he'd been hoping for.

"No one will ever suspect," he assured her.

Together they crept through the back door of the motel as stealthily as thieves. As if sensing the precariousness of her situation, Lucy stuck close to Jared until they were safely inside the room.

"We made it," Cat sighed in relief as she collapsed against their door.

"Of course," Jared said and dropped her suitcase on one bed and his duffel bag on the other.

While the dog joyously tracked every scent in the small room, an awkward silence fell between her two companions. Jared glanced about the room. He'd crashed in a lot of motel rooms in his life, but this one seemed smaller than any he remembered.

"Are you hungry?" Cat asked.

Jared's gaze snapped to hers. He was relieved to have the silence broken. "Actually, yes."

"Do you want to finish the food in the cooler or should we order out?" she asked, brushing by him to get to her suitcase.

"We passed a diner on the way in. Why don't I walk down there and get us something to eat?" Jared offered, anxious to be away from the two beds and the enticing female he was stuck with.

"You don't have to do that."

"I don't mind," he insisted.

"Well, let me give you some money."

"No," he refused. "I can handle it. Is there anything special you want?"

"Whatever you have will be fine," she said, taking Lucy's water dish into the bathroom to fill it. She paused and gazed at the bathtub with undisguised longing. Jared saw the look and inwardly groaned.

"I'll be right back," he said, in what he hoped was a discouraging tone.

CAT WATCHED THE DOOR CLOSE behind him. Jared seemed awfully tense. It was probably the long day on the road, but she wondered if it had anything to do with her. She supposed it could be the money. He hadn't been pleased when she'd footed the bill for their lodgings. Maybe if he bought dinner, he'd feel better.

She knew about men and their pride. Her former fiancé, the big dumb jerk, had plenty of pride. He used to spend five hours every Saturday cleaning and waxing his BMW. He was so proud of that car. Cat wondered how many hours of her life she'd spent buffing hubcaps and polishing the dashboard. Ugh! Letting him be the center of her world had been so foolish. She would never make that mistake again.

She unzipped her suitcase and pulled out her night clothes. Considering the close sleeping quarters, she chose summer pajamas, consisting of a navy blue cotton top and matching shorts. Conservative, but cool.

Any romantic notions she might have about Jared were obviously not going to be returned. It appeared she was the only one who'd felt a spark of awareness at the rest stop. Since then Jared had shown about as much interest in her as a woman as her brother would. Possibly even less. She didn't doubt for a second that sharing a room with him wouldn't be any more dangerous than sharing one with Cameron. And she had to admit that having a companion, especially an imposing one like Jared, made her feel safe.

"Everybody decent in here?" Jared called. He entered the room with one hand covering his eyes while the other clutched two large white bags and the room key.

"Lucy's in her birthday suit, but otherwise I think you're safe," Cat answered as she grabbed the bags from him.

"Shucks," he teased. Removing his hand from his eyes, he smiled at her. "I was hoping for better timing."

"Yeah, right." Cat shook her head at him and promptly dove into the bags of food. "What's the menu?"

"We have lasagna, garlic bread and a tossed salad," Jared answered as he helped her to unpack.

"Wonderful." Cat took the seat opposite him at the small table in front of the room's only window.

"You like lasagna?" he asked.

"Are you kidding? It's my favorite," she assured him and scooped up a forkful.

"I figured it was a solid choice," he said. "It was either that or liver and onions."

Cat chuckled. It wasn't the best lasagna she'd ever had, but when you're hungry enough to eat your shoes anything will do.

Replete with a meal in her belly, Cat eyed the puppy still tracking foreign smells in the carpet. Sleeping all day had stored up her energy. She was going to need a serious run in order to wear her out. Cat picked up her leash and called Lucy over just as Jared finished his meal.

"Where do you think you two are going?" he asked, stretching back in his chair.

"Somebody needs to get some exercise," Cat informed him over the puppy's head.

"You can't go out there alone." Jared frowned at her. "It's not safe. I'll go with you."

"What do you mean it's not safe? We're in a pokey little town in Pennsylvania. What could happen?"

"No wonder Cameron worries about you." Jared pulled the leash from her hand and led the way out the door. "Don't you watch the evening news?"

"Of course," she answered, following him into the deserted hallway and locking the door behind her.

"Then you should know that a woman alone, especially at night, is a walking target for bad guys," he chided as he hustled them out of the building only to have Lucy stop at the nearest patch of grass.

"I do realize that. That's why I have a dog."

Jared glanced at the black furball trying to yank him across the parking lot toward the woods. "She's not a dog, she's a puppy. What is she going to do? Eat the bad guy's shoes?"

"I bet she'd fight off anyone who tried to hurt me."

"Sure, she would." Jared laughed. "If she ever came out from under the bed."

Feeling her temper rise, Cat snatched the leash from his hand and stalked into the woods with Lucy at her heels.

"What kind of a name is Lucy anyway?" he continued to bait her. "That's a sissy name. You should call her something tough like Butch or Spike."

"For your information," Cat answered him in a clipped tone, "my students chose her name. We had a vote and they decided she was either a Lucy or a Wilma."

"As in Lucille Ball or Wilma Flintstone?"

"Yes, naturally, I was relieved when they chose Lucy. I just couldn't see myself yelling 'Wilma' out the front door."

"Naturally," he agreed with a snort.

His laughter didn't help her temper, and Cat had to fight the urge to kick him.

"I don't need you to protect me, you know." She spun around and glared at him while Lucy paused to sniff another tree.

"I know, you've got a dog." He rolled his eyes.

"More than that," she protested. "I've got common sense. I don't take stupid risks."

"Like walking into strange woods in the dark all alone?" he mocked her.

"I'm not alone," she ground the words between her teeth. "I'm stuck with you."

Her face felt hot and her chest heaved with suppressed anger. Shoving her hair out of her face, she glared at him. Jared's smile wavered and dimmed. His steamy blue gaze met hers and then skimmed down her body as slow and tangible as a caress. Cat gasped. This time she knew she wasn't the only one aware of the attraction snapping between them.

With a deep groan, Jared jerked his eyes away and glanced at the puppy sitting curiously between their feet.

"Look, it's late and we're both exhausted. I'm sorry if I was sarcastic," he apologized. "I don't want to fight with you."

When he glanced up, his gaze was neutral, revealing nothing but kindness. Disappointment rocked her. Had she just imagined the attraction? She shook her head. He was right. They were overtired. What were they fighting about, anyway? That a woman had to be careful in this world? Like that was news.

"I'm sorry, too," she said, following Jared out of the woods. "I guess you just sounded so much like Cameron that it got on my nerves. He's forever worrying about me. I appreciate it, but sometimes it's a bit smothering."

"Well, I'll try not to smother you." Jared grinned. "Unless, of course, you snore."

Cat caught her breath at his smile. A smile like that would be banned in Boston. It was charming and lethal and made her clothes long to fall off her body. Surely, she couldn't be imagining the spark between them. Could she?

She couldn't help but wonder, as she crept back into the motel behind him, what kind of worries had etched the tiny lines around his eyes? What painful lessons had he learned in his life that left him mum? And how could she get him to open up?

JARED EYED THE ROOM with renewed claustrophobia. He just couldn't sleep this close to a woman he'd seen practically naked. It wasn't right. Especially when the urge to share one bed was becoming increasingly tempting.

While Cat excused herself to the bathroom to change, Jared paced the room like a caged tiger. He switched on the television for distraction, but it was no use. Fearing she'd exit the bathroom in something sheer and lacy that would destroy his resolve completely, Jared yanked his bedspread off his bed and rigged it to hang like a curtain between the two beds.

It wasn't much, but it was something, he reassured himself as he sank down onto his own bed. He heard the bathroom door open and shut and felt his blood thud through his veins while he listened to Cat make her way to bed.

"This was thoughtful of you but unnecessary," she said as her mop of fiery hair and freshly scrubbed face appeared from behind the bedspread. "I'm not that modest."

Jared took in her navy pajamas while his brain flashed visions of a sodden cotton nightie, dripping in the glow of a morning sunrise. He licked his parched lips.

"Who says it's for you?" he asked, his gaze latching onto hers. The color in her eyes had deepened to reflect her navy pajamas, and they tilted up at the corners when she smiled.

"I'm sorry. I didn't realize you were shy." Her gaze roved doubtfully over his sprawled form.

"Watch that bold look of yours, lady, or you'll make me blush," he said.

"On which cheeks?" Seemingly shocked at her own words, Cat clapped a hand over her mouth.

With a laugh, Jared rolled up from the bed, took a step toward her and froze. Desire and his oath to his friend warred within him. The oath won and he spun away from her to trudge through her half of the room toward the bathroom, clutching his toothbrush in an iron fist.

Cat watched him stalk away and pondered this new piece of the puzzle that was Jared McLean. It was about as helpful as a round piece in a pile of squares. Shy her foot!

She climbed under the thin covers and waited for him to cross through the room again. He hurried by, actively trying not to look at her, or so it seemed.

She heard the rustle of his clothes as he undressed and wondered what he wore to bed. Was he a briefs or boxers man? She was betting on boxers. She glared at the bedspread he'd hung up. The creak of his bed signaled he'd climbed in.

"We have a long day ahead of us tomorrow," he said through the curtain. "We should get some shut-eye."

"All right," Cat agreed. She felt the foot of her bed dip as Lucy struggled to leap on it. She reached over and gave her a boost. "Good night, Jared."

"Good night," he answered and switched off the light, leaving the room in darkness.

Cat's eyelids drooped the moment her head landed on the pillow. It was hard and lumpy, but she didn't care. Exhaustion crept into her limbs, and her legs twitched as they relaxed. Her last conscious thought was how nice it was to have Jared nearby.

SHE WAS LOST. All around her were barren dunes of sand. They all looked the same. She uncapped her water bottle. It was empty. She was going to die of thirst. The lone cry of a coyote fractured the silence and she spun around with a start.

"Psst, Cat, wake up!"

"Huh?" Cat muttered.

"Wake up!"

Cat blinked. Jared was glaring at her from behind the makeshift curtain.

"If you don't want us to get kicked out, keep Lucy quiet."

Cat glanced at Lucy where she was sitting at the foot of

the bed. The puppy tipped back her head and began to howl.

"I thought she was a coyote," Cat said.

Jared looked at her as if she were a few sandwiches shy of a picnic.

Bang. Bang. Bang. A fist pounded on their door.

"Hey, open up in there," a man shouted.

Cat leapt from the bed. "That's the manager," she whispered to Jared. "If he sees Lucy, we'll get booted."

Jared reached for his jeans while Cat yanked down the bedspread. Lucy tipped her head back to howl again and Jared dropped his jeans and dove across the bed, dragging Cat and the bedspread with him. Down they went in a tangle of limbs and ugly motel blanket. Jared clamped a hand on Lucy's muzzle. Cat flailed her arms trying to get free of the blanket. When she did, her mouth popped open and she giggled. Jared was wearing boxers with big yellow smiley faces all over them. She knew he'd be a boxer man.

"Smiley faces?" she asked.

Jared opened his mouth to reply but was cut off by a fist banging on their door.

"What's going on in there?"

Jared let go of Lucy and finished pulling on his jeans. He helped Cat to her feet and grabbed the bedspread.

"Just go along with whatever I do," he whispered.

Cat nodded.

Jared flicked on the TV to a late-night movie. Then he tucked Lucy into the bed with her head on the pillow. He fluffed the comforter, making her look taller than she was.

"Hop into bed," Jared instructed. "Pretend you just woke up."

Cat crawled into bed beside Lucy and feigned sleep.

Jared went to answer the door. Cat watched him through her lashes. He rumpled his hair and let out a big yawn as he opened the door.

"What can I do for you?" he asked. The wiry little chicken of a manager burst past him.

"I got a call that there's a dog in here," he said. "We don't allow pets."

Cat pretended to awaken. "What's going on?" she asked.

"You're the young fella who booked the room," the old man accused. Then he squinted at Lucy. "Did you sneak a girl in here?"

Cat had her hand on Lucy's chest, keeping her still. Technically, Lucy was a girl and they had sneaked her in. She shrugged.

She heard Jared's snort, but didn't look at him for fear that she would burst out laughing.

"You need to keep a tighter rein on your boy," the manager said to Jared. "That'll be another ten dollars for the girl."

"Yes, sir." Jared fished his wallet out of his back pocket and slapped a ten into the manager's open hand.

Just then a howl sounded from the TV. The manager's head whipped around to look at the screen and Cat clamped a hand over Lucy's mouth.

"What are you watching?" the manager asked.

"Werewolf movie," Jared answered.

"Ah, so that explains it. Turn it down. I don't want to come back here tonight," the old man grumped and slammed the door behind him.

Cat and Jared each sagged with relief. Lucy leapt out from beneath the covers and licked Cat's face.

Jared began to laugh, tried to stop, looked at Cat and laughed harder.

"That old duffer thinks you're a guy," he howled. He laughed so hard Cat was afraid he'd injure himself. It wasn't that funny.

Feeling chagrined, she snapped off the lamp and pulled her covers up to her shoulders.

"Men who wear smiley-faced boxers should beware of being pantsed in public," she said.

"Huh?" Jared's laughter abruptly ended.

"You heard me," she said.

"You wouldn't," he protested.

"Keep laughing and we'll just see," she said.

A subdued Jared hung up the bedspread and switched off the TV.

"Good night...sonny boy," he said with a barely muffled chuckle.

"Good night...smiley," Cat answered with a snort.

3

JARED WANTED to blame their midnight shenanigans for his poor night's sleep, but he knew that wasn't it. It was his own fault. His own fault for agreeing to drive across country with a woman who made him laugh harder than anyone he'd ever known.

The sun was just lightening the sky when he rolled over and came nose to nose with Lucy. Her head rested on the spare pillow and her tail thumped on the mattress when his eyes met hers. Jared sighed. This was not the female he had pictured waking up with. A cold nose nuzzled his palm as soon as his feet hit the floor, and he glanced at the puppy through sore, sleep-deprived eyes.

"All right, I'll take you, but you have to be quiet," he whispered to the brown-eyed pooch.

Pulling on the jeans he'd tossed across his bed the night before, Jared stretched and tried to force the blood back into his limbs. Donning his T-shirt and sneakers with a hole in the toe, he led Lucy through the other half of the room, trying not to glance at the bed.

He failed. Cat was curled up in the fetal position with one hand supporting her chin. She looked cold. Jared pulled the remaining blanket off his bed and draped it on top of her. Her tousled hair splayed across the pillow, and her lashes nestled upon her cheeks. How the motel manager could confuse her gender was beyond Jared. She was one hundred percent Grade A female.

She looked as fragile as a buttercup, and Jared cursed

himself for the lecherous part of him that wanted to crawl into bed with her. Thinking the dog wasn't the only one who needed a leash, Jared swiftly clipped the puppy and led the way into the silent hallway. The door locked behind them, and Jared felt the tightness in his muscles ease as they left the motel in search of coffee.

JARED REENTERED THE ROOM with a steaming cup of coffee in one hand and a rambunctious puppy in the other. The room was still dark. Cat had uncurled and lay flat on her stomach. Her heart-shaped fanny was outlined by the covers, and it took all of Jared's resolve not to turn and run.

She shifted as soon as Lucy bounded up onto her bed. Jared placed the paper cup of coffee on the nightstand by her head and tried to escape before her ever-changing eyes found him. He was too late.

"Good morning," she said as she stretched beneath the covers and ruffled Lucy's ears. "Did you two have a nice walk?"

Jared glanced away from the curls that flopped over her forehead to the gaping neckline of her top, that offered him a shadowed view of her cleavage. He gulped.

"Yup," he answered and ducked behind the curtain to his side of the room. "It's time to get up. We have a lot of driving to do today."

"I know." He heard her sigh and shift in the bed. "I'm afraid I'm not a morning person."

"Really?" Jared asked, thinking of yesterday morning.

"Can I shower first?" she asked, poking her head around the curtain.

"Go ahead, but hurry. We don't want to fall behind on your schedule," he warned.

"Are you mocking me?" she asked.

"Me?" Jared blinked with innocence and then grinned.

"Oh...you," she said. "I'll be five minutes."

Jared watched her disappear into the bathroom. The attraction he felt for her was getting stronger with every moment they shared. He didn't want to know how soft she looked when she slept, or how her eyes snapped fire when she lost her temper, or how her body looked when it was next to naked.

Pulling down the makeshift curtain, he eyed the puppy, gleefully investigating his open duffel bag. "What am I going to do, Lucy?"

TWENTY MINUTES LATER, Jared and Cat entered the nearby diner freshly showered and starving. The van was packed with Lucy playing guard dog and all that was left to do was eat.

"Do you think she'll be okay in there all by herself?" Cat fretted her lower lip and glanced at the van worriedly.

"She'll be fine," Jared promised.

Jared steered Cat to a well-worn, red vinyl booth beside a large window that allowed them an unobstructed view of the van. A waitress approached them as soon as they opened their menus.

"Morning, Jared." The brunette smiled invitingly, and Cat could see where her magenta lipstick had smeared across her teeth. "Is this your wife?"

The waitress turned to smile at her, and Cat instantly regretted her unkind observation. Jared was gazing at her in amusement, and Cat felt herself blush at the waitress's spousal reference.

"We're not...that is, I'm not..."

"We're not married," Jared explained, taking pity on her.

"Oh, sorry." The waitress cast Cat a sympathetic glance and quickly turned away, muttering something about bringing them coffee.

Cat cleared her throat and said, ''I suppose it was a natural mistake.''

''Yeah,'' Jared agreed, hiding his amusement behind his menu.

That the waitress's assumption had rattled Cat so badly, that her kaleidoscope eyes were gray with guilty embarrassment, made Jared wonder if perhaps his attraction was returned in equal measure. The thought made the already warm morning grow hot. Shoot, it'd be hard enough to spend the next week resisting his own temptation, it'd be impossible for him to fend off hers.

The unhappy path of his thoughts made Jared grow silent and not a little surly. He all but growled his order to the waitress, while mentally cursing his longtime friend for getting him into this fix.

''Jared, is something wrong?'' Cat asked, breaking the strained silence that had fallen between them.

''No,'' he answered, unconsciously making his face blank.

''If you don't want to tell me, just say so.'' She glared at him. ''But at least do me the courtesy of not lying to me.''

''What are you talking about?'' He blinked.

''You aren't even aware that you do that, are you?'' she asked thoughtfully.

''Do what?'' he asked in exasperation.

''You shut down.'' Cat gestured, waving her hands in front of her face. ''It's like an impenetrable wall.''

''Have you been talking to my sister Jessica?'' he asked. ''She's forever nagging me to tell her what's going on inside me. I tell her nothing, but she never believes me.''

''So you have a sister?'' Cat smiled in triumph at the first bit of personal information he'd let slip.

''Yes, I have a sister,'' he acknowledged, trying not to laugh at the victorious glint in her eyes.

"Well, she's right. You should learn to share your feelings with people. It's not healthy to keep things bottled up."

"So, Freud, did you study psychology in college?" he teased.

"No, I didn't." She shook her head at him. "It's just common sense."

"All right, but what if the thoughts or feelings I'm having are private?" he asked. Unable to resist teasing her, he lowered his voice to a seductive murmur, "I mean, what if I'm having an incredibly hot, sweaty, erotic fantasy about a particular woman?"

CAT CHOKED ON HER COFFEE, and Jared reached across the table to thump her on the back. Slugging down some water, her gaze met his over the rim of the glass. His eyes were pure blue devil, and she longed to swat him. If he was sixty pounds lighter, she might have tried it. Still, she refused to be intimidated by the turn of the conversation.

"Trying to fluster me won't do you any good," she lectured him as sternly as she would any of her rebellious students. "You need to open up, Mr. McLean. You'll never have a completely fulfilling existence until you do."

"I like my privacy," he said in a case closed tone of voice.

When the waitress returned with their blueberry pancakes, he tucked into his food, not allowing Cat to keep up the thread of the conversation. The pancakes distracted her for a while. As she licked the last of the syrup off her fork with a hum of appreciation, she caught Jared watching her.

"What?" she asked.

"Nothing," he growled, resting his chin on his fist.

Cat mimicked his pose with a grin. She'd never been one to back down from a dare. "People tell me I'm a mighty good listener."

Scooping the check from the table before she had the chance, he rose from his seat and said, "Those people were probably badgered to death by you." He chuckled when her mouth popped open with indignation. "I don't badger so easily, lady."

Cat trailed him out of the diner with a muttered, "We'll see."

THEY AGREED to drive in shifts. Cat drove first while Jared dozed in the passenger's seat. Not wanting to wake Jared with the radio, she turned on the CB her brother had given her, keeping the volume at a low buzz. The CB remained silent, and Cat wondered if they'd ever hear any truckers.

The winding hills of Pennsylvania were intimidating, but Cat forged on, trying not to panic when the hills became steep and the oversized van had trouble chugging to the top.

Jared slept with his head slumped sideways. The sound of his deep breathing was comforting, and Cat tried not to envy Lucy's cushy seat on his lap. She was getting too big to be a lap dog, but she had yet to figure that out. She managed to curl herself into a ball small enough to fit across Jared, only her large feet poked out giving her away.

Jared had one hand wrapped around the puppy, holding her in place. He had a small smile on his lips and Cat wondered what he was dreaming about. She knew better than to ask, because he'd never tell her.

How could she break through that wall of silence? And what made her think she should be the one who tried? *Because you care for him.* She heard the voice in her head as loud as a scream.

It was true. From the moment she'd first seen him, at Cam's wedding five years ago, she'd been drawn to him. He had a gentleness about him that belied his size and strength. He was undeniably handsome, but there was a masculine energy about him that took her breath away. He was the kind of man who felt things soul deep. The kind of a man who would love only once and that love would last forever.

Now that's just pure fantasy, Levery, she chastised herself. She'd proven to be a lousy judge of character in the man department. And convincing herself that Jared was less likely to hurt her than the big dumb jerk was just asking for trouble. She should just stick to things she was good at judging, like melons in the produce department for example. Now cantaloupes, she could handle.

She felt his probing glance upon her face before he spoke. "Do you want to take a break? You've been driving all morning, and it looks like stormy weather up ahead."

"Thanks, but I'm fine." She shrugged. "It's not like I haven't driven in rain before."

As if to mock her, a huge clap of thunder boomed from above and the sky opened up with a deluge of rain as blinding as it was sudden. Cat gripped the wheel with white knuckles, determined to prove herself capable.

"Why don't you pull over?" Jared yelled over another clap of thunder. They were cruising down a steep hill that had no lane for emergency stops.

"Where?" Cat snapped, trying to see through the opaque sheets of gray water, streaming down the window, impervious to the wiper blades that beat a frantic tattoo across the glass.

They neared a sharp curve, and Cat clamped her lip between her teeth and gripped the wheel harder. She glanced at Jared. His own troubles were just beginning as Lucy, awakened by the storm, began to shiver uncontrollably with each clap of thunder. It was all Jared could do to keep the wiggling puppy from clambering into Cat's lap for comfort. Adding to the confusion, the CB crackled to life just as they began to round the bend.

"Breaker, breaker, if anybody's out there, beware of mile marker ninety-seven," an anonymous drawl filled the van. "The construction site is flooded and one vehicle has already skidded off the road."

Cat shot a wild-eyed look at Jared. "That's got to be up ahead. What do I do?"

"There's no place to pull over or turn around, you're going to have to drive through it," Jared spoke softly, as if trying to soothe her terror. "Just take a deep breath and concentrate on the road."

Flashing yellow warning lights began to blink at them from both sides of the road. The space between the concrete barriers didn't look large enough for a bicycle to pass through. The vehicle that hadn't made it through was lying on its side in the deep ravine to the right. Cat felt beads of sweat break out on her forehead. Every muscle in her body was clenched as tight as a fist.

"You're going to be fine," Jared coached her.

Cat slowed the van to a crawl. Unable to see through the blinding rain, she inched her way through the construction site while the water that filled the barriers slowly crept up the side of the van.

"The water must be covering the wheels." Cat let out a hiss. This was a trucker's route. If they stalled, they were goners, sitting ducks as the enormous trucks that rumbled along this road ran right over them.

Although it seemed like hours, in seconds it was over, and Cat steered the van onto an embankment at the end of the construction zone. Several other vehicles were parked there to wait out the remainder of the storm.

Cat put the van into Park and stepped on the emergency brake. She was shaking from the inside out. Her skin was clammy, and she felt nauseous. Jared took one look at her, unsnapped her seat belt, and pulled her into his arms, dislodging a quivering Lucy as he did so. The puppy immediately hopped into her lap and she cuddled Lucy as sweetly as Jared held her.

"That was some fancy driving there, Ace," Jared whispered against her hair. He rubbed her arms as if trying to warm her up. "I think I saw some people down by that car. Are you going to be okay if I run down and check on them?"

"I'll go with you," she volunteered between chattering teeth.

"No, stay here. I'll be right back," he ordered and placed a swift, comforting kiss on her forehead.

Cat watched him dart out into the rain and tried to pull herself together. They'd made it through the flooded road and everyone was fine. Concentrating on taking deep breaths, she felt her heart rate return to normal.

Although Jared had only been gone a few moments, it seemed like an eternity. The fogged-up windows made it impossible to see, and Cat felt panic begin to whisper along her already taut nerves. As a teacher, she'd made it her business to learn first aid. If people were hurt, they might need her.

"I'm going to go see if Jared needs help," she explained to Lucy. "You be a good girl."

She stepped into the warm rain and hurried to the side of the road. She reached the concrete barriers just as a trailer truck was passing through. He barely even slowed. As the water arched up and away from his tires, Cat felt a chill run through her. They could have been killed. So easily, they could have been killed.

Pushing the wet hair out of her eyes, Cat tried to control the trembling that racked her body. Jared. She had to find him. She scanned the road. The sheets of rain made it impossible to see. There was no sign of any trucks. If she was swift, she could make it to the other side of the pass. Without stopping to reconsider her actions, she began to run through the narrow cement barriers. The water was up to her knees, but she didn't pause long enough to notice. She had to get to Jared.

HE SAW HER RUNNING as he helped the stranded family climb up the muddy ravine. She was almost halfway across the narrowed roadway when Jared spotted an enormous eighteen-wheeler rolling down the opposite hill, headed straight for her at top speed.

"Catherine!" he shouted, but she couldn't hear him over the pounding rain. Thrusting the child he held into its mother's arms, Jared rushed up the steep hill alternately praying and cursing, hoping he reached Cat in time.

The truck was bearing down on her, but her gaze was focused on the car at the bottom of the ravine. He had to get to her. Jared scrambled up the muddy embankment, reaching the cement barriers just as Cat was about to rush past him. Reaching an arm over the cement wall, he grabbed for her waist. The hair on the back of his neck rose, as the rumbling truck bore down on them.

WHEN SHE FELT THE ARM lock around her waist, Cat opened her mouth to scream but no sound came out. Jerked off her feet, she flew through the air over the cement wall. Then to her horror she saw an enormous truck roll by. Cat knew, that if not for the arm wrapped about her waist, she would be dead.

She turned her head to shout a thank-you at her rescuer, but the sodden ground beneath her feet gave way, and she plummeted down the side of the hill, taking her rescuer with her.

The arm around her waist never loosened its grip, and as a result Cat landed with an indelicate thump on top of a very hard chest. Pushing the rain soaked hair out of her eyes, she raised her head to get a look at the person she owed her life to.

Her heart stopped in her throat when she recognized the pale-blond hair and broad frame. Jared. His eyes were closed as if in pain, and Cat felt a tremor of fear skitter through her. With a trembling hand, she reached out to touch his face, struggling to find the words to express her gratitude.

"Jared." Her voice was no louder than a raw croak. "Jared."

He didn't answer. Cat eased out from under his arm and grasped his face with both hands.

"Jared," she called, fear making her voice shake. "Oh God, I've killed him."

A slow rumble started deep in his chest, and Cat completely panicked. If he was going to die, it wasn't going to be because of her. Pressing her fingers against the base of his throat, she searched for his pulse.

"Damn you, Jared McLean, you wake up right now." Her voice cracked, but she continued to yell at him. "I am not heavy enough to crush you, so you'd better just wake up right now. Do you hear me? Wake up!"

"I'm awake." His blue eyes snapped open and pinned her with a glare. Fury crackled in his gaze, but Cat was too relieved to care.

She lifted her fingers from his pulse and sat back on her heels. "Well, you could have said something."

"I was trying to control my temper," he said.

"Your temper?" she repeated, irritated. "I thought you were hurt. Of all the rotten stunts to pull."

In disgust, she turned on her heel and began to trudge back up the slope. She only got three feet away when a hand clamped around her ankle and jerked her foot out from under her. She landed with an undignified splat.

All of her fear and panic twisted into fury, and she struck

out with her other foot only to have Jared pounce on her, trapping her body beneath his as he straddled her in the mud.

"Let me up," she snarled.

"No." His jaw was set and the muscles in his cheeks were clenched into knots. He was breathing through his nose. Each breath widened his nostrils, and he reminded Cat of a bull about to charge. She gulped.

"Please let me up?" she asked in a softer tone of voice.

"No. We're going to get one thing straight between us."

"What's that?"

"If you ever pull such a careless, boneheaded, stupid stunt again, I'll turn you over my knee. I swear I will." He lowered his head as he spoke, and Cat leaned away from him and deeper into the mud. It was cold and wet and did nothing to soothe her temper.

Who did he think he was? She'd stopped taking orders from anyone but herself the minute she'd crossed the Massachusetts state line. And she'd be damned if this freeloading hitchhiker was going to start doling them out now.

"Don't you dare talk to me like that," she argued. "You're not the boss of me. I'm a grown woman. I'm also trained in CPR and first aid. I was only coming to see if I could help."

"I didn't need your help."

"Well, how was I supposed to know that?" She reared up from the mud.

"I told you to stay in the van." He leaned forward until his face was just inches from hers. "I expect you to do what I tell you."

"Well, you're in for a mighty big disappointment," she snarled, refusing to back down. "I don't need your permission for anything. I do what I want when I want. Ha!"

"Really?" he roared. "So do I."

Before she could take a breath, Jared gripped the back

of her head with a muddy fist and captured her lips with his. At the hot, wet taste of her mouth, his anger fled like whispers in the wind. The only thing he felt was a gut-level need to kiss the woman in his arms senseless.

His kiss was savage in its fury. It was the kind of kiss meant to reprimand and tame, but with Cat, it didn't work that way. Her mouth, which was supposed to resist him, didn't. Instead she surrendered like liquid fire beneath his touch, scorching Jared with her response. Desire drummed through him like a runaway locomotive.

He knew he should pull away. This was Cat, for all intents and purposes, his charge for the next week. He was supposed to be protecting her, not cupping her head with his hand while his tongue ruthlessly plunged into her mouth. Reality was as quick and decisive as a slap. Jared released Cat as abruptly as he'd grabbed her.

His breath darted in and out of his lungs in quick gasps while he fought for control. Cat had no such trouble. Rising to her knees before him, she clasped his face between her two hands. Their gazes collided, hers filled with heat and his with warning. She didn't care a smidgen for his warning.

She let her lips hover just inches from his, and he felt her draw him in, not allowing him to refuse participation in a ritual that required two. She teased his lips with sweetly tender, testing kisses. No heavier than the brush of a feather, they wreaked havoc with his senses, giving him no choice but to respond.

Jared encircled her waist with his hands, splaying his fingers across her back and pulling her more tightly against him. Cat gasped.

His kisses didn't tease, they claimed. He held her still under the onslaught of his mouth. He probed, teased and laved her swollen mouth.

Jared heard the soft keening moan she made in the back

of her throat. His body responded immediately as all of the heat within him coursed to one central point. How had this happened? This wasn't supposed to happen.

But she tasted so good, and she felt so right, he'd have to be a saint to resist her. And Jared was no saint. Not right now. Not with this incredibly wild-eyed woman burning at his touch.

He deepened their kiss as his hands roamed restlessly toward her breasts. She leaned invitingly, and he almost answered, but a loud yell broke through his passionate haze.

"You folks all right down there?"

Jared and Cat broke apart like teenagers caught necking on the front porch. Still kneeling in the mud, they were covered in the dark brown muck from their hair to their shoes. Glancing at Jared through her lashes, Cat wasn't sure if she was more embarrassed, relieved or frustrated.

As if sensing her confusion, Jared grinned at her. Tilting her chin up with a finger, he placed a swift, searing kiss on her already swollen lips. "We'll discuss this later."

Pulling Cat to her feet, he led the way up the embankment toward the waiting spectators.

"We're fine," Jared answered as they reached the elderly couple at the top of the hill.

The man was tall and gaunt and sported a blue fishing cap festooned with a colorful barrage of lures. The woman was short and round, wearing a shiny purple raincoat and matching rain hat. Both were trimmed with silver rhinestones. If the sun came out, she'd be as blinding as the flash of a camera.

The woman elbowed the man in the ribs.

"I told you so," she said. "They're young and in love, probably on their honeymoon. The last thing they need is a couple of old fogies like us pestering them."

"There you go again. Nag, nag, nag," the man said.

"It's amazing I don't drown myself while fishing just to get away from you...honeybunch."

"You'd never be that thoughtful, pumpkin," the woman retorted.

"My name is Fly," the man said. "And this here is my ball and chain, Mabel."

"Humph," Mabel sniffed at her husband and turned to Cat and Jared. "How do."

"Nice to meet you." Jared shook Fly's hand. "I'm Jared and this blushing woman is Cat."

"Hi," Cat said, trying to mask her embarrassment by brushing the excess mud off her clothing.

"You're a mess," Mabel said. "You can use the john in our RV if you want to clean up."

"That's awfully kind, but we don't want to impose," Cat began to decline.

"It's not imposing," Fly insisted. "It's the least we can do to help out our fellow travelers."

"Then we accept," Jared answered for them. Cat frowned.

"Follow me," Mabel said and began to walk away.

Cat stopped by the van to feed Lucy and grab a change of clothes. She followed Mabel into the RV, while the men walked back to the car in the ravine to see if they could help the family with the tow truck that had just arrived. Thankfully, no one had been injured.

Cleaned up and in dry clothes, Cat examined the interior of the RV. It looked like something off of the showroom floor. There were no personal effects or homey knickknacks to be seen. Assuming Mabel must be a fastidious housekeeper, Cat was careful not to track dirt anywhere. Sinking onto a soft sofa with a steaming cup of coffee, Cat turned her attention to Mabel.

"Are you and your husband on vacation?" she asked, watching wide-eyed as the older woman lit a cigar off the stove burner. The pungent aroma of the tobacco filled the RV.

"Vacation? If you consider fishing in every watering hole in the United States a vacation. I hate fish."

"Oh." Cat slurped her coffee and glanced at the door. Surely, Jared would be here soon.

As if reading her mind, the door banged open and in strode Jared and Fly. Jared ducked into the bathroom and Cat gulped her coffee, hoping for a quick escape.

"So you kids are headed to Arizona?" Fly asked.

"How did you know?" Cat asked.

"The 'AZ or Bust' sign on the back of your van," he said.

Cat gave a nervous laugh. "Oh, yeah."

"Whereabouts in Arizona are you headed?" Mabel asked.

"Just outside Phoenix," Jared answered, stepping out of the bathroom. "Where are you two headed?"

"Arizona."

"Florida."

Fly and Mabel spoke at the same time. Mabel cast Fly a peeved expression and said, "Florida. We're going to Florida."

"No, we're not, sweetie," Fly disagreed.

"Yes, we are, honey pie."

"We've already discussed this," Fly said through gritted teeth. "We have to stick as close to our investments as possible, darling."

"But we don't want the whole world to know our plans, snookums," Mabel replied through an equally clenched jaw.

"Well, we'd better be on our way," Jared interrupted their disagreement. "Thanks for the use of your rest room."

"Yes, thank you," Cat echoed as she and Jared scrambled over each other to get out of the RV.

"Interesting couple," Cat said.

"That's one word for it," Jared said. "They remind me of that old radio program called The Bickersons."

Cat laughed. "That suits them."

Jared let Lucy out of the van so that she could run around and do her business. He took Cat's elbow to keep her from slipping in the mud. "I'm sorry about what happened before."

"You're sorry?" Cat repeated. "For yelling at me or kissing me?"

"Kissing you," he admitted, looking flustered. "I...we... that shouldn't have happened."

"Why not?" she asked, feeling contrary. Maybe they shouldn't have kissed, but hearing him say so made her feel compelled to argue.

"I'm your brother's friend." Jared waved an arm as if the answer were obvious. "It's part of the code."

"What code?"

"The best friends code. Guys don't hit on their friends' sisters."

"That's in the code?" Cat asked.

"Yeah, right next to the one that states you never date a friend's ex," Jared said.

"That one I know, but the sibling one? No, I've never heard of that," she said.

"It's a guy thing," he said. "Trust me. It exists."

"So?" She plunked her hands on her hips, trying to level him with a hard glare.

"So? I can't break the code. As your brother's friend, I should keep my damn hands off you." He walked past her and opened the passenger side of the van for Lucy to leap in. He motioned for Cat to follow. She didn't budge.

"Why?" She crossed her arms over her chest. "How does that have anything to do with us?"

"It's a safe bet that Cam wouldn't like me putting the moves on you," he explained, trying to propel her into her seat.

"Why? Did he say something?" Cat asked, feeling her temper burn. If Cameron had warned Jared away from her, she was going to wring his thick neck. She was a grown woman and she could take care of herself.

"He didn't have to." Jared snorted. "Now get in the van."

"Oh, I see, you're afraid of Cameron," she said, ignoring Jared's hand as he tried to bend her knee and get her to step into the seat.

"I am not afraid of him." He snapped to an upright position.

"Sounds like it to me." She shook her head in mock pity.

"I could whup your brother with one hand tied behind my back." He lowered his head to hers.

"Yeah, right," she said and stepped into the van. "Let's get going. We're behind schedule." She slammed her door in his face.

Schedule? Her and that stupid schedule. Jared stomped around the van to climb into his seat. He watched in consternation as she dug her index cards out of her bag and promptly began adjusting their time frame. The urge to jerk the cards out of her hands and toss them out the window was almost too strong to resist. He gripped the wheel tighter as they merged back into traffic.

Afraid of Cameron? Ha! By the time this little adventure was over, his good buddy was going to be afraid of him. He cast a fulminating glance at the caramel-haired woman beside him. She flipped through the cards, completely oblivious to him and his ire.

Jared felt his teeth clench. He wanted nothing but to pull over to the side of the road and kiss her until she was the same woman that had come apart for him while buried up to her neck in mud. He tightened his jaw and fought the impulse as if it were an addiction—second by second.

Cat was his best friend's sister. That made her practically a sister to him. Guys weren't supposed to have these sorts of thoughts about their sisters. How had this happened? He'd tried to be a good friend. He'd agreed to go on this damn hike across the country. But he hadn't expected to be lying to the first woman he'd found attractive in just about forever.

THEY ROLLED into Ohio late in the afternoon. Cat leaned out the window and took a picture of the sign welcoming them to the state. The storm had passed, and the day had become oppressively humid. Lucy spent the better part of the day leaning out the window, her usual goofy grin plastered to her face.

Cat envied the puppy's simple pleasure. The silence between her and Jared was heavier than the heat. The paperback she'd dug out of her purse provided no distraction, as Jared's brooding presence proved too potent to ignore.

"We'll be nearing Akron soon." She fidgeted with her book, waiting for him to respond.

Jared said nothing.

"Jared, I'm sorry about before. I don't think you're afraid of Cam."

"No need to be sorry," he said abruptly.

"Yes, there is," she persisted. "You were right. What happened shouldn't have. You're my brother's friend and I respect that."

"Fine. Let's just forget about it."

Cat agreed, but doubted it was likely. She'd never be able to erase the impact of his kiss. In all the years she'd been with Matthew, she'd never felt like that when he kissed her. Forgetting Jared's kiss would be like asking the Earth to forget its orbit—impossible.

Cat's gaze lingered on the pulse pounding in his jaw. She wondered if their kiss had agitated him as much as it had her. If it had, it would be a shame to let it go out of loyalty to her brother. Oh, who was she kidding? Their kiss was just a reaction to the heat of the moment. Nothing more. Wasn't it?

4

"WHAT IS THE most exciting thing you've ever done?" Cat asked.

They were sitting on the grass outside their room, enjoying the cool evening air while Lucy took her after-dinner stroll around the courtyard.

"Why do you ask?" Jared asked.

"Because this trip is the most exciting thing I've ever done," she said. "And I was wondering what was yours. It's called making conversation."

Jared glanced away. "I've never had much excitement in my life."

"Oh, come on," she said. "Enough of the strong silent stuff. Tell me a story."

She reached out and rested a hand on his forearm in a light caress. Jared glanced up. Her enormous eyes were soft and inquisitive. A man could get lost trying to follow the patterns of color swirling in her irises.

Think of her as a little sister, he told himself. An annoying little sister at that.

"Please, tell me," she said.

Jared moved away from her touch.

"Okay, I don't know if this was the most exciting thing that's ever happened to me, but it was the most profound," he said.

"I'm all ears," she chimed and propped her chin on her hand, poised to listen.

"My mother died when I was very young."

"I'm sorry," she whispered.

"No, it's all right. My father kept her memory alive for me with stories of how she used to sing to me when I was little and play games. I have nice memories of her. She was an amazing woman."

"That was good of your father."

"Yeah, he's the best," Jared agreed. "It wasn't easy for him. I was what you might call a handful."

"You?" Cat looked at him with mock surprise.

"I remember when I was seventeen and full of back talk and attitude." Jared gave Cat a wry smile. "I decided I didn't need to take orders form anyone anymore, especially from my father. Like all teenagers I bucked every direction he gave me and did my best to make our lives a living hell.

"He never gave in. He just worked me harder. I had packed a bag and was about to take off for parts unknown, when one of our mares began to foal. My curiosity dragged me to the stable, and my father immediately gave me the task of pulling a newborn colt into the world. To see a life begin…it was the single most amazing moment of my life." Jared paused, reliving that incredible day in his mind.

"My father never mentioned the packed bag I'd shown up with, and I never left. It was at that moment I realized, that despite the hell I'd put him through, my father trusted me enough, loved me enough, to let me perform one of the most vital functions on the ranch. I don't think I ever talked back to him again."

A cicada buzzed somewhere in the field behind them. Night had settled in and the glow of lanterns illuminating the courtyard made the moment intimate. Unaccustomed to revealing his innermost self, Jared felt intensely uncomfortable. Cat gazed at him with understanding, but still he felt raw and exposed.

"Your father must love you very much," she observed, squeezing his forearm.

Jared wrapped his hand around hers. The sound of her voice and feel of her touch soothed him. Her mysterious eyes were warm, and he knew she understood the memory still haunted him.

It was strangely uplifting to meet a woman so intuitive. There was no judgment in her eyes, just acceptance. She didn't try to tell him how he should feel. She just embraced what was.

She threatened a man's sanity with her taunts and her teasing, but her sensitivity and warmth just about unhinged him. And if he had to spend another night in a room with her, he was going to be a prime candidate for the ha-ha house.

Abruptly, Jared pulled away. His gaze was centered somewhere over Cat's left shoulder, and he muttered something about needing to clear his head. She watched in dismay as he began to walk away.

"But where are you going?" she protested.

"For a walk."

Feeling her temper rise, Cat glared at his back. He just couldn't stand to share one little crumb of his life with her, could he?

"Jared!" she yelled across the yard, oblivious to the other motel guests watching them with rapt attention. "Thank you for saving my life today."

If he heard her, he didn't acknowledge it. Unlatching the gate, he strode out of the courtyard without even glancing back at her.

Defeated, Cat sank back down onto the grass. When would she learn to butt out? She'd obviously driven Jared away with her incessant grilling about his life. Confidence had to be won, it couldn't be badgered out of a person. Unfortunately, whenever Jared was around, she seemed to turn into a world-class nag.

With a resigned sigh, she grabbed Lucy's leash and headed toward her. Suddenly, being in Ohio wasn't so thrilling anymore.

THE LATE MOVIE WINKED its blue gaze over the room, and Cat made a valiant effort to follow the plot. It was useless. She found the red digital clock built into the television's control panel infinitely more interesting.

Cat paced the tiny room with Lucy on her heels. It was two o'clock in the morning, and Jared hadn't returned from wherever he'd disappeared to. Cat's emotions had run the gamut from anger to worry and back. If he didn't show up soon, she was going to start calling the local hospitals as well as the police.

"How about another walk, Lucy?" she asked the puppy. "If I sit here for one more minute, I'm going to go out of my mind."

Leaping to her feet and rushing to the door, Lucy was eager to go. It was the third walk they'd taken in the past four hours, but she didn't seem to mind in the least.

The night was cool and quiet. Having no idea where to look for Jared, Cat let the puppy lead her around the brick building. The story he'd shared with her about his father had answered some of her questions about him, but it had also added a slew of new ones.

During the two days that they'd been driving, Cat had told him several stories about herself and her family. He'd never volunteered any. And now, tonight, when she'd finally pried open his shell a crack, he reacted by retreating completely.

Just where in Ohio had he gone, she wondered. And why did she care so much anyway? He was just a traveling companion—nothing more.

So what if his kiss had scorched her soul? She didn't want to get involved with him or anyone. She wanted to be on her own to prove that she could take care of herself and never risk the kind of rejection she'd suffered from the big dumb jerk. She couldn't handle that kind of pain again, especially with some close-lipped, relationship-phobic hottie like Jared McLean.

She sighed. The desire she felt for him made her other concerns seem trivial. If all she could have with him was a short-term affair, she knew deep down she'd do it.

An affair! Cat felt a flush fill her cheeks. She'd never considered a fling before—ever! But Jared was different. Somewhere down deep, near her heart, Cat knew that intimacy with Jared would never be casual.

She felt a connection with him, despite his silences, that she'd never felt with any other man before. Not even the big dumb jerk. She couldn't even think of Matthew and Jared in the same context. Sex with the big dumb jerk had been practically nonexistent. And, frankly, she hadn't missed it.

She couldn't even imagine what sex with Jared would be like. If it was anything like his kiss…it made her sweat just to contemplate it. She wanted him. And an affair would let her have him without having to risk being hurt. Could she do it? Could she be intimate with him and walk away? More importantly, could she live with never knowing what it was like to be loved by him?

Lost in thought, Cat followed her meandering puppy away from the motel and down the darkened street.

WHERE IN OHIO could she be? Jared checked the bathroom for the third time and resumed pacing. It was two-thirty in the morning and both Cat and the puppy were gone. His conscience kicked him with the thought that she'd probably gone looking for him, which only made him angrier.

Fighting to be rational, he tried to use logic to figure out where she could have gone. She hadn't gone to the van, because that's where he'd been. The bench seat in the van had been even more impossible to sleep on than the motel bed, and he'd finally given up, but when he'd arrived at the room, she was gone.

He called the front desk. The staff working the night shift said they hadn't seen her or the puppy. That left the pool area, but a glance out the window proved it to be deserted.

Maybe she just took Lucy for a walk, he hoped, trying to reassure himself. He headed out the door, determined to find the missing pair of delinquents.

He took a quick stroll around the building. There was no sign of them. Cameron was going to kill him. He'd promised to deliver her safely to her job in Arizona. Instead he'd been entertaining very unbrotherly thoughts about her and now he'd lost her in Ohio. Feeling his chest tighten with anxiety, Jared headed for the road. She couldn't be that irresponsible, he told himself while he scanned the surrounding area, looking for any trace of her or Lucy.

CAT FELT CERTAIN the way back to the hotel was to her right. Without hesitating, she pulled Lucy along with her. It was late. She was tired. And if Jared was determined not to be found, then the heck with him. What a fine companion he'd turned out to be.

She didn't care if he decided to desert her and hitchhike his way back to Arizona. Goodbye, good riddance and have a nice walk. She didn't need him anyway. At least, that's what she kept telling herself.

It wasn't until she heard the heavy footsteps, crunching on the road behind her that she reconsidered that opinion. The steps were moving fast and headed right for them. If she didn't pick up the pace, the stranger would be upon them in a matter of moments.

"Come on, Lucy," she whispered. The icy grip of fear had her by the throat, and Cat felt a ridiculous need to cry.

Jared had tried to warn her not to go out alone. But did she
listen? No!

A walking target for bad guys, wasn't that what he'd
said?

The person was drawing closer. Cat glanced over her
shoulder, but she couldn't see a thing in the dark. Her heart
was hammering triple time, and the only thing she knew
for sure was that she had to get out of there and fast. Scooping up Lucy, she turned on her heel and began to run toward the safety of the nearby woods.

The footsteps behind her echoed hers, and Cat knew with
sudden clarity that her number was up. So much for her
adventure west—she was never going to make it out of
Ohio.

"Catherine Levery! Just what do you think you're doing?" The voice jarred her to a stop, and Cat swung around
to see Jared striding toward her. Fury rang out with his
every step, but she was too relieved to care.

"Oh, it's you," she said, her knees buckling with relief
and the weight of the furball in her arms. "I thought you
were a bad guy."

"Don't be so sure I'm not," he snapped. "What are you
doing out here?"

"I…we…were looking for you," she explained.

"You were what?" He was just a few feet away from
her now, and Cat blinked at the rage in his eyes. "Do you
realize you scared the snot out of me?"

Cat smarted under his anger and felt her own temper
steam.

"Don't you yell at me." She shoved Lucy into his arms
and began to storm away. "If it wasn't for you, I wouldn't
be out here."

"Me?" Jared raged over the puppy's head. "What do I
have to do with your stupidity?"

"Stupidity?" Cat spun back to face him and planted her

hands on her hips. "If you hadn't behaved like such an immature adolescent, I wouldn't be out here looking for you."

"Immature adolescent?" His eyebrows lifted.

"Well, what do you call a man who runs off and sulks just because he confided a part of his precious personal life to someone?"

"Is that what you think?" he asked, his low voice becoming soft.

"Yes," she said, kicking the dirt at her feet as if it were him. Silence hummed between them as they watched one another, each refusing to take back their angry words.

Cat glanced up and caught Jared watching her with an intensity that made her mouth dry. A man really shouldn't look at a woman as if he were starving and she were a steak. Cat felt her skin grow hot and she pulled her gaze away from his.

"Look, it's late." Jared balanced the dog with one arm while he ran a hand over his face. "Why don't we go back to the motel and get some rest. We can discuss this in the morning."

"Fine," Cat agreed, pressing a hand to her galloping heart. Without glancing at him, she turned and resumed walking.

"Cat," Jared called, a hint of amusement in his voice. "The motel is this way."

She turned in time to see the suspicious shaking of his shoulders as he adjusted the puppy in his arms and led the way back to their room. He was laughing at her!

"I knew that!" she snapped.

"Uh-huh," he said with a snort.

Cat sighed.

"WAKE UP, SUNSHINE," Jared ordered as he crossed to his own side of the room, fresh from a hot shower.

"What time is it?" Cat groaned from beneath her covers.

"Time to hit the road," he answered. "If we are to maintain your schedule."

His shirt was only half on when Cat poked her head around the makeshift curtain.

"You're not going to yell at me again, are you?" she asked.

"No," he said with a smile. His dimples winked at her, and Cat felt her breath catch in her throat. She could smell his clean, male scent and the sight of his half-bare, broad chest made her toes curl into the floor. "But we are going to have a nice long chat."

"Good." She grinned at him. "You're overdue to spill your guts."

She ducked back behind the bedspread before he could respond.

What to wear? Standing in the bathroom, Cat examined the contents of her suitcase with a scrutinizing gaze. What did a woman wear when she wanted to have an affair?

Cat had decided that she did want to have an affair with Jared. The sight of his half-bare chest this morning had tipped the scale. She wanted him, and she was going to get him, with no strings attached.

She studied her naked form in the mirror. She was no voluptuous paramour, but she wasn't displeased with the shape she'd been given. Now all she needed was an outfit that would bring Jared to his knees. There wasn't a whole heck of a lot of time left for her to get him into bed, and that was precisely where she'd decided she wanted him.

She wasn't ready for a relationship, but that didn't mean she couldn't have a meaningful fling with Jared. She'd read *Cosmo*. Single, independent women did it all the time. And wasn't that what she was trying to prove? That she was, in fact, a single, independent woman?

With that goal in mind, Cat chose a bright blue, cropped

tank top and matching bicycle shorts. It was her workout attire, but it was sleek and tight and, with any luck, it would leave little to Jared's imagination.

THREE HOURS LATER, she realized she might as well have not bothered. He treated her with all the cordiality of a distant cousin. His gaze never lingered on her for more than a heartbeat and never in an intimate manner. As for the long talk they were supposed to have, that never materialized either. When Cat tried to attract Jared's attention with conversation, he was suddenly more interested in listening to the radio.

"How about some music?" he asked.

"Fine," she answered. If her response lacked enthusiasm, he didn't notice.

She watched his square fingers flip the dial, lingering only seconds on the stations as he passed.

"There we go," he said, finally settling on a station. The twang of a guitar and a nasal voice filled the van.

"Country? You like country-western?" she asked.

"Is there anything else?" Jared asked, turning to look at her for the first time that day.

"You probably wear a cowboy hat," she accused.

"When I'm working on the ranch," he confirmed. "Boots, too."

"Figures." Cat shook her head. The singer's voice blared into the silence, crooning about a love gone wrong, his pickup truck and his dog. "I can't listen to this," she announced and flipped the dial around until she found a contemporary rock station. The lead singer screamed his vocals to a primal beat that made the entire van shake. Cat bopped in her seat to the rhythm and shouted right along with the singer.

"No! No way!" Jared hollered over the music. "You leave that on and I'll have a headache in five minutes."

"If you play country, I'll die of boredom," she declared. They glared at each other over Lucy's head.

Jared flipped the dial to a news station. "Local authorities have released the sketches of the suspects, a man and woman in their mid-to-late sixties, wanted in connection with the Boston County jewelry heist last week. The thieves were reported to have stolen the famous ruby-and-diamond choker, last owned by Mrs. Gwendolyn Divine, while it was on display at the New England Heirloom Museum. The Divine choker is valued at three million dollars."

"No news," Cat said. "It's depressing and I'm on vacation."

"There has to be something we can both stand." Jared began to twist the dial again. "Ha! This is perfect."

A perky beat began to fill the cab, and Cat frowned, trying to recognize the song. It sounded suspiciously like… "Oldies?" she asked, wrinkling her nose in disgust.

"Oh, come on," Jared said. "This is a good one. Listen."

In spite of herself, Cat began to mouth the words.

"Ha! You know the words!" he accused, and she felt herself flush to the roots of her hair.

"This song is older than I am," she retorted. "I was weaned on this stuff, how can I not sing along?"

"You know the words. You know the words," he teased her in a singsong voice.

"So what?" she asked.

"So we're listening to oldies from now on," he declared with a laugh.

"Oh, goodie," Cat replied without enthusiasm.

Jared's teasing ended when they crossed the border into Illinois, and found themselves stuck in a major traffic jam.

"Shoot," Jared muttered, glaring at the endless stream of cars stopped in front of them. "What's the hold up?"

"This is really going to mess up our schedule," Cat fretted, once again pulling out her trusty index cards. "We might have to skip a rest stop to catch up."

"Let go of the schedule," Jared said.

"But I have it all planned out," she protested, flipping through the cards.

Jared scooped the cards out of her hands and tossed them under the seat. "You need to learn to be more flexible."

"I am very flexible," she said. "You're the rigid one."

"Am not," he said.

"Hey, isn't that what's their names?" Cat pointed out the window over Jared's shoulder. "The Bickersons?"

Jared turned just as the RV was pulling away.

"I couldn't tell," he said.

"I'm sure it was them," Cat said. "Those sparkly clothes of hers were pretty blinding."

"Breaker, breaker," the CB crackled to life. "If you're near mile marker seven, you'd better prepare for a wait. There's a major accident up ahead."

"Is anyone hurt?" Jared spoke into the CB's transmitter.

"I can't tell from here," answered the trucker. "But the meat wagon is on its way. I can see it coming up the breakdown lane."

"Thanks," Jared said.

"Meat wagon?" Cat asked.

"CB slang for ambulance," Jared explained.

"Oh, I hope no one is injured. Do you think we should go and see if we can help?" Cat chewed her lower lip and gazed down the road in front of them.

"We're too far away. The ambulance will be there before us."

Jared glanced at the concern in her eyes and could have kicked himself. Knowing Cat, she'd worry and fret about the accident the entire time they were stuck in traffic. He couldn't watch her worry; it would drive him crazy.

Switching off the engine, he rolled down his window and

motioned for her to do the same. A warm breeze drifted through the cab, ruffling Lucy's ears where she slept on the seat between them.

"So what do you want to do to pass the time?" he asked.

Cat turned in her seat and dug two sodas out of the cooler behind her. She handed one to Jared, considering him while popping the top on her own.

"How about that talk we were going to have?" she suggested.

"Are you sure you want to be lectured?" he asked.

"Me, lectured? I thought this was going to be your apology," she said.

"Apology?" He leaned over Lucy. "After you scared the bejeezes out of me and called me an immature adolescent? I don't think so, honey. If anyone is going to apologize, it's going to be you."

"You're right. How can I make it up to you?" she asked, gazing at him from beneath her lashes. Her lashes didn't quite hide the teasing glint in her eyes, but it didn't matter that she was teasing. Jared felt the sweat pop out on his brow. She leaned forward, giving him an unrestricted view of her cleavage. Rearing back from her, he slammed his back against the door and tried not to yelp when the door handle dug in between his vertebrae.

"Forget it," he ordered.

"All right." She grinned and shrugged. "How about you tell me another story?"

"About what?"

"Oh, I don't know, about you maybe."

Jared kept his gaze firmly planted on hers, fearing that it might stray to the blue stretchy material that fit her like a second skin. Think sister, he told himself.

"I'll make a deal with you," he offered. "I'll tell you about myself, if you tell me about Matthew Gerard."

"Matthew? How did you hear about the big dumb jerk?"

"Big dumb jerk, eh?" He laughed. "How do you think? Cameron."

"Oh, of course. All right, I'll take your deal, but I don't want to hear 'something' about you. I want to know your life story. You already know mine."

"I only know about your family," Jared argued. "You've been mum about your personal life."

"Why are you interested in my personal life?" she challenged.

"I'm not," he lied, in a voice more harsh than he'd intended. "It's just that it's the only thing you've left out."

"Oh." She blushed a beguiling shade of pink, and Jared was charmed. "Okay, I'll tell you all about my sordid love life, but remember you're going to tell me about all of your life. No assorted little tidbits. I want to hear it from birth to the present. Agreed?"

"Agreed." Jared nodded, taking a long sip from his soda. He was counting on the traffic being in motion before it was his turn.

Cat took a deep breath and appeared to gather her thoughts. Jared waited, but she wasn't talking. A silent Cat alarmed him.

"Don't tell me there are too many men for you to recall?" He frowned.

"Actually," she began with a nervous laugh, "it's quite the opposite. My history with men is brief to say the least. The big dumb jerk was first in a long line of one."

"Go on," Jared prodded her.

"I've only had one serious relationship in my whole life," Cat said on a sigh. "I dated a handful of guys in college, but the big dumb jerk was the only guy to ever call me for a second date. I always wondered if it was because I didn't put out on the first date."

Jared choked on his pop and it fizzed up his nose.

"Are you all right?" she asked.

"Fine," he said. "Go on."

"So, I dated Matthew from my third semester of college right up until I caught him with his assets in the air over his accountant."

Jared heard the wistfulness in her voice and felt his gut clench in a surprising twist of jealousy. The thought that Cat could still be pining for that big dumb jerk made him want to wrap his hands around something and squeeze— preferably Gerard's neck.

"What a mistake that turned out to be." Cat rolled her eyes at him. Jared felt his gut unclench and a subtle warmth infused him.

"So, you're not still in love with him?" he asked, studying the top of his can of pop. She was silent, and he glanced up to see her gazing at him. His gaze held hers, desperately trying to see into her soul. He didn't have to try very hard. It was all there for him to see.

"I never really was," she answered.

"But you were going to marry him," he said.

"All my life I've tried to be whatever was expected of me." Cat glanced away from him to the cars parked all around them. "Straight A student, band member, girl scout, all of that was someone else's wish, not mine. But because I knew it was expected, I did it."

"Why?" Jared frowned at her.

"To make people happy." Cat shrugged.

"Why didn't you just tell them all to shove off?" he asked, disturbed by the vision of an unhappy little girl, trapped into doing things she didn't like in order to please everyone else.

"Because I didn't have any backbone. Stop frowning." She reached over and smoothed the wrinkle on his brow with her thumb. His forehead was damp with sweat, and her thumb slicked across his skin, causing his breath to hitch. "I was never unhappy. It's just that there are things I wish I'd done that I never did."

"Like what?" Jared growled, his voice dipping low in response to her touch.

"You'll think it's stupid." She shook her head.

"No, I won't." He put his hand over his heart. "And even if I do, I promise not to laugh."

"All right." She tilted her head and her lips tipped mischievously. "I always wanted to play hooky."

"Hooky?" He gaped at her.

"Uh-huh." She nodded, watching him.

Jared tried not to laugh. He really did. He failed. Throwing back his head, he hooted with laughter until people in the cars surrounding them began to turn and stare.

"Hey, you promised," she chided him and reached over the puppy to poke him in the ribs.

"I'm sorry," he said, still chuckling. "But you're a teacher."

"So what?" she asked. "I believe the occasional day of hooky is necessary for both adults and children. Everyone needs a break. A day of escape from their routine."

"I'd be willing to bet you still don't play hooky," he accused. "I bet you haven't taken a day off since you began teaching."

"Wrong," she retorted. "Once, I took two days off in a row."

"For what?"

"I had the flu," she answered.

"That doesn't count." Jared shook his head. "There's no hooky in sick days."

"Says you," she replied.

"Yeah, says me." He winked at her.

Cat felt herself smile in return. Heavens, he had the most beautiful smile. Full lips parted over strong white teeth that were framed by a devastatingly deep pair of dimples. That was the kind of smile a woman lost her head over, not to mention a few of her more passionate body parts.

"So where does Gerard fit into the picture?"

"When I met the big dumb...Matthew—I really should stop calling him names," she said.

"Why?" Jared scowled. "If the name fits."

Cat snorted.

"When you met him, was it love at first sight?" Jared asked, shifting his gaze to Lucy.

"No." Cat shook her head. "He was too practical for that. But he was the first guy to show that kind of interest in me, and I was very flattered. I think I grew to love him, but it was more the love of a friend. I figured he was the only man who would ever ask me to marry him, so when he did, I said yes."

"That's the stupidest thing I've ever heard." Jared glared at her. "What kind of an idiot gets engaged because she thinks no one else will ever ask her?"

"You don't have to shout." Cat narrowed her eyes to match his. "I'm perfectly aware that it wasn't the brightest thing I've ever done. But at the time, it seemed reasonable."

"Well, it was stupid," he growled.

"Thank you very much," Cat snarled, pulling the puppy off his lap and turning to face the window. "Remind me not to tell you anything ever again."

"Fine," he agreed and looked up to see the traffic beginning to move. Starting the engine, he flowed with the traffic.

WHEN THEY LANDED in Effingham, Illinois, for their third night on the road, Cat was still stewing. Jared McLean was the most aggravating, irritating, attractive man she'd ever known. Absolutely the wrong man for her to get involved with, and still, she wanted him. With that thought in mind, she traded in her cotton pajamas for a frilly negligee. He didn't even flinch. She debated stripping naked and streaking around the motel room, but decided if he didn't notice, the humiliation might just kill her.

The air conditioner hummed, and Cat tossed and turned, tangling the light sheet that covered her. She could hear Jared's deep, even breathing and felt resentment swell within her. He'd hardly spoken to her since the traffic jam, he ignored her negligee, and to top it off, he snored! If he was going to ruin her night's sleep, the least he could do was be quiet about it.

Furious, she thrust the sheet aside and climbed out of bed. She didn't pause to consider her actions. She jerked the makeshift curtain aside and glared at the sleeping man before her.

Moonlight peeped through the window blinds, and Cat caught her breath as she gazed at the beautiful masculine form before her. She gulped. He was lying on his back, the thin motel sheet was wadded up around his waist, leaving his arms and the broad expanse of his chest bare. Wow!

Common sense told her to get back on her side of the curtain. Cat wasn't listening. Entranced, she sat beside the seductively warm sleeping body. She laid a hand on his shoulder and shook him, trying to rouse him without shocking him.

He grunted and rolled over, giving Cat a clear view of his back. It was warm and wide and hard, tapering down to a slim waist. Her fingers twitched when she reached for his shoulder. His skin was hot against her fingers and she sighed. He let out a deep nasal snore. The noise made her jump and then frown. That did it!

She reached across him, grabbed the extra pillow and smacked him on the head with it.

"Jared, wake up!"

"Huh?" He grabbed the pillow with one hand and her

waist with the other. His fingers tightened and then stilled as if registering the feel of her through the flimsy fabric she wore. His eyes popped open, his eyebrows shot up two notches, and he snapped upright, bringing his face within inches of hers.

"What are you doing on my side of the curtain?" he shouted.

"I can't sleep. I w-want to talk," she stammered.

"Well, get back on your side and talk from there." He waved his hand in the direction of her bed.

"Don't be ridiculous," she chided him and scooted closer to him on the bed.

"I'm not being ridiculous," he retorted, pulling the sheet up to his neck as he shot across the mattress away from her.

"Yes, you are." She followed him, trying to stifle a laugh at his prudishness. "I promise I won't touch you."

Jared eyed her in horror as she settled herself against the headboard, primly crossing her arms over her chest. Her negligee was as thin as tissue and just as revealing. Jared felt heat rush to parts of his body that had no business getting hot. He pinched the bridge of his nose between his thumb and forefinger and tried to concentrate on visions of snowdrifts and polar bears. It was useless.

"It's your turn," she declared.

"To what?" He dropped his hand to study her. "Hit you with a pillow?"

"To talk," she said. "You promised to tell me your life story this afternoon, but you never did. No time like the present, I always say."

"Talk?" he roared. "Are you out of your skull? It's the middle of the night!"

"Yeah, well, you snore and I can't sleep, so start talking."

"I snore?" he asked, appalled.

"You breathe heavy," she relented.

Jared studied her green-flecked eyes in amused horror. Only Cat would accost a man in his own bed at three o'clock in the morning to tell him he snored and demand he talk to her. He was sure it would never occur to her that when an exceptionally desirable woman climbed into a man's bed, the last thing he wanted to do was talk.

But then, Jared was beginning to suspect that Cat didn't think of herself as desirable, and certainly not as exceptionally desirable. That would explain the outfits she'd chosen today. From the filmy sleepwear she wore now to the tight, curve-hugging shorts and top she'd worn earlier, she'd shown an incredible lack of awareness.

And now she sat in his bed in that flimsy, frilly thing as trusting as if he were Cameron. And, if that wasn't galling enough, she had the nerve to sit there and say she wanted to talk!

Obviously, somebody had to teach her a lesson—for her own good. And Jared couldn't think of any soul more deserving of the job than himself. Catherine Levery had to learn once and for all that she was mind-numbingly attractive and that he was no eunuch!

CAT COULDN'T PINPOINT when the energy coming from Jared switched from annoyance to something much more serious. All she knew was that out of a sense of self-preservation, she began to scoot toward the edge of the mattress.

The blue gaze fixed on her mouth was predatory, and she felt her pulse pound in her throat while her breath stalled in her lungs.

"You know," she said, waving a finger thoughtfully in the air, "this may not be the best time for this discussion. It just occurred to me that you're probably tired. So, I'll just leave you to that. Good ni—"

"Not so fast." Jared gripped her wrist and tugged her relentlessly across the mattress. "I find I'm wide awake now, and it'd be a shame to let all of this energy go to waste, don't you think? Besides, we haven't finished our conversation yet."

"I said everything I had to say. Really." She nodded vigorously, trying not to get pinned beneath the incredibly warm, sculpted muscles of Jared's frame as it lowered onto hers.

He jerked the sheet from between them, and Cat felt his hot skin press against hers. She glanced down. All he wore was a pair of blue-and-white striped boxers. They weren't as funny as the smiley-faced boxers, but they were very sexy. He placed his hands on her hips and pulled her low onto the mattress while he shifted a leg over hers, effectively locking her into place.

Jared smiled at the look of dazed wonder on her face. Her taffy-colored hair was spread over the white pillow like waves of silk, and he indulged himself and pressed his cheek against her curls. They were soft and fragrant like the woman herself.

He nuzzled her ear with his lips and felt her start in surprise. He brushed his mouth across her face, soothing the wild look in her enormous eyes with reassuring caresses. Warnings about little boys who played with matches ran through his mind, but he was too drawn to the flame to worry about being burned.

Her lips responded sweetly, achingly sweet, to the lightest touch from his tongue. Lush lashes swept down, hiding her eyes from his gaze, but he didn't care. Her response to him was obvious in the way her body wrapped around his, holding him close.

A man could drown in such giving sweetness. Jared plunged his fingers into her curls, to hold her still, while his mouth ruthlessly courted hers. He didn't give her a chance to think or breathe, only to feel and respond. When she surrendered to the kiss, his hands skimmed down her body, searching out the curves that had taunted him all day.

Like a faithless friend her flimsy nightie gave way to his probing fingers. Cat felt a thousand tiny tremors build within her as he cupped one aching breast. His mouth left hers and his lips whispered across the peak, taunting it into tightening in response. The other nipple demanded similar treatment. He complied, circling the tip with his tongue. Cat found herself gasping for breath.

She'd never been loved like this before. Jared's intense concentration and pleasure in her responses was a revelation. His brilliant blue gaze was hooded in seduction, his low voice fathomless with harsh endearments, all of which sent her spiraling into a sirocco of passion she'd never known existed.

It was the soft, soughing sigh that escaped Cat's lips that brought Jared to his senses. She was feeling too much. Sharing too much with him. The woman had no sense of self-preservation, and he could never reciprocate that openness.

He pulled away from her with a shaky breath. She'd inadvertently held up a mirror to his soul, forcing him to look. In that dark reflection lurked the loner he would always be.

He wanted her more than any woman he'd ever known, but he couldn't be with her. He couldn't be what she needed. Cat would never be happy with a shadow of a man, and she deserved more than that.

"Jared." Her voice was soft and breathy, making Jared regret his scruples.

"Yes?" He touched his lips to hers, keeping it the caress of a friend and not a lover.

"What happened?" Her eyes were a luminous green and steeped in unspent passion.

"I got carried away," he answered, rolling onto his back and tucking her into his side.

"Oh." Cat pressed her cheek against his chest, as if seeking his warmth. "Jared, I've never...that is...nothing ever felt like...do you know what I'm getting at here?"

"I'm afraid so." Jared ran a hand over his eyes.

"I just want you to know how special that was," she mumbled into his chest.

"I know, honey, I know." Jared buried a kiss in her curls and sighed. Hell, yes, he knew. He'd been with a few women in his time, but he'd never felt like this. What was happening between them...scared the starch out of him!

"Can we talk now?"

"Not unless you want to get into trouble again," Jared warned her, trailing his hand up and down her spine.

"I wouldn't mind." She gazed at him through her lashes.

"That's it," Jared announced and sat up, abruptly hauling her out of the bed. "Back to your own side of the room."

Cat let him put her to bed, not protesting when he tucked the sheet so tight that escape was near impossible. His arousal was obvious against his shorts, and Cat felt a surge of female satisfaction swell within her.

Jared could protest and pull away as much as he liked, but it was obvious that he felt something for her. She snuggled under the cool sheet. She'd thought she was too aroused to sleep, but as soon as Jared stepped away from the bed, she fell into an exhausted slumber.

JARED WATCHED HER for a moment before he slipped back to his own bed. They'd be entering Missouri tomorrow, which meant they would be halfway to Arizona and he couldn't help but be relieved. He doubted he'd be able to keep his hands off her for the rest of the trip, but as long as they didn't end up sharing a bed his conscience would be quiet.

The Levery siblings had put him between a rock and a hard spot. He glanced down at his shorts and almost laughed. Hard spot was putting it mildly. He couldn't, and wouldn't, touch Cat while Cameron's lie stood between them. And he couldn't betray Cameron's trust. He'd tried to think of Cat as a sister. He really had, but the feelings, okay, the lust she brought out in him was anything but brotherly. Jared was certain that taking Cat to his bed would be the ultimate betrayal of his friend's trust.

He lay back on the bed and covered his face with his spare pillow. Letting loose a howl, he chanted, "Just a few more days."

But somehow, the thought of not seeing Cat every day didn't make him feel any better.

5

"GET THE CAMERA READY," Jared ordered as he maneuvered through the heavy traffic coursing into St. Louis.

"I'm trying," Cat said as she fumbled with the puppy and the camera in her lap.

"It's going to be to the right of us," Jared warned her.

"I'm going to roll down the window so I can get a better shot," Cat replied. "Can you hold Lucy?"

"Sure," Jared answered, scooping the puppy to him with his right hand.

"There it is!" Cat squealed in delight. "Can you see it?"

"I could miss that?" Jared asked. "Take the picture."

"Oh, yeah." Cat lifted the camera and snapped a series of photos. "Wow, isn't it remarkable? I can't believe I'm looking at the St. Louis Arch."

"Try to get some photos when we go over the bridge," Jared advised. "That'll be your best chance."

Cat lifted the camera back to her eye. As they crossed over the mighty Mississippi, Cat let the shutter fly. The August wind was hot in her face, and she watched in fascination as the sun lit up the massive silver arch. The river was crowded with boats and shimmered in the sun like a well-worn suit.

Her heart raced as she thought of all of the travelers who had passed before her through the grand gateway to the West. It still felt like a dream to her. The excitement she awoke with each morning hadn't ebbed. She'd been afraid homesickness would kick in as soon as she'd left Massachusetts, but that hadn't happened.

She didn't know how much Jared had to do with her state of well-being. She didn't want to know. He'd soon be back on his ranch, and she'd be facing her adventure alone again. Would homesickness catch up to her then? She didn't know.

What she did know was that the man beside her was a devastatingly good smoocher. Just thinking about his kiss made her toes curl against the floorboard.

She'd thought she could have an affair with him. She'd thought it could be something swift and sweet, but now she wasn't so sure. Sweet yes, but swift was doubtful.

Jared wasn't like anyone she'd ever known. And sleeping with him would be the greatest test of her newfound independence. It would be so easy to lose herself in him, even easier than it had been with the big dumb jerk. Could she be with Jared and walk away? Or would she become the pathetic, clinging vine she'd been before? There was only one way to know for sure.

"Cat," Jared interrupted her thoughts. "Are you planning on coming back in some time today? You're letting all of the air-conditioning out."

"Sorry." Cat pulled her head back in and turned to face Jared. "I got lost in thought."

"What about?" Jared asked as he released Lucy.

"Last night."

"What about it?" His intense blue gaze flashed to her, and Cat glanced down at her lap.

"I just wanted to apologize for waking you up." Cat fidgeted with the camera case in her lap. "It won't happen again."

"You're right it won't." Jared reached across the seat and brushed the windswept hair from her cheek. "I got carried away with you last night. I don't intend to make the same mistake twice."

"Why?"

"What do you mean 'why'?" He frowned at her.

"I mean," Cat paused to clear her throat, "why don't we just...you know?"

"You know?" Jared's frown deepened. "No, I don't know. Enlighten me."

Cat expelled a nervous breath, plunging ahead before she lost her nerve, "Why don't we make love?"

"Make love?" Jared hollered. "Are you nuts?"

Hot color flushed Cat's cheeks, but she persisted. "No, I'm not nuts," she argued through tight lips. "I am, however, very attracted to you, and I think it would be beneficial for both of us."

"Sweetheart, I can think of a lot of words to describe it, but 'beneficial' isn't one of them," he retorted.

"Are you saying no?" she pushed, wanting the conversation to die a quick merciful death.

"I'm not sure," Jared drawled. "When you say you want to make love, do you mean one time only, or were you thinking it could be a random hit-or-miss kind of thing? Maybe we could stop at a few rest stops along the way, or better yet, check into a sleazy by-the-hour motel."

"Never mind," she snapped, feeling foolish at his mockery. "You're obviously not as sophisticated as I thought you were."

"There's nothing sophisticated about sex." Jared shook his head at her. "It's purely an animal kind of thing."

"I'm sure it is for you." Cat sniffed and glared at the Missouri scenery outside her window.

ANGER WELLED UP in Jared, surprising him with its swiftness and intensity. He couldn't believe this sweet woman was offering him a cheap meaningless affair. With any other woman, he might have jumped at the chance. But the thought of Cat being like that with any man made his insides twist. And all because one big dumb jerk had thrown her away. Couldn't she see how special she was? How much she had to offer?

Cat deserved a whole man. A man that could give her all of himself not just bits and pieces. She deserved to be some guy's treasured wife. That guy wasn't Jared. And he'd be damned if he'd pull her self-esteem any lower by accepting her offer.

Reaching over the puppy, he captured her hand in his and placed a searing kiss against her palm. Her skin was warm against his lips, and his fingers tightened around hers in response.

"You deserve much more than an affair," he said. "Don't ever settle for less than you're worth."

HIS VOICE WAS A GRUFF GROWL that whispered over her skin, and Cat shivered. Who was she kidding? An affair with Jared would be like selling her soul to the devil. She'd be lucky to survive, never mind walk away. She ignored the regret that pinched her heart and nodded her agreement. "I hope we can still be friends."

"Of course." Jared smiled at her, unaware that his eyes contained a look of naked longing.

Cat felt her spirits lift at his expression. The man could resist the pull between them all he wanted, but it was there. And maybe, just maybe, she could seduce him into making love to her. Cat tucked away her smile and began to plot.

THEY STOPPED FOR LUNCH, gasoline and other necessities in a small town a few miles off Highway 44. The day was blisteringly hot, and Cat was pleased she'd thought to wear a pale-yellow tank top and matching shorts. Not only was it cool, but it had rendered Jared speechless when he'd seen her.

They agreed Cat would drive the afternoon shift. She listened to his thorough list of cautions and warnings, with an expression she hoped resembled grave appreciation. Really, the man was such a worrier. As if she would let them fall behind schedule! She watched as he belted himself into the passenger seat, pulled Lucy onto his lap, lowered his baseball hat over his brow and fell asleep.

She felt a twinge of remorse nip her conscience. Jared wouldn't be so tired today if she hadn't woken him in the middle of the night. As quietly as possible, she switched on the engine and belted herself into the driver's seat. Now if she could just remember the way back to the highway.

Cat searched vainly for road signs that would point her in the right direction. She took a left out of the grocer's lot, feeling certain that the on-ramp was just up ahead. Three turns and thirty minutes later, she wasn't so sure.

She sat at a crossroads, facing a dirt road that seemed to lead nowhere. This can't be right, she thought. Wouldn't she remember a dirt road if they'd been on one before? Cat pulled the travel map from the dashboard and tried to retrace her route. The map told her nothing. Putting the van into reverse, she backed up onto a pull-off area where she could turn the vehicle around, hopefully, without waking Jared.

As she maneuvered through the narrow rural roads, she tried to convince herself that she wasn't as hopelessly lost as it appeared. She retraced her route as accurately as possible, but instead of finding the grocery store as she'd hoped, she came face-to-face with an enormous cow.

Cat stood on the brakes while her right arm shot out to keep Lucy and Jared from being propelled into the dashboard. The van halted just inches from the large mammal that continued to chew its cud as though nothing unusual had happened.

"What the...?" Jared roared when Cat's elbow poked into his ribs, rousing him from his slumber.

"Sorry." She grimaced, hoping he wouldn't notice the rather large, black-and-white roadblock barring their escape.

"Where are we?" he asked, releasing his grip on Lucy.

"Missouri...I think." She shrugged.

"What?" He shook his head as if something was tampering with his hearing.

"I'm not certain where we are." Cat gazed at him as nonchalantly as the cow.

"We're lost? How could we be lost?" he asked in amazement. "All you had to do was take a right out of the grocer's parking lot, and we would have practically fallen onto the highway."

"I took a left. And we're not lost. We're directionally challenged." Cat tooted the horn to shoo the cow out of the road. It continued to chew its cud and watch her squirm.

"Call it what you will. We're lost. Why would you take a left?" he asked.

"I thought that was the way to the highway," she said. "Obviously, I was mistaken."

"How long have you been mistaken?"

"About an hour," she answered as she rolled down her window and stuck her arm out in an attempt to wave the cow away. It was useless.

"And you didn't wake me?" he shouted.

"I didn't think it was necessary," she answered. "I'd have found the highway eventually."

"Your brother's right," Jared marveled. "You have the sense of direction of a chicken with its head cut off."

"I do not," she protested.

"You do realize that we're headed north?" he asked.

"Yes," she lied.

"And when we left the highway, we were headed north?"

"Yes," she lied again.

"Then how are you going to find the highway if you keep traveling north and are, in fact, driving away from it?" he grilled her ruthlessly.

"I figured I'd run into a sign sooner or later," she explained lamely.

"Oh, you'd have hit a sign all right, probably one that reads 'Welcome to Iowa.'" Jared shook his head in disbelief.

Cat turned a serene glance from the cow to Jared and back again. A chuckle tumbled out of her lips, before she could stop it. Jared's eyes narrowed at her amusement and then he, too, began to laugh. He had a rich deep laugh that was as contagious as a tickle. They laughed at each other, glanced at the immovable cow, and erupted into laughter again.

"I'll say one thing for you, Catherine Levery," Jared said as he wiped the tears from his eyes. "You're never dull."

"I think I'll take that as a compliment," she retorted.

The cow, apparently bored by their laughter, resumed its walk across the narrow road and into the pasture beyond. Only after it was out of earshot, did Lucy leap up and begin to bark.

"Fine watchdog you are," Jared teased and ruffled her ears.

"I've been trying to retrace my steps," Cat said, taking her foot off the brake. "But so far, nothing looks familiar."

"Let's drive until we see someone, then we can stop and get directions," Jared advised.

"Sounds like a plan."

They traveled through the rolling hills until they saw two

men visiting over a fence. One was sitting on a tractor, the other stood on an overturned crate. Cat pulled over to the side of the road and waited while Jared went to get directions from them.

She saw the men glance at her and break into sympathetic grins. How annoying. It wasn't her fault that there was such lousy signage leaving the grocery store. If there had been a proper sign, she never would have gotten lost.

Jared thanked the gentlemen for their help and ambled back to the waiting van. How Cat could have taken the wrong turn was beyond him. It certainly validated Cameron's opinion of his sister's navigational skills. No wonder he worried about her.

Jared tried not to think of Cat alone in Copper Creek. He wouldn't be there to share her misadventures or rescue her when she got lost. It was disconcerting to realize not how much she would need somebody, but how much he wanted that somebody to be him.

Jared tried to shake these thoughts loose as he climbed into the van beside the woman who was beginning to torment his every waking hour. She was his friend's little sister and that was as far as it went. If he touched her, he was pond scum. He'd never forgive himself, and he was quite positive neither would Cam.

"So how far off are we?" she asked.

"Not terribly," he reassured her. "Just go straight until the road forks, veer to the left and that road should lead us to the highway."

"See? I told you I would have found it," she said.

Jared's mouth popped open as if he would protest, but then it slammed shut. Cat smiled.

A half hour later they were merging back onto the highway. Glancing at her side mirror, Cat saw an RV cross two lanes of heavy traffic to pull in behind them. She frowned. People were such reckless drivers. Then she noticed that the man driving looked familiar. He was wearing a fishing hat covered with lures.

"Jared, what color was the Bickersons' RV?"

"Um, white with a dark blue stripe," he said. "Why?"

"Because I swear that's them behind us, but they're in a different RV. This one is tan and green."

Jared looked at his side mirror. "The angle is bad. I can't see."

"I'm sure it's them. How odd. I thought Mabel said they were going to Florida. This isn't the way to Florida."

Jared rolled down his window and stuck his head out. The RV dropped back out of sight. "It must be someone who looks like them," he said.

"I guess," Cat said, unconvinced.

Trying to make up for lost time, they pressed on through the evening until they landed at a motel in Joplin, Missouri.

After they hauled their luggage and Lucy into the motel room, they each collapsed onto a bed.

"I don't think I've ever been this tired in my entire life," Cat observed with closed eyes. "Even with my eyes shut, all I see is the road in front of me, mile after mile of dotted white lines."

"I know what you mean," Jared's deep voice growled in agreement. "Fast food for dinner?"

"Definitely." Cat turned to glance at him.

"Do you realize we're only halfway there?" Jared asked, his forearm resting on his forehead as if to ward off a headache.

"You're kidding."

"Nope."

"Oh, God," Cat groaned and Lucy leapt up onto the bed and licked her hand in sympathy.

"Don't worry," Jared said. "We'll be there before you know it."

Cat studied the room around her. It was decorated in

deep shades of blue and green. Everything matched from the prints on the wall to the carpeting on the floor. Even the curtains and bedspreads matched. It screamed motel room.

But it was her motel room, and she shared it with the most attractive man she'd ever known. And she was sitting somewhere in the middle of the United States having a fabulous adventure. Life didn't get much better.

"We need to call Cameron," Jared said.

The adventure took an abrupt downward turn.

"Why?"

"Because I promised I would check in with him," he said. "To keep him from worrying."

Cat narrowed her eyes. "Fine. Call him. I'm going to take a shower."

She began to unzip her suitcase, and Jared jumped off his bed, pulled his bedspread free, and began to drape it between them. Although she knew it was childish, Cat was annoyed. He was just tucking the end of the bedspread behind a painting when she whipped off her tank top. She sent it sailing past his head. He glanced back to see her standing in her bra and shorts and his eyes bugged. She smiled.

Jared blinked and all but ran to attach the other end of the blanket to the mirror on the opposite wall. She heard him sigh once it was fastened. So, he thought he was safe now, did he? She began to hum, something slow and sexy as she rifled through her suitcase, looking for fresh clothes.

"I'M GOING TO CALL Cam now," Jared yelled and pulled the phone onto his side to the curtain. She hummed louder.

Jared punched the buttons on the phone as if the ten-digit number were 911. His friend's voice would jar him back to reality, he was counting on it.

"Hello?" Cameron answered the phone.

"Hey, buddy," Jared's voice sounded strained, even in his own ears. He glanced up. The bedspread was motel thin, and the light on the other side shined right through it, casting Cat's form into delicious, seductive shadow. "Oh, damn."

"What's that?" Cam asked. "Hey, where are you?"

"Joplin," Jared croaked, watching Cat bend over her suitcase. Her hum lowered to a purr as she arched her back, her fanny in the air, and stretched to lift items out of her bag. It was all Jared could do not to groan.

"Missouri?" Cam asked. "That's great. You're halfway there. How's Cat?"

"Fine," Jared gulped. He watched Cat's shadow as she shimmied out of her shorts with all the sensuality of a burlesque dancer. When she stepped out of them and tossed them onto the bed, Jared gasped.

"Can I speak with her?" Cam asked.

"No!" Jared snapped. "She's in the shower."

"Really?" Cam asked.

"We're sharing a room," Jared explained.

"Oh," Cameron said.

"But it's not what you think," Jared said. "Really. Nothing's happened."

"Okay," Cam said.

"Absolutely nothing," Jared said. "I'm treating her just like a little sister."

"I'm sure you are," Cam agreed.

"Yep, you don't have to worry about me making a move on her. No sirree," Jared said.

"It's okay, buddy," Cam said. "I believe you."

"You do?" Jared asked.

"Of course, I do," Cam said.

"Oh," Jared said. Glancing back at the curtain, he watched her unsnap her bra and slide it down her arms. He couldn't talk to his friend in this condition. As it was, he figured he'd have to go outside and bench press the van just to regain his sanity. "Look, we'll call you when we get to Arizona."

"Okay. And Jared?"

"Yeah?"

"Thanks," Cam said.

"Right," Jared said and hung up. He flopped back onto the bed and watched her pull on a short robe, tying it about her waist while still humming. The longing to rip the bedspread down, dive across the space between them, push her onto her back and climb on top of her was as primal an urge as he'd ever felt. Fighting it tooth and nail, he fisted the sheet in his hands and began to bang his head on the hard mattress. He doubted it would help, but at least it was something to do.

"WHO WAS THAT?" Julia asked her husband.

"Jared," Cam answered as he replaced the receiver. "He and Cat are in Joplin, Missouri."

"How's the trip going?" she asked.

"He's falling for her," Cam said. "I knew he would."

"You little matchmaker." Julia laughed and kissed her husband's cheek. "You're pretty proud of yourself, aren't you?"

"I just gave fate a helping hand," Cam said. "Those two are perfect for each other and by the end of the week they'll both see it, too."

"JARED, WHAT DO YOU KNOW about cars?" Cat asked.

"Why?" He glanced up from the map he'd been studying.

"Well." She grimaced. "I'm not positive, but I think the white puffs of steam coming out from under the hood are a bad thing."

"Pull over," he ordered, tossing the map aside.

Cat flipped on her signal and veered onto the shoulder. The steam was now billowing from beneath the hood. She glanced at Jared.

"Overheated." He frowned at her.

"Now what do we do?"

"Halfway across Oklahoma and our engine overheats." Jared ruffled Lucy's ears. "Doesn't that just figure?"

Cat glanced at the sparse scenery out the window. Oklahoma in August was as dry as dust and bone-wiltingly hot. The grass was bleached almost white and the few trees that broke up the arid landscape didn't look strong enough to support the leaves on their limbs.

"What are we going to do?" Cat asked.

"I'll take a look at it," Jared said and climbed out of the car.

Cat watched as he used the hem of his shirt to pop open the hood. A cloud of steam bellowed out. Cat gasped but Jared rolled out of the way and waved to her from the side of the van.

She rolled down the window and asked, "Well?"

"We have a broken hose," he shouted over the roar of the traffic. "I'm going to try to flag down some help. Sit tight."

It was a scorcher out there and Cat could see the sweat beginning to pour off of his brow. Did no one care that they were broken-down? Jared stood on the side of the road and waved but no one stopped. Cars and trucks streamed past him in an unending line. He looked chagrined and shrugged at Cat. She shrugged back. What could they do?

The van was beginning to heat up and Lucy licked Cat's hand and whined.

"I know, baby," she said and filled the puppy's water dish with some cold water. Lucy lapped at the water, spilling more than she drank.

Cat rolled down her window to offer some water to

Jared. She froze with her hand on the window crank. Jared was standing on the side of the road doing what looked like ballet moves!

Cat took a swig of the water and watched in rapt fascination at the sight before her. Jared had his hands extended over his head. He jumped in the air and wiggled his feet and then leapt from foot to foot. He looked like a frog on hot tar.

The cars that had been slowing down to observe their breakdown were now speeding up to get past the weirdo on the side of the road. Jared did a series of twirling leaps that looked as preposterous as a hippo in a tutu. Cat burst out laughing while Lucy watched him with her head cocked to the side as if uncertain of his sanity. When he attempted a split in midair, Cat cringed, fearing a nasty groin pull. Jared just bounced back to his feet and bowed. Some wise guy honked but didn't stop.

When Jared climbed back into the van, Cat was laughing so hard her belly hurt.

"What was that?" she asked.

"My attempt to get someone to stop," he said. "I was hoping someone would think I'd gone crazy from the heat and pull over to help."

"I think you scared away any Good Samaritans."

"Scared them?" he asked. "Does no one have a sense of humor?"

"Just me," Cat said. "Maybe if you showed a little leg someone would stop."

"You want me to show them the goods?" he asked, looking offended.

"Not all of the goods." She laughed. "That would land you in jail."

"You don't think I can do it, do you?" he asked.

"Uh…no," she said.

"Don't move," he said and hopped out of the van, slamming the door behind him.

He strode to the side of the road and pulled off his shirt. Cat felt her pulse thud in her ears. He was perfect. Muscle-hard and deeply tanned, his chest looked like she could bounce a quarter off it.

Jared struck a parody of a bodybuilder's stance. A lady honked and hollered her phone number as she drove past. He raised his arms and flexed. Another lady honked and threw a five-dollar bill out the window at him, but she didn't stop. Jared looked miffed.

He came back to the van and Cat handed him a cold bottle of water from the cooler. She tried not to stare at his chest.

"Nice try," she said. "But you should leave this to the professionals."

"Oh, is that so?" he asked. "You think you can do better? Be my guest."

Cat fished her lipstick and her hairbrush out of her purse. She fluffed her hair and reddened her lips. With a smile at Jared, she said, "Back in a jiff."

Jared watched her hop from the van. She paused on the side of the road to hike up her shorts and pull the straps on her tank top down over her shoulders. What was she doing?

She blew him a kiss and Jared felt his ears grow hot. She moved to stand in front of the van. She leaned back against the van so that her figure was shown to full advantage. She raised one knee and let her leg swing. She looked like a pinup girl from the forties, with her full red lips and her wild hair being teased by the breeze, not to mention the amount of female curves she had on display. She was every sexual fantasy he had ever had. Jared was transfixed at the sight before him.

The screech of brakes shattered Jared's lustful daze and

he frowned. One, no two, make that three vehicles pulled over onto the shoulder, leaving long black skidmarks in their wake.

Cat turned and glanced at him over her shoulder. Then she winked. That did it!

Jared stomped out of the van just as the first driver was approaching her.

"Cat, get in the van," Jared said.

She frowned at him.

"Do you need some assistance, ma'am?" A pimply faced kid, about sixteen, asked.

"No, she doesn't!" Jared snapped. "Get out of here."

"Jared!"

"Git!" Jared yelled and the young man ran back to his car.

"What seems to be the trouble?" the second driver, an older gentleman, asked.

"No trouble," Jared said. "Move along. She's fine now."

"Jared, have you lost your mind?" Cat asked. "We need help."

"No, we don't. Just move along, old man. Show's over."

"Humph." The old man stomped to his car and took off.

"You folks in need of some help?" A pretty young woman, wearing coveralls and baseball hat climbed out of the third vehicle.

Jared paused and Cat blinked.

"I saw your ballet moves," the woman said to Jared. "Pretty funny stuff. I was in the far lane so I had to double back to come get you. Can I offer you a lift?"

"No," Cat snapped, but Jared said, "Yes."

"Well, which is it?" the woman removed her hat and tossed a thick braid of honey-brown hair over her shoulder and looked between them.

"Yes," Jared said. "Definitely a yes."

Cat sat squished against the door with Lucy beside her. Jared sat in the middle, next to Molly, their rescuer.

"So, Jared, where are you and your wife headed?" she asked.

"She's not my wife," Jared said. A little too quickly, Cat thought. "No, Cat is more like a little sister to me."

Cat blanched. A little sister? How could he possibly think of her as a little sister? If he was sitting any closer to her, she'd bite him. Here she was smack dab in love with him and he thought of her as a sibling! Argh!

Cat stilled. In love with him? She felt her stomach flip over as if they'd hit a bump. She glanced out the window. There wasn't a pothole to be seen. Uh-oh. She'd fallen in love with the big galoot.

No, this couldn't be. That wasn't on her meticulously planned itinerary. Nowhere on her index cards did it read "fall in love." Ack! This was completely unacceptable.

"Cat, are you okay?" Jared asked. "You look pale. Did you get overheated?"

"In a sense," she said and he frowned. She turned away. "Don't worry. I'm fine."

6

THE REPAIRED VAN TOOK THEM all the way to Amarillo that day. The panhandle of Texas was just as hot and dusty as Oklahoma had been, and it was with relief that they finally stopped for the night.

They settled into their motel room after a quick bite at a diner and a brisk walk around the parking lot with Lucy. Jared watched Cat curl up on her bed with a book. She hadn't been herself since the van broke down. She was withdrawing into herself, and he felt helpless to stop her. He didn't know what had upset her, and he had no clue as to how to get her to talk to him.

There was no chatter before bedtime. No midnight talks or make-out sessions. Jared found himself at a complete loss. This was what he'd wanted, wasn't it?

In frustrated silence, he listened as Cat tossed and turned behind the blanket that separated their beds. He wanted to go to her, but common sense told him not to. Tomorrow would be soon enough to talk to her about Cameron.

Jared awoke to find the motel room empty. There was no sign of Cat, her voluminous overnight bag or the puppy. Panic struck him as hard as a hammer. Leaping from the bed, he grabbed his jeans and raced to the door.

He ripped it open to a wave of heat, and the sight of Cat and Lucy loping down the sidewalk toward him. Her eyes were on the two cups of coffee she gripped in her hands. Jared's gaze moved over her. Gone were the sexy tank tops and tight shorts he'd been tortured with for days. In their place, she wore blue shortalls and an enormous gray T-shirt. She looked cute.

"Where have you been?" he demanded more harshly than he intended.

CAT'S GAZE SHOT to where he stood in the doorway, and her heart stopped in her throat. Wearing nothing save a pair of unbuttoned jeans, Jared took her breath away. His hair was tousled from sleep, and the grouchy expression he wore resembled that of a grizzly interrupted during hibernation.

The man was tan all over except for a small patch of white skin just visible above his waistline. Cat felt heat creep into her face as she was riveted by that skin.

"Well?" He frowned at her, his arms folded over his chest.

Cat tried to walk past him, but he blocked her path, letting only Lucy slip into the room behind him.

"May I come in?" she asked, fighting to keep her gaze on his and not on his body.

"Sure." He smiled, but it was all teeth and no warmth. "When you tell me where you've been."

"Excuse me?" Cat raised her eyebrows and pushed past him. "I don't have to report to you."

"No, you don't." He nodded, slamming the door behind them. "But it would be common courtesy to let me know where you are going."

"You were asleep," she argued, puzzled at this new behavior of Jared's.

"You could have woken me up," he argued, grabbing his shaving kit and stomping into the bathroom.

"Next time I will," she yelled at the slammed door. She turned bewildered eyes to Lucy. "What do you suppose that was all about?"

JARED KNEW he'd overreacted. But when he'd awoken and she was gone, every protective instinct he possessed charged through him. It was impossible to pretend the feelings he had for her were merely that of friendship. Ever since the van had broken down, and he'd practically torn apart the two guys who had ogled his Cat, he'd known there was no going back.

He had no choice but to be honest with Cat, tell her about Cameron's lie, and hope she'd be willing to forgive him. How to tell her, well, that was a whole different barrel of pickles entirely.

They ate breakfast at a truck stop, chicken fried steak with gravy thick enough to clog an artery and biscuits. Jared tried to broach the subject then, but Cat was avoiding any and all conversation with him. Gone was the woman who badgered him incessantly. In her place sat a woman buried in a newspaper, making only monosyllabic grunts to his every attempt at conversation.

Before leaving Amarillo, Jared insisted they stop at Cadillac Ranch, hoping the tourist attraction would rouse the old Cat. With any luck, he'd be able to draw her into a conversation.

As they hiked across the working farm field, Jared watched as curiosity and amazement lit her delicate features. Silently, he congratulated himself on his genius. The ten classic Cadillacs, half buried nose-down in the field, were well-worn with age and vandalism, but the sheer preposterousness of the spectacle was remarkable.

"What a fantastically crazy idea." Cat laughed, letting Lucy lead her between the cars, whose metal tail fins stuck high in the air. The warm wind whipped her hair around her face, and Jared found himself returning her laughter.

"Cat." He reached for her hand and pulled her around to face him. "I want to…"

"Look, Mom!" A child, no more than four, came tearing around one of the cars to pounce on Lucy.

Following the child hurried a frazzled-looking mother

and father. They apologized for their son and tried to pull him away to look at the cars. Jared glanced down the path to see more tourists hiking their way to look at the cars. The moment was lost.

"Are you ready?" Cat asked, pulling her hand out of his.

"Yeah," he answered with regret.

Once back in the van, Jared tried to broach the subject again. He didn't particularly want to talk while driving, but if he waited until they reached Gallup, New Mexico, tonight, he might lose his chance.

"I'm so tired," Cat interrupted him and stretched in the passenger's seat. "I think I'll take a nap."

Jared frowned as she pulled his baseball cap down over her eyes. Why did he get the feeling she was thwarting him on purpose? Well, too bad, little lady. Like it or not, they were going to have this conversation.

"I don't think so," he said and tugged the baseball cap off her head. Her rebellious hair sprung about her head, and she had to blow some curls out of her eyes before she could glare at him.

"What's gotten into you?" Her quick-changing eyes flashed blue fire in annoyance. "First you bite my head off this morning, and now you won't let me sleep. What's going on?"

"I've been trying to talk to you," he growled. "But I get the feeling you're trying to avoid me. Want to explain why?"

"Not particularly." She crossed her arms over her chest and stared at the dashboard.

Jared leaned over the puppy to cup her chin and turn her face to his. "Aw, now what happened to the daring woman that crawled into my bed at three o'clock in the morning and demanded, of all things, conversation?"

"Just start the van," she ordered as her face flamed. "I already apologized for that, and you know it."

"I know you did, but I didn't." Jared's voice grew solemn.

"There's no need for you to apologize." She sighed. "I'm like a little sister to you. Right? Well, if we're family then you don't need to apologize."

"Ah, now I get it," Jared said. "Hold that thought, darling."

Cat felt her insides lurch at his endearment, and she watched in bemusement as he opened his door and came around to her side of the van. Without a word, he jerked open her door and pulled her out of her seat and into his arms.

Wedged between the vehicle and Jared, Cat was not given a moment to consider this abrupt turn of events. His lips landed on hers in a kiss that possessed her all the way to her toes. Her blood lurched in her veins, and she arched against him, a frustrated moan echoing in her throat.

He pulled back, and his blue eyes grew dark when Cat's only response was to wrap her arms around his neck and cling to his solid strength. His gaze pierced hers, with a look that bespoke sweaty passion and rumpled sheets. Cat shuddered. It was a look that scorched. Oh yeah, he wanted her all right.

"So, I'm more of a kissing cousin?" she asked.

"I'm sorry I compared you to a little sister yesterday. I was in denial," he said. "I've tried to think of you that way. Really, I have."

He leaned his forehead against hers. His breathing was uneven, and his hands shook as they trailed her spine. He had to come clean now, before he got even more carried away with her. Cupping her face with his palms, he drew a steadying breath and tried to ignore her heavy-lidded, passionate gaze.

"Cat, I have to be honest with you," he began.

She nodded, as if unable to speak.

"It's about Cameron," he began.

"What about Cam?" She went still, and Jared lowered his hands to grip her hips.

"About three weeks ago, he called me to ask a favor." Cat gasped, but Jared continued, "I agreed to do the favor, because he's my best friend."

"What favor?" she asked in clipped tones.

"I think you know," he said, watching her eyes turn blue with fury.

"Tell me," she demanded. "I want to hear it."

"He asked me to drive out west with his somewhat absentminded sister."

"You don't hitchhike, do you?" she asked.

Jared shook his head.

"And you don't have a place in Maine?"

"No," he admitted ruefully.

She shoved his arms aside and glared at him. "So this was to soften the blow?"

"No. I was trying to let you know how I feel about you." He ran a frustrated hand through his hair.

"How do you feel about me?" she snapped. "Never mind, it's obvious. You think I'm a scatterbrained nitwit who couldn't find her way out of a closet with the door open."

The hurt in her eyes hit Jared like a punch in the gut. He'd have preferred a punch—at least it would assuage some of the guilt he felt.

"I care about you," he said.

The veracity in his deep blue gaze was unmistakable, and Cat knew he was being honest. But it was too little, too late.

"Why?" she asked, her throat tight with angry tears. "Why did you lie to me? Do I really seem so feeble-brained that I can't be let out on my own?"

"No." Jared's voice was gruff. "Damn it, I never wanted to hurt you. But Cam asked me to protect you, and he's my friend."

"So your friendship with my brother is more important than being honest with me. Well, that tells me where I stand."

"It's not that simple," he protested.

"Isn't it?" she asked.

"I'm sorry, Cat," he said.

"Me, too." Pulling away from him, she climbed back into the van and slammed the door in his face.

THEY ARRIVED in Gallup, New Mexico, well after dark. This would be their last night together. Cat tried to feel better about that, but it just depressed her. She was supposed to have gotten Jared to make love to her by now. Ha!

They'd hardly exchanged two words all afternoon. Despite Jared's apology, she was still furious. She'd been duped. First by Cameron and then by Jared. It was like trying to swallow an aspirin that was lodged in her throat. A very bitter pill.

She'd thought Jared was different. He had seemed to believe she was just fine the way she was. But it had all been one big, fat whopping lie.

She'd spent the day mulling over what he'd said, and she understood his dilemma. But she also understood that he'd chosen his loyalty to her brother over his desire for her. And she was furious with him for it!

"What do you want for dinner?" Jared asked from his side of the room.

"I don't care," she said, patting Lucy as she moved across the motel room to stand by the window. She pushed aside the blinds and saw the neon lights of a honky-tonk bar flicker across the street. She let the blinds drop back into place.

"Order whatever you want," she said, feeling reckless. "I'm going out."

"What?" he snapped.

"I'm going out," she repeated.

"Where?"

"None of your business," she answered, pulling a clingy, tank-top dress out of her suitcase.

"What do you mean, 'none of my business'?" His eyes bugged.

"Exactly that." She grabbed the hem of her T-shirt and began to pull it up. "If you want to protect your friendship with my brother, you may want to turn around."

He narrowed his gaze at her and spun on his heel. "Cat, I know you're still angry. You have every right to be, but going off half-cocked isn't going to solve anything. We need to talk this out."

"Ha!" Cat laughed without mirth. "The quiet one wants to talk!"

"Cat." Jared peeked over his shoulder, but she ducked out of his line of vision.

"Ah-ah. No looking. What would Cam say?"

"Cat." This time his voice was a growl, and he spun around just in time to see her jerk the dress down to her knees. Stepping into strappy black sandals, she flipped her hair over her shoulder, pushing it into place with her fingers.

Grabbing her wallet out of her purse, she knelt down to scratch Lucy's tummy. "Don't wait up."

"Cat!"

She shut the door with a click. She was being petty, childish, immature and juvenile. Halfway across the street, she almost turned around, but the thought of facing Jared in retreat stayed her course. She was going out on the town by herself. That would show him!

Besides, how could she face him? She'd been throwing herself at him for days, and he'd merely been baby-sitting her. It was humiliating. Oh, sure, he'd said he cared for her and there had been moments between them when she'd thought something special was happening. But that was

Jared. She was sure any woman would feel swept away by him.

Pushing open the door to the Red Horse Saloon, she strode into the dimly lit, smoke-filled interior as if she were an experienced bar hopper. A jukebox blared out cowboy ballads that Jared would undoubtedly know the words to, while the television over the bar cast the room in an eerie blue light. A bar lined the wall to the right, while pool tables filled a room toward the back.

"Are you coming in or going out?" the bartender snapped.

"Coming in," Cat squeaked and stepped over the threshold.

"What'll ya have?" The bartender was short and stout and his bulbous, red nose indicated that he drank his share of the profits.

"What kind of wine do you have?"

"We don't got none," he said. "Hard alcohol and beer, that's it."

"I'll have a beer," Cat said and slipped onto a stool at the end of the bar.

The bartender poured one off the tap and smacked it down in front of her. "Two dollars." Cat handed him three.

A group of men were playing pool at the back, while two older men sat several stools down from her. Cat tried to relax, pretended to watch the football game on TV, and chugged half of her beer with a grimace, all the while wondering how long she had to sit here until she'd made her point.

"I can't finish it now, not with her sitting there."

Cat glanced up to see the chubbier of the two men pointing at her.

"Aw, come on," the other one chided, scratching his whiskers. "You can't leave me hanging for the punch line."

"Not with her there."

Cat glanced away, feeling as out of place as a rooster in a henhouse, or more accurately, a hen in a rooster house. She chuckled.

"It's just the punch line, spit it out!"

"Oh, all right," the man relented, casting Cat a sidelong glance. "So then the man says, 'Hey that's no lady, that's my wife!'"

"Heh, heh, heh," the whiskered one laughed and slapped his friend on the shoulder. "That's a good one, George."

"Thanks, Pete." The portly one grinned.

"That's the oldest joke in the book," Cat said, propping her chin on her hand. "I've heard that one a million times."

George spun his head toward her, his mouth gaping open as if he'd just seen a three-headed goat. Then his gaze narrowed, and he said, "Oh, and I suppose you've got a better one."

"You betcha," Cat answered and rose from her seat to move one seat away from him. "Want to hear it?"

"Sure," Pete answered for his friend. "And if it's better than George's, I'll buy you a beer."

"What if it isn't?" she asked.

"Then you'll buy me a beer."

"What about me?" George piped up.

"Shut up. Let the little lady tell her joke."

"Okay," Cat began. "What does a dog get when he flies?"

The men shook their heads.

"Jet wag," she said with a laugh. Pete and George looked pained, but she heard a snicker from somewhere.

"That was terrible," Pete said.

"I'm a fourth-grade teacher," Cat said. "Give me a break. Okay. Here's another one. Why won't sharks eat clowns?"

Both men shook their heads again.

"Because they taste funny," Cat said, slapping her hand on the bar with a laugh. "Get it? Clowns taste funny."

"Ugh." Pete lowered his head to the bar, and George looked away.

A second beer was plunked down before Cat and she looked up to see the bartender giving her a lopsided grin.

"That dog one was funny," he said shyly.

Cat smiled. What a nice man.

"Had enough?" A deep voice growled in Cat's ear, and she started, dousing George's shirt with her beer.

"Look what you made me do," she gasped and dabbed at George with a cocktail napkin. "I'm sorry, George."

"That's all right," he said. "I'll send him the cleaning bill."

Pete burst out laughing. Cat looked at George's shirt. It was a blue T-shirt with a large red arrow on it that read I'm with stupid. The arrow was pointing in Jared's direction.

"You do that," Cat giggled and turned to Jared. "How long have you been here?"

"Just in time for the jokes." Jared raised an eyebrow at her.

"Yep, he's been standing in the corner, glaring at you for quite some time," Pete confirmed.

"You want us to help him out the door?" George asked.

"No, he's a...friend." Cat wrinkled her nose as she said the word, hoping to make her feelings clear. Jared just sighed.

"Bartender, get these gentlemen two more beers on me," Jared said and threw a ten on the bar. "Come on, Cat, let's go get some dinner."

Dinner did sound like a good idea. Waving goodbye to her companions, Cat followed him out the door.

"If you wanted a beer, you should have waited until after dinner," Jared said.

"I didn't want a beer, I wanted wine, but they didn't have any," Cat said, letting him lead her into the motel's restaurant. "I was about to leave and come back to the room, but they bought me a beer, and I didn't want to be rude.''

"Heaven forbid," Jared mocked her as he helped her into a booth.

Cat curled her lip at him and snapped open her menu. She was famished! When the waitress appeared, she ordered a full dinner plus dessert.

"And I'd like my coffee now, please," she said.

"Make it a decaf," Jared said to the waitress.

"No." Cat shook her head. "I want regular."

"You'll be up all night," Jared argued.

"No, I won't," Cat insisted.

"Decaf," Jared whispered to the waitress.

"Regular," Cat said from between her teeth.

"Fine." Jared snapped his menu shut. "But I don't want to hear it when you're wide awake at three in the morning."

"You won't."

"How long have you two been married?" the waitress asked with a chuckle.

Cat and Jared glared at her.

"That long, eh?" the waitress asked as she walked away.

They ate dinner in silence, primarily because Cat was too busy eating to make conversation. Pleasantly full, she lingered over a second cup of coffee and a heaping helping of apple pie à la mode. Pausing, with her fork halfway to her mouth, she glanced at Jared. He was pinching the tips of his ears, looking completely agitated.

"Is something wrong?" she asked, expecting him to chastise her for her second cup of coffee.

"No," he snapped.

"Then why are you rubbing the tips of your ears?" she asked. "You're not getting sick, are you?"

"No," he said and then changed the subject. "Do you always moan when you eat?"

"No." Cat replaced her fork on the dish as she felt a

hot flush creep up her neck. "Only when I'm enjoying my food. Why, does it bother you?"

"Yes." Jared frowned, and then his mouth curved up into a slow, seductive and positively wicked grin. "That moan of yours makes the tips of my ears grow hot."

"Oh," Cat said, swallowing around the lump of apple in her throat.

On the walk back to the motel, Jared took her elbow and Cat let him. She was still angry with him, but it was nice to feel his callused palm against her skin. It seemed like ages, instead of hours, had passed since he'd kissed her, and she missed the feel of his mouth against hers like a physical ache.

"I can take care of myself, you know," she said, trying to pick a fight to cure her longing.

"I know," he agreed.

"Then why...?"

"Because Cameron asked me to," he said.

They entered the motel room silently. Cat paused. Lucy always greeted her at the door, but there was no sign of her.

"Lucy," she called. "Lucy."

Then she heard it. A grinding noise. Cat peered between the beds and found Lucy busily gnawing a rawhide bone.

"Jared, did you give Lucy a bone?" she asked.

"No, why?"

"Because she has one now," Cat said.

"Maybe the maid gave it to her," he said.

"Maybe," Cat agreed, unconvinced. "Hey, why is my bag on your side of the room?"

"I don't know," Jared said. "Why is my bag in your side of the room?"

"This is weird," Cat said.

"You don't suppose...?" Jared asked, looking pointedly at Lucy.

"Nah," they said together.

They undressed in silence with the bedspread hanging between them like a physical manifestation of the turbulence between them.

Good-nights were short. The light was flicked off with a snap. Cat lay in bed, studying the ceiling above her. It had all been lies, she thought. He didn't hitchhike. There was no cabin in Maine. He probably had money, too. She frowned.

If he had money, then there was no reason for them to be sharing this room now, except that she'd miss him if he wasn't there. But why hadn't he taken a room of his own? He'd been uncomfortable sharing a room since day one. Now that his secret was out, he could get another room if he wanted. Why hadn't he? She stared into the dark. Unless he didn't want to.

And if he didn't want to… No, it couldn't be. She glanced at the clock. The number on the digital clock changed, and she sighed. The caffeine was keeping her awake. So much for defiance, she thought. She turned onto her side. Her thoughts refused to be shut off or ignored. Like an itch that needed scratching her thoughts turned back to Jared. Why hadn't he gotten a separate room?

Perhaps it had been an oversight, but she doubted it. Jared was a watcher. He wasn't one to overlook the details. Maybe, just maybe, he'd been telling the truth and he did care about her and was just as attracted to her as she was to him. The thought flooded her with heat. She flopped onto her back. He was lying just four feet away, probably in boxers and nothing else. She had to know. Did he want her as badly as she wanted him? And if so, what would it take to make him do something about it?

She pushed the sheet aside, and sat up in bed. She'd been saying she wanted to prove her independence and take care of herself. Well, wasn't going after what she wanted a big part of that? And she wanted Jared. He'd lied to her, betrayed her trust, and conned her. He owed her!

She left Lucy sleeping on her bed, and ducked around the bedspread to Jared's side of the room. She stood by his bed as silent as a shadow, just watching him. He was lying on his side, facing her, with one arm under his pillow and the sheet knotted up around his waist. Cat reached out to touch him, but her fingers never made contact with his skin.

His hand shot out and clamped about her wrist. "Don't!" he said.

"Oh!" she started, but Jared didn't release her wrist. "You're awake."

"Your tossing and turning would keep the dead awake," he said.

"Sorry," she lied and took a step closer to the bed.

"What's the matter, coffee keeping you up?" he asked.

She let his sarcasm slide. She sank onto the bed, and used her free hand to trace a finger across his chest. "Among other things."

Jared's breath hissed from between his teeth. "Cat? What are you up to?"

"Up to?" She blinked. "Not a thing…yet."

"You're looking for trouble," he observed. "Why?"

"Because, as I figure it, you owe me, Jared McLean."

7

"OWE YOU?" he repeated. Releasing her wrist, he rose from the bed, folding his arms across his chest. "Just how do you figure that?"

"You lied to me." She glared up at him and crossed her arms over her chest, mimicking his stance.

"I explained about that," he said, taking a step forward. Cat took a step back.

"What more do you want me to do?" He took another step forward. Cat took another back.

"I want you to make love to me," she said, her voice gritty even to her own ears.

"Make love to you?" He took two steps forward. Cat took several back, until she felt the dresser at her back and knew she was stuck. "You don't know what you're saying."

"Yes, I do," she argued, not a bit intimidated when he placed a hand on either side of her, trapping her. "Are you attracted to me, yes or no?"

"Cat, how can you even ask that?" he groaned, lowering his lips to her throat.

"You wouldn't touch me because of your friendship with my brother," Cat said. "Are you worried about your friendship now?"

"Only with you," he muttered against the tender skin below her ear. "Cat, I never wanted to hurt you."

"Shh," she ordered, not wanting to hear the words. She

wanted only touches between them. Words hurt and, for once in her life, she was tired of them.

"Then make love to me. Please, Jared."

Her pleas were his undoing. Instinct and need overrode any honorable scruples he might have suffered. Primitive wanting pounded him. He couldn't fight it any longer. In the span of mere days, she'd wrapped herself around his heart like no one else ever had.

"Sweet, so sweet," he muttered as his lips descended to hers. She was so soft, so warm and fragile. He couldn't get enough of her. He buried one hand in the fine tendrils of her hair and curved the other around her hip, pulling her up against him until she cradled him.

As though she was caught in the same haze of heat that consumed him, Cat melted in his embrace. Passion washed over him in great aching torrents, leaving him feeling shaken from the inside out.

As his fingers cradled her scalp, he plunged his tongue deeply into her mouth and wooed her into a response. Jared felt the deep trembles that racked her body. With a moan, she wrapped her arms about his neck and returned his knee-wilting kiss with one of her own.

Their kiss broke off with their need to breathe. Still holding her hips against his, Jared ran his other hand through his hair. He was fighting for control, but the feel of her curves pressing into him was rapidly doing him in.

"I'm sorry," he said, trying to get his rioting desire under control.

"Oh, no you don't." She narrowed her eyes at him. They were green in passion, and Jared felt himself swallow nervously under her seductive gaze.

With the slow, deliberate movements of a woman who knew what she wanted, Cat buried both of her hands in his thick, blond hair and pulled his lips down to meet hers. Had she really thought she could deny her feelings for him?

Had she really thought she could just shut them down? This was Jared. She could no more deny him, or her feelings for him, than she could stop breathing. Her hurt and her anger vanished like shadows in the dark. The only thing she responded to now was the stark need in Jared's face.

She used every tool she knew. Every tool he'd taught her. As her tongue delicately traced the outline of his lips, she dragged her hips across his in an invitation he couldn't mistake.

"Oh, Cat," Jared groaned and leaned into her. Cat found herself pinned between his hot body and the dresser, but she didn't mind. His mouth savaged hers, and she arched into it, refusing to let him take charge of the kiss.

He ripped his mouth from hers and rested his forehead in between her breasts. She could feel his breath through her cotton nightshirt, and she shivered. She felt his body stiffen, and she decided to tip the scales. She lowered her mouth to his throat and nuzzled a path up his neck to his earlobe.

"Jared?" she whispered, her voice a husky alto.

"Hmm." His response was little more than a deep groan.

"I want you," she whispered into the shell of his ear. "Won't you please make love to me?"

His control, which had been teetering on the brink of submission, went careening over the cliff, pulling Jared with it. Hauling her up into his arms, Jared let the raging desire that had taunted him for days swell into a roaring tempest. There wasn't a part of his body that didn't ache or throb to possess this woman. He gritted his teeth as he tried to stifle the lust coursing through him. He was determined not to let his greed for her consume his need to show her how much she meant to him.

With ease, he laid her on the hard motel bed. She was breathtakingly lovely with her pointed chin and luminous eyes. Her hair spread out on his pillow just as he'd imagined it a thousand times. He hoped to be the gentle, ardent lover her former fiancé obviously hadn't been. But he hadn't counted on his desire for her.

The need he felt was almost painful in its intensity. He didn't know how long he could hang on or how good he would be able to make it for her. Especially if she kept looking at him with such tenderness and caring and…love.

It took his breath away, the realization that she did love him. He doubted she even realized it herself. But it was there, shining in her eyes as surely as the sun. He felt humbled by it.

He refused to examine his own feelings. To do so would be to shatter the beauty of the moment. He knew his feelings were deep. Deeper than they'd ever been for any woman, but love? He was afraid he was incapable of that intangible, evanescent emotion. Instead, he concentrated on the woman before him, with her arms open wide and willing.

The moment he lay between her thighs, Jared knew he was a goner. The steel control he'd always been able to maintain with the opposite sex evaporated like mist in the sun. His hands swept up her torso, his thumbs pausing to wreak havoc with her nipples, while his tongue once again claimed her mouth in the most basic way a man could claim a woman.

With a soft woman's sigh, Cat surrendered as Jared advanced upon her. She beckoned him closer by tightening her arms about him.

Hot sensations unfolded within him as she arched her back, pushing her breasts into his hands while her fingers sought his flesh.

She pushed at his boxers, until he let go of her long enough to shove them off himself. Cat sighed as her hands roamed and stroked and taunted at will.

Jared groaned at the feel of her questing hands. He pulled

his lips from hers and began to kiss a trail down her throat, while he unfastened the buttons to her nightshirt and yanked it over her head. He released a pent-up breath when at last his hands were able to caress the precious flesh that had been making his life hell for days.

Cat writhed beneath his touch. With callused fingers and a hot, wet tongue, he stroked her everywhere at once. As he ran his lips across one breast and then the other, she felt a liquid heat begin to pool and bubble low in her belly.

"Oh, Jared…please," she begged, reaching for him, but he eluded her grasp.

"Oh no, honey, I've waited too long for this to be rushed. We're just beginning," he said and splayed one hand across her abdomen, holding her still, while he kissed his way down her body. He kissed the inside of her thigh, and laughed when she bucked against him. "You're so beautiful, Cat."

She whimpered and he lowered his head to the curls at the juncture of her thighs. He sought out her secrets with his tongue, and she thrashed against the bed.

Cat had never been loved like this before. No one had ever made her feel this brand of pleasure-pain before. Heaven help her, she wanted more.

"Jared!" she wailed.

"Come for me, Cat," he coaxed, his mouth moving against her. "Come for me."

She had no choice. An explosion of heat rolled through her, and she arched taut as waves of intense pleasure convulsed within her.

She was breathing through her teeth, hissing with pleasure, but Jared gave her no chance to loiter in her solitary splendor. Lifting her knees, he pressed himself against her hot, slick opening with a groan that could have been ecstasy or agony.

"Cat." His voice was gruff with lust held in check. "Cat, look at me."

She did. Sweat coated him, causing their bodies to sizzle and stick together. Why this made Cat's insides knot, she didn't know, but they did just the same. She lifted her legs and wrapped them about Jared's waist, never breaking contact with his gaze.

"Hang on," Jared ordered, sounding as if he'd rather die than wait. He reached for his shaving kit, and Cat suddenly knew what he needed. Grabbing the kit for him, she pulled out a foil packet and ripped it open with her teeth. Her insides were still shuddering, and she couldn't think of any way to ease the throb except by having him come inside her.

She'd barely rolled the condom about him, when he shoved into her with one sure stroke. She tightened her legs about him while her body hugged his. Ah, this was bliss.

The scent of her, the softness of her, the feel of her skin beneath his. It ruined Jared. It beckoned to him like a siren's call and left him wasted upon the rocks. He couldn't get enough of her, and he thrust deeper and deeper into her tight, wet warmth.

Cat's response was to pull him closer. It was as if she, too, suffered from this need to be one. When he felt her stiffen, the walls of her insides milking him with their contractions, Jared exploded into her heat with a final deep thrust that sent his soul to spiraling to meet hers. When he collapsed on top of her, he captured her mouth in one last searing kiss.

They lay entwined for a long while. Neither one wanted to break the moment by speaking. It wasn't until Cat let out a yawn and snuggled closer to him that the ramifications of what they'd just done hit Jared like a sledgehammer.

What had he done? She'd gazed at him with those big

eyes of hers, and he'd allowed her to seduce him with his own need. He'd wanted her, and he'd taken her. But there was no understanding between them. She was still hurt and angry, and he was still uncertain that he could be the man she needed. What was he going to do now?

"Sweetheart," he whispered, rising up on one elbow. "We have to talk."

"I don't want to." Cat pushed his elbow and he collapsed onto the bed, stunned. Resting her head on his shoulder, she closed her eyes and sighed.

"You don't want to talk?"

"No."

Jared leaned over her and pressed his lips to her forehead. It wasn't a kiss. Cat swatted him away and sat up. "What are you doing?"

"Checking for fever," he said. "When you don't want to talk I worry."

"I don't have a fever," she said and then grinned. "Unless you want to give me one."

"Cut that out," he chided her, pulling her back down into his arms. "This is serious."

"Oh, phooey." She burrowed her nose into his neck.

"Cat, why did you come to me tonight?"

She stilled against him. His already deep voice had dropped an octave, and she knew her answer was very important to him. She guessed he was worried that she'd fallen in love with him. Well, she had. She'd known that since the van broke down, but there was no need to burden him with her feelings.

She knew him well enough to know that by making love with her, he was going to feel that he'd betrayed Cameron. He didn't need the added burden of worrying about hurting her. Besides, even though she loved him, she wasn't ready to relinquish her independence just yet. And she had no doubt that, if she declared her feelings for him, if for no other reason than honor, Jared would pursue a relationship with her.

She sought safety in a partial truth. "Because I wanted you," she said, her voice as low and gritty as his. She didn't say anything more.

"Why?" Jared felt his heart buck, and he cupped her chin with his hand. It was there in her eyes, but he wanted to hear her say it. He didn't analyze why her words of love were so important. He just knew that his desire to hear those words outweighed even his desire to have her body.

"I don't know. From the first moment I saw you, I wanted to make love with you." Her gaze shifted from his.

Jared felt his heart constrict at her words. What had he expected? That he would take her to bed, and she would suddenly declare her undying love for him? Disappointment rocked him, but he buried it where he'd buried every other emotion. He buried it in silence.

"I felt the same way about you," he said, lightening his voice. He traced patterns at the base of her spine and kissed her hair. Patience, he coached himself. She would open to him in time, he just needed patience.

She rose up on one elbow and placed a hand on his chest. "Your heart is thumping as loudly as mine. Hold me, Jared?"

Jared saw the damp shine in her eyes, and he knew he was lost. Pulling her on top of him, he buried his hands in her hair and kissed her with all of the desperation and longing he felt. What the future would bring he had no idea, but for the moment she was his and that was all that mattered.

"WE'LL BE CROSSING the Arizona border in a few minutes." Jared glanced at the woman beside him. She glowed this morning, and he was more than willing to take full credit. Every time his gaze rested upon her for more than a moment, she flushed a beguiling shade of pink, and he was charmed all over again.

"So soon?" she asked, pulling her gaze from the jagged, scrub-covered mesas surrounding them to look at him.

"We should arrive at your new home by early evening," Jared said, trying to gauge her response.

"All of a sudden, this seems very real to me." She bit her lower lip and glanced at the harsh scenery.

"You're going to be fine," he reassured her, placing a hand on her thigh. "You always have been." Cat shifted in her seat away from Jared's touch. His touch made her think of sweat-slick bodies and soul-deep shudders. His touch was not conducive to calm, rational reasoning. And that's just what she needed—calm, rational reasoning.

Last night had been the single most incredible experience of her life. Making love with Jared had been like running at top speed off of a mesa and soaring. She'd never flown so high or so free.

Unfortunately when she landed, she'd landed with a thump. A thump of reality. She could try and ignore her feelings as much as she liked, but the fact was, she loved him. Heart, soul, mind and body. And last night had only made it worse.

She'd thought she could be a woman of the new millennium, one who could have an affair with a man and then forget him. What a crock! If she had a lobotomy, she couldn't forget Jared, and now she'd be living as his neighbor for the next year!

"What are you thinking about?" he asked.

"That a year is an awfully long time," she answered.

"I'm willing to keep you occupied," he offered with a wolfish grin.

Cat felt a swirl of heat coil inside of her. The man was pure devil, and he knew it. But somehow he made her feel better.

THEY STOPPED at a Denny's in Holbrook at midday. Cat was too nervous to eat. She sipped an iced tea while Jared ordered a grand slam something or other. They were just hours from her new home and the anticipation was killing her. With three thousand miles of road behind them, it was hard to believe they were here.

The restaurant doors opened and Cat grabbed Jared's arm and pulled him down under the booth.

"Don't look but the Bickersons are here," she whispered.

Jared lifted his head and smacked it on the booth's table. "Ouch!"

"I told you not to look," she whispered.

"Why are we hiding?" he asked, rubbing his head.

"Because I think they're following us," she said.

"Why would they do that?" he asked. "That makes no sense."

"Well, neither does the fact that they keep turning up when they're supposed to be going to Florida, but they do," she said.

"That does it," Jared said and tossed his napkin aside. "Come on."

Jared took Cat's hand and led her over to the Bickersons' table. Fly was wearing his usual fishing cap and Mabel was wearing a denim shirt that sported a hot-pink fringe topped with magenta rhinestones. For a second Cat had trouble looking away from the dazzling sight.

"Hello, Fly," Jared said. "Mabel. What are you two doing here?"

Fly yelped and frowned at Mabel. "What'd you do that for, honeybunch?"

"Do what, sweetie?" She blinked.

"Kick me," he said. "You probably broke my leg."

"I did not," she snapped. "You big sissy."

"Sissy," he yowled. "Why I ought to—"

"Ha!" Mabel snorted. "You haven't got the nerve."

Cat squeezed Jared's hand. This was getting ugly.

"And you two are in Arizona because..." Jared interrupted them.

"Fly wants to see the Grand Canyon," Mabel said and glared at her husband. "Don't you, pookie?"

"Yeah, buttercup," he sulked. "That's right."

Jared looked at Cat with a raised eyebrow.

"I have to tell you that for a moment we were wondering if you were following us," he said.

Mabel choked on her tomato juice, spewing it across the table. Fly thumped her on the back none too gently.

"Why ever would you think that?" she gasped.

"You said you were going to Florida," Cat accused.

"We...uh...changed our minds," Fly said. "Isn't that right, peanut?"

"Yeah." Mabel barely acknowledged him and narrowed her eyes at Cat. "Where are you going?"

"The Phoenix area," Jared lied, squeezing Cat's fingers as if to get her to play along. "Just outside Phoenix actually."

"Maybe we'll see you again." Mabel smiled.

"Yeah, maybe," Cat agreed, hoping not.

"We'd better roll," Jared said.

"Good luck to you," Cat said to the Bickersons as Jared pulled her away.

"It's official," Jared said when they were out of earshot. "They're weird."

"Let's get out of here," Cat said.

"I'm right behind you," he agreed.

THEY DROVE SOUTHWEST from Holbrook, and Cat watched the scenery roll by. The dusty, scrub-covered hills rippled all the way to the horizon where she could see dark clouds looming ahead of them.

"Oh, no." She nudged Jared's arm. "Look ahead."

"Stormy weather." He nodded. "That's pretty typical during monsoon season."

"Monsoon season?" she echoed.

"Didn't your friend tell you?" he asked. "July and August are the rainy season for Arizona."

"No, Sally didn't mention that," Cat admitted.

"Be careful," he admonished her. "We have a lot of dried-up riverbeds, called washes, that fill up during a storm. A lot of people have been killed when they get trapped in the washes and swept downstream. They drown."

"I'll be careful," she promised, even though she suspected Jared was exaggerating.

The road they followed became mountainous, and Cat kept a watchful eye on the storm to the south of them. Occasional bolts of lightning lit the darkening sky, and she gasped at their brilliance.

"This is nothing like Massachusetts," she marveled. "Do you realize the sky above us is still blue, but I can see that storm as clear as if it were overhead?"

"There's a lot of sky out here," he agreed. "It gives you a nice feeling of space."

"I'll say," Cat agreed and then jumped when another brilliant bolt ripped through the sky. "Whoa! Did you see that? Are we going to drive through the storm?"

"No, it's moving south of us."

"Hey!" Cat sat up straight. "Isn't that the Bickersons?"

Jared looked at the white-and-black RV chugging along behind them.

"I can't tell. It sure looks like it."

Cat stuck her head out of the window to get a better look. The RV abruptly switched lanes.

"I'm sure it's them," she said. "And this is the third

RV I've seen them in. Something's not right. I think we should try and lose them.''

"What?" Jared looked at her as if she'd suggested they pull down their pants and moon them.

"I mean it. They're following us. We need to make a getaway.''

"You're joking," he said.

"Humor me," she asked and batted her eyelashes at him.

Jared sighed and hit the accelerator.

As they distanced themselves from the RV, it sped up. Like a game of cat and mouse they stayed just out of reach, swerving to block the RV when it got too close.

"It has to be them," Cat said. "But why are they after us?"

Jared frowned. There was something awfully odd about this.

They left behind open land and were enveloped amidst large pine trees. The road became steep and curvy as it wended its way through the mountains. Drop-offs punctuated every turn, and Cat held her breath while Jared navigated the steep climb. The van's engine was running at maximum. Their so-called high-speed getaway was going an absurd twenty-five miles per hour up the steep incline.

"This is ridiculous," Cat said. "I could run faster."

"You may have to," Jared said.

The road leveled off and they sped up. The RV followed. The road began to wind into hairpin turns and Jared lost sight of the RV in the third turn. He hauled the van into a small pullout and parked behind a thick cluster of pine trees. The RV rolled on by.

"Did we lose them?" Cat asked.

"I hope so," Jared answered, easing back on the accelerator. "I'm going to backtrack and take another route south. It'll take longer, but we won't be seeing them again.''

BROODING ABOUT the Bickersons, Cat didn't notice that they'd left the mountains behind until Jared nudged her with an elbow.

"Cat," he said. "Take a look."

Cat pulled the puppy in from her perch and glanced out at the hills surrounding them. The air coming in through the open window was scorching hot, but she was too engrossed in the scenery to notice. The land to her right was covered with tall, green, multiarmed cacti.

"Saguaro cactus?"

"Yes." Jared laughed at her surprise. "We've finally reached their latitude."

"There are so many of them!" she exclaimed. Her gaze ran over the view, and she noticed several other smaller cacti also dotting the hillside. "I always pictured the desert like the Roadrunner and Wile E. Coyote cartoons, you know, one cactus in the middle of nowhere. This isn't like that at all. It's beautiful."

"You really think so?" he asked her sharply.

"Yes," she answered with a note of awe in her voice. "Look, you can see the mountains in the distance. Aren't they amazing?"

"Sure are," he agreed, stretching in his seat, looking more relaxed than he had all day. "I'm glad you like the desert. Not everyone does. It's hot and rugged and leaves no room for ambivalence. You either love it or hate it."

"I think I'm one of the former," she assured him. The dimples in his cheeks deepened, and the grin he sent her was blinding.

They passed over a bridge, and Cat noted the narrow stream that trickled in the vast riverbed. She wondered what it would look like after a storm. Large wispy green trees sat along its banks and she noted in surprise that even their bark was green, or so it appeared.

"What kind of trees are those?" she asked.

"Palo Verde," Jared replied. "It's Arizona's state tree. The name means 'green stick' or 'branch'."

"So they really are green?" she asked.

"Yes," Jared laughed.

"Whew, I thought I was seeing things," she confessed with a chuckle.

"No, but you will in a moment," he promised. "We're about five minutes out of Copper Creek."

"Really?" She felt her stomach flutter in anticipation, and she dislodged Lucy so she could sit up in her seat. "I think I'm actually nervous. I mean this is going to be my home for the next year. It doesn't seem like a long time, and I know it will pass quickly, but what if it doesn't? What if no one in town likes me? What if I don't like the town…?"

"Cat." Jared reached over and gently tugged at the way-ward curls that danced on her shoulders. "You'll be fine."

"Sorry." She grimaced. "I'm just a little nervous."

"I know, honey."

Cat's heart flipped over at the endearment. She knew it shouldn't mean anything to her. This was supposed to be an affair, with no strings attached and no emotional com-mitment. But Jared wasn't playing by the rules, and she couldn't stop the warmth that flooded her at the tenderness in his voice.

As the van wended its way through town, Cat and the puppy kept their faces pressed to the window, eager to see their new home. Cat was delighted by the western flavor of the town. Most of the buildings sported square, false fronts, or stucco with red tile roofs.

Compared to New England, she felt as if she'd landed on another planet. Prickly pear cacti were planted beside a few of the stores, and Cat was pleased to see several leafy green trees, creating shade here and there. If it weren't for the cars parked along the side of the street, she'd almost think she'd stepped back in time.

"This is wonderful. I half expect to see the local sheriff and his faithful deputy strolling down the center of the street, looking for a shoot-out."

"I can't wait to tell my sister that." He laughed.

"Why? I don't think that's so funny," she chided him.

"It is, trust me, it is." He chuckled. "I'm not laughing at you, Cat, I'm laughing with you."

"But I'm not laughing." She tried to frown at him, but failed and turned her face back to the window before he saw her answering smile.

They left the center of town and turned onto a bumpy, narrow back road. Cat tried to ignore the nervous flutter in her stomach and restlessly began to scratch Lucy's head. She was sitting up on the seat, her ears perked up, as if she knew they'd arrived someplace important. Either that, or she had to take a leak.

Jared made another turn onto a short side street, and Cat held her breath as he pulled in front of the third stucco house on the right. The houses on the street were well spaced, and Cat was relieved to see that although she had neighbors on each side of her, they were far enough away to allow her some privacy.

"We made it." Jared switched off the engine and turned to face her. She didn't move. "Are you planning on getting out, Cat?"

Cat glanced at him and forced herself to pull it together. "I'm going. I'm going," she said. "I'm just a little stiff from the drive."

"Uh-huh." He looked dubious.

"Come on, Lucy." Cat fastened the leash to the puppy's collar and opened the door. "Let's go see our new home."

To Cat's delight, the quaint, stucco house boasted a red tile roof. A stone walkway led through an arched doorway into an enclosed courtyard. Cat promptly fell in love with it. A small fountain sat in one corner and wrought-iron patio furniture filled the other. On each side of the wooden front door were two flower boxes. Each was filled to bursting with scarlet Indian paintbrush.

"Oh, my," she gasped.

Jared heard Cat's sigh of appreciation when she walked into the courtyard and sent a silent thank-you to her friend for her good taste. He hoped the interior of the house was just as nice. It was important for Cat to love it here, more important than he cared to think about at the moment.

"Isn't it beautiful?" she asked. "I think every house should have a courtyard like this. I can't wait to see the inside."

Jared felt the tension within him ease. It was going to be all right. The nervous Cat had vanished and the daredevil was back. He watched her unclip Lucy and stretch her sore muscles. She put her fist in her back and arched against it. Jared felt his mouth go dry. The hot breeze drifting through the courtyard played havoc with her already disheveled hair, and she stopped stretching to push her curls out of her face.

Lust rooted Jared to the spot. Every cell in his body swelled with heat. It left him shaken and close to gasping for breath. The realization that he'd be leaving her soon only made his desire sharpen with an edge of panic.

Without pausing for thought, he left the archway and strode toward her. She'd paused in the doorway, as if uncertain. Jared was determined not to let her have any doubts.

Pushing both Cat and Lucy into the front room of their new home, he watched as the puppy began to sniff with blatant curiosity around the southwestern interior. Satisfied that Lucy was occupied for the moment, Jared grabbed Cat's hand and scanned the layout of the house. Finding a hallway to the right, he strode down it with a determined step, pulling a befuddled Cat behind him.

"Jared, where are you going?" she asked as she hurried behind him.

He didn't answer her. She'd know soon enough. Besides, he didn't want to give her a chance to think about it and reject him.

He strode past two bedrooms, stopping at the third and largest bedroom at the end of the hall. Not realizing he'd stopped, Cat plowed right into his back with a surprised "oomph!" Jared reached back to steady her with a hand. Glancing over his shoulder into the room, she smiled with delighted surprise.

The room was decorated Santa Fe style. The blond furniture was cut with jagged patterns and decorated in rich browns, reds and blues. The enormous bed in the center of the room matched the rest of the furniture with its carved wooden headboard. Jared liked it immediately.

"Isn't it wonderful?" she asked from behind him.

He didn't answer. He turned and before she could utter a sound, he lifted her up and tossed her onto the mammoth bed. Her mouth popped open in surprise, but his actions must have given him away, because her quick-changing, mercurial eyes flashed from angry blue to seductive green in a blink.

He advanced toward her, and she reclined on the bed, her arms outstretched and welcoming him. Jared felt a peculiar knot tighten in his throat. She thought this was goodbye. He had yet to inform her differently, but he would. Oh yes, he certainly would.

8

THE PREDATORY GLEAM in Jared's eyes sent a thrill rushing through Cat from her head to her feet. She hissed out a breath. Their time was drawing to a close. She tried not to think about it, but there it was. She studied him, trying to memorize everything about him from his white-blond hair to his low-slung jeans.

She wouldn't cry. She refused to cry. She swallowed her tears and concentrated on the man climbing onto the mattress beside her. His hair brushed her cheek as he kissed a path down her throat. The intimacy of that touch caused her heart to wrench. Oh, goodness, she loved him.

She gripped his broad shoulders for a moment, wanting to hold onto him. She forced herself to relax her grip and stroke his back, mimicking the caress of a lover. What she wanted to do was hang on and never let go, to lose herself in him. But no, she'd done that once before, and it had left her empty and alone, collapsed upon herself like a vine without a trellis. She wouldn't do that again.

Oh, but this man, he tempted her. To have him forever, to become one with him, it felt right. He was different, special, hers?

She wanted to remember everything about him, his strength, his warmth and his scent. She wanted to remember how she felt at this moment, just before they joined, so that in the future, when she was alone, she would be able to relive this moment. This man.

''Cat.'' Jared's voice was thick with desire, and he

leaned over her, cupping her face with his palms. "What are you thinking?"

Cat let herself be trapped by his cerulean gaze, and she knew she couldn't tell him what was in her mind, her heart, her soul. That she loved him. If she told him, he'd feel obliged to take care of her, and she couldn't allow that. Instead, she chose an answer guaranteed to coax a response.

"That I want you," she whispered and arched up against him, capturing his lips with hers.

"You're killing me, woman," he growled against her mouth.

"Yeah, well, ask a stupid question," she murmured, and Jared shut her up with a kiss.

His tongue wooed its way past her lips and into her mouth. It teased the roof of her mouth and tangled with her tongue, causing her heart to hammer triple time and her knees to shake.

"Cat." Jared ripped his mouth off hers and fought to catch his breath. "I don't want to steamroll you into bed. If you want me to stop, tell me now. I'll walk away, probably into oncoming traffic, but I'll walk away."

She squirmed out from under him and knelt to face him on the bed. Cupping his face with her hands, she pressed light kisses against his lips, his cheeks, his temple. Then she paused to trace the swirls of his ear with her tongue. He shuddered and she smiled.

In a voice as dusky as twilight, she breathed, "I want to be steamrolled. I want to be squashed flat by you."

With a groan, Jared pushed her back against the pillows. She'd robbed him of all reason, and he was helpless to stop it. He was supposed to be in control. He was supposed to make all the moves. But it seemed Cat had her own agenda, and keeping him distracted appeared to be on the top of her list.

He was rocked when she pulled his head down and

kissed him with a thoroughness that left him breathless. Before he could inhale, she had his shirt shoved up under his arms, and her questing hands were tracing the clenched muscles of his chest. Jared attempted to move away, but then her lips found the frantic pulse at the base of his throat and he was lost.

Pulling her hands away from him, Jared held them over her head while he tried to gain control of his rioting hormones. God, she was beautiful. Her fiery hair splayed out on the bedspread, and she gazed at him with half-closed eyes that shimmered a deep emerald green. Her lips were parted in invitation and Jared didn't have to be asked twice.

Rolling to the side, he jerked and tugged at their clothing, tossing it carelessly aside. When his bare flesh pressed hers deeper into the mattress, he felt her shudder and he smiled.

Jared caressed her soft curves, loving her warmth. He wanted to possess her from the outside in. He was seeking a mating of souls as well as flesh. With that goal in mind, he began working his way toward the core of her.

His lips burned a path down her throat to her breasts. When her nipples were slick and tight in response, he used his tongue to glide by her navel and nestle in the curls at the juncture of her thighs.

She opened her mouth to protest his complete possession of her, but his tongue flicked across the folds of her flesh, and she moaned instead. Jared chuckled at her response, and the reverberation of his voice against her skin caused Cat to grind her hips against the mattress.

She couldn't let him dominate her so completely. She had to meet him as an equal. Cat gripped the edge of the mattress and pulled herself out from under him. Always, she had been a passive lover, but with Jared she wanted to be the aggressor. She wanted to shake him down to the soles of his feet. When he looked at her, she wanted him to quake.

He watched her as she rolled up onto her knees and began to stalk him. He swallowed. He looked nervous. Oh, that was good, Cat thought, very good. She placed one hand on his chest and pushed. He fell backward amidst the pillows, his eyes wide.

Cat pressed her lips to the inside of his knee, and gazed at him through her hair. He groaned. She flicked his skin with her tongue, and he began to shake. She smiled and skimmed her mouth up the inside of his thigh.

"Cat." His voice held a note of warning, but it also held a plea for more. He fisted his hand in her hair, trying to pull her away. She forestalled him by taking him in her mouth. He writhed beneath her attention.

"Cat!" He released her hair and grabbed her about the waist, lifting her away from him.

He rolled until she was flattened beneath him, his chest heaving as he reached for the jeans he had dropped on the floor. Barely lifting off of her, he slid the condom on, cursing when his hands shook.

He pulled away just far enough to meet her gaze. His breath stalled in his throat. A woman shouldn't look at a man like that, he thought desperately. Like he was everything she'd ever desired, like he was every fantasy she'd ever had. Jared loved that look. That was his look, she looked like that just for him, and for the way he made her feel.

She shouldn't let him know so much, Jared thought as he eased himself back up across her body and lowered his lips to hers in a kiss designed to make her melt. She shouldn't let him witness her love or taste her need, not if she wanted him to let her go. Because when she gazed at him like that, with all of her love shining in her eyes, he knew he could never leave her. She was his. That look was his. And he had no intention of losing either.

Parting her flesh with his fingers, he slid into her welcoming warmth. She arched into his first thrust, and Jared wanted to shout. She was as tight as a fist and as hot as fire. It made his entire body throb. Determined to go slowly, he gritted his teeth and forced himself to glide in and out of her. He didn't want to rush this. He wanted to savor every sweet tortuous second.

Cat wasn't feeling that cautious, however. She wrapped her long legs around his waist and arched her back as she pulled him more deeply into her. Jared tried not to succumb to her seductive heat, but when her nails raked his back, he couldn't resist her.

With deep fast thrusts, he pumped into her, chasing her to the pinnacle of satiation. Only after her feminine muscles fisted around him in tight contractions, and she cried out his name as if it were wrung from her soul, did he follow her with his own shuddering climax.

He didn't want to leave her, but he was afraid his enthusiasm might have bruised her. He glanced at the woman beneath him. Her eyes were closed, her breathing ragged, her lips parted in a serene smile that bespoke bliss.

Jared smoothed a rebellious curl back from her forehead. She was gorgeous in her passion, and he felt a surge of masculine pride in knowing he was the man who had brought her there. She was his. The sooner she realized that the better off they'd be.

Her eyes blinked open and she caught him studying her. "What are you thinking?" she asked.

Jared knew she wasn't ready to hear it. Her blue-green gaze was watching him with a wariness that told him what he didn't want to know. She wasn't ready to admit to any feelings between them. Not yet.

With a sigh, he lied, "I'm thinking you shouldn't live alone."

"What?" Her eyes popped open, and she tried to shove him off her.

"It isn't safe." Jared frowned, ignoring her efforts to dislodge him.

"Don't say another word." She glared at him, her voice growl-deep and furious.

"It was just an observation." He relented and rolled off her. He cupped her chin and kissed her hard and quick. "Don't get so riled up. I just worry about you."

In spite of herself, Cat felt her heart soften toward him. He cared about her. Since when was that a bad thing?

"Well, all right," she conceded. "But don't get any ideas about trying to protect me. I can take care of myself, and I intend to prove it."

"I know, honey," Jared said as he hauled her off the bed and began to thread her arms back into her shirt. "I'll give you time."

Cat wasn't sure if that was a threat or a promise. Jared ignored her while he finished dressing her sans underwear. He remained naked, and Cat tried not to notice how utterly perfect he was. Her throat tightened, and she had to force herself to leave the room, afraid that if she didn't, she'd wind up in bed with him again.

She escaped the room with Jared's chuckle ringing in her ears. She found Lucy in the kitchen chewing on a dish towel. Retrieving the soggy rag from her with a halfhearted reprimand, she let her gaze roam over the kitchen.

White cabinets covered two walls and the floor was done in large square saltillo tile. A breakfast bar stood like an island in the center of the room, and Cat delighted in the copper cookware that hung from the ceiling over it. A note sat in the center of the table and she scooped it up.

Dear Cat,
Welcome home! I hope you love my place as much as I know I'm going to love yours. There is a pizza in the freezer and a bottle of pop in the fridge. I'll call

you as soon as I get to your place. I can't believe we really pulled this off.

Enjoy your adventure!

Love, Sally

Cat smiled as she put the note back. If she told Sally how her trip had turned out, Sally would never believe her. She could hardly believe it herself.

A screened porch led off the kitchen, and looking beyond it, Cat was thrilled to see the beautiful kidney-shaped pool and patio in the side yard. Turning back, she followed the steps from the kitchen to the large sunken living room that took up the rest of the house. Like the bedroom, it was decorated in blond woods and rich Southwestern patterns.

Sliding glass doors at the end of the room led to a backyard with a lush lawn surrounded by citrus trees. Lucy sat beside the door, her tail thumping as she gazed at her new yard.

"All right," Cat muttered and unlatched the door. "But don't get into any trouble."

Jared's hands slipped around her waist and pulled her back against his chest. She wasn't startled, for even though she hadn't seen him, she'd sensed he was there.

She shouldn't let herself feel this way, she thought. She wasn't ready. She had yet to prove that she could be alone, and she had to do that before she could find contentment anywhere else. Reluctantly, she tried to pull out of his embrace. He wouldn't let her. His arms tightened about her as if sensing her desire to escape. He placed a soft kiss in her curls and then loosened his grip.

"Do you want me to drive you out to your ranch now?" she asked.

"No, it's late," he answered as he followed her through the open glass doors and out into the yard. "We can do that tomorrow."

"All right," she agreed, annoyed by the relief that swept through her. The sun was just beginning to set and the air was still scorchingly hot. She walked to the corner of the small yard and glanced out across the neighborhood. Over the red tiled roofs, a range of purple-hued mountains were visible in the distance. Cat marveled at their sculpted features. This was certainly different from anything she'd ever known.

Her gaze strayed back to Jared. Wearing only jeans, he was on his knees, wrestling with Lucy. Though his hand was bigger than her head, he was incredibly gentle with the little dog. Cat felt her throat tighten. Oh brother, she was lost again. Lost in love for this wickedly handsome cowboy.

And what would her brother say about that? She knew Cameron considered Jared one of his closest friends, but would he approve of their...whatever this was? Not in this lifetime or any other. Well, too bad. If he didn't approve, he shouldn't have thrown them together in the first place. So there!

With new determination, she strode over to the two rascals rolling on the grass. Lucy was standing on Jared's chest, looking very much like the big conqueror, until Jared grabbed the puppy around the middle and leapt to his feet. Dangling from Jared's arm, Lucy looked about as chagrined as Cat felt.

Laughing with empathy, she rescued her puppy and led the way back into the house. "I don't know about you two, but I'm starving."

Dinner was eaten swiftly and with gusto. When Jared scooped Cat up and hauled her to bed, she put up a half-hearted protest about having to unload the van. He kissed her silent and spent the rest of the night making love to her. It was well into morning before Cat finally got some rest.

Cat awoke to find the other half of the bed empty. The pillow still bore the imprint of his head. Cat placed her hand there, seeking his warmth. It was cold. Loneliness filled her. So this was what it was like to be without him. She felt lost. Alone. Miserable.

She pulled her hand back. She would miss him. The sight of his dimpled grin, the scent of him, the feel of his rough hands on her skin, the sound of his deep reluctant voice, and the taste of his kiss—he filled every one of her senses until she was overflowing with him. How had he captured her heart so swiftly and so thoroughly? And how would she keep it from breaking when they said goodbye?

She started when a thump sounded down the hall. The bedroom door eased open, and she snatched the sheet up to cover herself as Jared strode into the room, carrying her suitcase.

Her heart pounded triple time, and a ridiculous grin lit up her face. Just the sight of him brought her an unequaled rush of joy.

''What are you smiling at, sleepyhead?'' He returned her grin.

''You,'' she whispered.

Jared felt a knot of heat tighten within him. The power she had over him stunned him. Just the sight of her lying in bed caused him to ache. Her caramel hair curled about her face in wild disarray and her lips looked kissably full, but it was her enormous eyes that were his undoing. They whispered the words that she would not say.

With a fierce growl, he dropped the bag and approached the bed. He hauled her naked body up against him, and his lips flattened hers in a kiss that was hot, wet and utterly possessive. When Cat went limp against him, he released her mouth and smiled in approval.

She was his. She belonged to him as no one else ever had, as no one else ever would. But Jared knew better than to try to rein her in too soon. She was running like a mare feeling freedom for the first time. She needed to tire herself out before he could claim her. Jared was patient. He could give her all the time she needed. But she would come to him, she would marry him, and they would be together.

He let her sink into the mattress, while bracing his hands on each side of her head. The desire to strip and crawl into the bed with her was overwhelming, but he resisted. She had to be tired from the previous night, and he'd be damned if he'd take advantage of her. Besides, he feared if he was with her now, he might never let her go.

In a husky voice that reeked of sexual promise, he crooned, ''If you want breakfast, be dressed and in the kitchen in ten minutes.'' With another swift kiss, he stalked out of the bedroom, leaving a bemused Cat sighing after him.

Breakfast consisted of pancakes, bacon, juice and coffee. Cat was pleased to discover that Jared was quite a cook. He'd also been a very busy man. Not only had he gone grocery shopping, but he'd also unpacked and cleaned the van. He'd left piles of boxes for her to sort through in the guest room, the den, and the living room.

Cat was disgruntled to have him doing all of her chores for her. The man was too competent by far. She supposed she should tell him just that, but one look at his broad shoulders, strong hands and devilish dimples, and she was rendered speechless.

The man was perfect. There was no other fit description for him. And she was going to miss him terribly.

''I suppose we should turn the van in,'' she said, trying not to sound depressed and failing miserably. ''And I should take you home.''

She turned from the sink to find Jared grinning at her. Great, all she had to do was mention home, and the man became deliriously happy. He probably couldn't wait to be rid of her. She turned back to the sink and began to exorcise her temper on the dishes.

"Uh, Cat." Jared's deep voice tickled her ear as he leaned his large frame against her back, propping his chin on her shoulder. "I think that's the plate's pattern you're trying to scrub away."

Cat stared at the sparkling dish in her hand. "I knew that," she snapped.

"I'm going to miss you, too," he said, sounding pleased and not bothering to suppress his laughter.

They spent the day returning the van and driving all over Copper Creek in Sally's SUV. Jared dragged her about town, introducing her to people he knew and pointing out things he thought she should know—the bank, the route she should take to school, the local grocery store, even the garage to take her car to if she had any trouble. And if that wasn't enough, they stopped at the town hall to pick up a map of Copper Creek for her.

When Cat protested, Jared said, "I just don't want you to get lost."

"In a town with only four main roads, that would be difficult even for me," she retorted. The dubious look he sent her would have been insulting if it hadn't been so funny.

It was late afternoon, before she finally convinced him it was time to head home. Jared resisted, but when she threatened to pull over and make him walk, he relented.

They returned to the house to pack up Jared's belongings. After taking Lucy for a long walk, they left for the ranch. West of town, they turned off the main road and traveled down a dirt strip for several miles before it came into sight.

An enormous two-story stucco mansion dominated the view, and Cat found herself gaping at it in wonder. Several large buildings were spread out behind it, but it was the main house that captivated her.

"It's like something out of a novel," she said. "It's beautiful."

"My father built it for my mother," Jared told her. "It's too big for my taste. I want my sister to have it."

"That's generous of you," Cat observed, turning off the dirt road and onto the gravel driveway. Huge cottonwoods lined the drive which swept in a circle in front of the house.

Cat pulled the car to a stop and turned to face Jared. "I want to thank you for traveling with me."

"Not necessary," Jared answered as he opened his door and stepped out. No goodbye kiss? Cat frowned when he slammed the door shut.

She watched him walk around the front of the car. He opened the door, giving her no choice but to get out. "I want you to meet my family," he explained.

"I can't," she said, scrambling to straighten her wayward hair.

Jared grabbed her hand and pulled her out of her seat. "Of course you can."

"But…" She began to protest when the sound of horse hooves pounding the earth brought her attention up short.

The woman galloping toward them was one of the most beautiful women Cat had ever seen. She was lithe and lovely, her hair was a thick raven mane that flowed behind her like a banner. She and the dark brown mare beneath her moved in perfect rhythm, as if they were extensions of one another.

Just scant feet away from them, she brought her horse to a halt with a spray of gravel and gracefully leapt to the ground. She was taller than Cat, and her curves were a nauseatingly perfect hourglass.

"Welcome home!" she cried and threw her arms about Jared's neck. Cat wanted to kick her. Jared didn't appear to have any such inclination. He held the woman close, and Cat could have sworn she heard him tell her he loved her. Jealousy twisted its way through her gut, and she cursed herself for being such an idiot.

She eyed the chocolate-brown horse beside her dolefully. Did she really think Jared had no women in his life? The man was perfect, for Pete's sake. He probably had a whole swarm of women after him.

"Now, would you like to tell me why you were galloping top speed down the driveway?" Jared bellowed at the woman, and Cat was suddenly grateful not to be on the receiving end of his attention.

"It's all right, big brother." The woman smiled at the giant looming over her. "I have my doctor's permission."

Brother? Cat's ears pricked up like Lucy's at the word dinner.

"In writing?" Jared scowled as he reached behind him to pull Cat forward.

"Yes." The beautiful girl laughed.

"All right, but I want to see it," he threatened. "Cat, this is my sister, Jessica. Jess, this is Cat."

"Nice to meet you." Jess turned and clasped Cat's hand warmly in hers. "I swear I don't know how you put up with him for eight days. If I'd been you, I'd have dumped him off in Ohio."

Cat laughed, noting that Jess's sparkling blue eyes were an exact replica of Jared's. His sister. She knew she'd like this woman the minute she saw her.

"It's nice to meet you, too," she answered.

"You're just in time for dinner. I heard Rosa ringing the chow bell. That's why I was in such a rush," Jess said, patting her horse's neck. "You'll have to stay and tell us all of your adventures on the trip."

"There weren't really any adventures to speak of," Cat answered politely.

When Jared began to choke behind his fist, Jess lifted an eyebrow in doubt. Cat gave him a quick jab with her elbow. ''Isn't that right, Jared?''

''Oh, definitely.'' He winked at his sister. ''It was an awfully dull trip.''

Jess let out a low, deep laugh. Leading her horse toward one of the buildings in back of the house, she said, ''Tell Dad I'll be in as soon as I can. I want to give Trixie a good rubdown.''

''Sure,'' Jared agreed and turned to take Cat's arm. ''Are you all right with staying for dinner?''

''Oh, you mean I have a choice?'' she asked.

''No.'' He shook his head. ''I just wanted to know how you felt about it.''

''I guess that depends on what we're having,'' she sassed him, delighting in his laughter. She didn't dwell on the fact that she was feeling unaccountably relieved to spend more time with him.

The interior of the house was sparsely decorated, but with a decided Western flare. It wasn't like the Santa Fe style that filled her new home, it was somehow more authentic. Just inside the front door a wide staircase swept up to the left while another set of steps led down into an enormous sunken living area.

The colors were vibrant shades of red, blue, green and black. A large leather U-shaped sofa filled the room and faced an enormous stone fireplace that took up most of the left wall. The mantle was covered in trophies and ribbons, and the walls were decorated with photos of what Cat assumed were the ranch's prize horses.

''You've won all of these?'' she asked in awe.

''Yes. Every one,'' he said with a grin.

''Don't listen to a word he says,'' a deep voice advised.

Cat turned to see an imposing man standing in the doorway. He was almost as large as Jared, his skin was deeply tanned and his midnight-black hair was peppered with silver. His eyes were beautiful. Like Jared's and Jess's, they gleamed like blue topaz.

Cat warmed to him immediately. "I've noticed that about your son. You can't believe a word that comes out of his mouth."

"Ah, so you've learned this about him in the short time you've known him." Mr. McLean shook his head in mock regret as he came to stand beside her. His eyes twinkled as he asked, "What has he said to make you believe this of him?"

"Well, he led me to believe that he was a poor rancher, living in little more than a thatched hut," she said.

"I did not," Jared protested. "That was your own miserable brother's idea."

"See how he refuses to take responsibility." Cat looked pityingly at Jared's father. "It's so sad."

"What else?" Mr. McLean asked, trying to hold back his laughter at his son's glare.

"Well, he might try to convince you that I have a problem with my sense of direction, but I can assure you, it's just another one of his outrageous fibs." Cat patted the man's arm in teasing conspiracy.

"You couldn't find the way out of a paper bag if you punched your way out," Jared retorted in annoyance.

"See?" Cat directed a pointed look at his father.

Booming laughter fell from the man's lips, and he boisterously threw an arm around Cat's shoulders. "I take it you're Catherine Levery?" Turning to Jared, he said, "I like this girl. When are you going to marry her?"

"As soon as she'll have me," Jared answered, his temper transforming into a deep dimpled grin.

Mr. McLean released a sputtering Cat to hug Jared. "Welcome home, son."

Dinner was served on the verandah, which was as long

as the house and half as wide. The meal was lively, and Cat was warmed by the affection so obvious between all of the McLeans. It reminded her of her own family, and she was surprised to discover that instead of making her homesick, it made her feel welcome.

"So, Cat," Jess said, between bites of her fajita, "how long will you be staying in Arizona?"

"Until next summer," Cat said. "My colleague and I have switched positions for the school year."

Mr. McLean and Jess exchanged a look that left Cat exasperated and Jared grinning.

"They're incorrigible," she muttered to Jared. "Now I know where you get it from."

"Forgive us." Mr. McLean smiled at Cat. "It's just that we're so pleased to meet you."

"Jess," Jared said, changing the subject. "Did I tell you what Cat said when she saw Copper Creek for the first time?"

"What?" Jess and Cat asked in unison.

"She said she half expected to see the local sheriff and his faithful deputy strolling down Main Street looking for a shoot-out."

Jess blinked and then let out a whoop of laughter. Jared and Mr. McLean joined her. Cat frowned at them in confusion and asked, "And just what's so funny about that?"

Jess waved a hand at her. "I'm sorry, it's just that, for all intents and purposes, I'm the faithful deputy."

"You're kidding." Cat bit her lip and felt her cheeks heat in embarrassment. She turned to Jared and scowled. "I can't believe you told them, you squealer."

Jared turned his gaze to his sister. "Well, I was kind of hoping she'd change her mind."

"Not a chance," she retorted. "As soon as I'm healed, I'm reporting for duty."

"Healed?" Cat repeated in surprise.

It was Jess's turn to flush now. "I...it...oh, damn."

Jared took pity on his sister and explained, "Jess is recovering from a gunshot wound."

"Oh, my," Cat gasped. "Are you all right?"

"Fine, thanks," Jess answered, looking rueful.

"But how...?" Cat dropped her fork onto her plate and fixed her gaze on Jess.

"Did I forget to mention how tenacious Cat is when she wants to know something?" Jared teased, deftly catching the napkin Cat tossed at his head.

"I used to be one of Phoenix's finest," Jess began. "But my career was cut short when I got embroiled in a drug bust that went bad. It was supposed to be an easy arrest, but in law enforcement things are seldom as easy as they seem. I took a bullet through my shoulder, and my partner was seriously injured."

Cat saw the stark pain flicker across Jess's features. Her black brows drew together and with a deep breath, she seemed to get herself under control. Cat wanted to reach out to her, but she suspected the overture wouldn't be welcome.

"Anyway, with a little nudging from Dad and Jared, I decided to work in Copper Creek instead," Jess said. "So, I left Phoenix and came home."

"A little nudging, eh?" Cat asked.

"Like a pair of bulldozers." Jess's eyes brightened, and she laughed.

"I know the feeling," Cat said. "I have a bulldozer of a brother myself."

"Hey, Cameron might be a bulldozer, but I have more finesse," Jared protested.

"Finesse?" Jess gawked. "You have about as much finesse as a wrecking ball. Nag, nag, nag. You're like a cranky mama hen pecking at her chicks."

"I am not," Jared protested.

"Are, too," Jess said.

"Am not," he said.

"Are, too," she said.

"Children," Mr. McLean interrupted them, but Cat burst out laughing.

"I'm sorry," she said. "But I'm having a flashback from the trip."

She and Jared looked at each other and grinned. "The Bickersons," they said in unison.

"Who?" Jess asked.

"This looney couple we kept running into on the trip," Cat said. "We first met them in Ohio, where they did nothing but squabble, and then we kept seeing them on the road. We even had to make a getaway in the mountains because we got so paranoid that they were following us."

"Following you?" Jess asked, frowning with concern.

Cat recounted all of their encounters with the Bickersons.

"What do you make of the different RVs we kept seeing them in?" Jared asked.

"Sounds like grand theft to me," Jess said. "I'll look into it and see if anything has been reported. If they have some kind of a stolen RV ring going, you two might be able to help out by giving a description."

"Let me know what you find out," Cat said.

"I will," Jess promised.

A soft breeze cooled the night air, and Cat felt a deep sense of contentment fill her as she sipped her coffee and watched the sun disappear behind the mountainous horizon. As if sensing her mood, Jared reached between their chairs and laced his fingers with hers. Cat made no move to resist. Knowing she would have to leave soon, she squeezed his fingers in return. Just to let him know she cared.

All too soon, it was time for her to go home. She rose reluctantly from her seat. Both Mr. McLean and Jess rose with Jared to walk her out. The conversation continued through the living room until they stopped at the front door.

"Come and visit again soon," Mr. McLean ordered her as he kissed her cheek.

"I will," Cat agreed.

"And if ever you need me, you know where to find me." Jess winked at her.

"Strolling down Main Street," Cat teased and wished them a good night as Jared took her arm and led her out of the house.

"I like your family," she told him.

"They like you, too," he said. "Give me the keys."

"What?"

"I'm going to drive you to the end of the dirt road and make sure you're headed in the right direction," he explained.

"I don't think so." She shook her head at him.

"You'll get lost."

"I will not," she argued. "You've got to have a little faith in me, Jared McLean."

"I do," he said. "That's why I'm letting you go."

Cat glanced at him and felt herself go still. He'd meant it. What he'd said to his father about marrying her. It was in his eyes like a silent promise. He loved her. He believed in her. He wanted to marry her!

"All right, how do you get home from here?" Jared asked, interrupting her thoughts. Cat described the route in vivid detail. He made her describe it again before he was satisfied, but he finally relented.

Cat didn't admit that she'd intentionally memorized the way because she'd wanted to know how to get to him. She didn't think his ego needed that much of a boost.

"Call me when you get home," he admonished.

"No," she argued. "I appreciate your concern, but I'm on my own now, and I want to act like it."

"Oh, darling, I'm going to miss you," he said.

"I'm going to miss you, too," she whispered.

Jared took her hand and pulled her close. She wasn't ready for a commitment yet, he could accept that, but he was going to make damn sure she knew how he felt about her. And if he couldn't tell her, he would show her. He cupped her chin in one hand and planted a kiss on her that made her knees buckle. He caught her before she fell.

"It's not over yet, sweetheart," he promised. "Not even close."

9

CAT SPENT the next few days preparing her classroom for the upcoming year. Her primary subject areas were to be reading and composition, and she decorated her room accordingly.

Lifting the long alphabet poster, she decided to tack it up over the chalkboard, but she didn't have a step stool. Pulling a chair over to the wall, she climbed onto it, hoping it would give her the height she needed. Stretching up onto her toes, she laid one palm flat on the poster while she used her thumb to push the tack in. It was like trying to push through concrete. She pushed harder. The toe of her left sneaker slid out from under her and Cat felt herself pitch off the chair toward the floor below.

Clenching her eyes tight, Cat braced for impact. It never came. A strong pair of arms caught her in mid-tumble and swept her up against a hard chest.

"Hello, sweetheart," a familiar voice greeted her, and her eyes popped open in surprise. "As graceful as ever, I see."

"Jared." Cat blinked and then grinned. "Nice catch."

"I think so." They watched each other, awareness crackling between them. Cat glanced away first.

"You can put me down now," she said as primly as possible, while brushing an invisible piece of lint from her shorts.

"No," Jared refused.

"No? What do you mean 'no'?" She frowned at him.

"Kiss me first." He leered.

"Jared! Not here. Someone might see us," she protested.

"The kids haven't landed yet," he said as he walked to the door and shut it with a kick. "Pucker up."

His dimples deepened as his gaze captured hers. Cat felt her heart slam against her ribs and wound her arms around his neck. Unable to resist him, she met his lips with hers.

Jared gave in to his desire for her and slid his mouth across hers. Pulling her close, he leaned against the door and let himself get his fill of her. His lips left hers and trailed a path of kisses just below her ear and down her throat. Cat hummed in response and lifted her chin to give him better access. Jared smiled.

"You drive me crazy," he said and pulled away, letting Cat slide down the front of him before he was tempted to go too far. The slide almost changed his mind.

"Ditto," she sighed as she stepped back on wobbly knees. Taking a breath, she motioned to the poster that still hung precariously on the wall. "Could you finish that for me? I don't think I'm steady enough to stand on a chair."

"Sure." He winked at her. "Want to hold the chair for me?"

"Humph," she grunted and returned to her box of supplies.

They spent the afternoon decorating Cat's room. She never asked him why he was there, nor did she try to kick him out. She was too happy to see him. It was all she could do to keep from grinning at him like a nitwit. It had only been a few days since she'd seen him, but oh, to her heart it felt much longer.

Jared left after seeing Cat to her car. She was surprised and not a little disappointed. She'd hoped to spend the evening with him, but with a quick kiss he was gone. Cat tried not to feel hurt, yet she couldn't help but wonder at his abrupt departure.

It was better this way, she told herself. This was what she wanted. If she got used to having Jared around or allowed herself to depend upon him, then it would defeat her entire purpose for being here.

She spent the evening eating a solitary meal on her patio. Yes, this was exactly what she wanted, she told herself, ignoring the misery that assailed her. The shrill hum of a cicada broke the evening silence.

Its annoying buzz magnified the loneliness Cat felt. She glanced around the small backyard. A bug, a dog and a couple of sparrows, flitting in the trees, were her only companions. It should have been enough, but it wasn't. A breeze ruffled the leaves of the lemon tree behind her chair, and she sighed. What was that old expression? Be careful what you wish for, you just might get it. Wasn't that the truth?

When she awoke with the sun early the next morning, Cat couldn't deny that something was missing. That something was Jared. Wistfully, she wrapped her palms around her mug of coffee and watched Lucy romp around the backyard.

Lucy had grown so much over the summer. With an acute pang, Cat missed the days when Lucy was small enough to climb onto her lap. Now the little moocher took up half of the bed. She remembered the night they'd first arrived. She and Jared had awoken in the middle of the night to find themselves separated by thirty pounds of canine.

"Good morning, sunshine." His voice was a whisper that swept over her skin.

Cat whirled around, one hand trying to fluff her sleep flattened hair while the other clutched her mug to her chest. Heat suffused her face as she fought to appear nonchalant at his sudden appearance. She failed miserably.

"Oh, hi." Her voice cracked. She wanted to throw herself in his arms, but her bare feet refused to budge.

Lucy had no such reservations. Barking a greeting, she rushed Jared, not pausing until she stood braced on her back legs with her front paws on Jared's hips as she begged for pats and tried to lick his face.

"Now how come you never rush into my arms like that?" Jared chided her as he hugged the dog.

"Bring me a treat and I might," she teased, feeling her equilibrium returning. She was heartbreakingly glad to see him. She wouldn't think of all of the reasons why this was bad. She would concentrate on him.

His blond hair looked windswept, and his bright blue eyes were shadowed with something akin to desperation. His hard physique was encased in a gray T-shirt, his usual faded jeans fit him like a second skin and were painfully familiar to Cat's lonely memory.

"Do you want some coffee?" she offered, wanting to lengthen his visit as long as she could.

"I'd love it," Jared answered, ruffling Lucy's ears one more time before pushing her feet off his hips.

Cat led him into the kitchen, aware of his every step, every glance, every breath. She poured his coffee with shaky fingers. "I wish we could have breakfast together, but I have to get ready for work."

Jared shook his head at her.

"What do you mean?" She narrowed her eyes at him.

In answer, Jared strode to her phone and dialed. Cat watched in horror as he asked to speak with Principal Horvath. She waved her hands, frantically trying to stop him, but Jared ignored her.

Cat listened as he told the principal that he was kidnapping one of her teachers for the day. He explained that this teacher was new and hadn't seen much of the desert and they couldn't have that, now could they? He then proceeded to charm the principal until Cat could hear the woman's laughter clear across the room.

As soon as he hung up, Cat launched into a sputtering speech, "Jared! You…how could you…I can't…this is irresponsible, juvenile and utterly reprehensible. My students are counting on me. What kind of example am I setting by pulling this kind of stunt? You'll just have to call back and say it was a gag."

"Cat, school doesn't start for two more days," Jared interrupted her tirade by pulling her into his arms. "Your room is ready. Your lesson plans for the first month are good to go. You even have your principal's blessing. Now come on, let's go play hooky."

Nonplussed, Cat felt his hands on her hips and promptly forgot her objections. "But…"

"No buts!" Jared spun her around and nudged her in the direction of her bedroom. "Let's go play hooky."

He remembered, Cat thought as she allowed him to nudge her toward her bedroom door. She ditched her robe and stepped into the shower. She was touched more than she could say. A whole day of being bad? Catherine Levery had never had the luxury. With a wicked laugh, she decided she was going to enjoy it. No recriminations, no guilt.

"What do you want to do first?" Jared asked her as soon as they were settled in the Jeep.

Straightening the hat and glasses he'd dropped on her head, she refrained from asking if they were the same ones they'd used to sneak Lucy into the motel.

"Let's just get out of town," she suggested, not knowing what she wanted to do. "And then I'll leave it up to you. You're the tour guide."

"Great," Jared answered with a wink. "I have a few ideas."

"I'm sure you do." Cat frowned at him and slumped in

her seat as the Jeep took off through her neighborhood. Playing hooky at her age—she must be out of her mind.

They stopped for coffee and donuts at a shop on the edge of town. Cat sat with Lucy while Jared dashed into the store. A whole day with Jared, her heart sang. Oh, how she'd missed him.

She wouldn't dwell on her need to be independent, not today. Today she was at Jared's mercy. It was disconcerting to realize there was no place she'd rather be.

"Plain or jelly?" he asked.

"Whichever you don't want," she said.

Jared glared at her. "Pick one."

"Jelly," she said.

"Good." He laughed. "I lied. They're all jelly."

"What if I'd wanted plain?" she asked.

"Much as it pains me to admit it, I'd have gone back in and gotten you one." He grimaced.

"I think that's the sweetest thing anyone's ever said to me." Cat laughed, biting into her donut with gusto.

"Nah," Jared disagreed. "That's just what you do for the people you love."

Cat choked, and he thumped her on the back, his dimples bracketing his rogue's smile. What did he mean? Was he trying to tell her...? No, he couldn't mean... Could he? Cat's brain stuttered to a halt.

A blue sparkle caught her eye as they passed the RV park at the edge of town. She was still mulling over Jared's words and it was a second before she turned her head to see what was making the blue flash. By the time she turned to look, it was gone.

Her first thought was that it was another of Mabel's outlandish outfits. Great. Now she was seeing things. The Bickersons must have made more of an impression upon her than she realized. Sometimes she was sure she was still being followed. But that was impossible. What could the Bickersons possibly want with her?

Jared turned down the lane to the ranch, parking beside one of the large buildings behind the house. Cat followed Jared through the enormous double doors. An office and tack room were on the right and just beyond Cat could see an endless row of stables. Lucy followed with her nose pressed to the ground.

"We need to get you some boots." Jared eyed her Keds with disdain and led her into the tack room. It was chock full of bridles, harnesses, saddles and a variety of other horse training equipment. The smell of worn leather and horse sweat filled her senses, and Cat felt a moment of exhilaration.

"My sister leaves her boots in here as do some of our students." Jared squatted beside a row of cubbyholes, full of boots and hats and riding crops. "What size are you?"

"Seven."

"Perfect." Jared returned with a pair of black, Western style boots in his hand.

Cat sat on the only bench in the room and removed her sneakers. The black boots were snug in the toe, but otherwise fine. She couldn't have cared less. She was too excited. When Jared plunked a large cowboy hat on her head, she peeped at him from beneath the brim.

"To block the sun," he said and covered his own head with a wide-brimmed brown Stetson. "Ready?"

Cat nodded and followed him out the side door to the yard. Waiting outside was a short, barrel shaped man, holding two of the most beautiful horses Cat had ever seen.

"Morning, Sirus," Jared greeted the older man. "I hope we didn't keep you waiting."

"Morning, Jared." The man's voice was gruff as if underused. "No, I just got here myself."

"This is Sirus." Jared pulled Cat forward. "Sirus, this is Cat."

"Nice to meet you, ma'am." The wrinkled face cracked in a smile, and Cat felt honored as if the old man didn't smile much and only when he meant it.

"Likewise…Mr…uh, Sirus." Cat nodded in return.

"This is your mount," Jared said, leading Cat to the smaller horse. "Her name's Cocoa Bar, and she's the sweetest mare in the stable. She won't give you any trouble."

"Hello, Cocoa Bar," Cat said and patted the horse's neck. "Aren't you a beautiful girl?" The horse nodded appreciatively, and Cat felt an understanding pass between them.

"I like her," Cat announced.

"Let me give you a boost." Jared crouched and cupped his hands. Cat placed her left foot in his hands and let him lift her until she could swing her other leg over the saddle.

Cocoa Bar stood perfectly still, and Cat felt herself relax. Somehow, she felt much higher off the ground than she had as a kid. Cat took the reins into her hands, trying to get used to the feel of them.

She'd always ridden English style as a child, and she noted the difference of the Western saddle. For one thing, it had a saddle horn. She wasn't sure what it was for, but it seemed like an awfully good thing to hang onto if she lost control of the horse or the reins.

When Jared finished fussing with her stirrups, she slipped her feet into them, remembering to keep her heels down and her toes up.

Jared mounted with much less fuss. His horse was equally well behaved, but there was a decided air of rebelliousness about him. Perhaps it was his coat of unrelieved black. Never had Cat seen such a dark horse. His bearing was regal, the power of his frame tangible, he was the perfect complement for Jared.

"What is your horse's name?" Cat asked.

"Diablo. It's Spanish for devil." Pride made his deep voice rumble, and Cat thought the name suited both the horse and the rider.

"Sirus, will you keep an eye on our girl?" Jared asked and pointed to Lucy who was sniffing one of the stalls.

"You bet," Sirus said.

"Ready?" Jared asked Cat.

She nodded and with a wave to Sirus, they left the stable yard and headed out into the desert. Cocoa Bar seemed content to follow Diablo's lead. Just like a woman in love, Cat thought with a quick glance at Jared's broad back. Her gaze strayed to the motion of his hips in the saddle, back and forth, back and forth. She gulped and shifted her gaze away.

They followed a well-worn path through the valley and Cat marveled at the scenery surrounding them. Every morning when she woke up and looked out her window, it took her breath away. Spiked cacti, large rust-brown mountains, and green-limbed trees. It was all foreign to her and so very beautiful.

"You know what I can't get used to out here?" Cat pulled alongside Jared as the path widened.

"The heat?" he guessed.

"No, the sky," she answered. "I mean from one shoulder to the other all I see is blue sky." Jared nodded, watching her with a tenderness that made her continue in a rush, "Back East, all you ever see is ribbons of blue through the trees." She sighed, tipping her head back while clutching her hat to keep it in place. "It's just amazing. It's impossible to be grumpy or depressed when you're inundated with sunshine like this."

"That's why so many people get hooked," Jared agreed.

"Some move here for a little while and find they never want to leave."

"Hmm." Cat could believe it.

They rode to the top of one of the nearby hills. There was a beautiful view of the ranch, and Cat was amazed at how high they'd climbed. The view of town was blocked by a series of larger hills that Jared called the Copper Creek Buttes. According to Jared, there was an excellent hike to the top of them, but the trail was not well marked and several people had gotten lost amongst them.

"You should always mark your trail when you're out in the wilderness," Jared said. "Bend a branch on a bush or make a pattern with some rocks, something that will remind you of which way you came."

Cat ignored the meaningful look Jared cast her as he imparted this information. Really, the man acted as if she couldn't tie her shoes by herself.

They rounded a bend and came upon a large clearing in which sat the wooden frame of a house under construction.

"Come here, I want to show you something." Jared motioned her off her horse.

Cat tried to swing her right leg free, but it wouldn't budge.

"Come on, Cat," Jared said, dismounting and tying Diablo to a Cottonwood tree.

Cat leaned forward. Her knees were locked and her legs felt as if they were tied to the saddle. She leaned backward, but her feet just slid deeper into the stirrups. She pushed up on the saddle horn. No luck. She could not get her legs free.

"Cat, are you okay?" Jared asked.

"I'm fine," she said, feeling her face get warm with embarrassment. "I'm just…I'm stuck."

"What?" he asked.

"You heard me, I'm stuck."

"Oh, that's right. You're a greenhorn." Jared laughed and strode over to stand beside the horse. He opened his arms and said, "Fall."

"What?"

"Let go and fall," he said. "Don't worry. I'll catch you."

With a frown, Cat did as he said. Jared caught her and gently set her on the ground. A shooting pain stabbed Cat in the posterior. It was all she could do not to hug her rump and moan.

"Come on, tenderfoot, walk it out," Jared said.

"Where are we?" she asked, limping beside him.

"This is my house," he said.

"You're building this?" She gasped in pleased surprise.

"You like it?" he asked warily.

"Are you kidding? It's gorgeous. The view alone is breathtaking."

Jared felt air sweep through his lungs and was surprised. He hadn't been aware he was holding his breath. This was good, he reassured himself, now all he had to do was convince Cat that she belonged here.

"Let me show you the rooms," he suggested and led her through the frame, telling her what had been planned and probing her for suggestions and ideas. Cat fell in with the plan immediately. She loved his ideas for the master bedroom, but was prepared to do battle with him over the kitchen.

"You can't put the appliances against the west wall," she argued, shaking her head. "You want windows on this wall. Just imagine the sunsets you'd miss if the appliances are here."

"I hadn't thought of that," Jared lied. She didn't need to know he was already planning to put windows there. "You're right. I'll have to tell the workmen to change it."

"Good." Cat nodded. "I'm sure you'll like that much better."

"Well, I don't cook very much for myself." Jared shrugged with false disinterest. "So, I don't suppose it will make much difference to me. But when I get married, I'm sure it will probably matter to my wife. Women seem to care about that kind of thing."

He watched her face fall. She looked as vulnerable as a little girl who's had her ice cream cone swiped. Silently, she turned on her heel and left the house.

"Cat." Jared stopped her with a hand on her arm. "What's wrong?"

"Nothing." She parted her lips in a smile that didn't quite reach her stormy eyes. "You have a beautiful house. I'm sure you'll be very happy here."

"No, I won't." Jared relented and cupped her chin, forcing her to meet his gaze. "Not unless you're here with me."

"What do you mean?" she asked.

"I mean that I've been trying to give you time to be on your own, but the truth is I miss you. I want to spend my life with you," he said.

"Oh, Jared, I...I can't."

She burst into tears, and Jared cursed himself for pushing the issue and making her cry. Pulling her into his arms, he rested his chin in her springy hair and hushed her with soft words and hands that swept up and down her spine.

He felt his throat tighten and he swallowed, sucking in a gulp of air. It was now or never. He had to tell her. His gut clenched, and he closed his eyes, battling the nerves that threatened to swamp him. He could do it. For her, he could take the biggest risk of his life.

"Cat, I love you," he whispered. She stiffened in his arms, and he knew she'd heard him.

"Don't!" Cat said, pushing out of his arms and turning

away from him. "I can't do this. I need to be on my own.
Damn it! I've waited too long to find my independence. I
won't give it up. Not even for you."

"Cat." Jared was in front of her in one stride. His hands
cupped her face, and he forced her eyes to meet his. "I
don't want you to give up your independence for me. I want
the pigheaded pain in the butt that fights me over where
the windows in the kitchen should be or what kind of music
she wants on the radio. I want the woman who is brave
enough to travel across the country by herself, but is kind
enough to take along someone who she thinks is stranded.
Don't you see you're different with me?"

With a shaky hand, Cat caressed his cheek. Oh, how she
loved this man. But she couldn't let him deceive himself.
She knew herself too well. She'd do what she always did
with the people she cared about. She'd let him become her
whole world. She'd lose herself in him, until he became so
bored he'd look elsewhere for amusement. She couldn't
handle that. With anyone but Jared, she'd survive, but to
have that happen to them, it would destroy her.

"Jared, I can't. I just can't." Her voice broke and her
tears flowed freely over both of them.

Her tears soaked his shirt, and Jared knew she wouldn't
change her mind. Belatedly, he realized the irony of having
the woman who opened his world be the same one to slam
the door in his face.

He had tried to give her time to be independent. Although, he supposed a few days wasn't a lot of time. But
he loved Cat. He loved her unreservedly and without fear.
For as long as he could remember, he'd been terrified of
loving anyone too much for fear that they'd be taken away
from him like his mother. But his love for Cat was so
strong, it wouldn't succumb to the fear.

He knew he was being selfish, but hell, when a guy finally finds his soul mate, he doesn't want to wait to start a

life together, he wants to start that life right now. But Cat wasn't ready. Maybe she never would be.

What was to become of them?

CAT PERUSED the produce aisle of the grocery store with an eye for something exotic. Cantaloupe, kiwi, rutabaga, it all seemed pretty bland. Then her gaze locked with a mocking blue one, and her heart skidded to a stop. But the gaze wasn't topped off by a head of bright blond hair; instead a black mane surrounded the face that grinned back at her.

"Hi, Jess," Cat said, biting back the urge to ask about Jared. It had been four days since she'd seen him. She missed him more every second that passed.

"Hi," Jess said, studying Cat's cart. "You cook?"

"I even enjoy it," Cat confessed.

"Eww!" Jess shuddered, clutching a six-pack of cola and a package of fig newtons to her chest. "How's school going?"

"So far so good," Cat answered. "The kids were a little rowdy on the first day, but they'll settle in. With one exception, of course."

"Of course." Jess grinned. "So who's the resident troublemaker?"

"Ty Peterson." Cat sighed. "Know him?"

"Actually, yeah." Jess frowned. "Very rough home life."

"I suspected as much." Cat chewed her lip.

"What are you going to do?" Jess asked.

"Love him as much as I can while he's in my class." Cat shrugged. "It's my job to teach him that he's valuable, and that school is his only way out of that so-called home."

"You'll do it." Jess nodded.

"How can you be so sure?" Cat asked. "I'm not even sure myself."

"Because I saw what you did for Jared," Jess answered softly.

"What did I do for Jared?" Cat wheeled her cart through produce toward canned goods, trying to feign indifference.

"I don't know exactly." Jess laughed. "All I know is that my brother has never, in all my life, told me that he loved me. Not even when I got shot."

Cat's gaze flew to Jess's in surprise.

"Oh, I always knew he did," Jess continued. "But he never said it. I think he felt too vulnerable. Like if he acknowledged how he felt, then it all might be taken away. He told you that our mother died when we were young?"

"Yeah," Cat whispered around the lump in her throat.

"Well, I guess he was always afraid that if he admitted that he cared, then Dad and I would be taken away, too." Jess paused. "That's just my theory, but it's totally irrelevant now. Thanks to you."

"I didn't do anything," Cat protested, her breath coming in shallow gasps.

"Yeah, right." Jess tilted her head and studied Cat closely. "When my brother showed up with you, that first night on the ranch, he told me he loved me. If he hadn't been hugging me, I'd have fallen down. I don't know what's happening between you and Jared or what will happen. All I know, is that you gave me a part of my brother I thought I'd never see. Thank you, Cat."

"I didn't. I couldn't. It's not what you think." Cat shook her head.

Jess gently pried loose the can of tomato soup Cat unwittingly clutched in her hands.

"Thank you, Cat," she repeated as she put the can in the cart, spun on her heel and left the grocery store.

Dazed, Cat followed in Jess's wake with nothing more in her cart than when she'd first spied Jess.

CAT SPENT THE AFTERNOON unpacking the last of her boxes with Lucy at her feet. Sally had cleared out some of her bookshelves and Cat was happily filling them up when she came upon a purple satin box, a bit larger than a shoe box, mixed in with her books.

The purple box! On the first day of their trip, Jared had said he found a purple box in the back of the van and had packed it in another box for safekeeping. Cat had completely forgotten about it.

She ran her hand over the smooth satin surface. She had never owned a box like this. She wondered if it was a present from Cameron and Julia. Cat flipped open the old-fashioned clasp and lifted the lid.

Winking at her in the late afternoon light from a bed of satin was the most breathtaking necklace Cat had ever seen. She slammed the lid down. This was not a gift for her. She opened the box again and lifted the necklace from its nest. It was cold and heavy and shimmered in the light as if it were alive. Three rows of small diamonds made up the choker and a large square ruby the size of Cat's thumb sat in the middle.

"Lucy, we're in big trouble," she said. "Come on, let's go see Jess."

Cat stuffed the necklace back into the box and raced out to her SUV. She opened the passenger side door and waited for Lucy to jump up. Lucy didn't budge.

"Come on, Lucy," she said. "We're going for a ride. Up! Hop up!"

Lucy growled at the interior of the car and still refused to move.

"Sweetie," Cat said as she put the box on the floor of the car and wrapped her arms around the dog. "I don't have time for this right now."

With a groan, Cat hefted the dog into the passenger's seat. She hurried around the front of the car. She climbed into the driver's seat and fastened her seat belt. Lucy was still growling so Cat turned on the ignition and pushed the button to roll down her window.

"It's all right, Lucy," she said and patted the dog on the head. Lucy ignored her.

Cat frowned and put the SUV into Reverse. She was halfway down her driveway when a head popped up from behind her seat. Cat screamed and stomped on the brake pedal. It was Fly! Her arm shot across the seat to protect Lucy. Fly wasn't so lucky and smashed his nose against the back of her seat.

A string of curses flew out of his mouth but Cat wasn't listening. She grabbed Lucy's collar and opened her door, planning to make a run for it.

"Don't try it," a voice instructed. Cat glanced around to see Mabel pop up on the seat next to Fly. She was holding a gun and it was pointed right at Cat. "It seems you've found our property."

"I'm sure there's been some mistake," Cat said.

"Yeah, trying to steal our goods was a big mistake on your part," Mabel agreed. "It took us a few days to get your name and address from the place you rented that moving van from, but as you can see persistence pays. Give it here."

"Give what?" Cat asked, rendered stupid by the sight of the gun.

"The necklace," Mabel waved the weapon impatiently. "Give me the necklace."

Cat grabbed the box off the floor and handed it to Mabel.

Mabel kept the gun trained on Cat while she unfastened the lid and examined the necklace.

"Ah," she purred. "You have no idea what I went through to get this."

"I'm sure I don't," Cat said, her fingers flexing around

the door handle. If she could just distract them maybe she could get away.

"Six months I spent scrubbing toilets, polishing glass and cleaning up little kids' vomit in that stinking New England Heirloom Museum just so I could get my hands on this beauty."

"It wasn't all you, dumpling," Fly protested. "I had to work security for six months, too."

"Security?" Mabel scoffed. "All you boys did was drink coffee, eat donuts and watch daytime TV. No, I had to do the hard part, sugarplum. And don't you forget it."

"I got you the codes, didn't I, dearest?" Fly asked. "You couldn't have broken in without me."

"All right, pudding," Mabel said. "You helped a little. But I'm the one who cut the glass and managed to lift out the necklace without setting off the laser alarm. These fingers might be old, but they're as steady as a twenty-year-old's."

"Just as pretty, too," Fly said. "See. You young folk don't pay us old folk no mind. You think we're just washed-up old has-beens sitting around in our wrinkled skin waiting to die. Well, phooey! Me and the missus have the lightest fingers in the fifty states and we've got the Swiss bank account to prove it."

"Oh, my God! You're the jewel thieves we heard about on the radio. But I don't understand," Cat said. "How did that necklace end up in my boxes unless…"

"We put it there," Fly said. "The heat was on us. The cops almost nailed us in Massachusetts. We had to keep switching vehicles to lose them, and we didn't want to risk them catching us with the goods. It's a lot easier to play the senile senior citizen with a stolen vehicle than it is with a necklace worth three million. We broke into your hotel room back in New Mexico to get it back but we couldn't find it. Still, with that 'AZ or Bust' sign we decided to use you to transport our latest acquisition since we're meeting our connection in Arizona.''

''Come on, we've got a meeting to get to,'' Mabel said with a wave of the gun.

''What about her?'' Fly asked.

''She's driving us,'' Mabel said. ''And we're bringing her little dog, too. Put it in drive, kiddo.''

Cat blanched but did as she was told. How was she going to get out of this one? She tried to think but her brain was clenched with fear and her thoughts were nothing but white noise.

''And don't try anything or you'll be sorry,'' Mabel said.

''What are we going to do with her?'' Fly asked.

''I suppose we'll have to shoot her,'' Mabel said.

Cat felt her head spin and she had to swallow to keep her lunch down.

''I want to be the one to shoot her, sweet pea,'' Fly said.

''No!'' Mabel said and then softened her tone, ''No, honeybunch, you know you're a lousy shot.''

''I am not. I can hit the diamond on the ace of diamonds at fifty paces.''

''More like five paces.''

''There you go again,'' Fly said. ''Miss Hoity-Toity. You always think you're so much better than me. My mother was right about you.''

''Don't you drag that old battle-ax into this, you mama's boy,'' Mabel said. ''That woman was nothing but mean to me from the first.''

''That's because she knew you weren't good enough for me.'' Fly sniffed.

Cat glanced in the mirror to see them glaring at one another. It was now or never. She braked the car in the middle of the road. Both Fly and Mabel were knocked to the floor. Cat opened her door and prepared to sprint.

''Run, Lucy,'' she ordered.

She only got three paces away when she heard a pitiful yip behind her. Cat turned to see Mabel leaning over the seat and holding Lucy by her ears.

"Get back in the car or else," Mabel said and pointed the gun at Lucy's head.

On knees that shook like loose change, Cat climbed back into the driver's seat.

Mabel leaned forward and pinched Cat's forearm with one of her age-spotted old hands. "No more stunts or else."

Cat nodded. She bit her lip to keep from crying. She had to keep her wits about her. She had to pay attention and look for an opportunity to escape. It was her only chance.

"TURN HERE AND PARK," Mabel ordered. Cat turned the SUV into the entrance to the Copper Creek Buttes State Park. A group of ramadas and a water fountain were all that marked the desolate camping area. Fly was following them in their latest RV, an Airstream trailer towed by a large pickup.

"Get out," Mabel ordered. "Take the dog with you."

Cat climbed out of the car, leading Lucy by her leash.

"Do you see our contact?" Mabel asked Fly as he joined them.

"Yeah, he's sitting over there," Fly said and pointed to the furthest ramada.

"Okay," Mabel said. "We're not going to kill you. But that's only because we don't want murder on our rap sheet. But it won't be our fault if you get lost in the desert and die of exposure. Right, Fly?"

Cat felt her knees sag with relief.

"That's right," he agreed. He was wearing a pair of binoculars around his neck, looking like a regular bird-watcher.

"So, start walking," Mabel said and waved the gun at Cat.

Anything was better than hanging around these two gun-toting old coots. Cat began to walk.

"Hold it," Fly said. He grabbed Lucy's leash out of Cat's hands. "Just so you don't get any ideas about not doing what we tell you. You keep walking or we shoot the mutt. Got it?"

"No—" Cat protested.

But Mabel cut her off, "Fly will watch you with his binoculars. If you try to turn around, and he sees you, I'll shoot your dog. Understand?"

Cat felt her insides twist. Lucy whimpered and Cat felt the lump in her throat harden. If anything happened to Lucy, she would hunt down these two geriatrics and she would make them pay.

Cat turned and began to walk in as straight a line as possible. How would she ever be able to find her way back? Then she remembered what Jared had told her. She knew the Bickersons were watching her so every few yards she carefully reached out and twisted the limb of a creosote bush, hoping that later she would be able to use the marker to find her way home.

CAT'S SUV was found at the base of the Copper Creek Buttes. There was no sign of foul play, but that did nothing to ease the terror that pounded through Jared like random cannon fire.

After questioning her neighbors, he discovered she'd been gone most of the day. She'd been seen about late afternoon, driving through town with an older couple. She'd taken Lucy with her. It was assumed she'd gone out for a drive with friends.

Assumed. The word sent waves of panic coursing through Jared's body. Assumed missing. Assumed dead. He hated the word "assumed." It was all his fault. He should have kept a closer eye on her.

The description of the older couple matched the Bickersons exactly. Jared remembered Cat's insistence that Mabel and Fly were following them. He called Jess. She confirmed what he feared. The Bickersons were felons wanted in connection with the heist of the Divine choker from the New England Heirloom Museum. They were last seen in an RV headed west.

The crisis was not alleviated by Cameron Levery's sudden appearance in town. On an unexpected business trip to Phoenix, he'd decided to surprise Cat with a quick visit.

"What do you mean my sister is missing?" he shouted. Having gone to her house and found her gone, Cameron had driven out to the ranch to visit Jared. It was then that Jess called to report that Cat's car had been found.

"We think she went for a drive." Jared said, not mentioning the Bickersons' possible abduction. He didn't think Cameron's nerves could take it. "But she's been gone all day, and no one knows exactly where she went."

"This wasn't supposed to happen," Cam said, pacing the room like a nervous father on prom night. "This wasn't part of the plan."

"What plan?" Jared asked.

"My plan to fix you two up," Cam said. "She was never supposed to be out of your sight. You were supposed to fall in love on the drive out and then you'd be together and I could stop worrying about the two of you. So, what's wrong with my sister that you didn't fall in love with her?"

"Who said I'm not?" Jared asked.

Cameron scrutinized his friend's face. Jared didn't need a mirror to know that his jaw was clenched so tight that lines of worry were creasing his cheeks and brow. He knew he looked as scared and desperate as he felt and he knew Cameron could see it, too.

"All right." Cam nodded. "Only a man in love could look as lousy as you do. Let's go find her."

SHE WALKED FOR HOURS. She had promised herself she would walk until the sun set and then she would turn around and go back the way she came. There was no way Mabel and Fly would be able to see her in the dark, assuming they were still watching.

The sun was just beginning to set and it was getting cooler when she heard a rustling in the scrub behind her. Cat spun around, looking for anything that slithered or scurried in the desert brush. All was still. She tried not to panic, but the rustling noise started again and it was getting closer. Did coyotes attack people? What if it was a rattlesnake? What could she use for a weapon?

Cat searched the ground looking for a big stick or a rock. There was nothing save dry grass and dirt. There were no large trees to climb, no water holes to jump into. Nothing.

The noise grew louder and Cat strained to see what was coming out of the bush at her. Didn't they have javelinas, wild pigs, out here? She turned and braced herself, ready to kick at anything that came within a yard of her.

The animal broke free of the bushes and launched itself at Cat. She had just a second to register the familiar yip, the soft black fur and open her arms. Lucy bowled her over right into the dirt.

"Oh, Lucy," she said. "I was afraid I'd never see you again. Did you run away or did they let you go? I bet you made a break for it. That's my good girl."

Lucy licked the tears off her face and Cat hugged her close.

They were standing a hundred yards away from a large flat-topped boulder. Knowing that the Bickersons couldn't possibly see them any longer, Cat hiked to the boulder. She climbed onto the rock and Lucy followed her. It was unlikely that anyone knew she was missing or would even know to look for her out here in the desert, but she figured her odds of being spotted were better if she was above the desert floor. Hugging Lucy close to her chest, Cat decided to wait out the dark night and to start back at first light.

There was no moon and the night was as black as tar, but Cat could discern the familiar forms around her. She sat cross-legged on the rock, her sleeping puppy nestled against her side. She'd had moments of sheer terror. Amazingly, it wasn't death that frightened her, but rather the fear that she might never see Jared again. Suddenly, it didn't seem to matter whether she was independent and self-sufficient or not. All that mattered was the man that filled her heart.

He was right. She was different with him. Why had it taken her so long to see that? With Jared, she never lost herself. With Jared, she never felt a need to subvert her needs to meet his. From the first day she'd met him, she'd been able to assert herself with him. He'd accepted it and loved her in spite of it. And he did love her. She knew that now.

Why hadn't she seen it sooner? Why hadn't she acknowledged all of the little ways she remained herself with him? He'd saved her life, yes, but she'd given him his. They were two halves of a whole. Yin and yang. Earth and sky. Sun and moon. And she was an idiot.

When the first pink fingers of dawn began to stretch across the sky, Cat opened her eyes. She was bone cold and her muscles ached. But, she reminded herself, they were alive. Curled up around the puppy with only a sweatshirt for cover, she rubbed Lucy's cold fur until they were both warm. They would be all right. They had to be.

"Let's go home," she said and Lucy jumped off the rock, eager to be on their way.

The morning chill soon dissipated, and Cat shed her sweatshirt, tying it around her waist.

They stopped to rest at the base of a hill that Cat was certain looked familiar. The bent limb of a creosote marked it as a place she had been. A cactus wren watched them from the tip of a saguaro, while Cat kept her eyes on the ground. She didn't want any surprises, like a rattlesnake, to leap up and catch her or Lucy unaware.

They walked on, following Cat's trail of bent branches, for most of the morning, until finally, Cat noticed the roofs of the ramadas off in the distance.

"Oh, Lucy, baby, we're almost home," Cat cried and dashed forward and down the steep hill with the last ounce of energy her body had. As if sensing her urgency, Lucy bounded along on her heels.

AT THE SOUND OF FOOTSTEPS, slamming into the rocky hill above, Jared's heart lurched into his throat. Please, he begged, please, let it be.

He saw her wild hair first. It was glinting in the sun in shades of copper and gold. She looked sunburnt and tired. There were scratches on her knees and a tear in her shirt.

Jared felt his throat close. She was all right. He told himself to breathe, but his lungs seemed to have forgotten how. She'd done it. She'd found her way home. A sweet rush of relief and thanks swept through him with an intensity that left him weak.

Her eyes were fixed on the ground. She still hadn't seen him. When her lashes swept up, and those quick-changing irises saw him, she froze in her tracks.

They stood gazing at one another as if they'd been apart for years and not days. And then Jared's arms were opening, and Cat was running to him. Their lips met in a kiss that bespoke fear and need and love.

When they parted, Cat was crying in great torrential sobs, the way she was wont to do. It sounded like music to Jared, and he laughed through the knot in his throat.

Lucy was not to be denied, and Jared reached down to scratch her head, never loosening his hold on Cat. Straightening back up, his lips swooped down on hers in a need to claim. Cat drowned in his kiss, all the while frantically touching his hair, his face and his body as if to reassure herself that he was indeed real.

When they broke apart, her tears were gone, and a smile lit her features. "What are you doing here?"

"Waiting for you," he said, his voice thready.

"The Bickersons…" she started.

But Jared finished, "Were picked up at the state line with a cool two point five million dollars in their possession. They told Jess that you were actually the one who stole the necklace. They were just working for you. What they didn't know was that their contact was actually an undercover FBI agent. They've got them dead to rights. They're going to be put away for a long time."

"They forced me to walk. They were going to shoot Lucy if I didn't," Cat said. Jared uttered an oath.

It was then that Cat noticed the large group of pickup trucks and horse trailers parked just beyond the ramadas.

"Organizing the cavalry?" she asked.

"I called in a few favors," he explained with a smile.

"I did it." She gestured vaguely to the rocky cliffs behind them. "I found my own way."

"I never doubted that you could," he said.

"I know." Cat cupped his beautiful face between her hands and peppered him with kisses. "I love you, Jared."

"Enough to marry me?" he asked, feeling as if his heart would burst.

"Yes, oh yes," she cried.

"That's good," Jared said. "Because your brother is here."

"Cameron is here?" Cat gasped.

"Yep, right down there." Jared pointed to his Jeep. "He set us up, you know."

"What do you mean?" Cat asked.

"The trip cross-country," Jared said. "He told me that he figured all along that we'd fall in love. In fact, that was his plan."

"His plan?" Cat repeated, but didn't bother to listen to any confirmation. Jared was left to follow in her dusty wake as she stomped down the hill toward her brother.

"Cat, I was so worried." Cameron opened his arms wide with relief. Cat stepped in close but instead of hugging him she stomped on his instep.

"Yow!" Cameron howled and danced around on one foot. "What did you do that for?"

"What's the big idea meddling in my personal life?" she asked. "You had no right setting Jared and I up like that. Do you have any idea the anguish you put him through? He was tormented about that stupid guy code that says a guy isn't supposed to touch his friend's sister."

"What?" Cameron asked and looked at Jared who nodded. "That only applies until such time as the brother gives his consent. I sent you cross-country with my baby sister, you dunce. You needed more consent than that?"

Jared shrugged.

"And what about me?" Cat asked. "You knew I wanted to be on my own to prove my independence, but you just couldn't let me be, could you? No, you had to send this big galoot with me."

"It's only because I care," Cameron protested. "After the big dumb jerk hurt you so bad, I wanted you to have the best guy I know."

"I know," Cat said. This time when she stepped in close, Cameron ducked but she pulled him into a big hug instead. "He's the best thing you've ever done for me. Thanks, big brother."

Cameron eyed his sister warily, as if looking for another stomp to his instep. But she just kissed his cheek and squeezed him harder.

"You love him, too?" Cameron grinned from ear to ear. "I knew it. I knew if you two were alone together for a couple of days, you'd fall for each other. Jeez, I am good at this. Maybe I should start a new business. A sideline…Fix Ups by Cameron. Or no, better yet, A Match Made by Cameron. What do you think?"

But Cat and Jared weren't listening. Jared took her hand and led her away from the others. He hadn't quite gotten his fill of her yet. He doubted he ever would.

"I love you," he said and scooped her up in a fierce bear hug.

"I never doubted that you did," she whispered in his ear.

It really didn't matter whether she believed him or not, Jared thought, for he intended to spend the next sixty to seventy years letting her know just how very much he loved her. And as his lips covered hers, Jared knew that now that they'd found one another, neither of them would ever be lost again.

HARLEQUIN® Temptation.

AMERICAN HEROES

**These men are heroes—
strong, fearless...
And impossible to resist!**

Join bestselling authors Lori Foster, Donna Kauffman
and Jill Shalvis as they deliver up

MEN OF COURAGE

Harlequin anthology
May 2003

Followed by *American Heroes* miniseries
in Harlequin Temptation

**RILEY by Lori Foster
June 2003**

**SEAN by Donna Kauffman
July 2003**

**LUKE by Jill Shalvis
August 2003**

Don't miss this sexy new miniseries by some of
Temptation's hottest authors!

Available at your favorite retail outlet.

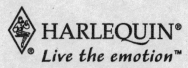

HARLEQUIN®
Live the emotion™

Visit us at www.eHarlequin.com

HTAH

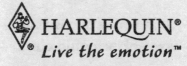

HARLEQUIN®

AMERICAN *Romance*®

celebrates its 20th Anniversary

This June, we have a distinctive lineup that features
another wonderful title in

The Deveraux Legacy

series from bestselling author

CATHY GILLEN THACKER

Taking Over the Tycoon
(HAR #973)

Sexy millionaire Connor Templeton is used to
getting whatever—whomever—he wants!
But has he finally met his match in
one beguiling single mother?

And on sale in July 2003,
Harlequin American Romance premieres
a brand-new miniseries,
Cowboys by the Dozen,
from **Tina Leonard.**

Available at your favorite retail outlet.

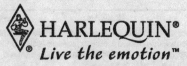

HARLEQUIN®
Live the emotion™

Visit us at www.eHarlequin.com

HAR20CGT